Philip Henry was born in 1974. He first started writing sketches while studying Performing Arts. After that he moved on to short stories and movie scripts. During long shifts at one of the more boring jobs he had, he began making notes for a novel, which he then wrote on his days off. That novel, *Vampire Dawn*, was released in 2004 and proved so popular it was extended into a trilogy with *Vampire Twilight* in 2007 and *Vampire Equinox* in 2009.

My Ivory Summer, Philip's first novel without a supernatural element, was short-listed for the Self-Published Book of the Year 2012.

Philip continues to write novels, screenplays and short stories, all based around his home on the North Coast of Ireland.

The North Coast Bloodlines Series:

The North Coast Bloodlines Series – Book Eleven

METHOD

PHILIP HENRY

CORAL MOON BOOKS
www.philiphenry.com

The North Coast Bloodlines Book 11: METHOD
By
Philip Henry

Published By Coral Moon Books
www.philiphenry.com

This is a work of fiction. Names, characters, places and incidents are either products of the author's imagination or are used fictitiously. Any resemblance to actual events or locales or persons, living or dead, save those clearly in the public domain, is purely coincidental.

Method Copyright © 2021 Philip Henry

ISBN: 9798510530698

10 9 8 7 6 5 4 3 2 1

Supported by
 The National Lottery® through the Arts Council of Northern Ireland

Description: Partial transcript of television interview from 'Parkinson' 03/12/04 between Michael Parkinson (MP) and Sean Black (SB). Additional comments by Britney Spears (BS) and Ricky Gervais (RG).

MP: Now, Sean, before we discuss your TV show, let's talk about your upbringing...

RG: Yeah, Britney and I have been a bit boring, best to move on.

(audience laughs)

MP: Not at all, not at all.

RG: You can't take it back now, Parky. There goes *your* cameo in my next series.

(audience laughs)

MP: Well, the acting world at least is probably breathing a sigh of relief.

(Gervais laughs)

MP: I did want to ask you, Sean – if it's OK with Ricky...?

RG: Oh, go on then!

(audience laughs)

MP: Thank you. You've been acting since you were very young. You started in school plays and local theatre productions when you were still in primary school. Can you remember when you first got bit by the acting bug?

SB: Yes, it was Halloween. There was this kid who always used to bully me. He was a couple of years older and he was always beating me up and taking my stuff.

RG: What was his name? Shame the little bastard on national TV.

(audience laughs)

MP: No, please don't. We don't want to get the lawyers involved.

SB: Anyway, it was Halloween and we were really poor so, I'd made myself a pretty rubbish Superman costume. It was just blue jeans, a blue sweater, a bit of an old red curtain I cut to the size of a cape, and I just drew and coloured in the S symbol on a piece of paper and pinned it to my sweater with safety pins.

BS: Oh, I bet you looked adorable.

RG: Did you have the red underpants?

(audience laughs)

SB: I *did* have the red pants, and let me tell you, it took a lot of guts to pull them on over my jeans and walk outside, but I figured if Superman could do it, so could I. So off I went trick or treating and got my little plastic carrier bag filled with sweets. And as I was walking home, who do I run into, but this...

RG: Wanker?

(audience laughs)

SB: Exactly. So he pushes me down and takes my bag of sweets from me. And as I'm lying there on the ground, I look at my costume and I think, *What are you doing? You're Superman! Don't let this baddie push you around.* And I don't even remember what happened next, but by all accounts, I jumped to my feet and socked him in the eye.

(audience applauds)

BS: That is so cool.

SB: Apparently he went down like a bag of spuds. I took my sweets back from him and walked home.

2

MP: You say 'apparently'. Don't you remember any of it happening?

SB: No. It must be like they say, you know, you get the red mist and anger just takes over. The next thing I remember, after being on the ground, is being back in my living room eating sweets. But he never bothered me again after that day.

MP: I should think not.

(audience applauds)

SB: And that was the first time I saw the power of acting, of becoming someone else for a little while.

……………transcript ends.

Description: statement from former detective Joseph Taggart.

We found William (Billy) Docherty late on Halloween night 1984 behind a hedge near the local park, a couple of hours after he'd been reported missing by his mother. He'd been brutally bludgeoned with a brick, which we found at the scene. There were no witnesses to the crime and there was no CCTV in those days.

In the following weeks and months we did numerous appeals for witnesses to come forward with any information they thought could be helpful, but nothing panned out. Sean Black was interviewed at the time, as he was one of the many children that the victim bullied, but he accounted for his whereabouts that night and it was confirmed by multiple sources. We saw no reason to pursue that avenue of inquiry.

We never made any arrests connected to the assault on Billy Docherty. I see his mother from time to time. He still lives with her as he requires twenty-four-hour care. The assault caused permanent brain damage, so Billy was never able to tell us what happened. He hasn't spoken since that night and his motor-functions are limited. He has spent a good part of his life in various mental health facilities and hospitals. His condition is not expected to improve.

1997

01.

The knife slipped from his fingers and fell silently to the floor. He stumbled back a couple of steps and dropped to his knees.

His eyes were fixated on the space before him. He wiped his bloody hand on the leg of his trousers, his gaze still straight ahead. At the body. The corpse. No longer a person, now just an object. An object to be examined. Studied. To be scrutinised for clues. Evidence. He looked at where the knife had fallen. He swallowed, trying to draw spittle to his mouth.

Was he really going to do this? He'd sat through enough Sunday School to know what he *should* do, but his instincts for self-preservation were much stronger than any two-thousand-year-old book of do's and don'ts. If caught, he would tell them he thought long and hard about doing the right thing, but that wasn't what really happened. The truth was, even before her body touched the floor, he'd already started thinking of places to hide it. He hadn't intended to kill her, but there was no way he was going to jail for her death.

He watched her breath mist in the basement air. The clouds getting smaller each time she tried to exhale. Her lungs were filling with blood. Later, much later, when working out his back-up plan, he would tell them he tried to call an ambulance but couldn't get a signal. He'd tell them he sat beside her, holding her hand. He'd tell them she begged him not to leave her alone in her final moments. He'd tell them she wasn't scared because she'd known it had been an accident. He'd tell them all that and more.

But only if they found the body.

The last breath from her lips was barely visible. She had fallen facing away from him, so this had been his only way of gauging her condition. He sat up on his haunches and looked over her body. He saw her mouth full of blood, the overflow running down her cheek and pooling on the dirt floor. A chill ran round his veins. He took a further step back on his knees and lowered himself to the ground again.

It still wasn't too late to do the right thing.

He could abandon all the plans that had flooded his mind in the seconds since the knife pierced her chest. He could call the police and explain.

He looked at his watch.

He had about three hours before he'd be missed.

He got to his feet quickly... *and froze.*

7

'Very nicely done, Sean.'

McMaster turned and cued the rest of the class with a few half-hearted claps of her own. She couldn't clap properly with the remote control still in her hand. The rest of the class dutifully gave their applause.

Sean Black gave a modest smile and hung his head slightly. He knew at least half the class hated him. The male half predominately. Most of the female actors in the class had been guests in his bed at one time or another, and those who hadn't were either still on his TBF list, or weren't worth the effort.

Whether they liked him or not, they couldn't deny he had owned that scene. The playback and close-ups of his reactions only confirmed what he had felt on the day; he had blown everyone else off the stage. McMaster had done her best with the others, but there was only so much you could teach. The rest was instinct. Natural ability.

'So,' McMaster said, gesturing at Sean's face still paused on-screen, 'what do we think happened?'

'He stabbed someone, and then felt bad about it,' Alison Edwards answered.

'No he didn't,' Emily Williams said. Her eyes met Sean's and she gave him her cutest smile. 'He murdered someone.'

'What's the difference?' Alison asked.

'The difference is, he didn't try to help her. He just sat back and watched her die.'

McMaster looked around the class. 'Do we all agree?' There was a general mumbled consensus around the class. 'Why she?' McMaster asked.

Emily raised her eyebrows at the teacher.

'You said: "he didn't try to help *her*" and "watched *her* die". What makes you think it was a woman he murdered?'

Emily looked at Sean again, but he had lowered his glance, giving away nothing. 'There was tenderness in his gestures. When he stabbed her, he didn't just let her drop; he lowered her, gently. He loved her.'

'Loved her enough to kill her,' Alison added, getting a laugh from the class.

'He loved her *once*,' Emily said.

McMaster looked at Sean. 'Mr Black?'

8

'Spot on, Emily.' He gave her a quick smile and she responded tenfold. She'd been one of his first conquests. Early September. He'd given her a four out of ten at the time, but she'd been around the Media Studies block a few times since then. Maybe it was time for a rematch. She had a Reader's Digest face but a Playboy body.

'This is what I meant when I said tell a story without dialogue,' McMaster said. 'So many of you took that to mean mime, but Sean's piece told us a story that wasn't about walking in the wind or being trapped inside a box.'

A few of the class laughed, a few others looked embarrassed.

'And look at his gestures,' she went on. 'He keeps everything small and subtle. That's what screen acting is all about. If you want to do big over-the-top flourishes and wave your arms around so that the wee man in the back row can see, you should be in the Theatre Studies class. Screen acting is intimate. It gets right in your face, so you only need the smallest of movements to convey what you're feeling. High-Definition television will be in every home in a few years. Consider *that* when you think you're doing too little. Less is definitely more.' She turned to Sean. 'Mr Black, would you care to let us in on your process?'

Sean got up and did his best to look humble. He reckoned if he threw in one of those James Dean downward glances every once in a while, that would do it. 'I just imagine it all. Everything. I really see it. There was no woman, no knife, no blood in that scene, but I saw it all in my mind. I remembered where everything was. How the body was lying on the floor. How the knife felt. The blood seeping into the dirt floor. Her last breaths misting in the cold basement air.' He felt like he was teaching now, and he could see his peers didn't appreciate it, even if most of them needed some tips. He lowered his head. 'That's just what works for me.'

'Imagination is one of an actor's most powerful tools, and it's going to become much more important in years to come.' McMaster gestured Sean to return to his seat as she made her way back to the podium. 'The biggest film of last year was *Independence Day*. Large portions of it shot against green screen. And I'm sure you've all spent hours downloading the trailer for the *Star Wars* trilogy special editions coming out soon. Looks like green screen has been used to create the new scenes they're sticking in. It's not going to be long before CGI becomes more cost-effective than building massive sets. That means you won't have your environment to help get you into

9

character, and you might be acting opposite a completely computer-generated character a few years after that.' She tapped her temple. 'And that's when your imagination is going to become essential. Instead of another actor, you might just have a stagehand reading the lines that some cartoon and a voice actor will fill in later. *Jurassic Park* changed everything, folks. There are strange times ahead for this profession. Future-proof yourselves as best you can.'

The bell rang.

'OK, everyone. That's it for today. We'll watch the rest next time. Good Friday tomorrow and the start of your Easter holidays.' A muted cheer went up from the exiting students. 'Enjoy yourselves. I'll see you all in a fortnight.'

McMaster pulled on her coat and grabbed her briefcase. She turned to leave and then grabbed the remote. She looked at Sean, still frozen on the screen, and then over at the young actor. She made an O with the thumb and forefinger of her free hand and smiled at him. He nodded his appreciation. She turned the TV off and set the remote control down as she hurried from the room.

Sean looked up at the seats in the auditorium and saw everyone else had left.

Except Emily.

She was pretending she was still trying to gather up her belongings. How long did it take to lift a coat and a bag? Much longer than it had taken everyone else apparently. God, she was a terrible actress. But a terrible actress with a killer body, an on-again/ off-again boyfriend, and self-esteem issues. Sean smiled.

02.

'What's taking you so long? I need a piss,' Sean shouted at the bathroom door.

The door opened and Emily came out, blinking. One of her eyes was bloodshot. She was wearing a T-shirt that ended a few inches below her waistline. 'Sorry,' she said. 'Some of it got in my eye and it was kind of stinging, so...' Sean walked past her, still naked. She looked around the corners of the room quickly. It was OK to see him naked while they were in bed, but she didn't know where to look when he was just walking around like that. She heard the sound of him peeing. She turned her back to the open door and rubbed her watering eye. 'You know you don't have to do that. There, I mean, on my face. I mean, I'm on the pill, so it's OK to... but if you prefer... I'm easy either way.'

The toilet flushed and Sean walked out. 'Yeah, I noticed.' He walked over to the bed, pulled his boxer shorts on and sat down. He picked his socks off the ground and started putting them on.

'Are you leaving?'

'Looks that way.'

She pulled the hem of her T-shirt downwards. 'I thought maybe we could have dinner or something. I'll pay. What do you like? Chinese, or Indian, or pizza? I have menus. They deliver. We wouldn't even have to...'

'Where's what's his name; Dick, is it?'

She looked at the floor. 'Rick. Ricky. He hadn't any classes today so he went home yesterday. He's got a job in a bar over the holidays. He's saving up so we can...'

'So why are you taking facials from me?'

After a few seconds staring at her feet, Emily walked over and sat on the end of the bed. Sean continued pulling his jeans on. She looked down and started picking at her nails. 'That first time we got together, at the start of term, you were only... that was only my second time.'

'You don't say. This is my surprised face.' Sean pulled his T-shirt on.

'My first time... it wasn't very... I didn't enjoy it. But that time with you...'

'I rang your bell a couple of times, didn't I?' He chuckled.

She continued worrying at a hangnail intently as she said, 'I liked being with you. I like you. Ricky's a nice guy, but... if you wanted to see what it'd be like with us as a couple I would...'

'Who's this?' Sean pulled a blu-tacked photo off the mirror. 'I've seen her around.'

Emily raised her head for the first time since sitting down. 'That's Kelly. She's my roommate. She's already gone home for the Easter...'

'She's tasty. You think you could talk her into a threesome?'

'What?'

'A threesome. Me, her and you. You think she'd be up for it?'

Emily's mouth hung open for a few seconds and then she lowered her head and started picking at her nail again.

Sean pulled his jacket on and slid across the bed to her. He took her chin in his thumb and forefinger and gently turned her head towards him. 'Hey, it's no big deal. It's just something I've never done before. I thought we could do it together. It might make us closer.'

She looked into his eyes, wanting to believe him. He kissed her lips softly. She gave him a weak smile. A tear ran from her bloodshot eye. He rubbed it away with his thumb. Something beeped on the other side of the room. He looked suspicious.

She shook her head and smiled. 'It's just a text message.'

'Oh my god, you haven't got one of those mobile phones, have you?' He shook his head. 'One born every minute.'

'I know, the calls are very dear so everyone mostly texts.' She read the message. 'That's my mum thanking me for the flowers I sent for Mother's Day. Did you get your mum anything?'

'My mum ran off with a British soldier when I was only a wee'un. Haven't heard from her since.'

'Oh. Sorry.'

'Don't be. If you knew my da you wouldn't blame her.'

She bit her lip. 'Of course, the good thing about these phones is you can get hold of someone pretty much twenty-four/ seven. If you want to.' She reached over to the desk and grabbed a pen and pad. 'I'll give you my number. Just in case you ever need to...'

'Nah, you're all right.'

She finished writing the number and ripped off the page. 'Well, you never know when you might need... me.' She offered the piece of paper and looked him in the eyes.

'OK, I'll take it. *Jesus.*' He snapped the page from her and stuffed it in his jacket pocket.

She looked at her feet again. 'Sean, you do like me, don't you?'

'Of course, but I can't stay tonight. I have to be somewhere. Can't get out of it. OK?' She looked up and nodded with a brave smile. 'Atta girl. And you'll ask your roommate about the threesome?'

After a momentary pause, she nodded.

'You're amazing.' He kissed her cheek and stood up. He gave his pockets a quick pat. 'Ah, you couldn't sub me some bus fare, could you?'

'Yes, of course.' She got to her feet and quickly ran to her coat. She pulled out her purse. He followed her over and saw the wad of notes. She reached him a fiver.

He took it and smiled. 'Cheers. Oh, and you said you would buy me dinner? Do you still want to do that?' He nodded at her purse.

'Er, yes, OK.' She reached him another tenner. 'Is that enough?'

'Yeah, should be.' He took the note but made no motion to move.

After a few uncomfortable seconds, she reached him another tenner. 'Maybe just take that to be sure, then. If you have any left over you might be able to get a pint.'

'You're a fuckin' angel, you know that?' He took the second tenner and kissed her cheek. 'We might not be able to have dinner together, but I'll be thinking about you the whole time I'm eating. You can be sure of that.' He gave her a hug. 'OK, so I guess I'll see you in a couple of weeks.'

'You know, I could stay an extra day or two if you wanted to...'

'No point. I'm going home.'

'Oh, right. I... then I'll see you back in class and we can talk then.'

'Right.' He opened the dorm room door and checked the hall was clear. He gave her a nod. 'See ya.' He walked out. She held the door, stopping the counter weight from closing it automatically. She watched him walk down the hall until he was out of sight. He didn't look back.

03.

Sean was lucky enough to get a seat with a table on the train home. He took his personal CD player out and put his earphones on. He had time to listen Def Leppard's *Slang* and the most of *Recovering the Satellites* by Counting Crows on the journey from Belfast to Coleraine. Despite there being a couple of prospects in the same carriage who looked over and giggled a few times, he kept his head against the window, watching the countryside go by.

During the Christmas holidays he had stayed in Belfast, but now, with his student loan running low, he had to go home. He'd brought a bin-bag full of washing with him. At least that would save him a few quid on the laundrette.

When the train pulled into Coleraine, he watched at least a dozen other students with dirty clothes, dirty hair and bags of laundry, jump off the train and run towards taxis and buses. Sean was last to get off. He walked up the platform. He looked at the row of buses. One left for Portstewart about every half hour. He decided to go for a walk.

He trudged the streets of Coleraine wearing a heavy backpack and carrying a bin-bag full of dirty clothes for over an hour and didn't see anyone he knew. He stopped for a coffee at one end of the town and made it last half an hour, glancing up every time the door opened. Then he had a cup of tea and a caramel square in a café at the other end of the town and made it last forty-five minutes.

Where the hell was everyone? It used to be that he couldn't walk down this street without stopping to chat a dozen times to different people, and then maybe he'd go for a drink with some of them, or back to their place for a smoke.

The waitress was giving him unsubtle glares whenever she passed. His purchases didn't justify the time he had spent at the table by the window. He was sure his bag of stinky clothes probably wasn't endearing him to her either. That was a shame, because she wasn't half bad looking. He might've had a go if he wasn't already on the back foot with her. He got up and left.

He walked to the nearest bus stop and got the next bus to Portstewart. Instead of getting off at the stop nearest his house, he got off in the middle of the promenade and lugged his washing up to the top of the street, then crossed the road and went back down the street on the other side. He didn't see anyone he knew.

He went into Morelli's and let Emily treat him to a generous portion of fish and chips. He ordered a second Diet Coke when he was done and sipped it slowly over his empty plate for another twenty minutes before leaving.

As he got closer to his house, he felt sure someone he knew would cross his path, but the only familiar face he saw was Alex; local 'character'. He was swigging from a bottle wrapped in a blue plastic bag and shouted something Sean couldn't understand as he passed. Sean gave him a nod and a smile without breaking his stride.

The old place didn't look much different. Maybe a few more burst bags of rubbish in the front yard amongst the dog shit, but it was pretty much as he remembered it.

No lights on. That could mean no one was home or they'd been cut off again. His heart sank at the thought of having dragged this washing all the way from Belfast and having no electricity to wash it. He turned his key in the door and pushed. The pile of letters, flyers and magazines wedged under the other side offered some resistance, but he put his shoulder to it and got it open.

He closed the door, dropped his washing, and took off his backpack. He lifted the mail from the floor. Even at a glance he saw a lot of red writing in bold letters on the front of brown envelopes. He flipped through it quickly and saw nothing written by a female hand.

He expected his mother would get in contact at some point. When he was a rich and famous actor, she'd probably show up with her hand out. It was ridiculous to think a letter would arrive at this house anyway. She had never lived here, and thanks to his dad's debts, Sean had moved several times since she had headed for pastures new. There was no way she'd know to write to him here. And yet he still looked a second time, more carefully. There was nothing personal. All official typed letters. He left the pile on the hall table for now. He'd go through them later and see if any of it was for him.

He flicked the hall light switch. Nothing. Typical.

'Da? Are you home?' he shouted up the stairs.

No answer.

The house was cold, like it hadn't been lived in for months. He walked to the kitchen. When he opened the door, the smell hit him immediately. There was dog shit all over the floor. Sean put his hand over his mouth. There was a whimper from the corner.

'Marlon? Is that you, boy?' He negotiated the minefield of crap towards the corner. The dog cowered away from him. Sean knelt down in front of him. 'Hey, it's OK. I know it's not your fault.' He put a hand out, and when the dog realised he was being petted, not punched, he relaxed and put his head on Sean's shoulder. Sean rubbed the dog's belly and felt his ribs. He looked over his shoulder and saw the dog's water and food bowls both empty. Licked clean and dry.

'Fuckin' hell, da,' he whispered.

Sean walked away from the local shop with four bags of groceries. There was nothing in the house to eat, for him or the dog. There was no washing powder or softener either. Plus, he had to buy enough electricity to wipe the arrears from the keypad and put him in credit, and when he came to pay for his groceries, the shopkeeper refused to sell him anything until he had paid off the £33.60's worth of stuff his dad had bought on tick, so he had to dip into the remains of his student loan a lot deeper than he intended.

So much for coming home to save money.

Marlon wolfed down the dog food so quickly that he threw it up again almost immediately. Sean could only wonder how long it had been since he'd been fed. The next time he tried him on dry kibble, a little at a time, and when he saw the dog was keeping that down, he gave him a little dog food. It was a good thing he hadn't cleaned up the dog shit from the kitchen floor already, so now he was able to clean the vomit as well. He scraped it all up and threw it outside – the back garden looked worse than the front. Then he washed the kitchen floor thoroughly with a good dose of bleach in the mop bucket.

By the time he was done it was gone eleven. Still no sign of his dad. He went to the living room and turned on the TV. Of course, there was no heating oil left, but at least the little space heater would keep him and Marlon warm. He flicked around the remaining TV channels – the satellite had been cut off as well – and found Hitchcock's *Psycho* was just starting.

He curled up on the sofa, and Marlon jumped up next to him. The dog rested his head in Sean's lap and they watched the film.

04.

When he woke the next morning to the sound of Marlon barking, the heater and TV were still on. He quickly turned both off and opened the front door for the dog to go out and do his early morning business. A couple of fresh bills had also arrived, which he added to the pile.

Sean went upstairs and saw to his own morning business. He'd only come up here once last night, to empty his bladder, but now he had a better look around.

The stink from his dad's bedroom hit him as soon as he opened the door. Sean held his breath and hurried over to the windows, opening them wide after pulling the curtains. The smell still lingered. He'd have to open all the windows upstairs to get some kind of draught going. He walked over to the rumpled sheets on the bed and saw several stains of different ages. That explained a lot. His dad had a new girlfriend. Sean stripped the bed and threw the bundle over the banister on the way to his room.

At first glance it looked almost the same as he'd left it; his TV and VCR were gone, but he'd almost expected that; the pawn shop was like a second home for them. It was only on closer inspection he began to see the smaller changes. Firstly, the sheets smelled. Not the same aroma as down the landing, but not the fresh sheet smell it should've been. Cigarettes and sweat were the main offenders, but when he pulled back the duvet, he saw actual dirt around the bottom of the sheet. His dad must've let one of his loser friends sleep over, and the dirty bastard hadn't even taken his shoes off. Sean pulled the clothes off the bed and flipped the mattress before throwing them over the banister as well.

When he came back in and sat on the corner of his bed, he noticed how many of his CDs and videos were missing. On his cluttered desk there was a thinner layer of dust in a large rectangle, marking where his boom-box had once sat. His guitar stand no longer held a guitar. Some of his more quality items of clothing were missing from his wardrobe. An expensive watch he'd been given for Christmas one rare year when his dad was flush, was missing from his drawer, as were a few other items of jewellery he'd bought himself. He took a deep breath and hung his head.

The first time he could remember something like this happening was when he was eleven. He'd won twenty pounds for coming first at the school's talent show by re-enacting Elliot's tearful speech from E.T. Dave Maxwell had actually got the final line of the scene, so it looked like he was getting all the applause just for sitting up and saying: 'E.T. phone home' with several Christmas lights taped to his belly, but the judges had recognised the real talent on stage.

Sean had got off the bus and ran all the way home to tell his dad. Dessie Black had patted his son's back and said all the right things about being proud and congratulating him. Sean went to sleep that night looking at the twenty-pound note, which he had propped up on his bedside locker. It wasn't the value of the note he was so proud of; it was what it represented. He, Sean Black, son of drunkard, drug user, gambler, philanderer, and all-round fuck-up, Dessie Black, had talent. He wasn't going to end up a failed musician and career dolie like his old man. He was going to have fame and fortune and everything he ever wanted. That twenty was proof of it. Sean went to sleep that night smiling, with his head full of dreams. He woke the next morning to find the note gone. He searched frantically for it, fearing some errant breeze had carried it off, and also worried about how his dad would shout at him for losing so much money.

He'd already missed the bus, but this was more important than school. After searching his room thoroughly and finding nothing, he opened his bedroom door and walked out to face the music. He would've kept on searching, but he needed to pee and could hold on no longer. He hoped he would've time to use the bathroom before his dad questioned him about the missing money, so he kept up a brisk pace towards the bathroom, only glancing into his dad's bedroom as he got close.

His dad's bed was empty.

And in the blink of an eye, the missing money was explained. The boy's heart sank. There was only one reason his father wouldn't be in bed at 9.20am. He hadn't come home.

Sean felt dizzy. He saw dots of light, like tiny kaleidoscopes, as the world slipped out of focus. His breathing was weird too; fast and shallow. He was shivering. He rested his shoulder against the jamb of his dad's bedroom door and tried to take deep breaths to get it back to normal. After a few minutes he felt a little better. He walked into the bathroom and held onto the sink as he peed. He was still off-balance, and there was a strange pain inside his head. He sat down in the corner, wedged between the toilet bowl and the wall. The floor was cold and wet through his pyjamas. He drew his legs up and hugged them with his arms, and then lowered his forehead down on top of his knees. The pain in his head was getting worse. He kept trying to breathe slower. That seemed like the right thing to do. He felt sure that would make him better.

Two days later, his dad returned home and found him still sitting in the corner of the bathroom. He'd peed and soiled himself at least a few times. When Dessie Black lifted him, he feared the boy was dead. Sean was in a stupor. But after finding a pulse, he gently slapped him until he came round. Sean believed it to be the same morning and couldn't account for the previous two days.

Even Dessie Black could see the boy was cold to the bone, and hadn't had any food or water in at least two days. He quickly put him in the shower and made the water as hot as the boy could bear. As well as washing the filth from the boy's shaking, skinny body, he also hoped this would heat him up and bring some colour back to his skin.

When he'd towelled the boy off, got him into some fresh, warm clothes and parked him in front of the electric heater in the living room, his dad had gone out and brought back fish and chips for them both as well as renting a copy of *Return of the Jedi*. He made sure the boy ate it all. Sean forced it down. Not because he was especially hungry, but because he could see real worry in his father's eyes. Dessie had fucked up badly and he knew it.

That night he had sat next to Sean on the sofa with his arm around him as they watched Luke Skywalker and his friends defeat the Empire. When it was over, he even let him stay up and watch *Sledge Hammer!* after the ten o'clock news. When Sean laughed at the gun-toting detective's comic antics, his father finally relaxed a little. That night his dad tucked him into bed and kissed his forehead.

The missing twenty-pound note was never mentioned, and Sean seemed to need no further medical attention. His dad thanked his lucky stars for the resilience of children, but he knew how close he'd come to tragedy. He vowed to never leave his son alone again.

That lasted almost a fortnight.

Sean slapped his face with both hands. He couldn't let himself go to the dark place again. He looked around his looted room and decided to be thankful for all the stuff his dad hadn't taken. He had to hold on just a little while longer. Everyone in his class saw his talent, his teachers all saw it, and when he finished this term and got out there into the world of auditions and casting calls, the whole fucking business would see it.

Then all this shit would just be a memory.

He got up off the bed and opened the windows of his room. The breeze soothed his stinging eyes. He opened the window in the bathroom as he passed on his way to the stairs. He went down and put the bedclothes in the washing machine.

He'd make himself some breakfast and then take Marlon for a nice long walk.

05.

Sean had been home for five days. His dad still hadn't made an appearance, but more importantly, he'd been going to bed alone all week. He'd forgotten how hard it was to score in his home town with his family's reputation following him everywhere. When he'd gone to uni he'd reinvented himself. No one had known him, and he'd used that to his advantage.

The previous evening he'd gone to a local nightclub. It was free entry if you showed your student card. There was a long queue outside populated with lots of short skirts. If this were uni, he'd have called this a 'fish in a barrel' venue, but it only took half an hour of standing at the bar nursing a pint to realise this was a bad idea. Faces he vaguely remembered, now with a little more make-up or a different haircut, walked past giving him snotty looks. He was back to who he was before he left; not Sean Black, who could charm his way into even the most conservative pants, but Dessie Black's son, who would probably give you a dose of something nasty and then rob you blind for good measure. He gave it another half hour and then walked home and dug into his dad's porn collection.

Among the videos was nothing he could pleasure himself to. Sean didn't see anything sexy about women being bound and gagged, but at least there was some nudity. It was when the male performer brought out knives and razor blades that Sean quickly turned it off. He tried to finish himself off by replaying the memory of him and that freaky hippie chick in her tent at Glastonbury in '95, but ended up falling asleep.

He woke the next morning with his trousers and boxers still around his ankles. His mouth was dry and the whole room smelled of stale beer. This was humiliating. Sean Black reduced to this. If the uni crowd could see him now. He got to his feet and pulled his trousers and boxers up. He waddled to the kitchen and made himself a strong mug of coffee. As the caffeine slowly brought his senses back to life, he began to wonder who he could call. There was no one in his home town. He had several casual relationships going with girls at uni. The problem was, he didn't know where any of them lived when they weren't at uni. The bigger problem was, he didn't know any of their surnames, even if he did know what town they lived in.

But then there was Emily.

Emily and her mobile phone.

As he went through the pockets of the jacket he'd been wearing that day, he tried to remember where she lived. Was she anywhere near him? Did it matter? She had a car. She'd probably drive from Cork if he asked her. He laughed. He found the scrap of paper and saw the number, her name and three kisses. She was going to be tough to get rid of if he invited her here, but it was either that or go a full two weeks without getting laid.

He filled his pockets with change and set off towards the nearest phone box.

'Hello?'

'Hi, Emily. It's Sean.'

'Sean! I didn't recognize the number. This isn't the number I have for you.'

'No, I'm in a phone box. Our phone has been... it's not working. BT are taking forever to sort it out.'

'That's why McMaster couldn't get hold of you. She's called me three times since yesterday asking if I'd spoke to you.'

'Why's McMaster looking for me?'

'I don't know exactly, it's something to do with a film role. She's been calling everyone trying to get hold of you.'

'Did she leave a number to call her back on?' Emily read out the number and Sean scribbled it on the back of his hand. 'OK. Cheers. I better call her and see what this is all about. Bye.'

'Wait! Sean, why were you calling me?'

'I... I'll call you back after I speak to McMaster.' He hung up and dialled the number on his hand.

'Hello?'

'Hi, it's Sean. Have you been trying to...?'

'Sean! My god, where have you been?'

'The house phone is...'

'Never mind about that now. What time is it? OK, you still have time to make it if you go now.'

'Make what?'

'I was having dinner the other night with a friend I went to college with. He works as a production manager now. He's over here filming some Troubles drama. Anyway, I told him about you and never thought anything more about it, but yesterday he calls me up and tells me they need someone immediately. One of the actors got sick and had to drop out. It's only half a dozen lines, but it's a proper movie, and they'll give you a few quid, I'm sure. So what do you think?'

'Yeah! I mean, of course. Where is it and how long do I have to get there?' McMaster gave him the details and he wrote them on his arm. 'What about the script; my lines?'

'Do you have the Internet at home?'

'No, I don't. Listen, don't worry, I can pick up lines easily. Just call the guy and tell him I'm on my way.'

'OK, I will. Break a leg!'

Sean slammed down the phone and ran from the phone box. Four hours later he was on-set memorizing lines.

Colm walks through the run-down housing project, unfazed by the graffiti and garbage everywhere.

He is stopped by an intimidating youth called MICKY. The kid is 20, and wears the cuts and bruises of several different fights like badges of honor.

> MICKY
> Where do you think you're going, mate?

> COLM
> I'm going wherever the fuck I want, son. What business do you think it is of yours?

> MICKY
> This is my estate, mother-fucker. You want to come in here, you pay the price or I'll fuckin' shiv you where you stand.

MICKY pulls out a switchblade.

That was it. That was the key to his character. He didn't have a lot to work with, but that was the most important phrase. What McMaster called his character-defining moment. Micky believed he owned this estate. He was the gatekeeper. No bad guy thinks he's a bad guy. This guy probably imagines he's keeping the other residents of this place safe. That's who he is. That's who Sean had to become.

He was acting opposite a guy he had last seen in a Channel 4 drama. They were introduced and shook hands, but he said little as the cameras prepared to roll. He was staying in character. Sean could respect that if that was his process.

As they got their final make-up touch-ups and the director took his place behind the camera, Sean felt his bladder screaming to be emptied. He couldn't halt things now. What would they all think of him? Unprofessional. Just a kid. He looked at his co-star. Cool as a fucking cucumber. A pro, through and through. He knew to take a piss before he left his trailer. Shit, what was he going to do? How long would this take? Could he hold on? Use it. That's what

McMaster would say. Use that nervous energy in the character. Sean had already decided he would be a bit twitchy. He was probably on drugs. Use it. Use it and nail the fuckin' scene in one take. That was what he had to do. That would get him back to his trailer the quickest.

'All right, are we ready for one?' the director asked. After getting the required nods from the heads of department, he said, 'OK.'

'Rolling,' the cameraman said.

'Sound-speed,' the boom operator said.

The clapper loader stepped into shot and held the board in front of the camera. 'Scene thirty-two, take one.' He brought the clapstick down on the board making the required clap and stepped out of shot.

The assembled crew got very quiet. The director said, 'OK, and... action.'

The director had gone over the blocking and given him a few ideas on how to play the character, now it was down to Sean to bring Micky to life. Forget about the growing pain of needing to piss. He took a deep breath and walked forward, a little twitch, a sniff to imply his nose-powder habit, and said...

'Boom's in shot,' the cameraman said.

'OK, cut,' the director said. 'Reset. First positions again, please.'

The make-up girl walked in to touch him up again for some reason Sean couldn't fathom. The boom operator was laughing about spoiling the shot.

Fuckwit.

Sean wanted to go over there and break his fuckin' nose. He wasn't going to be able to hold on much longer.

'OK, everyone ready to go again?' the director asked.

Everyone checked in.

'Scene thirty-two, take two.' Clap.

'OK, and action!'

'Hold on. Motorbike,' the sound man said. Everyone waited as the sound of a motorcycle a couple of streets away came and went.

Fuckin' asshole soundman again. Who gives a fuck about motorbikes in the background? There are motorbikes in real life.

'Ok, third time's a charm,' the director, who seemed unflappable, said with a grin.

For a third time everyone checked in.

'Scene thirty-two, take three.' Clap!

23

'Action!'

The cameras were rolling. Everyone was silent, waiting for Sean to step forward, and that's when he turned around and stepped backwards. He unzipped and relieved himself against the alley wall. No one said anything. The director wasn't yelling cut. Sean glanced over his shoulder and then gave a quick shake and walked toward his co-star.

'Where do you think you're going, mate?'

'I'm going wherever the fuck I want, son. What business do you think it is of yours?'

Sean stepped closer and gave him an unscripted poke in the chest. 'This is my estate, motherfucker! You want to come in here you pay the price, or I'll fuckin' shiv you where you stand.' Sean pulled out the knife and flicked it open just under his co-star's head. The point of the blade missed his chin by millimetres, but he never broke character, and they finished the scene glaring at each other.

For ten seconds. For twenty seconds.

The director hadn't called cut.

'Oh, sorry. Cut.' The director got up from his chair and looked at his department heads. 'Please tell me you got that.' They both nodded and he broke out in a huge smile. He ran over and threw an arm around each of his actors. 'That was incredible! Sean, where... why did... how did you come up with that, to start with him pissing?'

'I don't know. It just came to me that it seemed a bit contrived if he was just standing in this alley for no reason, so I figured he ducked in to take a piss, and also it would be a territorial thing.'

The director was shaking with excitement. 'It was incredible. That was a true moment. No bullshit. Totally real. Just... of the moment. Thank god we got it and it was a two-shot. We'll shoot the singles and a couple of inserts, just for safety, but I'm already sure that's the take I'll be using.' The director hurried off to talk to his department heads.

Sean's co-star leaned in and said, 'I think you made his day. That was pretty good, son. Even I'll admit that.'

They did the scene again in single shots and filmed close-ups of the knife being pulled and the knife point being pushed under his co-star's chin. Sean watched closely, enthralled by the marriage of technical and creative disciplines on the set. He also didn't mind all the attention he was being paid.

That night the cast and crew went to the pub. Sean didn't have to put his hand in his pocket once. He got nicely drunk and ingratiated himself with the whole production as they played darts, sang songs, and gave the landlord his best Tuesday night takings in a long time. By the time he fell out of the pub around one a.m. Sean had a very cute First A.D. on his arm. He spent the night in her room, and despite the fact they were both quite drunk and tired, they managed to have sex twice before falling asleep.

The next morning she was gone before seven for the early call. Sean stayed in the room until checkout, ordering breakfast and watching TV. He found some money in her bag, but didn't take it. No point burning his bridges with a company who might hire him again. Besides, he was getting paid for this gig anyway.

When the cleaner knocked on the door at midday, he let her in and let himself out.

He took the train home.

He was happy in a variety of ways.

POLICE APPEAL FOR WITNESSES IN BRUTAL MUGGING

Detectives based at the Strand Road RUC station are appealing for witnesses to a brutal mugging which took place in the early hours of Wednesday April 2nd in the city centre.

Thirty-four-year-old Fergus Connolly was attacked while walking back to his hotel after a night out with work colleagues. Mister Connolly was in town working as a sound recordist on a feature film currently shooting in the city. After being jumped from behind and beaten with a blunt object, the victim had something sharp inserted into both ears. Doctors at Altnagelvin Hospital report his condition as stable, but are unable to comment on whether he'll ever be able to hear again.

Lead detective Bernard Canning described the attack as: 'A senseless and brutal assault on a visitor to our city.' He added that, 'The city should be welcoming outside productions like this to help Derry's economy. The person or persons who carried out this mindless act need to be brought to justice, and I urge anyone who saw anything on the night in question to contact the RUC immediately. We will not stop until we track down those responsible.'

Derry Chronicle, 10th April, 1997

06.

Sean was woken by the sound of breaking glass in the middle of the night.

He jumped out of bed and quickly grabbed the hurling bat behind his bedroom door. He looked out the window but saw no cars or flashing lights. He turned and ran out his bedroom door and across the landing. He looked over the banister, gripping the bat tightly with both hands.

'Who the fuck's down there?' he shouted down the dark stairs.

The shambling silhouette answered his question even before the light went on. The older man blinked as his eyes became accustomed to the light. Sean looked down at the ageing Teddy Boy in his blue and red zoot suit and lowered his bat.

'Hey, da.'

'All right, boy. Are you home?' He turned and pushed the door closed. He pointed a thumb at the broken pane above the door handle. 'I suppose that's why the deadbolt was on.'

Sean started down the stairs. 'I've been home for nearly a fortnight. I go back to uni tomorrow. Where have you been?'

'Been on the road, haven't I?' he smiled and slicked back his unnaturally black hair. 'Johnny Cosmos and the All-Stars. We've been all over the south for the last month.'

'How? Your drums were repossessed.'

'Borrowed Jimmy Sticks's kit. He's in hospital with a hernia.'

Sean exhaled and looked at the broken glass on the floor. 'Go put the kettle on. I'll clean this up.'

'I'd prefer a wee nip of something. Is there anything in the house?'

'No there isn't. Make the tea, da.'

They sat at the table drinking tea and saying little. Dessie Black dropped his cigarette butt on the floor and stubbed it out with the heel of his tiger-print suede creepers. He lit his third cigarette since walking through the door, and inhaled deeply.

'There's a bunch of bills and letters for you.'

'Right. I'll have a look in the morning.'

'There's a few from Sycamore Acres. Sounds like Uncle Ronnie isn't in good form.' Dessie nodded vaguely at this news of his brother. 'They reckon you should maybe go and see him before it's too late.'

'Aye, I'll try to find the time.'

If his dad hadn't been staring into his mug, he would've seen Sean smirk. Find the time? Like his dad had such a busy schedule.

Uncle Ronnie had been in Sycamore Acres most of his life. Sean never really knew the full story behind it, but his dad referred to the place as *the nuthouse* and his brother as a *mental case*, so he guessed they weren't that close. Sean had vague memories of the man from when he was very young. Mostly Christmases spent together. Coloured paper hats. Everyone drinking Shloer. His mum singing ABBA songs at the piano when she ran out of carols. That was in the other house. When they still had a piano. When they still celebrated Christmas. Before everything changed. Before the shouting. Before the screaming.

'What time are you off tomorrow?'

'Early.' Sean stared into his mug. 'If you're going to swan off again, don't leave Marlon locked in. He was nearly fuckin' dead when I got home.'

'Shite. Did I leave him inside?' He chuckled and shook his head. 'It was such a last-minute thing. I must've rushed out and forgot about him. Is he OK?'

'He is now.'

'And how's university?'

'Yeah, I'm getting distinctions across the board. On track for a First my teacher thinks.'

'You get that from me. I was surprised how quick I picked up the songs again after all this time.' He drummed on the table with his forefingers. 'But you never forget the important stuff. This might turn into a regular gig with Johnny.'

'I got a wee part in a film.'

'That's good. You getting your end away plenty?'

Sean smiled a little. He could tell stories that would impress even his dad, and he was just about to when...

'I'll tell you this, boy, it was great being back on the road. I forgot how much pussy you get after gigs when you're in a band. Now I admit, they're not the teenagers I used to get, but you get these horny oul housewives out for a night without the husband. Fuck, I had manys a knee-trembler in the last month. My sack's empty. They're not the tens I used to get, but they're solid sixes and sevens. What you lose on the young body, you make up for with experience. Middle-aged women know things young girls don't, boy.' He drained his tea and put the mug down on the table as he stood up. 'Right, I'm for bed. If you're away before I'm up in the morning, best of luck with it all. When are you back again?'

'I don't know. Summer, maybe.'

'Right, I daresay I'll see you then.'

'Night, da. I'll get a bit of wood from the shed and cover that hole in the door, then I'll go to bed too.'

Sean walked Marlon to the supermarket early next morning. Along with a few groceries, he bought a small, ready-cooked chicken from the hot food bar and then walked back home through the woods. He stopped in a quiet area, unwrapped the chicken and set it on the ground in front of the dog. Marlon looked at it, and then at his master with a *What, really?* look in his eyes. Sean nodded. As the dog feasted on the chicken, Sean dug into the loose earth with pieces of branch and his bare hands.

He sat under a tree when he was done, with the dog in his lap. Sean stroked it for a long time before lifting its head and looking Marlon in the eyes. 'I can't take you with me. And if I leave you with him, you're just going to die a slow, painful death. So this is the best thing for both of us.' The dog leaned forwards and licked the tears from his cheeks. Sean hugged him tightly. And then tighter. The dog's paws started to claw at the ground beneath them, trying to get away. Sean held on as it squirmed harder. It yelped, unable to bark because of the grip Sean had. He swallowed hard and gave the dog's head a sharp twist. He heard the crack, and the dog went limp in his arms. And then he cried, openly and audibly.

After he'd buried the dog, he walked home.

His dad would sleep until noon at least. He stuck another £20 on the electricity keypad, and put a few essentials in the fridge and cupboard. He'd already packed up anything from his room that he wanted to keep. Despite what he said last night, he didn't think he'd be back. He left £40 under the saltshaker on the table and left.

1999

01.

The quiet suburban street looked like any other. Lawns were neatly mown; gardens were tended and weeds were quickly evicted. Paintwork was never allowed to get to the flaking stage. Dogs barked. Cats walked along fences. Curtains twitched and housewives gossiped. That was all par for the course, but today the routine of their lives had an added element of excitement. Half a dozen cars were parked outside number thirty-seven.

They were making a film.

Her son was at university doing Media Studies.

No one had seen anyone famous yet, but apparently one of the cast had a small part in a film once. It was cut from the final edit, and his scene had been trimmed to one shot of him in silhouette with his back to the camera having a piss in an alley.

They had arrived early this morning and hung a large black blanket over the outside of the upstairs bedroom window. They'd carried lots of equipment inside and apart from seeing a couple of people (that they didn't recognise) out for a smoke, that was the last the neighbours had seen of them.

They had no idea what was going on in there.

```
06. INT. BEDROOM - NIGHT

David, a man who looks like a hunky computer
programmer, is waiting on the bed when his wife
Judith comes home.

                    DAVID
          Your late, Judith. Don't
          try to make up and excuse.
          Theres no point lying to
          me, Judith. I know you've
          been with John. I know
          you've been having an
          affair with him for the
          past six months while I was
          working hard at my computer
          firm for our family. Just
          tell me why you had an
          affair, Judith. I've always
          treated you nicely and been
          a good husband and John is
          my best friend who I grew
          up with and now works with
          me at my computer company.
```

Sean looked up from his script wondering how he was ever going to make this dialogue sound natural. For the past two days he had been trying to make it work, but the nineteen-year-old director yelled 'cut' if he changed anything. He seemed to think that was a director's job; pulling actors up when they said a wrong word. On the first morning, Sean had tried to tell him that it would sound more natural if he said the same thing in his own words. The director was not in agreement. This story was based on his own family's break-up, and no one knew this material better than him. So Sean had shut his mouth and taken the meagre payday.

He had to stop doing these student films.

At least this was the last scene they had to shoot. He looked over at the director, pacing nervously in his black polo-neck and beret. That would be pretentious enough for most people, but the viewfinder hanging around his neck really topped off the look. He ended up in the corner of the room, rubbing his forehead with his eyes tightly shut, doing his best to look like a misunderstood genius.

Sean had been on these student projects before. Nine times out of ten they were terribly written, but at least the college or university usually had good equipment, so if the crew knew what they were doing there might be some usable visuals for his showreel. There wouldn't be any usable dialogue, though. Not from this project.

The other good thing about doing student films was the chance to meet some college girls. His knowledge of directors, from Aronofsky to Zemeckis, had gained him admittance to many dorm rooms on previous films. There were only two women on this shoot. The lead actress, who was obviously the director's girlfriend, because 1) she couldn't act, and 2) between takes the director held onto her like she was a helium balloon that might float away. The boom-operator was the other option, but he was getting a distinct man-hating-lesbian vibe from her. He'd given her a smile and a nod 'hello' on the first day and got a disgusted look in return.

Bad dialogue. Low pay. And not even any prospects in the cast and crew.

It was a hell of a way to make a living.

The bedroom door was knocked and a third option presented itself. The producer – a short guy with bad acne, holding a clipboard and trying to look busier than he was – immediately blushed and hurried over to intercept her. She was carrying a tray of tea and home-made buns.

Sean looked her up and down. She was at least twice his age, but it looked good on her. The third finger of her left hand was naked and still cinched-in near the knuckle. She hadn't been here when they arrived this morning. The boy producer had probably ordered her to clear out. He spoke to her in quick sentences through gritted teeth, but she ignored him and proceeded to hand out tea and buns to the cast and crew. Everyone welcomed the refreshments except the director, who sighed loudly and shook his head in disbelief as if this were the hundredth interruption today and not the first.

She leaned over and offered the tray to Sean. He looked down her blouse and saw a cleavage college girls couldn't compete with. He took a bun and made sure he brushed her fingers when he took the cup of tea from her. He saw her eyes glint and she smiled.

'Do you go to college with...?' She left the sentence hanging, as if she had forgotten her son's name temporarily.

'No, I left uni a couple of years ago,' Sean said. 'I'm just a jobbing actor now.'

'That must be... hard.' She smiled.

'It can be. It can be *really* hard.' Sean smiled at her and she visibly flushed.

They both suddenly became aware that the whole set had gone quiet and everyone was looking at them. This time she was blushing instead of flushing. She stood up and moved on to serving the rest of the gobsmacked students.

Sean was outside having a smoke when his mobile phone rang. He saw the caller ID and his heart skipped. Avi Goldman. His agent. Not only an agent, but an American agent. He might live in Belfast now, but he was still an American with American contacts. This is one reason why Sean had gone with him ahead of other, bigger agencies. Several of the top casting agencies had shown interest in him when he left college, but he'd got a good vibe from Avi. He was old, and his agency was small, but to Sean that just meant he had experience and he would spend his time working hard to get him auditions. And he *had* been getting him auditions, but Sean just wasn't getting the parts. Maybe this was the phone call that would change that. He pressed the little green phone button.

'Avi, how's it going?'

'I'm... I'm OK, kid.'

He didn't even have to say it. Sean could tell by his tone that it was bad news. 'Another knockback?'

'I'm sorry, kid.'

'Shit.' Sean flicked his cigarette across the lawn. 'Which one?'

'Ballykissangel.'

'I fuckin' nailed that in the audition.'

'They just... they went another way with it.'

Sean took a deep breath. 'What the fuck I'm I doing wrong, Avi?'

'Nothing, kid. These things take time. You've seen interviews with all your favourite actors. How many of them said it was easy? How many of them said they got the first job they went up for and it was plain sailing after that? Well, how many?'

'None.'

'Exactly. You got talent, kid. I'm going to keep sending you up for everything I can. One of these directors is going to see what I see eventually. Trust Avi. Do you trust Avi?'

Sean smiled. He knew he was being handled, but it didn't matter. The old guy knew what to say and how to say it. 'Yeah, I trust Avi.'

'Fuckin' A! How's the short going?'

Sean looked around to make sure he wasn't being overheard. 'It's fuckin' shite. The dialogue's a joke. Thank fuck today will finish it.'

'You think there'll be anything for your showreel?'

'I doubt it. The director climbed up his own arse on the first day and he's been there ever since.'

The old man on the other end of the phone laughed and then broke into a phlegmy cough. Sean could imagine the fat cigar he was sucking on. 'Well, hang in there, kid. Some of the biggest assholes go on to become very famous. Bite your tongue. Do the work and take the paycheque.'

'I will. Thanks, Avi.'

'I'll talk to you later, kid.' With that he hung up.

Sean thought of Avi sitting in his little office. He seemed most at ease there. He hated going out in public. Sean wondered if he might be a little agoraphobic. Or maybe he just valued his privacy.

Sean had done a Cinemagic workshop the year before, teaching some kids drama. It was the sort of event that the press lapped up, and Avi had been there to make sure Sean got as much publicity as possible. While photographing Sean teaching the class, one of the photographers had inadvertently caught Avi in the back of the shot. Avi had immediately asked him for the film. The guy refused point blank and Avi had shrugged and walked away with a smile, but Sean had seen him later. Avi had followed at a distance until the guy changed camera and then, while he was shooting the kids being cute, Avi had stepped in and taken the film from the camera. Sean saw him hurry into the nearest toilet where he assumed the film met a watery fate. No one else had seen it happen. It was only by chance that Sean had seen him do it.

That was why Avi wasn't on set with him now. Sean wondered if he would still stay in the office when he hit the bigtime. Would the old man still avoid the photographer's lens if he was on a red carpet?

Sean looked back at the suburban house and saw just how far away the bigtime was from here. He walked back to the front door and leaned on the jamb, looking around the little collection of houses. He saw two women talking over their fence. They looked over at him frequently. They looked suspicious, or maybe even jealous. He understood. This was an event for them; a release from the daily routine of washing, cooking and cleaning. Some of them probably envied him for pursuing such a tough but ultimately glamorous career, others probably hated him for the same reason. These people were everything he didn't want to be. If a crappy little short film shooting on your street was the most exciting thing to happen in your week, what the hell was the point of living?

Someone lightly cleared their throat behind him.

He turned and saw the producer's mum standing at the base of the stairs.

She smiled. He noticed she'd put on fresh make-up. 'Hello again.'

Sean nodded and smiled.

She took a step towards him and put her hands behind her back, pushing her chest out. 'Is there anything you need?'

The washing machine banged against the utility room's wall in rhythm with Sean's hips. Her breasts were huge when he had unleashed them. They rippled with every thrust. Her stomach looked like she spent a lot of time in the gym trying to halt the effects of time. Considering the size of her breasts, her waist was disproportionately tiny.

He'd never had sex with a woman this old. He expected her to show him a few tricks, and maybe she would've if he'd let her take the lead, but Sean was in no mood to be submissive. The washing machine door banged against his knees as the appliance rocked back and forth.

He looked at her face. She was ruddy in the cheeks and breathing hard trying to keep up with him. If she thought this was going to be some sort of Mrs. Robinson scenario, she was wrong. Sean seized her around the throat and began to close his fingers. She stopped the panting and moaning first. Then the excitement in her eyes turned to fear. Sean thrust harder, faster. Her mouth was open. Maybe she was trying to speak. Or scream. Or maybe she was just trying to breathe. Sean leaned in closer and looked into those frightened eyes. He looked into her open mouth and spat in it. She looked really terrified now as she started to choke on his spittle. Her hands slapped his shoulders repeatedly.

In the space of a few seconds Sean growled through gritted teeth, released his hand from around her throat, stopped thrusting, and stepped back. The middle-aged woman lay there for a few moments, letting the oxygen back into her lungs. When she sat up, she pulled her blouse tightly across her breasts. Sean wasn't sure if she was crying or if her eyes were just watering from the choking. Either way, he was sure he'd given her an afternoon to remember. She might look scared now, but he was sure, before the week was out, she'd be bragging about this encounter with her friends.

By the time Sean had buckled up his trousers and lit a cigarette, she was still sitting in the same position watching him intently. Neither of them spoke. Sean gave her a smug smile before leaving.

The shoot didn't finish until after eight that night. Pizzas were ordered at suppertime. The producer's mum brought refreshments once more after that. Her hair was still damp from the shower. She had a silk scarf tied around her neck. This time she didn't make eye contact when she gave Sean his tea.

02.

It was after nine when Sean got back to the flat. The director had actually given them a speech when they wrapped, about how much he appreciated everyone's help in bringing his vision to life. That was followed by much hugging, backslapping and fake congratulations.

Were they really so deluded that they truly believed this film was going to be good? Sean wondered if he had ever been that naïve. Still, he had played along shaking hands with his co-stars and making promises to see everyone at the premiere screening. Avi was right about assholes sometimes getting the breaks, so it did no harm to stay chummy with these talentless wannabes.

Kelly was passed out on the sofa with the TV on. He saw the Beano annual with all the components for making joints laid out on it sitting on the floor. She'd gone through a lot of that Soft Black since he left this morning. She'd probably called in sick to work again. It was only a matter of time before she was fired. Even if her mum was friends with the owner, no one wanted to be sold the latest fashions by someone looking like that.

She was wearing one of Sean's T-shirts which had rode up her body as she had gradually slid down the sofa. Other than that, she was only wearing pants. Pants that Sean had once described as sexy – maybe that's why she wore them so often – but since it had been at least two weeks since she had changed them, they were the furthest thing from sexy now. Her hair was thick with grease. She had really bad acne around her mouth from huffing glue. Her armpit hair was gross. She was a million miles away from the sexy girl Emily had introduced him to before their threesome.

Emily.

He wondered where she was now.

In the last couple of years phone technology had moved on a lot, and the mobile number he had for her no longer worked. She had undoubtedly upgraded to a flip-phone by now. This wasn't the first time he'd thought about her. He'd often wondered if he chose the wrong girl after that night in their dorm room. He was quite happy to keep seeing them both, singly or together, but Emily and Kelly's relationship deteriorated quickly after that night and she had given him an ultimatum. The choice was easy at the time because Emily said she would never want to do anything like that again. Kelly, however, was starting to use ecstasy regularly and had no such restrictions. She was up for anything and that suited Sean.

He looked at her now and found her repulsive. If it hadn't been for her parents paying the rent on this shithole he would've walked long ago. They didn't even screw anymore. She had little to no sex-drive, and he found her repellent.

Sean lifted the Beano annual and started skinning-up. At least there was always dope in the house. Kelly's dealer, Marvel, was a regular visitor to their little flat. Sean was pretty sure Kelly had blown him a few times when they were out of money and she needed some hash. If Marvel thought that was a reasonable deal, Sean had no problem with it. All he needed was one plum role and he'd leave this place for good and never look back.

His spliff completed, Sean left the annual back on the floor and got up gently. Kelly stirred but didn't wake. He used her lighter to spark it before turning off the TV, the light, and closing the door as he left the room.

The bedclothes stank almost as badly as Kelly did, but he didn't care. He turned on the portable TV and VCR. After scanning the titles available in his small collection of VHS tapes he chose *Being John Malkovich*. It was a pirate copy – something else Marvel dealt in – but the quality was pretty decent. He loved this movie. Cusack, Diaz, Malkovich, Spike Jonze, Kaufman's script. It was all perfect.

After pressing play, he wrapped the dirty duvet around himself, took a long hit on the joint and entered that other, fantastical world.

Sean had put it down to the squalid conditions in the flat originally. But even after repeated showering and scrubbing, his penis still itched, and there was now a burning sensation when he peed. He still hoped it would go away – whatever it was – by itself in time, but when puss oozed from the tip of his penis one morning, he decided it was time to see a doctor and made an appointment immediately.

Thankfully, the doctor was male, but this was causing shrinkage and recoil in the small, cold office. The doctor put his glasses on and had a quick look. The two men exchanged a glance. Sean stretched it out. The doctor took it in his rubber gloves and examined it. Sean stared at the ceiling tiles and gritted his teeth as the doctor took a sample of the discharge.

When he stood up and pulled off his gloves, Sean quickly wriggled back into his jeans. The doctor dropped the used gloves into the hazardous waste bin and said, 'We'll have to wait for the test results to be positive, but I'm almost certain it's gonorrhoea. Have you had unprotected sex recently?' He sat down and started making notes in Sean's file.

The only person Sean had had sex with in the last three weeks was the producer's mother on the short film. Had she dosed him? 'Yes,' he said quietly.

'Girlfriend?'

'No. She was a… I didn't… it was a one-off.'

'I see.' The doctor's voice was monotone. No judgement. No reproaches. Just the facts.

Sean finished buckling up his belt and sat down next to him. 'I've heard of gonorrhoea, but… I mean, it's treatable, right?'

'A course of antibiotics should clear it up.'

Sean exhaled deeply. 'Jesus! Thank fuck for that.'

'There is something else we should discuss.' The doctor took off his glasses and made eye-contact with Sean. 'In these cases, where an STD has been passed on through unprotected sex with an unknown partner, it's standard practice for us to suggest an HIV test too.'

Sean's stomach filled with maggots. He felt bile rise in this throat but choked it back. He felt his eyes stinging, but blinked away the tears. He could barely get the words out. 'You think I have…?'

'Not at all, this is just precautionary.'

'How… how long, before…?'

'It'll take about a week for the results to come back.'

Sean nodded. A tear escaped his eye. He wiped before it made it halfway down his cheek. He nodded at the doctor and sniffed back hard.

It was like being high. The door to the doctor's office blurred so much he missed the handle the first time he reached for it. As he walked up the corridor the walls seemed to pulse in and out with his breathing. The receptionist said something to him as he passed, but it sounded far away and muffled. He didn't stop to ask her to repeat it. He needed to get outside. He needed air. He made it to the car park before dropping to his knees and vomiting. There were sounds all around; muffled like he had water in his ears after swimming. He looked down at the pool of half-digested food below him. He wiped the strands of sick hanging from his lips and got to his feet. He had to put out a hand and steady himself on the nearest car to stop himself from falling. Breathe. Breathe. He forced long deep breaths, just like McMaster had taught him. This was just like dealing with stage fright. Fright was fear. Fear was fright. This was fear. Breathing would help. Breathe. Just breathe.

He must've started walking at some point, because the next thing he remembered he was sitting in a cinema at a matinee showing of *Dogma*. He looked around and saw a couple of stoners sitting together, one conservative old lady who seemed to be making notes on the film, and a couple sucking face in the back row. He looked at the screen and was calmed.

He'd seen this film already, which was a blessing because he couldn't follow the story this time. There was too much else going on in his head. He could've left, but he couldn't think of anywhere else he'd rather be. He thought about getting those results next week. He imagined the worst, the slow painful death that awaited him. He imagined some grief-stricken female crying inconsolable tears at his graveside, but he couldn't imagine who she might be. Not Kelly, that's for sure. Maybe Emily. But then again, maybe not.

Between showings he hid in the bathroom, but when he heard Alanis Morissette's excellent song *Still* play over the end credits for the fourth time that day, he knew he had to leave. The lobby lights were off. The staff had their jackets on. He was the last customer to leave. Those who had come on during the evening shift eyed him with suspicion because they didn't remember him coming in, but no one said anything.

Sean walked out into the cold night air and took several deep breaths just to make sure he didn't freak out again. Seeing a film where there was undisputable proof of God had done nothing to sway his atheist tendencies, but he had reached some level of acceptance. He began the long walk back to the flat.

03.

Apart from telling Kelly to fuck off when she tried to come into the bedroom, Sean didn't speak to anyone for the next two days. He hadn't told her about visiting the doctor or the worst-case scenario when the results came back. If it was the producer's mother who had dosed him, he hadn't touched Kelly since then. She was so out of it these days he wouldn't expect the gravitas of the situation to register with her anyway.

So, he stayed in bed. He watched the eleven films he had on VHS one after the other. When he'd watched them all, he started with the first again.

Then the phone rang and the caller ID said it was Avi. Sean looked at the ringing phone and knew it was going to be good news. That would be typical if he got his big break and died before he got a chance to show the world what he could do. Like Alanis said: 'Isn't it ironic.'

He pressed the green button. 'Hi, Avi.'

'Hey, kid.' It was his consolation voice. For some reason that made Sean feel better. He wasn't going to miss his big opportunity, because there was no opportunity.

'Someone else turn me down?' He was actually smiling for the first time in two days.

'I'm sorry, kid. The sitcom guys went with Michael Smiley for the bike courier guy. You didn't want that role anyway. It's not leading man material.'

'I'd take anything right now, Avi. I'm going out of my fuckin' mind sitting here. Get me something, anything!' He took a breath and calmed himself before adding, 'Please.'

'Look, I know you've said no before, but there's so little going on in Northern Ireland right now, it's all I can get you.'

Sean's heart sank. 'Extra work?'

'It's money kid, and a chance to meet people in the biz.' He laughed. 'And with your looks and that permanent hard-on of yours, I'm sure there's someone you could charm.' The old man chuckle-coughed.

There were stories of extras who had gone on to become proper actors. Oliver Reed was one. But they were few and far between. Sean hadn't spent all this time honing his craft to stand in the background with a group of wankers and be directed by a First AD.

He looked around the bedroom. Filth and stink from corner to corner. The walls felt closer this morning. Being an extra was degrading, but sitting in this room was driving him batshit.

The Third AD threw the wad of toilet paper into the bowl. She pulled her jeans and pants up as Sean rinsed his fingers under the tap. She looked at the bulge in his trousers.

'Are you sure I can't return the favour?' God, he loved her accent. He'd grown up equating American accents with beauty and glamour. She popped her breasts back into the cups of her bra and pulled her T-shirt down. 'You look like you're about to rip your jeans open.'

41

Sean grabbed a paper towel and dried his hands as he turned to her. Her name was Lauren. She had perfect hair and perfect teeth. Anywhere else in the world she was beautiful enough to be an actress, but in LA she was a Third AD. He reached around to the small of her back and pulled her close. 'That's what you do to me.' She smiled and he kissed her. 'But I don't want to fuck up this money. I'm counting on it.'

'You think they can tell?'

'They said they could, and I'd be removed from the trial if I did any private experiments.'

'How do they count sperm anyway?'

'A pair of tweezers and a calculator?'

She laughed again. She had a cute laugh. She put her arms around his neck and looked him seriously in the eyes. 'How much longer do you have to... abstain?' It sounded so dirty when she said it.

'Five more days.' That would finish his course of antibiotics. 'Can you last that long?'

'No problem to me, as long as you keep doing what you just did. The question is, can you last that long?' Her lips brushed his.

'Get away from me, devil woman,' he whispered with a grin.

The headset around her neck crackled and instantly wiped the smile from her face. She stepped back and put the earphones on, then adjusted the mic position in front of her mouth. She pressed the talk button. 'I'm here, Damian. Yep. I know. I'm just rounding up the last of them now. OK.' She nodded at the door. 'I have to have all the extras back on set in five. I have to run.' She leaned in and kissed him quickly. She unlocked the door and almost hit the man in the wheelchair. She locked eyes with him. She blushed, wondering how long he'd been out here. The man nodded at the disabled sign on the door.

She gave him an apologetic smile and ran off before he could say anything else.

Sean wandered out seconds later, smiling. He gave the man in the wheelchair a pat on the shoulder as he passed. 'All yours, man.'

The man rolled forward a few inches to the threshold of the door and sniffed the air. His face winced.

Sean had been on this medical drama pilot for two days now. They had built an elaborate mock-up of an E.R. in the Paint Hall studio in Belfast. The production was American, so it was an E.R. rather than a Casualty Department. There were a few minor TV celebs swanning about like they were doing everyone a favour by being here. All the speaking parts had to be Americans. They'd probably got some funding or tax break which said they had to shoot some percentage of it in Northern Ireland, but they were doing their best to disguise that fact in the finished film.

He'd actually been in a couple of scenes that were filmed, but he was so far from camera in one, and had his back to camera in the other, that he was beginning to doubt this endeavour would provide him anything useful for his showreel.

The extras had their own area to relax and wait, far from the stars in case any ordinariness might infect their talent. Sean went there after he'd walked off his erection. He made himself a cup of tea and sat among the extras. This wasn't his area. He shouldn't be here. He'd listened to them talk for two days, but rarely joined in. These people weren't actors. They were housewives, plumbers, civil servants, and fuck knows what else. Day trippers.

He didn't like downtime. His thoughts always went back to those test results he was waiting on. He'd tried to convince himself that the odds of a randy, old housewife from a quiet suburb of Northern Ireland having HIV or AIDS were highly unlikely. But then again, she hadn't got gonorrhoea from baking scones. His next few years, which he had always imagined spending climbing the acting ladder to bigger and better roles, might instead be spent in hospitals. Looking like a zombie as he tried new therapies and drug cocktails. He took a long drink of his tea, hoping to chase away the shivers running up his back.

Sean saw Lauren running across the soundstage looking panicked. She was glancing in all directions and holding a clipboard close to her chest; it acted like a shield as she bumped into people along the way. Sean knew this wasn't good.

Had the disabled guy ratted them out? Was the disabled guy someone? Was Lauren someone? Maybe the director's daughter or the producer's niece? Sean had never thought to ask if she was related to anyone that could potentially fuck up his career.

She spotted him and her haphazard course received a solid direction. Sean got to his feet, preparing for the worst.

She ran into the extras area, raising a few heads from their knitting and newspapers, and grabbed Sean by the arm. She dragged him out of the area and rushed him towards the set. She pushed the talk button on her walkie and said, 'I've got him, Damian. We're on our way.'

Sean swallowed hard. Americans carried guns, didn't they? 'What's going on?'

'Johnny Casper got arrested at the airport with a bag of coke.' She didn't look at him when she spoke; she was too busy trying to negotiate the quickest way through the set.

'Who's Johnny Casper?'

'He was supposed to be doing his big scene today. Our lawyers can't get him out. The producers made the call to replace him and I suggested you.' She yanked him in another direction when she saw a crane parked in their path and continued at speed across the massive set.

Sean wasn't being dragged anymore. He was keeping pace. 'Shit. Really? Fuck. What's the part?'

'Damian will explain all that to you. Can you do a convincing American accent? I told him you could. Don't make me look like an asshole.' They saw the director now, huddled in a serious conference with the producer and heads of department thirty feet away. Lauren jerked him to a stop and pushed him behind a rail of costumes. She looked him in the eyes, no longer playful. 'Are you as good as you think you are?'

'I'm better.' He gave her a grin, but she was too scared to return the gesture.

'I vouched for you. Do you understand what that means? What it *could* mean? To you *and* to me?'

Sean stepped forward and kissed her gently. 'I won't let you down.'

She dared to give him a cautious smile. 'OK, are you ready?'

Sean nodded and she led him around the rail towards the director.

The first person in the huddle saw them approaching. Then, like a ripple, heads all turned and stared at the Third AD approaching with the actor. They were all judging him on his appearance now. If he didn't look right for the part it wouldn't matter how good his accent was, or his acting. The director smiled and Sean relaxed a little.

This was it.

His looks passed the test.

A few minutes later his accent had passed the test. They only ever heard him speak with an American accent. He never let them hear his native accent and never would, that way they would never know how much or how little he was acting. They just accepted it.

For the next few minutes, he answered questions as quickly as they were thrown at him and always answered yes. Did he have an agent? Can you give me his details? Are you a member of Equity? Will you work for Equity minimum rate? Do you have experience with emotional scenes? Can you cry on cue? Are you free for the next few days to film the rest of these scenes?

Then the director asked him how quickly he could learn the dialogue. Sean told them to start setting up the scene – he'd be ready when they were. The director laughed. He had to admire the kid's balls. He gave him a copy of the sides and showed him to the trailer they had hired for Johnny Casper.

04.

Sean didn't even look around the opulent dressing room on wheels. He walked in, pulled the door closed behind him and sat down on the first thing he saw. He started reading the lines. Halfway down the page he laughed in disbelief.

SAINT JUDE'S - SHOOTING SCRIPT - (PINK PAGES) 9/21/98

11. EMERGENCY ROOM - CURTAINED AREA - DAY

Blake and Connors come back into the curtained area. Josh sits on the bed holding hands with Brooke, dressed and anxious to leave. They stand as the doctors enter.

              JOSH
       So, doc, you figured out what
       these purple spots are?

              BLAKE
       I think maybe we should talk
       to Brooke alone.

              BROOKE
       What? No. Whatever you have to
       say, Josh can hear it. We're
       getting married. We have no
       secrets.

              CONNORS
       Brooke, I really think we should...

45

                    JOSH
          Look, she said it's OK.

Josh takes Brooke's hand in his and squeezes
tightly.

                    JOSH (CONT'D)
          Whatever it is, we'll face it
          together.

Brooke nods her agreement at the doctors.

                    BLAKE
          Brooke, I'm very sorry but, you've
          tested positive for the HIV virus.

As the shock hits the young couple, Josh
stumbles backwards against the wall. Brooke
tries to hold on to his hand but he shakes it
off.

There are a few seconds of awkward silence as
the news is digested.

                    BLAKE (CONT'D)
          Have you two been having
          unprotected sex?

Josh is still leaning against the wall, staring
at the floor. Brooke looks at Blake and the
gentlest of nods frees a tear from her eye.

                    CONNORS
          Look, the first thing we need to
          make clear is, that this is not a
          death sentence.

Josh lunges forward and punches Brooke in the
face. Blake and Connors grab him and try to
restrain him as they shout for security.

Brooke, her nose bloodied, climbs back on the
bed and cries openly as Josh is dragged away
screaming obscenities at her.

That scene alone would've been a dream come true for a promoted
extra, but he had three further scenes. One of them was where he
talked with Connors in the hospital chapel about his fears as they
waited for his test results to come back. There was no one better
prepared to play that scene than he was. The dialogue was mostly

46

his. That was where he'd prove himself. That's where he'd show the world what he could do.

By the time Lauren knocked on his door to take him to make up, he pretty much had the first scene down, but he kept re-reading it as she led him through costume and make-up, so by the time he arrived on set he was confident he could nail this scene in his sleep.

He met his co-stars. The doctors were familiar from various TV shows popular ten years ago. His screen girlfriend introduced herself as Brooke and asked that he not call her anything but that until the shoot was over.

Sean smiled and nodded, though inwardly winced. Fuckin' method actors.

The director ran through the blocking for the scene and the stunt co-ordinator showed him how to throw a convincing punch. Since they were now behind schedule, the director asked if everyone felt comfortable trying to do the scene in one take. The DoP had to get a second camera running for coverage, but was excited about the hand-held feel of the scene adding an unpredictable energy. They ran the scene through twice to get the blocking straight, and they all seemed to know their lines. Everyone was ready.

Sean took deep breaths as the director gave the cameraman last-minute instructions. He looked over at Brooke sitting on the gurney. She gave him a quick nod backwards. He walked over and she beckoned him closer with her finger.

'When it comes to the punch, I want you to really hit me,' she whispered.

'What? No fuckin' way. I'll get fired,' Sean whispered back.

'You won't. It's a single take shot. They'll understand if your adrenaline kicked in and you misjudged the punch.' She grabbed his hand. 'I need this for my process!' she said through gritted teeth. She exhaled quickly and her face softened slightly. 'Please,' she added in a more affable tone.

'OK, first positions, everyone,' the director called.

She held his gaze as he stepped back to his mark. The bell rang ordering quiet on the stage. She was still looking at him as the boom operator positioned the microphone above them. Sean closed his eyes as the make-up girl ran in and did some last-minute touch-ups. When she was done, Sean sat down on the gurney next to Brooke and looked at her like he was in love, but worried. To his surprise, the same look was returned. They sat there, gazing into each other's eyes in silence.

'OK, everyone, settle. Everyone ready?' the director asked. The camera operators gave him a nod. The boom operator gave him a thumbs-up. 'OK, action!'

The curtain was pulled open and Connors and Blake stepped in. They pulled the curtain closed behind them and looked concerned. Josh got up quickly and faced them with an optimistic smile. Brooke remained sitting on the gurney.

'So, doc, you figured out what's going on?' Josh asked.

Doctor Blake's poker face gave away nothing as he said, 'I think maybe we should talk to Brooke alone.'

Brooke's glance quickly flitted between Josh and the doctor. 'What? No. Whatever you have to say I want Josh to hear it. We're getting married. We have no secrets.'

The younger doctor stepped forward. She was slim and pretty, and her glasses gave her a sexy secretary look. She gave the patient a tight-lipped smile. 'Brooke, I really think we should...'

'Look, she said it's OK,' Josh shouted. He was worried now. Doctors never wanted to speak to the patient alone if it was good news. This was bad. Now it was just a question of how bad. Still, Brooke was his fiancée. He loved her. He'd stick with her through anything. He took her hand and squeezed it tightly. He nodded at the doctor and said, 'Go on. Tell us.' Brooke looked up at him from the gurney. Tears were in her eyes and he felt the love, almost tangible in the space between them. She smiled at him, but he could see the same fear behind those eyes he knew almost as well as his own. She turned to the doctor and nodded for him to go ahead.

Doctor Blake cleared his throat, and then said, 'Brooke, I'm very sorry, but... you've tested positive for the HIV virus.'

Josh felt his heart quicken. He felt his stomach turn and for a moment he thought he was going to be sick. His vision blurred. He felt light-headed and stumbled backwards, knocking over a drip-stand before steadying himself against the wall. He started taking breaths, trying to calm himself, but it wasn't working. He saw the doctors saying muffled words. They sounded underwater. He looked over at the love of his life, now just an out-of-focus blur he didn't recognise. He took deeper breaths, but as the nausea passed it was replaced by something much stronger. Hate. Anger. Fear. They all swelled up inside him, and as he heard the younger doctor say something about a death sentence, all those things suddenly had a focus and he lashed out with his fist.

The punch hit her square on the nose. He heard it crack and felt satisfied. She looked shocked and confused as she fell backwards. He drew back his fist to throw another and it was caught. He didn't look back to see who had caught it; he just shook it free and punched her again. This time hitting her eye. As he drew back for a third punch two hands seized him, and this time they really seized him and yanked him backwards. Someone was screaming for security behind him, but he was trying to get free to hit her again. She, who had done this to him. Given him this death sentence. He struggled to get free but the arms around him were holding him fast.

'I'll fucking kill you, you bitch. You fuckin' whore! I'll fuckin' kill you, I swear to god, I will!' He saw her start to cry but didn't care. She *should* feel bad. Fuck her. Fuck that stupid slut's feelings.

'Cut!'

Josh was released by the actors and fell to the floor. He lay face down with his hands over his head. He took deep breaths and swallowed hard. He wasn't sure how long he lay there, probably only a few seconds, but when he got up, he was Sean again. He looked back at the set and saw the First Aid nurse attending to Brooke. Now he remembered. The acting wasn't over yet.

'Oh my god, are you all right? Did I hit you?' Sean ran over to her. Brooke laughed and edged the First Aid nurse out of the way as she hugged Sean.

'Don't worry about it. It was just an accident. It's OK, I'm fine. You barely touched me.' With that statement, the rest of the crew seemed to relax and even broke into applause.

The director was looking at his heads of department. 'Please tell me we got that.' They all nodded and the director smiled widely.

Brooke laughed and hugged him again, tighter. This time she whispered in his ear, 'Thank you.' She released her embrace and let the nurse carry on trying to stem the bleeding from her nose.

Sean stepped back and had his hand grabbed and shook by the other two actors in the scene. The older man looked excited, like Sean had just reminded him of what real acting was all about. The younger one looked like she wanted to fuck him right there and then.

The director ran over and hugged him. 'That was fucking incredible, Sean!' The guy was shaking he was so excited. He leaned in and whispered, 'Just between us, did you mean to peg her?'

Sean gave him a cheeky grin and said, 'Of course not. It was an accident.' He gave him a quick wink.

The director laughed and shook Sean's hand with both of his own. He leaned in again and whispered, 'The make-up's going to look so much better on top of a real broken nose. We'll hardly have to use any at all!'

When the director had gone back to his heads to organise the next shot, various members of the crew approached Sean and congratulated him. Sean saw Lauren at the back of the crowd smiling like a proud parent. He gave her an appreciative nod.

Brooke was led past a smiling man with a stainless-steel briefcase. The nurse had her head tilted back and was pinching the bridge of her nose while holding a piece of gauze under her nostrils. The man winced as he got a closer look and then made a bee-line for Sean.

He stuck his hand into the midst of the group congratulating Sean and grabbed his hand. 'Sean, babe. Can I have a word?' Keeping a hold of his hand, he pulled him from the circle.

'You really blew them away in that scene. And me, if I'm honest. Johnny Casper, huh? What an arsehole. Lucky for you, though, right?' he said in a chirpy, Irish brogue.

Sean looked at his cheap suit and knock-off Rolex. 'Sorry, who are you?'

He still had hold of his hand and gave it another shaking as he introduced himself. 'Paddy Hancock. Hancock Artists Representation. I saw you in a couple of shorts years ago.'

Sean broke the agent's grip and shook his head. 'I already have representation.'

'I know. Avi Goldman, right. He's a fucking dinosaur, babe. Plus, he's a fucking yank. He doesn't have the connections I have around here.'

Sean smiled. 'And what connections are those?' Paddy's mouth opened and closed without making a sound. 'Because you look to me like you're six weeks out of uni looking for a break. Go on then, impress me. Who else do you represent?'

'Well, at the minute...' The sentence and his confidence trailed off to nothing.

'That's what I thought.' Sean gave him a pat on the shoulder as he left. 'I'll stick with Avi. Good luck to you, Paddy.'

The young agent watched him disappear back into the congratulatory huddle.

05.

Lauren was waiting outside his trailer when he finished changing back into his own clothes. It was possibly the first time he'd seen her without her walkie and headset. She had her coat on. She batted her eyelashes at him and smiled coyly. 'Please, Mister Black, can I have your autograph? I'll do *any*thing you say.' She laughed.

Sean smiled. 'My mother warned me about girls like you.'

'Big day, huh?'

Sean exhaled. 'Yeah, I can hardly believe it. I can't thank you enough for putting in a word for me.'

'Well how about treating a girl to dinner and a show?'

Sean winced and the smile on Lauren's face slowly fell. 'Sorry, I really think I need to stay in tonight and work on tomorrow's scene. I did today on fear and adrenaline. I'd like to be a bit more prepared tomorrow.'

Lauren was nodding. 'No, no, that's fine. Totally understandable. This is your big break; you don't want to fuck it up.'

Sean took her hands in his and looked her in the eyes. 'When my scenes are finished I'll take you somewhere really nice to say thank you. A really swanky restaurant.'

Lauren forced a smile. 'Sounds good.'

'And since I'll be in the money, I'll even let you super-size your meal. How about that?'

Lauren hit him playfully and laughed. 'Go home. Learn your lines. I'll see you tomorrow. You have a 10am call. Don't be late.' She leaned in and gave him a quick kiss, and then walked away with a spring in her step.

The light was still on in her trailer. Sean spat out the chewing gum and checked his breath was suitably minty. He knocked on the door. She was just wearing a silk dressing gown when the door opened.

'Josh. What are you doing here?'

Sean leaned into the open doorway. 'I just wanted to check you were OK. How's the nose?'

'It's fine. I'll see you tomorrow, Josh.'

51

She tried to pull the door closed and Sean grabbed it. 'I wanted to say you were really excellent in the scene today. I'd love to talk to you about...'

'Look, I can't fuck you, if that's what you're after. Think about where my character is at right now. You punched me in the face today and called me all sorts of names. It would make no sense for us to fuck now. Come back after we film the reconciliation scene and we can fuck then, OK?' She slammed the trailer door.

Sean turned away from the door and whispered to himself, 'What the fuck?'

It was nearly 9pm when Sean got back to the flat. That morning's mail was still lying on the hall carpet. He sifted through the bills, flyers, and offers for credit cards and saw the letter with the hospital logo on it.

His mouth had gone dry. He tried to swallow but couldn't. He felt cold all over, but there was sweat on his forehead. He turned the letter over and put his finger under the flap... and stopped. His big scene in the chapel was tomorrow. The scene where he's waiting for his test results to come back. He looked at the envelope and turned it over a few times in his hands. Then he folded it in half and put it in his back pocket.

He was shocked when he looked into the living room. It was clean. Well, as clean as it was possible to make it. Kelly was sitting on the sofa smoking a cigarette. She was clean too. She'd showered and even dressed for the first time in weeks. He recognised the outfit. He'd complimented her on it once. He said her ass looked amazing in those jeans and that top hugged her curves in indecent ways. The jeans were loose on her now and her curves were considerably smaller. Her hair was clean, but now that it was tied back it revealed just how pale and sick she looked.

She noticed him and sat forward to stub out her cigarette. She smiled and he thought her face had cracked in a dozen places. Where had all those lines come from? She was so dark around the eyes she looked almost skeletal. 'Sean. How was today?'

'Good. Better than good, actually. What's going on, Kel?'

'I just got sick of living in filth. I ordered some Chinese food. It's in the oven. Are you ready to eat?'

'Yeah. I could eat.'

She smiled and ran out of the room to the kitchen. Sean sat down on the sofa and waited for her.

As they ate their Kung Po chicken and Beef Chow Mein, Sean told her (most) of what had happened that day. She was attentive and encouraging. When they finished, Kelly reached for her cigarette pack. Now it made sense. She was out of weed and was being nice to him so she could hit him up for a loan.

'How come you're not having a joint?' She froze momentarily with a cigarette between her lips and a lighter halfway to her mouth. She lit the cigarette.

'Don't feel like it.' She stared straight ahead.

'You always have a joint after you eat. Are we out?'

'Yes. But that's not why.' She sucked hard on the cigarette. 'I think I'm going to knock it all on the head for a while.' She still hadn't looked at him.

'Was your mum round?'

'No. Not today.' She filled her lungs with the toxic chemicals again.

'Then what's brought about this change of heart?'

She took another long drag for courage and said, 'I hit bottom.' It was little more than whispered, but the truth of it echoed around the room like she'd screamed. She wiped her cheeks and sniffed. 'I called Marvel this morning. I needed some gear, but I didn't have enough money. He said if he could come round we'd work something out.' She wiped her eyes again. 'So I said he could.' Her voice was cracking now. She didn't dare turn and see the look on Sean's face, so she just kept talking while staring at the faded wallpaper opposite her. 'When he came round, Razor was with him. They gave me a hit of ecstasy. It was strong shit. After a while I let them tie me up and then...' Three short drags on her cigarette. 'Then... they did things to me.' She was so close to breaking down now. 'Both of them... and they took pictures of me on their phones.' Her cigarette had burned down to her fingers. She stubbed it out. 'They laughed. They laughed while they were doing it. They laughed when I cried. They laughed.' She turned to Sean.

Sean's face was giving nothing away. He knew she'd been blowing, and probably screwing, Marvel before now. That part of it didn't really bother him. Their relationship was over long ago as far as he was concerned, but anything she'd done in the past was consensual. And though some scumbag lawyer might argue that today's events were also consensual, Sean knew they weren't. There was a line and Marvel had crossed it. Sean thought of the couple in the scene today. How would he feel if someone did that to Brooke? What would Josh do?

Sean opened his arms to Kelly. The look of relief on her face was instant and released all the emotion she had been holding on to. She fell into his arms and buried her head in his chest. She cried until she couldn't cry anymore. They must've sat like that for an hour or more.

She'd been quiet for a long time. He thought she'd fallen asleep. 'Kel?'

She looked up at him. Her eyes were bloodshot.

'I have to learn my lines for tomorrow.'

'Of course.' She sniffed and sat up. 'I love you, Sean.'

He didn't know what to say. Even in the early days, when they'd been inseparable and had sex all the time, she'd never said that. What would Josh do? 'I love you too, Kel.'

She smiled. 'I've fucked everything up, but if you're still with me, I know I can kick that shit and get back on track. I was even thinking about going back to college and finishing off my degree.'

'I think that's a great idea.' That's what Josh would say.

She smiled and he saw a glimmer of the girl he'd been attracted to a long time ago. 'Can I help you run lines?'

'Yeah, I guess.' Pure Josh.

They lay in bed that night sharing the script. Kelly read all the other parts and Sean read Josh's lines. He couldn't help but smile after a while. Even on the first read through he frequently thought – I knew that's what Josh would say to that line.

Kelly fell asleep first. She must've been exhausted physically and mentally after today. She had helped him memorize the lines. The rest was up to him.

Next morning Sean silently packed everything that mattered to him into a holdall. He left his key on the hall table and closed the door as gently as he could when he left.

06.

Josh's heartfelt confession to Doctor Blake in the chapel scene reduced some of the crew to tears as they watched. The director knew how hard it was to pull out that kind of emotion, but he had also seen what Sean was capable of, so again he opted to get all

Sean's coverage in one take, and he was glad he did. When he hugged Sean afterwards, he called his performance: 'Pure fuckin' gold!'

They also did some of the earlier scenes with him getting a phone call at work – another convincing office set that had been built in the north corner of the soundstage – and a few short shots of him running down corridors and into the E.R.

He was so well-rehearsed, by the time the First AD called lunch they were actually ahead of schedule, so everyone got an extended break. This made him extremely popular with cast and crew, and he got many pats on the shoulder, and approving smiles as he walked back to craft services. He picked up a sandwich and an apple – he felt Josh would eat sensibly with a wedding coming up – and headed back to his trailer.

He passed the script supervisor on the way and she said, 'Great work today! We'll have to start calling you single-take-Sean,' as she hurried past to get lunch.

Sean thanked her, but as he walked on, he wondered why anyone would call him that when his name was... oh no, it did work. Of course! He laughed to himself and shook his head.

When he got to his trailer, he found Lauren lying on the small sofa wearing nothing but a smile and some skimpy red underwear. 'What are you doing here?'

She sat forward and said, 'Well, I was thinking, since you've got this acting job now, do you really need the money from the fertility study?' She got up and strode towards him slowly. She reached out to put her arms around his neck, but he stepped back.

'Lauren, I'm sorry but I can't do this. Not now. Please don't ask me to explain, I just... I can't. OK?'

She blushed and quickly tried to cover up the body she had been so proud of only seconds earlier. She pulled on her clothes, apologising every few seconds, and then made for the door. She grabbed the door handle and then stopped. 'Are we... do you still want to have our date when you're done or are we...?'

'No, we can still do that. God, I owe you that much.'

Lauren's lips tightened but she said nothing. She slammed the door behind her as she left.

Sean wondered what Brooke would say if she'd seen that. If he were Josh. And Brooke was his girlfriend. She wouldn't have liked that at all. He would've felt horrible if he'd cheated on her, considering her diagnosis. He couldn't do that to her. It would've broken her heart. If Brooke was his girlfriend.

And if he were Josh.

Sean lived in his trailer for the next few days. The production had some guest stars coming in who they only had for a short time, so they had to give their scenes priority. Sean didn't care. He was living rent free and getting fed for free every day.

The folded envelope was still in his pocket. He took it out and looked at it every once in a while. He was pretty sure it said he was clear. It was a thin envelope. Thick envelopes were the ones you had to worry about. Thin envelopes said: All clear, sorry to have worried you. But thick envelopes contained pamphlets and sheets about What Happens Next? What's My Prognosis? and the dreaded FAQ list. This envelope was thin. It couldn't possibly contain any of that shit. It could contain a referral to a specialist. That would be thin. But more than likely he was going to be OK. He had none of the other symptoms that Brooke had in the script, and his penis looked normal again. He'd take the last day of the antibiotics just to be sure, but he was pretty sure they'd already done their job.

He had his final scene today. What Brooke called their reconciliation scene. Josh would find out that his test results were clear and declare his love for Brooke and vow to stand beside her through her coming treatment. Sean planned to look at his own results just before the scene, and then he and Josh would share the relief of getting an all clear.

Of course, if his results were different to Josh's... well, he didn't know what he'd do.

The scene was blocked and rehearsed. The cameramen and boom operator were set. The make-up girl ran in for some last-minute touch-ups. As she moved on to Brooke, Sean took the well-crumpled envelope from his pocket and discreetly opened it. He unfolded the page and attached it to the clipboard hanging from Brooke's bed.

As he walked back to the waiting room set, the nervous excitement and fear in his stomach lurched. He thought he needed the toilet, but held on. The director was smiling and chatting casually with his department heads. Sean saw the clipboard hanging from bed, thirty feet away. He was starting to sweat. They needed to start this take now or his make-up would run. He felt light-headed. It reminded him of smoking dope with Kelly.

Kelly.

For the first time he wondered how she was taking his departure. She'd be OK. Kel was tough. She'd probably go back to her parents and get straightened out. They'd take care of her. She'd be fine. His stomach cramped again. He could see the letter across the set and turned away quickly.

Even from this distance he could tell it was a short letter. A brief paragraph, a small table with the results, and a final short paragraph. That was good. Brief was good. There had been no pamphlets in the envelope as he suspected. That was good. Unless his diagnosis was too complex to go into in a letter.

'OK, are we all ready for one?' the director asked and received nods from everyone.

Sean's stomach twisted and the sour taste of bile rose in his throat. He choked it down. He saw Brooke sit down on the bed. The letter hung only a couple of feet away. An AD pulled the curtain around her cubicle and the letter was out of sight. Sean tried to slow his breathing. The AD was Lauren. She gave him a professional nod and smile. He lowered his head and became very aware of how fast his heart was beating.

'Action!'

Sean slowly raised his head as the camera dollied in on him. He was doing his best to hold it together, but he was close to vomiting. He swallowed hard and got up quickly. The hand-held cameraman followed him as he marched across the set and pulled open the curtain of Brooke's cubicle. She looked surprised and maybe even a little scared to see him.

She did her best to look emotionally detached when she asked, 'So what did your test results say?'

'They're not back yet.' He took a couple of steps and knelt down before her. He took her hand. It felt cold. 'I've done a lot of growing up in the last twenty-four hours, and I wanted you to know that I love you, and if you want me to, I'll stand by you through everything that's to come.' He touched his forehead to the back of her hand. 'I wanted you to know that before my results came back. Whether I have it or not, I want us to spend our lives together.'

Tears rolled from her eyes as she pulled him to his feet. They kissed, not with passion, but with love.

When their kiss ended, they remained close, looking at each other. They both glanced over and saw the doctors approaching. She could see the fear in his eyes, but also the bravery. They both closed their eyes and touched foreheads briefly.

Blake cleared his throat and they stepped back from each other. 'Josh, if we could have a word in private?'

Brooke sat down on the bed and Josh sat down in the chair. His knee touched the hanging clipboard and made it sway. He swallowed hard. He looked over at the love of his life and smiled at her. 'Whatever you have to tell me, you can say in front of Brooke. We're getting married, remember?'

She smiled at him, tears escaping her eyes. He reached out to her and she took his hand and squeezed it tightly.

Josh turned to Blake and Connors. 'Go ahead.'

Josh lowered his head and saw the letter in the corner of his eye. As soon as Blake started to deliver his line he glanced over and saw three key phrases: *pleased to inform you*, *Negative*, and *no trace*.

'You don't have the HIV virus, Josh,' Blake said.

Josh's body, which seconds ago had been so taut, now relaxed and tears flowed freely. He felt relieved, but as he felt the hand gripping his, he also felt guilty that he had been lucky and she hadn't.

'You've been very fortunate, and you're going to have to take precautions in future. I've got some literature here for both of you to read.'

'What about Brooke?' he blurted out. He didn't even know if it was part of the script. It was just what Josh wanted to know. Connors answered his question so she was either improvising brilliantly or it was in the script. The rest of the scene needed some reshoots from various alternate angles, but the director was happy. He said he'd got the gold on the first take and wouldn't ask his actors to try to replicate that emotion again. The final shot was of their backs. Brooke and Josh walking out the hospital doors with their arms around each other.

There was no dialogue in the shot, so the boom operator missed Brooke whispering to him, 'When we're done here, come to my trailer and fuck me.'

07.

She insisted he wear a condom, because that's what Brooke and Josh would have to do from now on. After the events of the last few days, Sean didn't need much convincing.

Only seconds after climaxing, she got out of bed and went to her flight bag. Sean watched her naked form with admiration. He'd been with girls of all different body-types, but she was flawless. Not an ounce of fat, not a birthmark, not a spot or pimple anywhere, and not a trace of hair anywhere but on her head.

'So, am I allowed to know your real name now?'

She continued rummaging in her luggage. 'Bethany Ross.'

'And am I allowed to call you Bethany?'

Still with her back to him. 'Beth is OK.' She unzipped a make-up bag and said, 'Yes!' She came back to the bed with a joint in her mouth and a lighter in her hand. 'Do you get high?'

'Sure.'

'I've been dying for this for weeks, but I figured Brooke was a bit of a straight arrow. In the character profile I built for her, she was raised by a strict Baptist preacher. She fell for this small-town bad boy that she thought she could reform. *That's* who she contracted the virus from.' She lit the joint and took several short drags. 'But he dumped her and left her alone in a strange city. She was too ashamed to go back home to her father, so she got a job waiting tables in a diner and that's where she met you. Josh, I mean.'

Sean smiled. 'God, you really believe the whole method acting shtick, don't you?'

'Of course.'

'Does that mean you have sex with all your co-stars?'

'No, it depends on the part.' She picked a little strand of tobacco from her tongue. 'I did this play once where I played a novice – that's like a trainee nun – and for the whole three-month run of the play I stayed in character.'

'You didn't have sex for three months?'

'Didn't have sex, didn't smoke, didn't drink, didn't even masturbate. I drank water. I ate the kind of simple foods nuns eat. No make-up or cosmetics. Bathed in a bath of cold water. I went back to my room every night and read the Bible. I can quote you chapter and verse now. I read it so much it was like learning lines; it stuck after a while. It was a tough run, but I got great reviews.'

Sean was laughing as he took the joint from her. 'That's fuckin' mental.'

'Everything tasted sweeter when I did finally go back to normal.' She smiled smugly, and repeated, '*Every*thing,' as she nodded at his crotch.

'Yeah, maybe, but why put yourself through that? I just act. It's much easier.' He toked hard on the joint.

'Not today you didn't. I saw the letter, Sean.' His smile fell. 'Don't tell me that didn't help you through today's scene. I was watching. You held off reading the results of your own HIV test. That is fucking hardcore, dude!'

'Wait, you don't mind? We just had sex.'

'Yeah. So? Your results were clear and you rubbered up. Why should I care? I figured this is what Brooke and Josh would do when they got home. They'd fuck. And he'd *have* to wear a rubber from now on, so it's all good. It's what I call giving closure to my character.'

Sean shook his head and chuckled. 'Fuckin' American girls.'

'I'm Canadian.'

'Whatever. All I know is, if an Irish girl knew I was the sort of guy who needed to get tested for HIV; that there was even the slightest possibility I had it, they wouldn't let my dick anywhere near them. Rubbered up or not.'

She took the joint back from him. 'Well, that's their loss.' She sucked hard on the joint. 'You know I used to be like you. I used to just act. But when I watch that stuff back it just makes me cringe. It looks so phoney. When I watch myself in a method part, it's real, because I was fuckin' living it. You know the first time I tried it?'

Sean turned on his side and faced her. 'Go on, tell me.'

'My third movie. Four lines I had. Four lines to prove myself. The first two movies I'd done were similar, small roles and I was fine, but... that's all. So this third movie I'm playing a hooker and I have no idea how to play that. I was a good girl. I went to catholic school.'

'Do you still have the uniform?'

She lightly slapped his chest and continued, 'By that stage I'd only ever slept with two guys and they were both long-term boyfriends. So I get this idea...' She passed the joint back to Sean and crossed her legs sitting in front of him. 'There was this guy who lived on our block. He was a year younger than me, and I knew he'd always had the hots for me, but this dude was large – you know what I'm saying? He must've weighed at least three-hundred pounds. So I go round there one night when I know his parents are out and I say to him: "Give me fifty bucks and you can fuck me any way you want." Well, shit, the guy couldn't get his piggy bank smashed fast enough.' She laughed and Sean choked mid-drag as he laughed too. She patted his back until he got his breathing regulated.

'And you really went through with it?'

'Damn right I did. Of course I insisted he wore a rubber. He was clumsy, and over-eager, and didn't take very long.' She took the joint back and finished it off with a few short drags. 'But as I lay there afterwards, naked and vulnerable, feeling used and debased, he handed me the money, and I knew what it felt like to sink that low.' She stubbed out the joint. 'He even offered me a hundred more for another go, but I'd got what I needed. I had four lines in that movie, and one of them got cut, and I still won the Rising Talent Award at the Indie Film Awards. Up until then it was the only thing of mine I could watch without wincing at my performance.' She lay down next to him and rested her head on his chest. 'So when you see this thing back on TV, just compare it to what you've done before and you tell me which is better.'

Sean stroked her hair gently as she lay there, and thought about what she had said.

42DD HOUSEWIFE: I TOOK SEAN BLACK'S VIRGINITY!
EXPOSED! FILM STAR'S WASHING MACHINE ROMP WITH OLDER WOMAN!
Weekend Gossip, March, 2012

BELFAST SUICIDE VICTIM IDENTIFIED

Police were called to a flat at an address in lower Belfast late on Sunday evening after neighbours noticed the house lights had been on all day from the previous night and there was no response at the door.

After gaining forcible entry to the property, police found the body of a young girl hanging from a light fixture in the kitchen. The girl has now been formally identified as Kelly Russell (21) from Antrim town.

Police have found no evidence to suggest foul play. A note was found at the scene, but the RUC have not released the details of its content.

Kelly had been studying Fashion and Design at Queens University until recently when she dropped out. She was described by her teachers as an intelligent and studious girl with a promising future until her unexpected departure from college. Close friends say they knew she was struggling with a drug problem, and her recent separation from a long-time boyfriend may have been more than she could handle.

A spokesperson for Aware NI said: 'Not enough is being done to reach out to young people dealing with depression and suicidal thoughts. We urge the government to look more closely at this growing problem.'

Belfast Echo, 22ⁿᵈ April, 1999

TWO DEAD AFTER SUSPECTED PUNISHMENT BEATING

The two men found nailed to trees in Victoria Park in Belfast have now been identified as Marvin Walsh (34), known locally as Marvel, and Jonathan Sharpe (32), known locally as Razor.

Police say the two men were viciously beaten and tortured for hours before being nailed to the trees. However, the medical examiner believes they were still alive at this point and could have survived these injuries, but after their hands and feet had been nailed in place, both men had their genitals removed by a large-bladed instrument, possibly a hunting knife. The resulting blood loss was found to be the eventual cause of death.

So far, no paramilitary group has claimed responsibility for the murders, though police are investigating claims that the pair were dealing in various controlled substances and recreational drugs. The working theory is that this was a warning given to deter drug dealing in Belfast.

Colin McCollum, local MLA for the area said: 'In these fledgling days of the Good Friday Agreement, we cannot allow these remnants of the dark times to stifle progress. Those responsible for this atrocity have no political agenda to hide behind that will be recognised by any court of law. They are criminals and will be treated as such when caught.'

Belfast Echo, 22ⁿᵈ April, 1999

"I'd like to believe that everyone gets what they deserve, but in my experience, sometimes karma needs a push."

Sean Black (actor), Quotables Vol. 5

2000

01.

'I hate these places. They give me the creeps.'

Emily took his hand. 'Just sign the papers, say a quick hello, and we can go.'

Sean slammed the steering wheel with his free hand. 'This is my da's responsibility. I hardly know the guy.'

'They can't find your dad. You're the next of kin. They need you to authorize changing his meds in...'

'Yeah, yeah, yeah. I know.' He exhaled. 'I just thought when I moved out I was done cleaning up after him. Fuck knows who he's shacked up with now or what he's doing. You'd think he'd check in on his own brother at least once in a while! He probably owes them money like everyone else.' He turned to Emily. 'If they ask me for money, I'm not paying. This has nothing to do with me!'

'I don't think they'll expect you to pay for anything. They didn't say anything about money on the phone. This consent is just a legal formality. He *is* your uncle. If this new drug treatment will improve his quality of life, shouldn't you try to help?' Sean saw that familiar sympathetic smile. She only ever wanted to help. It was hard not to love her for that.

They had met again at Kelly's funeral. It was the first time they had spoken since falling out after the threesome. Both girls had become possessive over Sean. It had all blown up when Kelly spilled everything to Emily's then-boyfriend Ricky. Ricky quickly ended their relationship and dropped out of university. Emily vowed never to speak to her ex-roommate again after that. A couple of months later Emily switched to Theatre Studies and did her best to ignore Kelly and Sean when she saw them on campus.

When she had read about Kelly's death in the paper, all those old hostile feelings seemed petty and insignificant. She and Kelly had shared a room for almost a year and become good friends before the threesome. She went to the funeral to make her peace and say goodbye.

She hadn't expected Sean to be there. In amongst the grieving friends and relatives, they only knew each other, so they sat together in the church. They held each other, crying at the graveside, they sat at a table by themselves at the wake. By the time they parted ways that day they were on hugging terms and had agreed to meet up again to talk things through. By the time they left each other after that rendezvous, they were on kissing terms. A week later Sean moved in with her, which was fortunate, as that was the same day the trailer he had been living in on-set was due to be taken away.

Since then they had been happily living together. Emily was now teaching drama to primary school children on a freelance basis. It was steady money, which allowed Sean to pursue his less reliable career. She knew how much acting meant to him and supported him without ever complaining, and now it looked like he might finally be getting a decent break. That last thing he needed while preparing for this film role was a distraction like this.

He looked over at the imposing concrete structure. It looked more like a prison than a hospital. He turned to Emily. 'OK. Come on. Let's get this over with.' He opened the car door and got out. They met at the back of the car and she took his hand again as they walked towards the entrance.

The building was large and Victorian with blank grey walls surrounding it. It was a purely functional piece of architecture designed with one purpose in mind – to keep those inside from getting out. Sycamore Acres was carved into the stone above the gates. Emily could tell he was nervous, though she didn't know why.

'You never told me, what's he in here for?'

'I don't really know myself. My da never talked about him much. I just remember a guy who used to show up at our house every once in a while, and then he just stopped coming. It wasn't until years later that I found out he was in here. My da said he used to get into fights a lot and one of them got him arrested, but when some police psychiatrist examined him, he diagnosed him with... I don't know. Something or other. So he ended up here rather than prison.'

'That sounds horrible. How long's he been in here?'

'The last time I remember seeing him was when I was... I don't know, seven or eight?'

'They were never able to cure him, or at least get him on meds to help him?'

'My da said he got worse when he went in here. It's probably why he's chickened out from seeing him now.' Sean squeezed her hand. 'It's also why I'm in no rush to see him.'

They stopped at the iron gates and the guard came out with a clipboard. 'Name?'

'Sean Black and this is my girlf...'

'*Patient's* name?' the guard corrected.

66

'Oh, Ronnie, Ronald Black.'

The guard made a tick on his clipboard and then opened the gate. He reached into his small office and grabbed two laminated lanyards with VISITOR written on them. He handed one to each of them. 'Wear these at all times. Follow the blue line on the ground to reception,' he said, and then wandered back into his office without waiting for a reply.

Sean and Emily followed the faded blue line painted on the ground across the courtyard to the main building. A large, no-nonsense woman sat behind the nurses' station and gave them an unwelcoming look that silently asked why they were cluttering up her ward.

'Hi, my name is Sean Black. I got a phone call to come in and sign some forms about my Uncle Ronnie?'

'Oh yes.' She sized the pair of them up, suspiciously. A quick rummage in her inbox produced the forms. She dropped them on the counter and slapped a pen down on top of them. 'Sign and date where you see the red cross.'

Sean took the pen and signed where indicated. He handed the forms back to her and she checked them. When she seemed satisfied, she dropped them in her outbox. 'Is that it?'

'Yes. Unless you'd like to visit your uncle?'

Sean's mouth dried and his lips froze. Emily stepped forward and said, 'Well, maybe just a quick hello.'

The nurse looked like she'd heard that one before. She grabbed a large bunch of keys and came out from behind the desk. 'OK, follow me.'

As they walked down the long corridor behind the stout woman, Emily saw Sean wipe the sweat from his brow twice, even though it was anything but warm in here. His face was devoid of expression. She took his hand again and gave him a supportive smile, but this time he was too scared or preoccupied to respond.

The nurse stopped outside a door and turned to them. 'Do you have anything for him?'

Emily winced and looked at Sean. He was still staring blankly ahead. She looked at the nurse apologetically. 'Sorry, we didn't bring anything.'

'All gifts must be approved by myself or another senior member of staff.'

'Well, like I said we forgot to...'

'This includes flowers, food, drink, cigarettes, magazines, books, music, music players or any other form of gift.'

Emily winced another smile, shaking her head.

'In short, nothing is to be passed to this inmate without my knowledge, do you understand?'

Emily nodded.

The nurse didn't seem convinced, but turned and unlocked the door anyway. 'The door will remain open and you will be constantly observed by me from the door. In case of an emergency with the patient, you are to leave the room immediately. Do not try to help in any way. Is that understood?'

Emily nodded again.

After giving one final check through the small window in the metal door, the nurse pulled it open and beckoned them inside. Emily put her hand in the small of Sean's back and gave him a little push to get him moving.

The man sitting on the bed in hospital-issued pyjamas was painfully thin. His grey hair was thinning on top and his face was wrinkled beyond his years, but Emily saw some family resemblance. He was smiling. He looked like any other kindly old uncle. Emily heard a bleep and turned around. She saw the nurse was blocking the doorway with her considerable girth. She had her arms folded across her chest and was now holding a charged Taser gun.

Emily turned back around and looked at Sean. He still seemed to be in a daze. She squeezed his hand until he turned to her, and then she nodded towards the man on the bed. Sean took a deep breath and stepped closer. He knelt down before the man on the bed.

'Uncle Ronnie? It's me, Sean.'

He looked bewildered and studied Sean closely.

'Dessie and Maddie's boy? You remember me, don't you? You used to come and stay at Christmas. One year you gave me an Action Man. Do you remember that? He came with a frogman's outfit and I left him swimming in the jelly overnight while it set. We had to eat him out on Boxing Day. He always smelled of strawberries after that. That's why strawberries always make me think of you.'

The older man winced, trying desperately to remember. His face brightened. 'I know who you are.' He reached forward and touched Sean's face. The nurse's plimsoles squeaked on the floor as she tensed. Emily turned and held up a halting hand to her. Ronnie leaned forward and whispered, 'I know who you are.' He leaned back again and put a finger to his lips and said, 'Under the blue elephant. Shhh.' He smiled and gave Sean a quick wink, just like he used to. There was still something of his uncle left inside this shell.

Sean turned to the nurse and said, 'Blue elephant?'

She shook her head. 'That's a new one on me, but he often comes out with stuff that doesn't make sense.'

Ronnie's gaze turned to Emily. He tilted his head, trying to place her.

Sean turned back and saw him looking. 'Oh, right, ah, this is my girlfriend, Emily.'

Emily smiled, stepped forward and extended her hand.

Ronnie looked down and started undoing his pyjama cord. Sean stood up quickly in front of Emily and backed away with his hands up, 'Whoa! Hold on there, Ronnie!'

But it was too late. For someone whose movements had been so slow, he got his pyjama-bottoms pulled down in amazing time and was soon pulling on his limp penis trying to coax it back to life.

'All right, that's enough. Time to leave,' the nurse said.

Sean and Emily hurried to the door and the nurse closed and locked it quickly once they were outside.

Sean turned to Emily. 'Are you OK?' She nodded. He turned to the nurse. 'What the fuck was that?'

'That was him on a good day. Have you seen all you need to?'

Sean glanced through the small window in the door and saw his uncle's face slam against it, leaving a bloody stain on the glass. It made him jump.

The nurse extended her arms like she was herding sheep and gently edged Emily and Sean away from the door. 'OK, you've over-stimulated him. I'm going to have to deal with this. Follow the green line back to reception, then the blue line back to the main gates. Thank you.' Her words may have said thank you, but her tone said thanks for making this shift even more unbearable.

Sean walked back up the corridor and out to the gates in a semi-daze. He didn't even remember giving his visitor pass back, though he assumed he must have. They sat in the car park for a long time, saying nothing. Emily waited patiently for him to process what had just happened.

It was nearly half an hour later when he turned to her. 'I'm hungry. What do you fancy for dinner tonight?'

'What?' Emily had not tried to force him to speak after seeing his uncle. She thought they would have a long heartfelt talk when he was ready. She wasn't expecting this.

'I don't fancy cooking. Let's just get a burger and chips or something on the way home. It might be my last chance for a while.' He smiled. That same childish excited smile she only ever saw when he was talking about acting. 'Em? Chippy on the way home?'

Emily nodded and forced a smile.

Sean started the car and pulled away.

They never talked about that day again.

02.

The young black guy threw punch after punch at Sean, faster than he could avoid, and his feet never seemed to settle in one place, so any punch Sean threw back missed and threw him further off-balance.

The black guy tagged him once, twice, thrice, fourfivesix times more in the face. Sean swung again and missed. He swung his left at him, trying to catch him off-guard, but he was already gone before the punch could find its mark. The black guy moved in close and landed a succession of lightning-fast punches to Sean's torso.

The bell rung. An unenthusiastic voice said, 'Time.'

The black guy stopped bouncing around and landing punches. He resumed a normal posture and put up his glove. Sean tapped it with his glove and then walked back to his corner.

His coach was there waiting and gave him an insincere smile. 'Nice goin', kid. We're getting there.'

He helped Sean off with his face mask and then took out his gum-protector. Sean's hair was soaking with sweat. 'We're not getting there. That guy's running rings around me and I'm lumbering around like Godzilla!'

'Calm down, OK? He's been training for years to get that good. We've got six weeks to make you look like you can box. And that's the key difference – we're only trying to make it *look* like you can box. You don't actually have to be able to box. You just need to look like you have some skill and technique.'

'Jesus, we've been at this for two weeks and I haven't got any better,' Sean shouted. 'I eat what you tell me to, I do all the exercises and road work you tell me to, so why can't I fucking do this?'

The coach put his hands on Sean's shoulders. 'You're getting there. Just take a breath.' Sean took a long, deep breath and felt calmer. 'You're too hard on yourself. I see improvement. We all do. But you can't expect to be Rocky Balboa after two weeks.' The coach gave him a grin. Sean smiled and nodded. 'Go hit the showers and get a rubdown. That'll do for today.'

Sean left the ring and walked back to the changing rooms. He might look like a boxer, but he didn't feel like one.

Despite having spent most of the day throwing punches, as he stood under the changing room shower, he really wanted to punch something, hard. The white tiles before him were inviting just such a punch, but he had to restrain himself. A broken hand wasn't going to get him anything except fired from the film.

He turned up the heat as hot as he could bear. The projectiles of water were hitting his skin like red-hot pellets, but that's what he deserved. He should be able to get this. When they had started, the coach told him it takes most actors about four weeks to get the hang of it. Sean had wanted to prove he could do it in half the time and now he had failed. His fist clenched tightly. His chest was red from the water. He shut it off with a swipe of his hand. He put his back against the tile wall and slid to the ground. He sat in the dregs of water and soap residue and watched the water drain down the hair-clogged plughole.

He couldn't blow this. It wasn't a big budget movie, but it was the sort of film that got noticed for awards. Not just the TV guide, women's magazines and other meaningless awards he had won for his role in St. Jude's, this could get him serious recognition.

And he was fucking it all up because he couldn't learn how to box.

The film was called *Wee Barry* and was a biopic of Barry McGuigan, the Irish boxer who had won the gold medal for boxing at the Commonwealth Games when he was only 17. He had gone on to win the World Featherweight Championship in 1985, and all this during the most tumultuous time in Northern Ireland's history. McGuigan was from the south of Ireland, but since his father had been from the north, he was allowed to fight for British titles, which annoyed both nationalists and loyalists, making him the subject of death threats from both sides. McGuigan had no interest in politics, only boxing. He was a catholic who married a protestant when such a thing was grounds for your community to reject you... or worse. In the end, McGuigan's tenacity had won out, and when he won a fight, both north and south felt like they had won with him. He united the people of Ireland in a way no politician ever did.

Sean had fought off hard competition to win this part, and slept with a couple of producers who were well past their sell-by date, but it would all be worth it if he could pull this off. McGuigan himself was booked to help choreograph the fight scenes once principal photography started, but until then it was just down to the coach, who Sean felt was purposely taking things slowly to get more money out of the production.

'Are you still in here, Sean?'

'Aye, coming now, Charlie.' Charlie was there to give him his rub-down. A retired boxer himself, he was old-school and didn't sugar-coat anything.

Sean walked in and loosened his towel as he lay down on the table. Charlie started massaging his tired muscles. 'Jesus Christ, son, what temperature had you that fucking shower at? You're red raw.'

'I just turned it the wrong way as I was getting out.' The grey-haired man mumbled something to himself that could've been acceptance of that lie or dismissal of it.

'How'd you think I looked out there today, Charlie?'

'You were a right fucking shambles, son. But I suppose I've seen worse who ended up better.' He kneaded the skin on Sean's back hard, deep into the muscle.

'How long did it take you to get good?'

'I don't know if I was ever good, but I could hold my own. Still, I don't suppose they'll ever make a film about me.' He moved down to Sean's legs and started on his hamstrings. 'I wasn't brought up fighting in a gym, so I learned faster.'

'Faster?' Sean arched his back and turned his head to Charlie. 'How did you learn faster?'

Charlie pushed his head down to the table again and kept going. 'We used to fight for money to eat. My dad was killed in the war. My mother did what work she could, but there were seven of us to look after. So as soon as we were old enough to work, we were pulled out of school and sent to the shipyards. At fourteen I was supporting my family. So if I wanted a few shillings for myself, I had to box.'

'When did you find the time to train?'

Charlie barked the first note of a laugh into the air. 'I spent all day shifting sections of iron around the shipyards. That took care of the weight-training, and I had to walk four miles to my work every morning, so once I got a bit more serious about the boxing, I ran that. Four miles in the morning and four miles home after a fifteen-hour shift. That took care of the roadwork. All that left was... well, what you're missing.'

Sean turned over and sat up. 'What am I missing?'

Charlie wiped the massage oil from his hands with a rag. 'Look at you!'

Sean looked down at his physique. That was the one thing he thought he had done well. At least he looked like a boxer. 'What? Too muscley? Not muscley enough?'

'No! Look!'

Sean looked down and failed to see what Charlie was talking about. He shrugged.

'How many times do you think you got hit today? Five hundred? A thousand? Where's the marks?'

'He's not allowed to hit me hard. The insurance carrier won't allow it. They don't want my nose busted or me covered in bruises before we start filming.'

'That's why you're not fighting out there; because you're in no danger of getting hurt. Fighting ain't about knowing the moves and the steps, that's fucking dancing. To know what it is to fight, to be in that moment, you have to know fear. You have to know that you might get seriously hurt, or worse. You don't know how to act out there because you don't know what it's like to stand toe to toe with another man who is determined to fuck you up as bad as he can.'

Sean sat up and watched the old man walk over and sit on the bench by the lockers. He took out a tin of tobacco and rolled himself a thin cigarette with the skill and speed of a magician. He lit it and sucked the noxious smoke into his already struggling lungs.

03.

Sean was late home again.

Emily had three chicken fillets cooked for him and a generous helping of mixed vegetables. He'd been on this same diet now for five weeks. She didn't know how he wasn't sick of it. She put the plate in the oven on a low heat.

The house was a small mid-terrace built in the 1950s. Emily's grandmother had lived there most of her life. When she had to move into a care home, Emily had inherited the place. Like all terrace houses it was small and cramped, but it was enough for her and Sean. There were two bedrooms, but they only needed one. For now.

The second bedroom was a junk room at the moment. Sean had got great reviews and even some awards for his role on Saint Jude's, which had gone on to be picked up by a major network and was now filming its second season. He kept the awards in one corner of the junk room. He said he wasn't affected by awards, but Emily knew he went in there sometimes just to look at them.

She walked to the front window and looked out on the street in the direction of the bus stop. There was no sign of him yet. She opened the door and wrapped her cardigan tighter around her as she buried her hands under her arms. The evenings were starting to get longer, but it was still dark enough for the street lights to come on.

Mrs. Murphy came walking up the street burdened down with shopping. Emily had exchanged brief hellos with her on several occasions. She lived three doors down with a husband Emily had yet to hear speak. Any time she had seen him he was either reading a newspaper or carrying one back from the shop. He would nod to acknowledge her presence but no more. Emily wondered what sort of home life the pair had.

'Evening, Mrs. Murphy,' she said as the woman got closer. 'How are you?'

The beleaguered woman shook her head. 'Och, I'm still waiting for an appointment at the hospital to get myself sorted out.'

Emily didn't know what she was waiting to get sorted out, nor did she want to. 'Ah, well, I hope it's not much longer.'

'Are you looking for that man of yours?'

Emily's heart went from zero to sixty in three seconds. She swallowed hard, not sure if she wanted to know the gossip on Sean. 'Yes.'

'He's in the church, so I'm sure he'll not be long.'

'The church? Are you sure it was Sean?'

'Oh, aye, plain as day. I always nip in on the way past, to say a prayer for my sister and her trouble. I've seen him in there before.'

'What church?'

Mrs. Murphy nodded over her shoulder. 'Saint Peter's just at the end of the road. Anyway, I must go and get his tea on. He'll be home before long, and if his tea's not ready I'll never hear the end of it. See you, love.' Mrs. Murphy waddled on to her front door. Emily waited until she had gone inside before grabbing her keys and coat and pulling the door closed behind her.

She hurried up the street towards the church. Mrs. Murphy must've been mistaken. Maybe one of her many ailments was her eyesight. Sean wasn't religious. He had never even mentioned church, or God, or anything of the sort to Emily. On the rare occasion when they had dipped a toe into the possibility of getting married, he was adamant about a secular registry office ceremony, if they ever had enough money to get married.

Emily hurried up the steps and into the church. She felt like she was crossing enemy lines. A protestant didn't go into a catholic church. Not in Belfast. Not anywhere in Northern Ireland. She crossed the threshold and looked in at the rows of pews.

There were only about a dozen people. They were all facing forward so they had their backs to her, but Emily knew what jacket Sean had been wearing when he left the house and spotted it immediately. OK, it was the same top, that's probably how Mrs. Murphy had been mistaken. She moved over towards the left side to get a better look at his face. He had the same colour hair as Sean. Even the same style. The man was praying with his head bowed into his folded hands. It was only when he finished and sat up that she saw his face clearly.

Even though it was unmistakably Sean, she continued to look at him for almost thirty seconds, because he just didn't look right. In this context, it looked like someone with all Sean's features, but not Sean.

Her first thought was that maybe he had changed his mind about a church wedding and was putting in the required hours to declare himself a member of this church. Could that be it? She smiled to herself and her heart started racing again, but this time there was also a warm tingling in her chest.

Sean got up from his seat and she ducked behind a pillar. If he turned to leave now, there was no way she could beat him outside without being seen. But he didn't leave immediately. He walked up to the front to light a candle. That was when Emily snuck out and hurried back to the house.

She closed the door, took her coat off and hurried to the kitchen. She opened the oven door and checked the chicken and vegetables were OK. The door opened and Sean walked in.

'Hi. You're a bit late so I had to keep these warm, but I think they're OK.' She took the plate from the oven and placed it on the table.

Sean took off his jacket and hung it over the back of the sofa. 'Yeah. Bus was late again.' He walked into the kitchen and kissed Emily hello.

'Good day apart from that?'

'Yes, five weeks of training and I think I'm finally starting to get the hang of it.' He sat down in front of the plate. 'I'm ready for this.' He tucked into the food as Emily sat down opposite him.

Sean sniffed the air. 'Go on then, tell me what you had.'

'Lasagne and garlic bread,' Emily said apologetically.

'God, I'll be glad to get back on real food after this shoot.'

And that was as much as he said about religion.

An after-dinner ritual had developed when Sean was working. They would run lines until Sean knew the entire script off by heart. Emily enjoyed it as well. Even though she found her work with children rewarding, there wasn't much opportunity to go deep into character motivations and gestures. She was just lucky if they remembered the lines and didn't wet themselves onstage. With Sean's parts they would dissect every line, every stage direction and he seemed to appreciate her notes and ideas.

She curled up on the sofa next to him with the script. This close to shooting, he was already off-book and rarely needed to refer to the script.

Emily flipped through the dog-eared pages scanning the numerous marks and comments. 'So, what do you want to work on tonight?'

'Let's do the scene where he goes to church to talk to Father D'Arcy again. I don't think I have that the way it should be.' Sean saw Emily's face change. 'What's that look?'

Emily shook her head. 'What look?'

'That! You look like you just remembered where you hid a bar of Dairy Milk.' He smiled.

'Well maybe I did!' She leaned in and kissed him.

76

Thursday was the last day of training. Principal photography started on Monday and they wanted him to have a long weekend off before starting shooting. The fight scenes were all being done first, so it was crucial that he was in top shape. The trainer seemed pleased with how he had trained Sean, and various lackeys echoed his praise.

They were taking it easy on him today. Sean had done his usual warm up and some light sparring and was feeling good about how well he was moving in the ring. He was ready to take it up to the next level when the trainer said everyone could take an early lunch. He called Sean over to the corner and told him the press were coming to do some publicity shots with him and the real Barry McGuigan.

Sean was momentarily annoyed that his schedule was being interrupted, but he took a deep breath and thought about the benefits of talking to Barry and really getting inside his head. They might even do some sparring, and he would be able to see how well Sean had copied his style and movements.

The trainer clicked his fingers and a woman in her mid-twenties stepped forward with what looked like a tool box in her hand. 'The producer sent over this make-up girl to give you a quick once-over and rub some coconut oil over you.'

'Coconut oil?' Sean asked in disbelief.

The trainer shrugged and climbed out of the ring.

Thirty minutes later the make-up girl had greased him up, styled his hair and blended out any imperfections on his face. When Sean went back out to the ring the press were already there and started snapping pictures of him. He smiled and indulged them. A few seconds later the camera lenses all changed direction as Barry McGuigan came in the door. As soon as Sean saw he was wearing a suit, his dreams of sparring all but disappeared. Sean heard him talking with the reporters as he entered. 'Well, I wish all I had to do for my money was dance around a bit and throw some fake punches.'

'I bet there's a time or two you would've like someone to call cut and you could have another go at it.'

'Aye, you're right there. And a wee latte and a massage between rounds wouldn't've gone amiss either!' McGuigan joked. The reporters laughed and lapped it all up.

Sean wished he'd put in his gum-protector. His teeth were grinding together. After what he'd put himself through for the last six weeks, this was what McGuigan thought of him?

McGuigan saw his doppelganger and immediately came towards him with his hand outstretched and a smile on his face. Sean bumped his glove to McGuigan's fist as a dozen cameras clicked and flashed.

'What do you think of him, Barry?' someone shouted.

McGuigan turned and put his arm around Sean as he faced the press. 'Well, he's taller than me...'

'Who isn't?' someone else shouted. Everyone laughed.

'He's got the moustache right, though!' McGuigan said, pointing to it and causing more laughter. Several reporters scribbled on notepads.

Sean looked at the boxer beside him and wondered if he threw a punch what would this man in a suit do. Would this man, who had retired from boxing eleven years ago, still be able to defend himself? Sean was wearing boxing gloves, but his fists were clenched as tightly as possible. McGuigan said something else and the press-monkeys were laughing again. Laughing at him. They thought he was a poor imitator, but Sean could drop anyone in this room in less than a minute. He looked at McGuigan again from the corner of his eye.

Anyone in the room.

If the producers wanted publicity for the film, he would give them something that would go national, maybe even international. Sean could imagine the headlines and his face on the front pages. There was always the chance that this could kill the movie, but it was much more likely that it would give the film an international profile and potential sales in territories that the producers hadn't even dreamed of. But more important than that, much more important than that, it would show McGuigan that he wasn't some poncy actor going through a dance routine. It would show McGuigan that...

'Sean?'

'Sorry, what?'

One of the reporters waved to him. 'I said, what have you done to get into character?'

I found some really hard-working actors and said some really patronising shit to them about their profession!

Sean took a deep breath.

And smiled.

'Well, a couple of weeks ago I stole his credit card and PIN number, so that's helped a lot.' The reporters laughed and scribbled the sound bite.

'I wondered where that went!' McGuigan played along with the gag.

'And I've made a point of falling out with the actor who's playing Barney Eastwood.'

More laughter. McGuigan hung his head but couldn't stop himself from grinning. He had no comeback for that one.

When the laughter died, Sean continued, 'No, I've just been reading every interview I can get hold of, and we've been training really hard here at the gym. I'm going to try my best to put Barry on the screen. I think he's someone everyone in Ireland – north and south – can be proud of, and it's an honour to share his story with the world.'

Scribbling. More photos. Barry turned and gave Sean a hug and slapped his coconut-oiled back.

For the next half-hour they took photos and Sean chatted to the man he would be portraying. They did the classic face-to-face in profile shot and then there were some shots of them in the corner of the ring with Sean sitting on his stool and McGuigan whispering in his ear. Sean bombarded McGuigan with questions and the ex-champ was happy to answer. He even told Sean the prayer that he said with Father D'Arcy before every fight. Sean memorised it, just like his lines.

By the time they all left, Sean was ready to pummel the heavy bag until his arms were tired, but Charlie came out and shook his head. 'If you still want to do this, hold on to it, son.'

Sean crouched down and took several deep breaths.

'Unless you want to call this off.'

Sean stood up and turned to him. 'No. We go through with it.'

The old man looked unsure, but gave him a nod. 'OK. I'll pick you up at seven. Be ready.'

As Charlie walked away Sean felt a little better. He had something real to focus on again after all the artificiality of the afternoon.

He and Emily ran lines after dinner. They were interrupted by phone calls from the producer and Avi, both congratulating him on what a great job he had done with the press. They had loved him and lapped up his sense of humour and repartee with McGuigan. His face would be all over the papers this weekend.

Avi also told him he had been receiving some other interesting offers. The good buzz around the McGuigan biopic was turning heads, and he predicted after the photos of Sean, oiled-up, looking toned and taut hit the shelves, he would probably have more offers. Sean said he couldn't think about his next role yet. He had to concentrate on getting this one right first. Avi knew the schedule for the shoot, so Sean asked him to set aside any interesting scripts that he would still be able to read for when *Wee Barry* wrapped.

Sean hung up the phone and looked at the clock for the hundredth time that night. He needed to time this just right. Emily had gone to the kitchen to wash the dishes while he had talked with Avi. He got up and joined her.

'That was a long one.' She sat another plate on the drying rack.

Sean sidled up behind her and put his hands on her hips. 'Avi's seeing dollar signs for my next three movies before I've even finished this one.' He slowly smoothed his hands around her waist, gently pulling her close to him. She was still wearing her work trousers. They were a snug fit and made her bum look great. He rubbed his crotch lightly against the smooth material. Emily stopped washing the dishes and stepped back into him. He kissed her neck from behind as his hands crept up to her breasts. He cupped them with his hands and felt the lacy material of her bra through her blouse. She leaned her head back and closed her eyes as he kissed her neck more passionately. His hands quickly ripped her blouse apart and she gasped as the breath caught in her throat. He grabbed her breasts again and squeezed her nipples through the thin material. She felt him grow harder through his jeans and gently coaxed it by rubbing herself against him. She wanted him. She needed him. Right now. She tried to turn, but he gripped her firmly and kept her back to him. His right hand made its way down her naked belly inside her trousers. His fingertips lightly combed through the soft hair and inside her. She moaned now, feeling hot and breathless. Enjoying the moment, but also craving the real thing. This wasn't something Sean had done before so she had no idea how long he was going to tease her before...

There were two faint parps of a car horn and Sean quickly withdrew and stepped back. He was breathing heavily as he stumbled back against the wall. Emily turned to him, still gasping. She looked at him, her brow furrowed. Sean looked away and then

80

hurried out of the kitchen. Emily went after him, but was just in time to see him run out the front door with his sports bag.

The door slammed shut.

Emily stood in the kitchen doorway and pulled her ripped blouse closed as best she could in case he was going to come back in with company. Instead, a few seconds later she heard the sound of a car driving away.

04.

There were at least a few dozen cars in the car park. The old linen mill had been abandoned years ago and was far enough out of Belfast to avoid anyone stumbling across it walking their dog. People only came here deliberately, and for one reason. The large open spaces and the fact that it was still watertight made it ideal for these events. Tonight was mild, so they wouldn't have to listen to the rain machine-gunning off the tin roof. Several generators took care of the electricity and lighting, and it seemed to be a case of bring your own booze as most people had a blue plastic bag at their feet.

Sean walked in behind Charlie, who nodded at the right people and led him to the makeshift ring. A fight was already in progress. A tall, muscular man with a buzzcut was pummelling a much smaller squat man, who, though built like a tank, was slow on his feet and had a face like roadkill.

Charlie nodded that Sean should stay here and watch the fight. Sean watched as the old pug approached a man in a cheap grey suit and trilby. Occasionally Charlie nodded or pointed in Sean's direction. Sean could feel the excitement building in his chest. He turned his attention back to the final seconds of the fight.

The first thing he noticed was, he wasn't going to need his shorts or boxing boots. These men were just stripped to the waist, wearing jeans and trainers. At least they were wearing gloves and gum-shields.

Sean sized up the bigger fighter. The squat man wasn't going down, but he was also too tired or hurt to raise his own gloves. Sean saw a group of men on the other side of the ring cheering on the larger fighter. They all had buzzcuts, and even though they weren't in uniform, they stuck out a mile as squaddies.

The bell finally rang and even though the squat man had resisted the call of the canvas (or concrete in this case), there was no way he had won. The referee – a man who looked like he was probably an accountant by day – stepped forward and lifted the squaddie's glove in the air. His friends cheered and Sean saw money getting shared out by a small man in a 70s style leather jacket. He was flanked at all times by two huge men with unsmiling faces.

Charlie was back at his side. 'OK, son, it's all set. The Brit has twenty minutes recovery time and then you're up against him.' Charlie glanced over at the victor of the last fight and watched as he swigged beer with his mates. 'You can still call it off. I'm starting to think this was a bad idea.'

'Don't worry about it, Charlie. I can take him.'

'Jesus Christ, son, he's got six inches and forty pounds on you. You're not even in the same weight class. This is fucking mental.'

'Win or lose, I'll have got what I came for.' Sean pulled off his shirt and started stretching. The group of squaddies looked over, pointing and laughing.

Keep laughing, motherfuckers. Keep laughing.

Sean started rolling his head around and doing stretches.

More laughter from across the ring.

Charlie stuck a roll-up in his mouth and tried to light it, but the lighter wouldn't spark. He threw it to the ground. 'Shit! You wanna know what it's like to stand toe to toe with a guy like that? I'll tell you. It's fucking scary. There. Take that piece of wisdom and go do your film.'

'I have to feel it, Charlie. Listen, will you go and…'

'If you get hurt in there, it's my fucking arse that'll get it. I'll lose my job for a start, and fuck knows what all those Hollywood types will do to me for getting you fucked up and unable to do the film.'

Sean grinned. 'This film has fuck all to do with Hollywood, Charlie. I wish it had.' He reached into his pocket and brought out a wad of notes. He pressed it into Charlie's hand. He clamped his own hand tightly over it and looked Charlie in the eyes. 'That's all the money I have. Three hundred and forty quid. See that man in the leather coat? See what kind of odds you can get.'

For a few seconds, hope blossomed on Charlie's face. He smiled. 'I don't know if he'll take this big a bet against an upstart.'

'Not against me, *on* me, Charlie.'

The old man's face sank. He hung his head and shook it from side to side slowly.

Sean grabbed him by the jaw and lifted his head. 'I'm going to win, Charlie, but even if I don't, you're safe. Worst case scenario: if he fucks my face up so badly I can't do the movie, I will never, never, mention you had anything to do with this. OK?'

Charlie exhaled slowly and then nodded.

'Go put on the bet.' Sean patted his shoulder and the old man shuffled away.

Charlie knew the boy's heart was in the right place, but he also knew, even if the boy did keep his mouth shut, it wouldn't take Columbo to figure out who told him about this place and brought him here.

The small man in the leather jacket saw Charlie approaching and gave him a quick upward nod, like a rat sniffing for cheese. Charlie thought about walking away. At least when the boy was carried out of the ring, he'd only have lost the fight and not the money too, but as leather jacket gave him an impatient second twitch, Charlie knew Sean wouldn't thank him for it. The lad was all or nothing.

Charlie leaned in to be heard over the crowd. 'The young boy fighting the Brit next, he wants to bet on himself.'

He grinned, showing his little rodent teeth. 'How much?'

Charlie showed the cash. 'Three hundred and forty.'

Now he was suspicious. He quickly brushed his nose twice with the back of his hand. 'He ever fight before?'

'Just sparring, no full contact.'

'Well, what the fuck's he doing here?' He was almost laughing.

'He's an actor. He's playing McGuigan in a film. He wants to know what it's like.' Charlie watched as the little rat-man ran the numbers in his head.

'How's his form?'

'He's been training hard for six weeks. Sparring, weights, the lot, but he's never been in a real fight. Your guess is as good as mine.'

'Six to one.'

'Ach, come on. For a first-timer?'

'That's the best I can do. He's an unknown quantity.' He glanced down at the cash in Charlie's hand. 'That's a bigger wager than I'm used to. I have to think about what I can cover.' He rubbed his nose with the back of his hand again and quickly looked left and right.

Charlie thought about it and then nodded. 'Six to one.' He handed over the cash and it was stuffed into the leather jacket. The little rat-man wrote him a hasty slip and walked away flanked by his goons.

Word got around about the six to one odds. Sean saw people sizing him up, pointing and shaking their heads for the most part. The twenty-minute break was closer to thirty-five by the time the little man in the leather coat gave the nod to the organiser that all bets were in.

The ring was little more than a length of rope tied around four ceiling supports. The floor was concrete and would hurt a lot more than canvas if you fell face first onto it. Sean ducked under the rope and got into his corner. He started to dance from toe to toe, buzzing with energy. Charlie appeared behind him and slipped a gum-shield in his mouth.

'All right, son. You just feel him out in this round. He's taller than you and he's got a longer reach, so get to know how far away from him you need to be to be safe. Throw a few jabs and watch his face. See how hard you need to hit for him to feel it. Don't let him put you in a corner. Keep moving, keep swinging, and above all, keep your fucking guard up.' Sean nodded at the wrinkled face that was looking older now than it had ever looked before. Charlie stepped back. Sean turned and put one knee on the ground. He bowed his head into his gloves.

Oh, angel of God, my guardian dear
To whom God's love commits us here
Ever this day be at my side
To light and guard, to rule and guide.
Amen.

The referee called seconds out.

Sean got up and turned to face his opponent. He could see the smug grin on the Brit's face, even with his gum-shield in. Fear and excitement fizzed in Sean's chest. His heart was beating at triple speed, pumping blood and engorging his muscles. The crowd were screaming for the match to start.

If he busts my lip, I'm fucked.
If he messes up my teeth, I'm fucked.
If he busts open my eye, I'm fucked.
If he breaks my nose, I'm really fucked.
If he hits my face at all, I'm probably fucked.
I can't let him take this opportunity away from me.
I won't let him take this opportunity away from me.

The bell rang.

The British soldier came shuffling towards him. A soldier like the one Sean's mum had run off with. Sean met him halfway. He saw an opening in the taller fighter's defence and threw a hard right hand into his stomach. He twitched. His face definitely twitched. He felt it. The Brit lowered his gloves to protect his mid-section and Sean threw a left hook at his head. It connected and knocked him off-balance. Sean didn't give him time to recover and started landing punch after punch to the bigger fighter wherever he saw an opening. This wasn't boxing. There was no strategy or skill involved. It was pure rage. Sean landed one, two, three unanswered blows to the other boxer's head. He saw his feet stumble, trying to regain his balance. Sean stepped forward and threw alternating punches to his body and face. The bigger fighter was caught off-guard by this style. There was no sense to it.

The soldier knew his opponent couldn't keep up this level of attack, but he also knew he couldn't take much more. The young mick was coming at him again. He couldn't tell if he was going for his head or torso. He lowered his guard to protect his ribs. A short jab flattened his nose and it exploded with blood. The Brit's eyes welled up with tears and he tried to blink them away to regain focus. He saw his opponent moving in again and threw a punch. It connected with Sean's jaw, but only partially. He heard the smaller fighter say something. He wasn't sure because of the gum-shield and the rage in his voice, but it sounded like: *Where's my mum?* What the fuck was he talking about? Was this guy fuckin' insane? The Brit put up his gloves defensively as he came at him again, stronger, harder.

If this were a proper boxing match the ref would've called it long ago. Now the Brit was just praying to hear the sound of the bell being struck. He felt like he'd been in here for six rounds already. The smaller fighter kept raining punches down on him wherever he saw an opening. The Brit was trying his best to keep his gloves up and his face protected. Sean pummelled his body with combination lefts and rights. The Brit pushed down with his gloves, trying to stop the assault on his stomach. Sean saw an opening and threw all his rage into his right fist and upwards. He caught the Brit under the chin and knocked him six inches off the ground before he fell in an awkward heap on the concrete floor. Sean rushed towards him with his right hand cocked and ready to strike.

Two men grabbed him from behind and pulled him back. Sean struggled against them until he realised one of them was Charlie. He took a few breaths to slow his heart rate. He glanced around and got his bearings. The crowd wasn't cheering anymore. They looked like they'd just witnessed a car crash. Maybe a fatal one.

Sean hadn't heard the bell being banged repeatedly.

The squaddies ran over to their fallen comrade and checked his injuries, but there was no question of him going on. The referee held Sean's glove in the air and declared him the winner. The majority of the audience threw tickets at the floor and looked annoyed.

Sean got dressed and the squaddies carried their friend towards a car bound for the nearest hospital. Charlie found the little man in the leather jacket.

'What the fuck was that?'

Charlie shook his head. 'I don't know.'

'If you think I'm paying you after that, you're fucking dreaming. We had three more fights scheduled for the Brit tonight. Now look! The fuckin' night's over. I'm keeping your winnings as compensation for my loss of earnings.'

Charlie nodded slowly. 'Maybe you want to tell that to him.' He flicked his head in the direction of Sean.

'You threatening me, old man?' He clicked his fingers and his two goons came up and stood behind him. The little man pointed backwards. 'Your boy's good, but he isn't that good.'

Charlie curled a finger, beckoning the little man to come closer. After a few seconds deliberation, he came. Charlie whispered, 'That boy's not kin to me, so I don't really give a fuck, but from what I know of him, and after what I've just seen, I'd suggest you don't get on the wrong side of him. You might have these two with you tonight, but that boy strikes me as the kind that holds a grudge, and the kind that'll wait for his moment. Now, he's done what he came here to do. You pay him and you'll never see him again. You stiff him, and I'd be pretty sure you *will* see him again. Probably when you least expect it.' Charlie held up his hands. 'It doesn't matter to me either way. It's your decision.'

The little bookie rubbed his nose with the back of his hand as he ran the odds in his head for a few seconds, and then glanced at the squaddie being carried out with his face in a bloody mess. He checked over his shoulder to make sure his goons didn't know he was being strong-armed. He reached into his pocket and quickly counted out Sean's winnings. He held out the wad of cash. Charlie reached and took hold of it, but the little man didn't let go of his end. 'Don't bring him back here, old man.' Charlie nodded. The bookie released the cash and watched Charlie walk away.

Emily had gone to bed early but was still reading when Sean came in. He stood in the bedroom doorway with one hand behind his back. She put her book down and looked at him, tight-lipped. He smiled at her.

'Where've you been, Sean?'

As he walked towards her, he took his hand out from behind his back and raised it high in the air. He released the wad of cash and let it fall down on her. She looked up with wonder, like a child seeing snow falling for the first time.

'What is this?'

'This,' Sean said as the last notes fell out of his hand, 'is two-thousand, three hundred and eighty pounds.'

'Where did you get it?'

He lay down on top of her. 'I'll tell you about it later.' He kissed her. 'I think we had some unfinished business.'

'You might have. I finished myself off.' She smiled.

'Oh, you dirty girl.' He smiled.

He got off the bed and extended his hand to her. She took it and got out of bed. She stood facing him. He pulled her nightie over her head. She pulled his T-shirt over his head and put her hands on his chest.

'My god, your heart's racing.'

He pulled her close and kissed her roughly. When they broke the kiss, he pushed her backwards onto the bed of money. As he kicked his trainers off and pulled down his jeans, Emily slipped off her panties and rubbed her naked body with handfuls of money.

Sean pounced on her.

PRODUCTION: 'Wee Barry'   DIR: N. VIRTUE   PDR: P. WELLS

SHOOT DAY	SC.#	CAST	LOCATION	CALL TIME
9 OF 23	06	Sean Black	Boxing Club	10am
	06	Shelly Marcus	Boxing Club	10am
	06	Cormac Dennis	Boxing Club	10am
	06	Extras (30)	Boxing Club	10am

05.

Avi Goldman stood outside the Holy Family Amateur Boxing Club smoking his fifth stogie of the day. He was early. He didn't need much sleep nowadays, but a phone call he'd received late last night kept him awake longer than usual. He'd been popping his heart pills like M&M's. Sean Black was as close as he'd ever come to the bigtime, and if he didn't put out this particular fire it might all be over before it properly started.

He checked his watch again. Still early. He sucked hard on his cigar and paced back and forth outside the front door. Across the road a black Chrysler pulled in and stopped. Avi winced at the oddity. It wasn't the sort of car you saw in Northern Ireland very often. The driver got out. He was formally dressed and put on his cap before opening the back door and looking over. Avi looked up and down the street and saw no one else. He put a finger to his chest. The driver gave him a single nod. Avi dropped his stogie into the gutter.

As he walked towards the car all sorts of possibilities crossed the old man's mind; was this an expensive lawyer? A movie star who had heard about him or Sean? Or was it some rich producer with plans for Sean? Avi could only imagine good things as he got into the car, smiling. The driver closed the door after him and remained standing outside.

The man sitting next to him was in his mid-thirties, wearing a dark-navy suit and with dark hair slicked back with product. He closed the cardboard folder on his lap and flashed his pearly whites as he stuck out his hand. 'Mr. Goldman. Pleasure to meet you.'

Avi shook the hand lightly. As discreetly as possible he checked the door locks were still up.

'I'm Josh Peterson from the U.S. Embassy in Belfast. I've been assigned your case.'

Avi swallowed hard and looked for a bulge in the man's jacket. 'What happened to Paulie?'

'Agent Scott took early retirement three years ago.'

'And you're only telling me now?'

'We're not obliged to tell you about personnel changes, Mr. Goldman. However, as per your plea bargain with the FBI's field office in New York, I am required to inform you that Joseph Bianchi was released yesterday from Rikers Island.'

Avi's hand was shaking as he reached into his pocket for his pill box. He flipped the lid off and it fell to the ground. His thumb and forefinger fumbled to pick up one of the small tablets and put it below his tongue.

Agent Peterson folded his hands across his lap and waited patiently for the old man to compose himself. Avi's hand was still shaking as he reached down and picked the lid from the floor. He clipped it on and put the pillbox back in his pocket. He looked at the smiling agent opposite him.

'So, what does this mean?'

'I'm sorry?'

'What do we do?'

The agent smiled wider as he furrowed his brow. 'We don't do anything.'

'What?'

'Mr. Goldman, I'm only telling you this because it was part of your agreement that you be informed. Nothing else has changed. We have no intelligence to suggest that your identity in Witness Protection has been compromised. No one knows you're here and we don't foresee that changing. Added to which, Mr. Bianchi is seventy-six years old now.'

'You think any of that matters?' Avi leaned towards the young agent. 'You think he'll just forget what I did? He's Italian. Those guys don't forget. Even if his hands are crippled with arthritis so bad that holding a feather caused him pain in every cell of his being, he'd still find the strength to pull the trigger on me. You guys have to give me some increased protection or something.'

'I'm afraid that would just call unnecessary attention to you and invite the kind of scenario we're trying to avoid.'

'Scenario?' Avi shook his head and took another stogie from his jacket.

'There's no smoking in here.'

Avi lit his cigar. 'You're a poor replacement for Paulie, kid. At least he pretended to give a fuck.'

Peterson was waving away the cloud of smoke from his face. 'We have fulfilled all the conditions set out in your agreement with the US Government and we will continue to update you if and when...'

'You can take all that bullshit and shove it up your ass, kid.' Avi opened the door.

'Do you have any comments you want me to pass on to my superiors?'

Avi paused halfway out the door. 'Yeah. Fuck you, and fuck the FBI.'

The old man got out and slammed the door behind him. He walked back across the road and heard the Chrysler drive away in his wake. He checked his watch. He was still early. He walked to the end of the street and found a payphone that hadn't been vandalised and called his office.

'Goldman Talent, how may I help you?' He savoured the voice of his secretary. She had been with him for thirty years and though her waistline had grown considerably over the last three decades, he still got a little rush every time he saw or heard her. 'Hey, it's me. Any calls?'

'Just a young actress looking for an agent. I put her name down on the list for the open casting day next month.' The line stayed silent for several seconds. 'Avi?'

'Yeah, I'm still here. Listen, you think your old man is likely to pop into the office this afternoon?'

'No, he's in Dublin today. He won't be back until late.'

'Book our room.'

Her voice lowered even though she was alone. 'On a weekday? Are you sure?'

'Yeah, I'm sure.'

'For the lunch hour?'

'For the rest of the day.'

'You want me to close the office?'

'Yeah, close the office and book our room. I'll meet you there for lunch.'

'Avi, what's wrong?'

'Nothing's wrong, sweetheart. Everything's fine. I'll see you there at lunch time. We'll get some room service sent up, so don't bring your sandwiches. OK?'

'OK.'

There was a brief pause, and then, 'I love you, Aileen.'

Her mouth slowly fell open. By the time she said, 'What?' he had already hung up.

Avi walked back to the boxing club. The last words he had heard his previous boss say, or shout, actually, were across a crowded courtroom. They echoed in his head.

'You're dead! You hear me, you Jew motherfucker? You're fucking dead! Wherever you go, wherever you run, it'll never be far enough. I'll find you. You hear me? I'll find you, you miserable rat fuck! I'll find you!'

Two cars passed the club before Sean's taxi arrived. Avi eyed each of them with suspicion and his heart quickened the closer they got. He was relieved to see Sean so they could get indoors.

'Avi, what are you doing here?'

'We got some business to attend to. Come on, let's get off the street.'

06.

Sean walked in and saw the place was empty. No cameras, no crew, no extras. 'Where is everyone? Did they change the time of the call?'

Avi kept pushing him towards the office at the back of the gym. 'Yeah, it's pushed back to midday. Everyone will be here then, hopefully.'

'Hopefully? What do you mean, hopefully? What the fuck is going on, Avi?'

'Just something we have to clear up, kid.' They stopped briefly at the office door and Avi knocked. Without waiting for a response, he opened the door and entered. Sean walked in behind the old man and saw his co-star Shelly Marcus. Her lips were pursed tightly together and her arms were folded. Next to her was her agent, Kathy, and at the head of the table was one of the producers; the one who Sean had last seen making her O face. She blushed slightly as he looked at her.

Avi gestured Sean towards a seat. 'Sit down, kid.'

Sean walked in and dropped into the seat as Avi closed the door. 'What's this all about?'

'You know fine fucking well what this is about, Sean,' Shelly shouted. Her agent put a calming hand on her arm to stop her from getting up. She shook her head and folded her arms again.

Avi sat down next to Sean. 'Sean, Shelly says you made some unwanted sexual advances towards her in her trailer yesterday.'

Sean smiled, shaking his head.

'Oh, you're going to deny it?' Shelly shouted.

Avi held up his hands and the girl sat back in her chair. 'Sean, why don't you tell us your side of this story.'

'There aren't any sides, there's only...'

'Please, Shelly,' the producer said. 'You've had your say; it's only fair Sean has his.'

The young actress shook her head and sat back in her chair again. The producer nodded towards Sean.

'OK,' he began. 'Yesterday I did go to Shelly's trailer, because I knew we had this kissing scene coming up and I wanted to rehearse it. Now I know that sounds like the plot to a bad porno, but it's the truth.'

Shelly squinted at him. 'Yeah, *then* what happened?'

'Well, I already knew you had a boyfriend. He's working on *Fair City* at the moment, right? And you know I have a girlfriend who I live with. But you're playing my wife Sandra in this film, so I didn't want it to look like our first time kissing. We're supposed to be completely at ease with each other. So I said we should rehearse how we were going to do it, just to get comfortable with each other.'

The producer looked around the room and saw no objections. 'OK, so what happened then?'

'She agreed. We started blocking out how we were going to do the kiss and then she freaked and threw me out.'

'You fucking liar!'

'Please, Shelly. Try to remain calm.'

'But he's fucking lying. He's been trying to get in my pants since day one. He kept giving me all this "what happens on-set, stays on-set" shit. Last night he said he had to fuck me, he just plain *had* to. For his "process." That's why I threw him out. He's obsessed.'

Sean was shaking his head and smiling.

Shelly's eyes went wide as the realisation hit her. She leaned forward and put both hands on the table as she stood up. 'Are you the one who's been phoning my house? It fucking is you, isn't it? I should've known. It all makes sense now.'

Sean turned to Avi and the producer in disbelief.

'Shelly, please sit down,' the producer said.

'Sit down, nothing! I want to file a restraining order against him. He's fucking crazy.'

'How are we going to work together on a film if you have a restraining order against me, genius?'

'Fuck off!'

'Please sit down, Shelly,' the producer repeated.

'Fuck you, Sean!'

'Shelly! Please!' She sat down. The producer took a deep breath. 'Now, is it *possible* that you misconstrued Sean's rehearsing as sexual advances?'

'No, it isn't. I know what he did and I know what he said.' She looked over at his innocent smiling face. 'And so does he. Smug bastard.'

The producer took another approach. 'Is there any way you two think you can get past this and continue working together?'

'I'm quite happy to work with Shelly. I think she's a fine actress. She's proving that right now.'

'Fuck you, Sean.'

Silence filled the air like carbon monoxide fumes. No one spoke as each second dragged forward. Sean sat forward. 'Shelly, would you be willing to speak to me alone? I think we could clear the air about some stuff if we could just talk without an audience.'

Shelly eyed him. Kathy put her hand on her client's arm and gave it a gentle squeeze. 'You don't have to if you don't want to, Shelly.'

After several more painful seconds she finally said, 'Why not. This doesn't seem to be getting us anywhere.'

Avi stood up. 'OK, why don't we step outside and give them a few minutes.' Avi knew Sean. He'd seen him charm the pants off a woman at fifty yards. He didn't know what had really gone on last night, but he had faith in his star. He gave him a pat on the shoulder as they left.

'We'll be right outside,' Kathy said before the door closed and silence returned to the room. They sat looking at each other across the desk.

'Well, are you still going to deny what happened when it's just us?'

Sean sat back in his chair. 'Are you sure you want to be an actress?'

'What?'

'I ran into this girl I knew from uni a few months back. After she graduated she went off to LA to seek her fortune. Rich parents paid for it all. Now this girl, she was beautiful. I'm sure she was the primo wanking material for her whole high school when she was there. When she got to LA, how many producers do you think wanted to see her act before they cast her?'

Shelly leaned back and folded her arms. She knew where this was going.

'I'll give you a clue,' Sean continued. 'It was less than one. Now how many of them do you think wanted to fuck a pretty little Irish girl who'd just fell off the shamrock truck?'

'And I'll bet she screwed them all.'

'Nah. She had a boyfriend back here. She was loyal. She came home after eight months and got a job in a bank. But the girl she shared a house with in LA sucked and fucked everything that was unzipped in front of her, and she's been in a list of TV shows and films as long as your arm.'

'So you were, what, preparing me for what's to come?'

'I'm just saying, when you're dealing with millionaires and billionaires, the only real currency you have is between your legs. That's a fact. And if you don't like it, there're plenty more banks needing cashiers.' Shelly was about to answer when he continued, 'You think I got this job without servicing her?' He pointed to the empty chair where the producer had sat. Shelly looked genuinely shocked. 'That's because I know how the game is played, and I play it. Now, you're going to get over this little tantrum and finish the movie.'

She looked surprised. 'Am I?'

'You are if you ever want to work again. If it comes down to me or you, who do you think is signing-on come Monday morning?' Shelly's face dropped slightly. Sean leaned across the table. 'They've invested a lot of time and money in me. We've already shot all the fight scenes and the finale of the fucking film! You're replaceable. You've got six lousy scenes in the whole show. So take the high ground if you want. I'll even apologize in front of everyone if that's what you need, but you have to say it was all a big misunderstanding or so help me, you'll regret it.'

Shelly was trying to swallow but her mouth seemed to have no spit. She felt colder the longer he looked at her.

'The sooner we get this film finished, the sooner we can go our separate ways and you never have to see me again.'

The chair Shelly sat in felt bigger now. The room felt bigger. Sean looked bigger and more dangerous than he had last night. She couldn't look at him as she gave him a subtle nod.

The sound of his chair screeching backwards made her jump. 'Smile when they come back in.' He opened the door and she smiled.

'Is everything OK?' the producer asked.

'Of course it is, we're the best of friends,' Sean said. He ushered them back inside as they all breathed a sigh of relief. Avi gave the kid a quick wink when he walked past him. He knew he could do it.

Smiles were exchanged between everyone. The producer breathed a sigh of relief before saying, 'OK, I'll make some calls and get everyone here as soon as possible. We don't need to waste any more time.'

'There is just one more thing.'

Everyone froze and looked at Sean.

'Well, since you're all here. Chaperones, if you will, maybe we should rehearse this kiss.' He looked around the uncomfortable faces. 'Just a suggestion. But we are shooting this scene today and given all that's happened, I certainly don't feel confident about it looking natural.'

Everyone looked at Shelly. She felt as if there was a rock in her stomach. Gooseflesh rose on her arms. If she didn't do it, it would just add more credence to his story. She forced a quick grin and nodded.

Everyone exhaled. Sean found a space at the end of the table and Shelly joined him. The two agents and producers positioned themselves to watch.

Sean took her hands. She fought the bile rising in her throat. He nodded at her, smiling. The last time he was this close to her was last night. Her heart quickened. She looked at the door.

'OK, I'll feed you the line before the kiss and then we'll just go for it, OK?'

Shelly nodded.

Sean took a cleansing breath. *'Sandra, I'm not fighting for the trophy or the money when I'm in there. I'm fighting for you. For us. For our future.'*

'I love you, Barry.'

She closed her eyes and they kissed. She felt his tongue try to part her lips, but her jaw was clenched shut. She could only think of what he'd said last night when they were this close. When she was pressed against the wall of her trailer. She swallowed, remembering his hand around her throat. She opened her eyes and found she was looking at the door.

Sean stepped back and turned to the spectators. 'Well, how was that?'

They all looked at each other, hoping someone else would say it.

'Yeah, that's what I thought. It was shite. This is what I was worried about.' He turned to her. 'How did you feel, Shelly?'

She shrugged and shook her head.

The producer took half a step forward. 'It's like you said, Sean, it's just unfamiliarity. You just need to feel comfortable with each other.'

'OK, so go again?'

The producer nodded.

Sean stepped in and raised his eyebrows to Shelly. 'You good to try again?'

She nodded.

'Sandra, I'm not fighting for the trophy or the money when I'm in there. I'm fighting for you. For us. For our future.'

'I love you, Barry.'

They kissed and this time she let his tongue slide between her lips and probe her mouth until it touched her own tongue. She fought back the nausea. A nest of snakes was writhing around her stomach, but the quicker she got this right, the quicker she could get away from him.

Sean stepped back and looked at the three again. He saw their expressions and turned away from Shelly. 'Look, I'm trying to be professional here, but I'm getting nothing back. It's like kissing a fucking corpse.'

Shelly was staring at the door. At the handle.

'Shelly?' She turned and saw the wincing face of her agent. 'If you feel like you're being unfaithful, maybe you could just pretend he's your boyfriend when you're kissing.'

Before she could answer Sean said, 'It's not just her. It's me too. I feel really self-conscious about touching her after what she accused me of.'

The room fell silent and everyone looked to Shelly for her response. It took everything she had not to cry. She looked at the door and then turned her attention to Sean. He was making a case for having her replaced. She wouldn't let that happen. He wasn't the only one who wanted this as a career.

She stepped forward. 'I'm sorry to all of you. But I'm mostly sorry to you, Sean.' He turned and faced her. 'I'm sorry to put my personal hang-ups on you. You're right; we need to be professional about this and that means it has to look real. So let's try this again, and this time

I want you to forget all about what I said and just kiss me. Kiss me like you'd kiss your own girlfriend and don't worry about what you can or can't touch. Just do what feels natural.' The two agents and producer were smiling broadly.

Sean turned back to her and smiled. 'If you're sure?'

She nodded. 'I'm sure. Let's get on with it.'

He stepped close and pushed a strand of hair behind her ear. *'Sandra, I'm not fighting for the trophy or the money when I'm in there.'* He puts his hands around her waist and slowly pulled her closer. He touched his forehead to hers. With his lips almost touching hers, he whispered, *'I'm fighting for you. For us. For our future.'*

She looked into his eyes as her own welled up. *'I love you, Barry,'* she whispered.

They kissed. Lightly at first, then becoming more passionate as his hands pulled her closer. She responded by putting her arms around him and holding tightly. Their tongues found each other quickly and they were lost in the moment. When they broke their embrace they touched foreheads again and remained close for a few seconds before the sound of applause made them step apart.

The agents and producer were all beaming with smiles as they clapped.

'That's what we need,' the producer said. 'Do that on screen and we'll all be very happy.' Sean went over to Avi.

Kathy came over to Shelly. 'That was so convincing,' she said, rubbing her client's arms with excitement.

The producer was already pressing buttons on her mobile phone. 'OK, it's going to take me at least an hour to summon the troops, so if you want to get a coffee or have a nap, whatever, feel free, but be back by eleven for make-up.'

'I should get back to the office. Are you all right now?' Kathy asked. Shelly nodded. Kathy hurried out, making a phone out of her little finger and thumb and wiggling it at Shelly as she went.

Shelly gathered her jacket and bag and walked to the door. Sean turned and gave her a wink and a smile as she left.

Shelly walked out of the gym. She hurried along the street until she found a café. She went inside and ran past the counter to the toilets. Once inside the cubicle she dropped to her knees and was sick. When she was sure there was nothing left inside her, she flushed and wiped her mouth with toilet paper.

Then she sat down on the cold tile floor and cried.

07.

Aileen was sitting on the edge of the bed when Avi came in. She had taken her coat off but nothing else. Usually when they met here every second counted and she would be undressed and in bed if she was here ahead of Avi. She had her hands in her lap. She raised her head briefly when he came in, but when she saw the flowers, she lowered it again.

Avi took off his coat and hung it on the hook on the back of the door. He dropped the flowers on the bedside table and sat down next to her. He looked down, wondering what she was finding so fascinating on the floor.

She twisted and tore at the tissue in her hands. 'What happened with Sean?'

'All sorted.'

In a room somewhere nearby, the maid was vacuuming. They listened for a few seconds.

'Carnations?' she asked without looking up.

'I thought they were your favourite.'

She nodded lightly. She sniffed back hard. 'What's her name?'

Avi looked at the profile of the woman he loved. 'Who? The actress who complained about Sean?'

'No. Not her.'

'Who then?'

She finally turned to him and he saw the tears in her eyes. 'Whoever you're replacing me with.' She looked at the old man feigning confusion. 'Younger, I'll bet. Thinner, I'm sure. Was she one of the actresses you saw last month? It's OK. I don't blame you. I've been expecting it for a while.'

'Will you shut the fuck up?' he said, quite matter-of-factly.

Her mouth fell open. Avi swore like a teenager, but never at her.

'I didn't call you here to break up with you. Jesus Christ, don't you know I fuckin' love you?' She smiled and the tears she had been preparing for an entirely different purpose, escaped her. He edged closer to her and put his arm around her.

She rested her head on his shoulder. 'I was so...' She made a noise somewhere between a laugh and a cry. She sniffed hard and wiped her nose and cheeks with the shredded tissue. She raised her head and looked him in the eyes. 'Then what's this all about?'

Avi looked into those beautiful, vulnerable eyes and didn't want to lie, but lying would keep her safe. 'A few days ago I heard someone I knew died.'

'Oh, Avi!'

'No, no, it's OK. I hadn't seen him in years. Not since I lived in the States. But he was the same age as me and it got me thinking about a lot of things. So I've made arrangements. If anything happens to me...'

She shook her head. 'No, Avi...'

He took her firmly by both shoulders and made her face him. 'Yes, Aileen! You have to hear this. Now, if anything happens to me you're going to get a letter and a key. The key is for a safety deposit box and the letter inside will explain everything else.' She still looked confused, but she'd also worked for Avi long enough to know when to not ask questions. He moved closer to her, and to those eyes that hadn't aged since the first time he'd looked into them three decades earlier. 'I love you. No one else in this world. Only you.' They kissed.

Avi kicked his shoes off and slid back to the head of the bed. Aileen did the same. She lay with her head on his chest. 'You ready to order lunch?'

'I can wait a while if you can,' she said.

'OK,' he said. 'Let's just lie here. I just want to hold onto you, OK?' He felt her nodding against his chest. He tightened his arm around her. 'I just want to hold onto you,' he repeated.

POLICE CALLED TO McGUIGAN HOME

Police were called to the home of former world champion boxer Barry McGuigan on Friday night when the security system was triggered. The alarm, which is directly linked to the local police station, registered the attempted break-in at 11.04pm.

Local RUC officers were on the scene within minutes and found a broken window and footprints to the rear of the premises, but they are confident the intruder did not gain access to the property and was probably scared off by the alarm.

Also found at the scene was an undisclosed item, thought to have been dropped by the intruder as they ran from the scene. Though the police are reluctant to specify what this item is, detectives are thought to be very concerned by its discovery, suggesting this may have been more than just a robbery attempt.

The McGuigan family were at home during the incident but were unaware of the intruder until the alarm sounded. No members of the household were hurt, but sources close to the investigation said they were 'noticeably shaken' by the experience and were very appreciative to the officers who responded so quickly to the call.

McGuigan, who now lives in Kent, had been renting the Belfast property during an extended stay back in his old stomping ground while he acts as a consultant on his upcoming biopic *Wee Barry*. Filming wrapped almost two weeks ago, but the McGuigan family had decided to stay on in the province for the summer, though this incident may now alter those plans.

A spokesman for the RUC said they would be keeping a close eye on the McGuigan home from now on, and were pursuing several possible avenues of investigation about the attempted break in.

Barry McGuigan, the Clones Cyclone, retired from professional boxing in 1989 to become a boxing promoter and manager. Most recently he has been in the news promoting his upcoming biopic *Wee Barry*, due in cinemas next year.

Belfast Echo, April 17, 2000

BOXING BIOPIC IS A KNOCKOUT!

There can be few better examples of the rags to riches story than boxing. When your main character isn't only figuratively, but also literally, fighting for a better life, audiences can't help but root for the underdog.

I'm sure I won't be the only critic to compare this film to the original (and best) *Rocky* movie from 1978. Before the gloss and extended 'music video' sections that some of the sequels indulged in, we had a simple story of a little guy given a big chance, and that's what *Wee Barry* gives us too.

Newcomer Sean Black is astonishing in the title role as the diminutive boxer from Clones who got his shot at the World Featherweight Championship in 1985 against Eusebio Pedroza. McGuigan himself helped choreograph the fight sequences, and director Neill Virtue gets right into the ring with him with some truly astonishing camera shots. I'd be embarrassed to admit I actually found myself ducking from left to right in my seat at the press screening, if I hadn't seen so many of my peers doing the same.

The supporting cast also excel for the most part, with Jim Broadbent as Barney Eastwood and Christopher Eccleston as Father Brian D'Arcy particular standouts. Faring less well is newcomer Shelly Marcus, who plays McGuigan's wife Sandra. The actress seems out of her depth at her best, and wooden and uncomfortable at her worst. Insider gossip tells us her role was scaled back as much as possible in the edit, which was probably a good thing if what remains is anything to go by.

But when all is said and done, this is Black's film, and he couldn't have picked a better way to introduce himself to the world. No doubt Hollywood will be calling soon and he'll be off to do blockbusters in Tinseltown. Until then, we'll savour this young Northern Ireland actor in whatever he chooses to do next.

Wee Barry will inspire and excite boxing and film fans in equal measure, and we fully expect to see some tuxedos on the red carpet representing this movie come award season. Sean Black is one to watch in 2001.

The Imperial Verdict: 4/5

Imperial Magazine, November 1, 2000

TEN QUESTIONS

In real life, Sean Black seems as humble and self-deprecating as the boxer he played in *Wee Barry*. The role seems tailor-made for him, so it's no wonder he's setting the box office on fire with his portrayal of the boxing legend. We caught up with the young actor to ask him our famous Ten Questions!

01. Favourite Film: The first *Rocky* film. I've seen it dozens of times.

02. Favourite Band/ Musician: My dad!

03. Favourite Food: Grilled chicken.

04. Favourite TV Show: *Ballykissangel*. I know a few people who've been on it so that's always fun seeing them. I also like repeats of *Minder*. It's on one of the satellite channels. I like the old ones with Terry, but I like the newer ones with Ray too. And George Cole is a legend in the role of Arthur.

05. Favourite Drink: Diet Coke. Sorry to be boring. I'm not much of a drinker.

06. First Celebrity Crush: Oh, God! Let me think. Probably Keren Woodward from Bananarama. I had her poster on my wall for years. I might still have it somewhere, but don't tell my girlfriend.

07. Person You'd Most Like To Meet: Apart from Keren? [laughs] Muhammad Ali. I'll bet he has some stories.

08. Last Time You Laughed: Em (his long-time girlfriend Emily Williams) and I watched *Meet the Parents* the other night. We both laughed a lot at that.

09. Last Time You Cried: At the wrap party for *Wee Barry*. I blubbed like a baby. I'd got really close to a lot of the cast and crew and it was weird to be saying goodbye to them. Shelly (Marcus) was worse than me, though. I remember her crying a lot.

10. Favourite Quote: 'You haven't failed until you stop trying.' I don't know who said it, but it's good advice, especially for actors.

Wotz on the Box? Magazine, 18, November 2000

SEAN NOMINATED FOR A 'WEE' STATUE

Portstewart actor Sean Black has been nominated for a BAFTA in the category of Best Newcomer for his portrayal of Barry McGuigan in the biopic *Wee Barry*. The film, which is proving a hit both with critics and audiences, follows the boxer from his humble roots to winning the word Featherweight Championship in 1985. In a statement released from his agent earlier today Black is said to be 'extremely honoured to be nominated for this award.' With a BAFTA nomination in the bag, there are already rumblings of an Oscar nod for the actor as well. We've got our fingers crossed for you, Sean!

Weekend Gossip, December 3, 2000

IT'S A BUM DEAL FOR SEAN!

After a couple of months full of awards and acclaim, Sean Black, the hunky star of boxing biopic *Wee Barry* has won possibly his most important award to date; The Bestest Bum Award 2000. Almost

40,000 votes were cast when the contest was announced in Galz Stuff Magazine, with The Northern Irish beefcake scooping the top prize by a considerable margin. Second place went to ex-Take That star Robbie Williams and our favourite dumb-but-lovable Friend Joey Tribbiani (Matt LeBlanc) took third place.

Galz Stuff Magazine – The Big Christmas Issue! December 21, 2000

PORTSTEWART ACTOR IN COURT

Sean Black, star of *Wee Barry* has been fighting again, but this time it wasn't for the world championship, it was for his reputation. His co-star Shelly Marcus alleges that Black sexually harassed her during the making of the film and even at the wrap party, claiming he became violent and abusive when she refused his advances.

The High Court in Belfast is to hear testimony from Marcus and Black this coming Monday when they reconvene. When asked for a statement leaving the courthouse today Black said: 'I'm sorry things haven't worked out the way Shelly thought they might after the release of the film. But I hope she sees this isn't the way forward. I wish her all the best.' Miss Marcus refused to comment.

Belfast Echo, 12, January, 2001

IT'S A NICE DAY FOR A BLACK WEDDING

In a secret ceremony at Belfast Registry Office on Saturday morning, Sean Black married his long-time girlfriend Emily Williams. Emily's parents and sister sat on the bride's side, but no one from Black's family was in attendance. The star's agent, Avi Goldman, served as his best man.

The bride was dressed modestly in a white skirt and jacket, with a small hat and veil. Black was dressed in a navy-blue suit with a red tie. Details about the reception or honeymoon destination remain a mystery.

Sunday Echo, 14, January 2001

BLACK CASE DISMISSED

Those expecting to hear lurid details about Sean Black's on-set shenanigans were left disappointed this morning when a packed courtroom was told that all charges had been dropped against the actor.

Black and his barrister looked as shocked as everyone else when the bailiff made the announcement. Shelly Marcus had claimed multiple counts of sexual harassment against the *Wee Barry* star, but neither she nor her representation were willing to make any formal statement about the matter as we went to press.

At the gates to the courthouse Sean Black said: 'I don't know what happened. I'm in the dark as much as you guys. I guess she changed her mind. I'm glad she saw sense. Maybe now I can get on with my honeymoon.'

When asked for his honeymoon destination, Black laughed and said, 'Wouldn't you guys like to know!' as he walked away.

Wherever he goes, we're sure he's happy to be leaving these unpleasant accusations behind him.

Belfast Echo, 15, January, 2001

<u>2001</u>

01.

Sean exhaled long and slowly.

His heart had been beating in double-time all morning, and now he was here it had gone up another gear. The London offices were huge. Glass-walled offices held the executives inside like terrariums.

The men were all shapes and sizes, but the women were some of the most beautiful he'd ever seen. Even the secretaries, who seemed to do little else but answer the phone and say, 'Hold please,' could have been catwalk models; skinny, dressed in the latest fashions with flawless hair and make-up. They answered their phones with disdain, but when anyone in a suit approached their desk, they would show their unnaturally white, perfectly straight teeth, framed in a lipstick smile. That was enough to make any man's day a little brighter.

Everyone was in a rush. No one walked from place to place, everyone ran. Couriers ran in with a parcel and one of the supermodel assistants would hurry as fast as her four-inch heels allowed to take it the last leg of its journey.

Sean glanced at Avi. He looked like a man at a poker table holding a royal flush but trying not to give too much away. He sat with one leg crossed over the other and his hands in his lap. How could he be so calm?

One of the glass doors swung open and a harried looking woman marched out followed by an even more distressed-looking agent, tripping after her like a dog on a leash. Sean recognised her. He'd seen her in a film recently. More importantly, he'd seen her breasts in a film recently. He couldn't place her name. She wasn't quite A-list, but she was very well-known, and her topless scene was something her male fans had waited a long time to see. It was a weird feeling to be in the same room as someone he'd never met, but had seen naked in a very erotic shower scene.

Sean tried to catch her eye as she passed. She glanced at him and dismissed him a second later, never breaking her stride towards the glass exit doors. Her agent, for that is what she just had to be, followed carrying a dog-eared script under her arm and trying to not look as pathetic as she felt.

Almost imperceptibly, Avi's knee nudged Sean and he turned to see a woman walking towards them with a clipboard. She looked like she'd escaped from Robert Palmer's *Addicted To Love* video.

'Mr. Greenberg will be ready for you soon, gentlemen. He's just finishing up a phone call. Can I get you any refreshment for your meeting?'

Sean imagined the polite thing was to say no, but his mouth was so dry he feared he wouldn't be able to speak once he got in there. 'Just some water would be good.'

She made a tick on her clipboard. 'Still or sparkling?'

Sean shrugged. 'Still.'

She made another tick, and then turned to Avi. 'And for you, sir?'

'Nothing for me, thanks.'

She gave a brief smile, probably only twenty-five percent of a full smile, but still enough for them to feel it. She turned and walked away. Avi and Sean admired the firm buttocks in the tight black dress until they were out of sight. They looked at each other and smiled.

Seconds later a different Palmer girl approached them and said, 'Mr. Greenberg will see you now. If you gentlemen would like to follow me.'

Sean was on his feet before she had finished talking, but Avi took his time getting up, and Sean knew it was nothing to do with his age. He didn't want to seem too eager. Sean tried to remind himself to do the same as they followed another set of perfect buttocks towards Greenberg's office.

She opened the door and gave them a fifty-percent smile as she ushered them inside.

The large man behind the desk stood up. He was wearing red braces holding up his oversized trousers. He had his shirt sleeves rolled up and was chomping on a more expensive cigar than Avi could afford. What little hair he had left was curly and unnaturally dark for a man who must've been easily pushing fifty. He opened his arms wide as Avi and Sean approached.

Next to Greenberg was a thin man with grey hair parted to one side. While everyone was shaking hands, he was introduced as Michael Murphy. Sean couldn't help but think they'd dragged this poor bugger in from some obscure department just because of his surname; to make Sean feel more at home. He imagined it was the sort of thing Americans did, and Greenberg was as American as you could get; big, brash and rich.

With the introductions complete, everyone was taking their seats when the first Palmer girl came in with Sean's bottle of water. This time she gave him the full smile as she delivered it, and it was as dazzling as he'd imagined. Sean thanked her and couldn't help but watch her buttocks walk back to the door. When the door closed and the show was over, he turned back around to see the other three men had been looking at the same thing. They all laughed at how easily they had been hypnotised by her figure.

'Jesus, that ass!' Greenberg declared. 'You think I'd be used to it by now.'

'I think that's the most perfect arse I've ever seen in my life.'

Greenberg laughed. 'Listen to that accent! I love this kid! Arse!' He laughed again, and then leaned forward. 'Listen, Sean, we look after our actors here, so any time you want that ass – or arse! – parked on your face, or anywhere else, you just let me know. I guarantee you, you won't be disappointed.'

Sean smiled at him. 'You know from experience?'

Greenberg licked his lips, 'Kid, that girl has the tightest ass I've ever had the pleasure of, and I go to Thailand twice a year!' He laughed again. The other three men smiled and nodded.

In truth, the thought of this huge man grunting and grinding on top of that skinny little girl had put Sean off the experience completely. He was wondering how to steer the conversation away from this subject when Avi did it for him.

'So, now can you tell us what this big hush-hush project is that you're considering Sean for?'

'Avi's all about the business,' Greenberg said with a touch of admiration. 'OK, the reason we couldn't say on the phone was because we were still haggling; trying to secure the rights. There was this big auction in New York and everyone wanted this property, but in the end, we got it, and after seeing Wee Barry, we thought Sean would be perfect for the role. You were dynamite as that boxer, kid.' Greenberg threw a few air punches just to remind Sean.

It sounded wrong when he said *Wee Barry*. It was such an Irish word and Americans had no experience using it. It didn't even sound like he knew what it meant. The way he pronounced it sounded like he thought it was something someone might say to a kid named Barry as he came down a slide. Sean just nodded and said, 'Thank you.'

Greenberg smiled at him as if enthralled by a magic trick. 'Look at that face. This is our guy. This is our fucking guy, Murph!' His accountant nodded.

'So, this hot property was…?' Avi asked.

'The Crying Garden!' Greenberg said, throwing his arms out like a ringmaster. 'It was the biggest novel of the year. Sold zillions. Won every award there was. The critics loved this fucking thing, kid. This is real literature. This is the kind of shit that wins awards.'

Sean had been trying to catch Avi's eye, but thankfully the old man knew what to say without being cued. 'I'm sorry, I'm not much of a reader. Not novels anyway. I spend most of my time reading scripts,' Avi said. 'I think Sean is probably the same.' He lifted his bushy grey eyebrows in the direction of his client.

Sean shrugged. 'Yeah, same here. Sorry. Emily's probably read it. She reads a lot. What's it about?'

Greenberg waved his hands dismissively. 'Don't worry about it. You think I read the fucking thing? It's like a house brick.' The executive laughed his way back to his seat and plopped down. 'Give 'em the short synopsis, Murph.'

His accountant sat forward in his seat and said, 'It starts off with a little nine-year-old girl going missing. The whole town is out looking for her and when they find her, two weeks later, she's been raped and murdered. The rest of the book is about how her sister grows up without her and eventually becomes obsessed with the case and tracks the guy down who did it.'

'And that's where you come in!' Greenberg bellowed.

Avi sat forward, shaking his head. 'Sean would be like a cop or something that helps the sister find the guy?'

'No, Sean would be the guy. That's the lead. There is no cop part. It's basically a two-hander between the sister and the killer. Half the film is with her trying to find him, and the other half is with him doing some really nasty shit to little kids.'

Sean realised he hadn't breathed for some time and made a point of it. The breath didn't come easy. He felt like there was a noose around his neck. He pulled at his collar and tried to breathe again. The breaths were short and irregular.

There was a school less than a mile from his house. Some of those kids walked home alone.

His eyes were starting to water. He could see the mouths of the others still moving, but their voices were muffled, like he was listening to them underwater.

Emily was out all day. He would have the house to himself for all those hours.

His mouth was dry and hot. He fumbled with the lid of the bottle the girl had brought him and took a long drink of cold water. He dragged the back of his hand across his forehead and found it slick with sweat.

The walls of the house were thin though. He and Emily could hear the neighbour's TV when their own house was silent. But with some duct tape no one would ever hear...

His vision was drifting in and out of focus. He took another drink of the water. He was very aware of how fast his heart was beating.

And then when he had them alone...

When he had them alone...

The vomit rose in Sean's throat. He pursed his lips tightly and forced the acidic liquid back down.

'Three of this director's last five pictures have been Oscar nominated,' Greenberg continued. 'We haven't secured the lead actress for the part yet, but every hot twentysomething in Hollywood is desperate to play the part. Some of them are *real* desperate, so if there's any particular actress Sean fancies having a private... Jesus, kid, are you all right?' The executive furrowed his eyebrows at the pale and sweating actor.

'I'm OK, but this isn't. Thanks. But, no. I... I don't think I can do this part. What else have you got for me?' Sean tried to smile.

Greenberg glanced at Murphy and then at Avi. Avi got to his feet. 'Sean, I think we need to talk privately before you make such...'

'I don't give a fuck, Avi. I'm not playing that part!' He turned to Greenberg. 'What else have you got for me?'

Greenberg spoke softly for the first time today. 'I don't have anything else for you, kid. This is the part we like you for.'

'Well fuck you, I'm not doing it.'

Avi was hurrying across the room towards Sean.

'What the...? You talk to me like that? In my office? Avi, if this is some sort of joke, I'm not laughing.'

Avi held his palms up. 'The kid's just nervous. Please, just let me talk to him alone and we can sort this all out.' Avi tried to take Sean's arm and the younger man shrugged it off.

'I'm not playing no fucking paedo, Avi.' He pointed to Greenberg. 'You tell him. You tell him to find me something else, Avi.'

'Jesus Christ, kid. Calm down. No one's going to make you play any part you don't want to.'

Greenberg poured himself a generous drink and downed it. 'Avi, I don't know if this is some kind of negotiating tactic or if your guy's just fucking nuts, but this is getting old fast.'

Avi looked at his client, pleading with his eyes. 'Sean, just take a deep breath and think about what you're turning down.'

'You listen to Avi, kid. This is your ticket to Hollywood. To the big leagues.' Greenberg poured himself another drink and downed it in one. 'There might come a day when you can pick and choose your projects, but you're a hell of a long way from there right now.' Greenberg got up from his chair and loomed over the young man. 'Now, I've gone to a lot of time and trouble to line you up for this project, and if you're smart, you'll apologize, take the part, say thank you, and shut the fuck up for the rest of this meeting.'

Sean got to his feet and stood face to face with the much larger man. 'I'm not doing it.'

'If you ever want to work again, you will. Trust me, kid, I can fucking destroy you in this business. I've had some of the biggest stars in the world on their knees before me, offering to suck my dick to be in one of my movies. And I'm not just talking about women, and I'm not talking about fags. And yet you, *you*, think you can turn me down?' He lowered his voice again, but this time it was sinister not sympathetic. 'You think hard about what you do next, kid.'

The room fell silent for a few seconds.

And then Sean punched Greenberg as hard as he could in the face.

SEAN GONE!

One-hit wonder, Sean Black has been voted off Celebrity Big Brother with a staggering 81% of the viewers votes. Black, 23, is the first to go in this latest series. The actor who starred in the film *Wee Barry* was described by most BB fans as boring and bland. He refused to get involved with the tasks set out in the show and rarely spoke to the other housemates. Page 3 girl Becky Bounce said he was an 'arrogant t**t' after she had to cook a meal with him. It doesn't look like the young actor will be missed from the BB house.

Daily News, 11 August, 2001

Just when you think *Gunge Factory* (Saturday, Channel 5) can't sink any lower, either in terms of ratings or my personal opinion, they've now switched from dragging has-beens out of retirement homes to giving never-beens a chance to be part of their humiliating show.

This week's desperado was Sean Black, who you might remember from the film *Wee Barry*. It was a great film and the lad turned in a great performance, so what he's doing slumming it in this excuse for entertainment is anyone's guess.

First they dressed the poor sod up as Dorothy from *The Wizard of Oz* and then sent him down this yellow brick road where the dregs from some council estate (or contestants if you prefer) squirted him with water pistols full of slime. I swear as he sat in that chair at the end, waiting to be dropped into a bath full of green gunge, I could read his mind, and he was thinking: *How did it come to this?*

How indeed, Sean.

Dickie Spatz Tells It Like It Is, 14 October, 2001

'We've had another text for our Celebrity Spotter competition. Kath from Belfast says she spotted Wee Barry actor Sean Black at her local cinema. No, not on the big screen, he was the one serving at the Pick N' Mix scales. Oh, it's not all glamour this acting lark, is it? Maybe he's researching the part of a Pick n' Mix guy for his next movie. That would be a sweet role! Let's just hope he's not punching above his weight! You're listening to Jimbo on Drive Time.'

Jimbo's Drive Time, Radio 99, 11 November, 2001

COMING CHRISTMAS 2001!

PUSS IN BOOTS at The Lyric Theatre, Belfast

Starring Jane McLean, Russell Arthur and Tom Bradley

With Special Guest Appearances by Wee Barry star Sean Black &

Pop Idol quarter finalist Jim Kennedy!

Tickets on sale now!

PUSS IN BOOTS REVIEW (excerpt)

...did some topical material about the break-up of Tom Cruise and Nicole Kidman, Angelina Jolie kissing her brother, and Peter Jackson's *Fellowship of the Ring* movie, but perhaps the biggest laugh of the night was unscripted.

In the final act when Puss (Jane McLean) has to fight the Ogre (John Lindsay), she calls to the wings for help and out comes Sean Black dressed as Barry McGuigan in full boxing gear. There was a great cheer for the actor, but when it died down a rather slurred voice near the front shouted: 'Oi, Sean! Where's your career? It's behind you!' The theatre erupted in laughter. Black seemed to be taking the whole thing in good humour, but who knows? We may have been lucky he was wearing a gum-shield and unable to talk.

Belfast Echo, 16 December, 2001

FEAGAN GETS 'GARDEN' ROLE.

Hollywood sources have confirmed that after an exhaustive search, Ciaran Feagan will play the lead role in the much-anticipated screen adaptation of the best-selling novel *The Crying Garden*. Only recently the part was hotly rumoured to belong to *Wee Barry* star Sean Black; a casting decision that had the novel's author Christy-Marie Schultz's full backing. How she feels about Feagan now taking the role is unknown, and Sean Black's management refused to comment on why he seems to have pulled out of the project.

Imperial Magazine, 16 December, 2001

What was Sean Black doing on *Silly Oul' Granny* last night? The inexplicably long-running Irish 'comedy' series wheeled him out dressed as McGuigan (yet again) for a scene so badly shoe-horned into the narrative that it made me feel genuinely embarrassed for the young actor.

Black looked ill at ease in the usual mix of camp humour, circa-1970s gags and sub-par acting that this show has become known for. What's next, Sean? Maybe a novelty single with B*Witched for Christmas would get you some credibility back.

I don't know who's steering this poor lad's career, but my advice is they get back on their meds as soon as possible!

Dickie Spatz Tells It Like It Is, 18 December, 2001

RIVER BODY IDENTIFIED

The remains of a body dragged from the River Lagan early yesterday morning have been identified as Robert 'Bertie' Ellis from Stranmillis. Mr Ellis went missing on a night out with work colleagues. As part of their Christmas celebrations the work outing had visited several pubs, an Indian restaurant and finished the night off seeing a local pantomime.

He was last seen shortly after midnight when he left his colleagues to walk home. His work mates described him as 'great craic,' and 'the life and soul of every party.' Company boss John Butcher said: 'Bertie always brightened up the office with his humour. We are all terribly saddened by this news. He will be greatly missed.'

The PSNI are investigating his death, though it is thought to be accidental at this time. A spokesman for the police said: 'Mr Ellis had consumed a lot of alcohol and then walked home by the river. Those two facts, plus the heavy ground-frost that night lead us to believe this was nothing but a terrible accident, but we will investigate fully, nonetheless.'

Anyone who thinks they saw Mr Ellis walking home on the night of December 15th is urged to contact their local police station.

Belfast Echo, 21 December, 2001

2004

01.

Emily climbed on top of Sean and kissed her way up his chest to his mouth. Her tongue probed his mouth deeply. The coarse hairs of his moustache scraped at her face. His hands slid up her taut torso and cupped her breasts before darting around to her back. He pulled himself up and faced her. He kissed her passionately again and then threw her backwards onto the bed. Her breath caught in her throat as her heart raced. He moved towards her, parting her legs.

And then he stopped, as if someone had hit the pause button.

'You OK?'

He nodded quickly. 'Yeah, just give me a second.' He grabbed his flaccid member and started stretching it out. He closed his eyes tightly and gritted his teeth.

Emily eased herself up onto her elbows and looked down at him tugging his limp penis. She sat forward. 'Let me do that.' She reached forward but he knocked her hand away with his own. He turned away and sat on the edge of the bed.

She left it a few seconds and then moved over and sat behind him. She put her arms around him and rested her head on his back. 'It's OK. It happens. It doesn't matter.'

'I think you'll find it does matter if you want to get pregnant, Em.'

'You're just over-worked. Eight shows a week is enough to tire anyone out. When was the last time you had a day off? That's what understudies are for, Sean.'

'Ha! If you think I'm letting that little bitch get one foot on my stage you're mistaken. It's what he's been waiting for. This is my part, Em. I want producers to see I'm not going to fold when things get tough. Some of those West End shows play for years. This was only four months.'

'It lasted a lot longer than anyone thought it would and that's due to you. It was your performance; your reviews, that got those bums on seats.'

'Not for much longer.'

'I'm glad it's coming to an end. You need a break. When this is over and the pressure's off, you'll be back to your old self and I'll be pregnant in no time.'

'I hope you haven't got too used to eating and paying bills while I've had this gig, because I don't know what I'm going to do next. I don't know how we're going to afford a baby, either.'

She kissed his back. 'Other people manage. We will too. We'll be OK. I'm still working and I've been putting a little aside every week for a holiday. It's maybe not enough for Barbados, but it'll get us a long weekend in Portrush. We'll make it work. I love you, Sean.'

He was silent for so long she was tempted to get up and see his expression. Eventually he just mumbled, 'I don't know why,' and then got up and left the room. Emily heard the shower turn on a few seconds later. She lay down and wrapped her naked body tightly in the crumpled bed sheets.

The small basement flat reeked of damp. Mould was climbing the lower portion of the walls and the carpet felt wet under bare feet. Robin hurried back, the noise of the toilet still echoing behind him. His painfully skinny frame and hairless chest made him look like a greyhound when he was naked. He tip-toed quickly across the sodden carpet and jumped back into bed.

Sean stroked his hair as Robin laid his head down on his chest. He wrapped his bony limbs around him for warmth while Sean continued smoking a roll-up.

'Are you hungry?'

'Not really,' Sean replied.

'I've made some Saturday Pie. I found the recipe on the Internet. Apparently it was very popular in post-World War One Britain. It's basically just leftovers from the week thrown into a pie and covered with mashed potatoes, but it'll make a change from all that corned beef and pea soup you've been living on.'

'My farts are getting pretty bad.' Sean smiled as Robin laughed on his chest.

'Did I tell you I'm down to the final three for a role in *EastEnders*? My agent thinks I have a good chance of getting it. Do you know what you're doing when this run finishes?'

'Avi says he has some stuff for me to consider.'

'You don't sound too excited.'

Sean put on his best indignant Richard E. Grant accent. 'The last thing Avi offered me was a tampon commercial. Bastard. It wasn't even the lead.'

Robin laughed. 'You know I could always ask if there's anything else going on *EastEnders*. It might be pretty cool, you and I working downt market together.'

'I think you're confusing a Yorkshireman with a Cockney.'

'Maybe you're right. Maybe you could be my dialect coach.'

Sean stubbed the last quarter inch of the roll-up out on the wooden bedhead. 'Well, that'll always be the dream.'

Robin put one leg over Sean, straddling him. He looked him in the eyes. 'Doing this play with you... it's been the best time of my life. I don't want it to end.'

Sean kissed him tenderly and then slid out from below him and started to get dressed.

'We need to talk about this, Sean. You need to tell Emily about us. It's not fair to her.'

'I'll tell her.' He turned and gave him a smile. 'I promise.'

Robin looked unsure, but returned the smile.

Sean looked in the bedroom mirror. 'I'll tell you one thing I won't miss, is this fucking moustache. It was bad enough wearing the 1980s McGuigan moustache for three months, but this big bushy fucker is a nightmare.'

Robin smiled. 'I think you look cute with it.'

'Well take a picture, because as soon as this play closes I'm shaving the bastard.'

Robin considered his next statement for at least ten seconds. Something inside him told him not to say it, but he said it anyway. 'I love you, Sean.'

Sean paused momentarily as he pulled on his shirt. 'Come on, we have to get to the theatre.'

'Is that all you have to say?'

Sean sat down on the edge of the bed and took Robin's hand. 'Give me time. I'm getting there. I have a longer journey to make than you.' He kissed him. He gave him another grin and Robin smiled back, wanting to believe it. Sean slapped Robin's naked thigh. 'Come on, let's not get fired this close to the end of the run.'

Sean sat at his dressing table finishing off a letter. He was wearing his uniform, waiting for the curtain. The letter was a reply to one he had found waiting for him at the theatre when he arrived. Last week they had done some matinee performances for the local schools. A young boy who had been in the audience, had written to Sean asking for his advice about coming out to a father he knew wasn't going to understand. Sean did his best to offer him good advice. He hoped it was enough. The poor kid sounded like he was at the end of his tether. He licked the envelope and sealed it.

There were two quick taps on the door and then it was opened six inches. Dougie, the production manager, stuck his head in the gap and said: 'That's fifteen minutes, Sean.'

'How's the house?'

'Maybe a quarter full. We'll sell some more last minute at the door.'

Sean smiled and gave him a nod. Dougie closed the door as quickly as he'd opened it and disappeared.

Sean turned to the mirror and checked his make-up again. It was fine. He took out his tobacco tin and started rolling a cigarette. He heard the door open behind him and turned, fully expecting to see Dougie. He definitely wasn't expecting to see his dad standing there with a programme in his hand.

Sean got to his feet and straightened his uniform as if he were a soldier being inspected. His dad didn't look impressed. The two men stared at each other.

Sean studied the man he hadn't seen in five years. The dye in his hair was even more obvious than before, but his Teddy-boy clothes were the same.

Dessie Black raised the programme and opened it to the first page. He started reading: '*Shrapnel from a Rainbow* tells the story of two young men returning from the trenches of Europe in 1918 having to hide a love that was forged in battle. This exploration of repressed homo...' He cleared his throat. '...homosexuality is by turns funny, poignant and tragic, but is never less than mesmerising.' He closed the programme and put it under his arm. He stared at his son.

Sean recognised the look. It was the same look he had given him when Sean had cracked one of his dad's cymbals when he was young. He had been trying to emulate Animal from *The Muppet Show* on his dad's practice kit and toppled the Zildjian cymbal in a frenzied attack, cracking it when it hit the floor. Sean had put the cymbal back up and even turned the crack to the back, hoping it wouldn't be seen.

When his dad got home and saw the damage, he'd come up to Sean's bedroom and said, 'Have you got something to tell me?'

Sean had gone to bed uncharacteristically early, hoping if he was asleep when his dad got home, he would save the interrogation until the following day, and then maybe forget. The young boy shook his head. His dad had taken a seat and given him a look. This look. He didn't say another word for what seemed like hours, until Sean finally confessed. His dad pulled the bed sheets back and produced a leather guitar strap from behind his back. He'd beaten him for a long time. The boy had rolled and squirmed, screamed and cried, but his dad had continued beating him until he was out of breath.

And now here he was again. Giving the same look. Playing the same game. Waiting for a confession.

Dougie popped his head around the door again. He acknowledged the older man with a quick smile and said, 'Sorry.' Dessie Black returned his smile and gave a dismissive shake of his head. Dougie turned to the man in uniform. 'Sean, the leg on that Bentwood's come off again. It's not worthwhile fixing it at this point in the run, so just use the Carver in act three, OK?'

Sean was glaring at the old man in front of him, but gave Dougie a quick nod. The production manager turned slowly and looked at Dessie Black again. 'Is everything OK, Sean?'

Sean just continued glaring at his father.

Dessie Black smiled and extended his hand to Dougie. 'There's no problem, son. I'm his dad.'

Dougie relaxed and shook the proffered hand. 'Oh, right. Glad to meet you. Are you staying for the show? Do you need a ticket?'

Fear flared in Sean's eyes and Dessie Black saw it. 'No, you're all right, son. I've seen it already.' Dougie nodded and then hurried off.

Dessie Black turned and meandered into the room. 'Aye, that's right. I've seen it already. I came a couple of weeks back. Wasn't many in, but I kept to the back row anyway. Seen you prancing about like a fairy, kissing that other fella for all the world to see. Some of them smooches go on for a while, don't they? I could barely keep my dinner down. I didn't hang around afterwards. Didn't want anyone knowing you were my son after that exhibition.' By now he was face to face with his son, barely an inch between them. 'To tell the truth, it's been bugging me ever since. I know your teachers said you were good at this acting lark, but I don't know if you're that good. I don't know if anyone is. So I thought I'd just come here and ask you to your face, because I know you can't lie to me. So tell me, boy, are you a faggot now?'

Sean's mouth was dry. The truth was he didn't know what to tell him. He thought about telling him the response most likely to make him stay away forever. He thought about telling him about Emily and how they were trying for a baby. He thought about telling him it was just a role and he really *was* that good an actor.

'Sean, do you fancy hitting a club tonight with Bruce and Colin? They've got tickets...' Robin stopped in his tracks when he saw the older man and Sean nose to nose. He stood there wearing nothing but his boxer shorts trying to read the situation. Dessie Black took one look at him and then turned back to his son shaking his head. He grabbed the lapel of Sean's uniform. 'Your grandfather wore this uniform. Not on a stage, but on a battlefield!' He leaned in and whispered, 'You're a fuckin' disgrace!' With that, Dessie Black turned and walked out, giving Robin a contemptuous look as he passed.

Robin watched him go and then turned to Sean. 'Who the fuck was that?'

Sean sat down at his dressing table. 'My dad.'

'Shit. Are you OK?'

Sean looked at himself in the mirror and saw the thick layer of make-up covering his face. 'I'm fine. I just need some time alone.'

'OK,' Robin said. He was tempted to launch into his own oft-told tale of coming out to his dad, but decided now was not the time.

Sean grabbed the tub of cold cream and smudged it over his face. He started wiping off the make-up with cotton balls in harsh rough strokes. 'Tell Michelle to get back in here and do my make-up properly this time. I look like a fucking clown.'

Robin nodded and left.

Sean threw the cold cream against the nearest wall, smashing the tub.

02.

Sean and Robin walked to the train station together.

'I'm sorry about tonight,' Sean said. 'I was fucking shite. You had to carry me most of act three.'

For the first time since the dressing room Robin felt confident enough to put his arm around Sean. He didn't shrug it off. Robin laid his head on Sean's shoulder as they walked. 'Everyone has a bad night once in a while.'

'It was my fucking dad showing up that threw me. I haven't seen the bastard in five years and he lands on me like that, right before a fucking show. Dickhead!'

'I'm sure he'll come around.'

'Come around to what?' Sean stopped walking and looked at Robin.

The skinny actor shrugged and nodded at Sean, still unsure if his lover wanted those life-changing words to be said out loud. 'You know.'

Sean laughed and they started walking again. 'I don't think so. He's a fucking dinosaur. I don't really give a shit what he thinks.'

'Sure you don't.'

Sean let that sink in for a few seconds before agreeing. 'Shit! You're right. Why do I care what he thinks?'

'Because he's your dad.'

They walked into the station and Robin saw the conductor giving the platform a final check. 'Shit, that's my train. I have to go. I'll see you tomorrow?'

Sean nodded. Robin gave him a quick kiss and ran to the train, just making it through the door before the conductor stepped on board. The train pulled out. Sean had a twenty-minute wait for his train so he turned to find a bench and that's when he saw them.

There were three of them. They were huddled in a corner passing a bottle in a brown paper bag around. They were nodding at him and talking amongst themselves. Sean walked over to the closest bench and sat down. Apart from the drinkers, there were only two middle-aged women and one pensioner on the platform.

Sean kept an eye on the drinkers from the corner of his eye. The swigs from the bottle got longer as their gestures became more animated and frantic. Their glances at Sean became more frequent. Inevitably, when the bottle was empty and dropped at their feet, the three men made their way towards him.

'All right, mate!' the alpha male said as they came close. 'Nice 'tache. Let me guess, your name's Frankie and you're going to Hollywood?' His two cronies laughed. 'Hey, I'm talking to you!'

'You got a problem, guys?' Sean asked.

'Yeah, we got a problem, Freddie Mercury. You and your faggot friend kissing in public like it's fucking normal or something.'

Sean's fist clenched. He took a deep breath, trying to calm himself. 'You really need to walk away from me right now.'

Alpha turned to his friends and they all shared a laugh. 'Why, what are you going to do? Chase us around with a feather duster?'

The cronies were still laughing when alpha's nose got flattened and blood exploded across his face. He was falling backwards before the cronies registered what had happened and moved to react.

Sean kicked the closest one in the balls. He folded in half and Sean pulled him face-first into the bench. The remaining crony, though obviously scared by this point, put up his fists and tried to properly fight Sean. The *Wee Barry* training came back in an instant. Sean ducked and dodged the first two punches thrown and then led with a succession of quick jabs, finally following through with a strong right hook. The crony stumbled backwards but didn't fall. Sean grabbed his jacket with both hands and head-butted him, breaking his second (possibly third) nose of the night.

The express train rattled through the station and while he was still disoriented, Sean threw him head-first at the speeding train. The train hit his head like a steel pinball, knocking him backwards and across the platform where he dropped to the ground.

Sean was making his way back to alpha when he was charged by the crony he had thrown into the bench. His nose definitely looked crooked. He ran screaming at Sean with his fists in the air. Sean stepped forward and punched him in the throat. His expression immediately changed as he dropped to the ground, fighting for breath.

Sean continued to alpha. He was still rolling around the ground holding his flattened nose. There was at least half a pint of blood on the ground below him. His eyes had teared up from the impact. He couldn't focus when Sean stood over him.

Even though alpha's hands were slick with blood, he managed to reach into his jacket and pull out a large knife with a retractable blade. He clicked a button and the blade extended. He pointed it in front of him and lunged blindly. Sean grabbed the knife and took it from him. Now defenceless, alpha cowered into a ball as best as he could.

Sean knelt down next to his head and whispered, 'I want you to remember tonight every time you look in the mirror.' Sean poked the tip of the cold blade into his cheek. 'I want you to see how unattractive intolerance is.'

'No, please. Please don't. I'm sorry,' alpha whimpered.

'Sometimes sorry doesn't fucking cut it!' Sean rasped.

'Drop it!'

Sean turned and saw two police officers coming towards him.

'Drop the knife right now!'

Sean looked at the pathetic specimen shuddering under him, begging to be put out of his misery, and then at the two cops advancing on him. And then at the two middle-aged women huddling next to the pensioner, all looking terrified. Sean smiled at the PSNI officers and dropped the knife beyond alpha's reach. He stood up and put his hands behind his head.

The attack at the train station had made the papers and guaranteed that the last few nights of the play were sold out. There really was no such thing as bad publicity. If only he'd thought of doing it earlier. The papers were selling it as a hate-crime against a gay man, and Sean was happy to let them keep thinking that. His barrister had told him, with that defence there was a good chance he'd get off if it went to trial.

It also helped that none of the witnesses on the platform saw the first punch being thrown, so when Sean said he was attacked by three drunken homophobes and defended himself, it seemed like the most plausible explanation. None of the three injured men had made any sort of statement, public or otherwise yet, as they were still in hospital.

The biggest problem with playing along with the media's narrative was finding a way to explain it to Emily. He eventually settled on a narrative that was closer than what the newspapers were reporting, but still wasn't the whole truth.

He told Emily he had walked with his co-star to the train station. Robin had kissed his cheek – because he was one of those luvvie-type actors – before getting on the train and these three apes had taken exception to it. He also confided in her that he had in fact thrown the first punch and that was why he had bent the truth slightly. Emily not only believed him, but was proud of him for standing up for the gay community in Northern Ireland. Avi had already been in touch to say that *Gay Times NI* wanted to do an interview with him for next month's issue. Given the amount of whooping and cheering when he and Robin kissed onstage, it was members of the gay community who had bought up the tickets for the remaining shows.

The final show went brilliantly. The crowd were enthusiastic and gave Sean the longest standing ovation of his life. Emily came and stayed for the cast and crew wrap-party. She met everyone, including Robin, who she suspected might have a crush on Sean. It was probably best that she was there or the young boy may have made a fool of himself given the amount he drank.

When Emily woke on Sunday morning Sean wasn't lying beside her. She got up and walked to the bathroom. She saw him standing at the sink and gave him a little wolf-whistle.

Sean turned and gave her a smile. His moustache was gone. He wiped the remaining shaving cream from his face with a towel and kissed her.

'Hmm. That's better,' she said. 'May I have another?'

He kissed her again.

'I hope the next character you play is clean-shaven.'

'I hope there is a next character.'

'When are you seeing Avi?'

'Tomorrow morning.'

She wrapped her arms around his neck. 'So I have you all to myself today?'

'To do with as you please, but first... I think we have some unfinished business.'

She looked down and saw a wigwam over the crotch of his pyjamas. She looked at him, smiling. Her eyes twinkled. He picked her up and carried her to the bedroom.

Some time later Emily got out of bed. She turned to him with a dreamy, satisfied smile before continuing to the bathroom. Sean heard the shower turn on. He'd give her some time to get wet and soapy then he'd join her. He could already feel the first beginnings of himself stiffening up again.

His phone bleeped and he looked at it. There were eighteen unread messages and four voicemails. All from Robin. He deleted them all and then blocked the caller.

And then he followed Emily into the shower.

03.

They decided to go to a nice hotel for Sunday lunch. Unless Avi had something already set up for him tomorrow, they were going to have to tighten their belts until some more acting work came in, so this could be the last extravagance for a while.

The restaurant area was mostly filled with families. Wrinkles and grey hair sat across from exhausted new parents and crying babies, while elsewhere older children ran around the maze of tables like it was the greatest game in the world. Emily watched them with a smile and the sort of inexhaustible patience only the childless know.

'Can I get you something to drink while you look at the menu?' He was a teenage boy who covered the worst of his acne with the wrong shade of foundation. It was probably borrowed (or stolen) from an older sister, and despite it not blending into his natural skin tone, it was probably an improvement on what it was covering.

'I think I'll have a glass of white wine,' Emily said. The waiter made the appropriate scribble on his notepad and then raised his eyebrows at Sean.

Sean looked at the different styles of glasses on the table, and then he looked over at the bar, and then at Emily. 'What do you think I should have?'

'Have whatever you like. That's why I left the car at home.' She smiled.

Sean looked around the other tables to see what other people were drinking. An old man was drinking brandy. A young father was drinking lemonade. A fat man with a beard was drinking Guinness. A man around Sean's age with a similar build was sitting with his girlfriend. He had a pint of lager.

'A pint of lager.'

'We got there in the end,' the cynical teen said with a smile, instantly losing him any chance of him getting a tip. 'Have a look at the menus while I get your drinks. The specials are on the back.' He walked away.

Emily smiled like it was her first time in a restaurant. She opened the menu and looked at Sean. 'You look so handsome.'

'If you say so. You're the one who has to look at me.' She smiled. Apart from losing the moustache that morning, Emily had also played around with his hair. For months now it had been in a side parting, slicked back with Brylcreem, she had given it a trim and some minor rearranging to make it into something more modern. She also said he would look good in his dark suit and the tie she had got him for his birthday, and he hadn't argued.

'You look every inch the movie star.'

'Maybe I should wear this to see Avi.'

'I don't know why you think Avi's going to have nothing for you. Whenever I've spoken to him on the phone he says he's got lots of stuff waiting for you.'

'That's just agent bullshit. It's what he's paid to do; bolster my ego and flatter me.'

'I thought that was my job.'

'It is, but you don't get paid.'

'Well, let's see what he says tomorrow before you decide to chuck it all in. After all, it's your rule that he not show you stuff while you're in character.'

'I suppose you're right.' Sean looked at the menu. 'What are you having?'

'The roast duck with hoisin sauce sounds nice. Expensive, though.'

'Let's not worry about the cost today. Yeah, I might get the duck too.'

'You don't like duck. You had it on my birthday two years ago and threw up afterwards.'

'Oh, right. Of course. I forgot. What do I like?'

'Have whatever you fancy.'

'Yeah, yeah, but... what do I usually eat? What's my... go-to dish, would you say?'

She grinned at him shaking her head. 'Don't you know?'

He closed the menu and sat back in his chair. 'Look, why don't you order for me? My brain is still frazzled and to be honest, I've been on World War One rations for so long anything is going to taste nice. So you just pick whatever you know I like and I'll eat it. I really don't want to have to make a decision like this today. I just want to relax, OK?' His tone had got slightly louder and more intense during that little speech and Emily knew not to push him. She'd seen him like this before. He called it decompressing after a role. His behaviour would be odd for a few days while he readjusted.

When the waiter came back, she ordered him a medium–rare steak with pepper sauce and chips, and Pecan Pie for dessert.

His favourites, she thought.

Avi had asked him to drop by the office any time after nine on Monday morning. Sean walked in at eight-forty, when Aileen hadn't even finished her first cup of tea of the day.

'Hello, Sean.' She glanced at the clock on the wall and then checked her watch to make sure they agreed.

'Hi, Aileen. Is he in?'

'Yes, but I'm not sure...'

Sean was already walking towards the connecting door. 'Thanks,' he said over his shoulder and hurried through without knocking.

The old man was at his desk opening the day's mail. It was a mix of bills, junk and aspiring actors' CVs. He looked up and smiled. 'The office opened ten minutes ago. I'm surprised it took you this long.'

Sean shrugged and smiled. He sat down opposite his agent and leaned forward. 'So, what have you got for me?'

Avi finished his first coffee of the day and buzzed Aileen to bring more before answering with a nod. Sean looked at the three stacks of scripts on Avi's desk before him.

'These are all for me?'

'Seems like a lot of influential people saw your play, or at least read the reviews.' Avi slapped a hand down on the first pile of scripts. 'Plays.' He slapped the middle pile. 'TV shows.' And then he slapped the final, and admittedly smallest, of the three piles. 'Movies.'

Sean let his eyes move over the stacks of opportunities. 'There must be...'

'Thirty-seven in all,' Avi said. 'Do you have any idea what sort of thing you want to do next?'

Sean shook his head, still staring at the mounds of pages. 'I don't really mind as long as it's something I haven't done before.'

'And it pays the bills?'

'Yeah, of course.' Sean ran his fingers over the scripts. 'Have you read all of these?'

Avi nodded. 'That's why I get paid the big bucks.'

For the first time Sean lifted his gaze and looked Avi in the eyes. 'What do you think I should do?'

It was music to Avi's ears. He leaned forward and pulled the top script from the movie pile and the top one from the TV pile. He handed them to Sean. 'Do the movie first. It's not the lead, but it's a good part and it's a good way to dip your toe back in that world. It's going to shoot in London, but it's mostly an American cast, American director, and most importantly, American money behind it. It's a solid script. I think it's going to do well.'

Sean read the title: *Shards*. He furrowed his brow at Avi. 'Slasher movie?'

'Psychological thriller. Amnesia. Dream sequences – that sort of stuff. You'd play this petty crook, lowlife scumbag. You're basically the red herring of the story. Everything points towards you being the killer, but surprise – you're not.'

'I could be that,' Sean said, more to himself than Avi.

'There's a character description on page one. That's something you don't see very often. Writer must be a newb. Kid's talented though.'

Sean almost ripped off the title page getting to page one as fast as he could.

'Connor O'Malley,' Avi said.

Sean scanned down the names until he found it. He didn't hear Aileen bring the fresh coffee or ask him if he wanted milk and sugar. He didn't smell the strong aroma when it was set in front of him. He just read the short description over and over.

Connor O'Malley. Connor is from Northern Ireland and was a member of the IRA before being disavowed by the organisation after a mission went spectacularly wrong. Despite the things he's done (and continues to do) he still considers himself moral and a good catholic. He fled to London where he changed his name. He found cash-in-hand work on building sites, where he learned the skills crucial to the plot in Act II. But the murder of his parents when he was just a kid has left deep psychological scars. Sometimes Connor wakes up in strange places with no recollection of how he got there, and sometimes he has blood on his hands. This has caused him to lose any form of steady employment, so he has resorted to petty crimes to keep himself alive. He has no moral compass about who he steals from. The heist he is offered at the beginning of Act I is the biggest thing he's ever been involved in, and he's out of his depth. Even when he was in the IRA, he specialized in intimidation, and never actually pulled the trigger. (Except once, which we find out about in the denouement).

He didn't count how many times he read that character description before he looked up, but by the time he was done, Avi was halfway through a stogie and Sean's coffee was cold. He nodded at Avi. 'I'll do this.'

'You sure? Before you've read the script?'

'I trust your judgement. I'll do it.'

'OK. Great. I'll call them and confirm. I'll let you know your travel and accommodation details by Wednesday because they need you in a couple of weeks. Is it OK to tell you about the other one? They need to know pretty soon. The movie is yours if you want it, but this one they need you to audition for if you're interested.'

Sean nodded. 'OK, give me the outline.' Sean shuffled the second script to the top and read the title: *Savage M.D.*

'OK, so this is a six-part TV show for the BBC with the option for further episodes if it's successful. You'd play Doctor Richard Savage, he's a specialist consultant the cops call when they get a weird murder and they can't figure out how it was done. He's sort of like a Sherlock Holmes character, only he sees these little forensic details that don't add up in the body, instead of the crime scene. It sounds a bit corny, but it's really well written. It's a very clever pilot. So every week there would be another one of these cases, but throughout the six episodes there's another cold case related to Savage personally that he's trying to solve as well. You'd be partnered with this female detective, who you don't get along with, of course. I think they're talking to Sarah Alexander for that part. You know the sexy little blonde from that sitcom *Coupling*?'

Sean nodded vaguely.

'Well *Coupling*'s ending this year and she wants to move into drama. I've read the script and I think you and she would be a great fit together.'

'She's the romantic interest too?'

'No, they're more like a brother and sister who argue all the time over the stupidest things. Those bits are really funny. I think this show could be a big hit.'

'When's the audition?'

'A few weeks.'

'After I do the movie?'

'Ah... yeah, I can probably swing that.'

'OK, set it up.'

Sean walked down the stairs from Avi's office. His agent rented the space above a butcher's shop. Tony was a nice guy and had been very generous with his portions when Sean was going through lean times. With two scripts under his arm Sean felt like celebrating. He went into the butcher's shop. According to Avi, he had been here at least thirty years and so spoke in a weird mix of Northern Irish and his native Italian accents.

'Sean Black! Where have you been? You forget all about me now you are famous treading the boards?' He was a big man with a ruddy complexion. Some dark curls poked out from beneath his white hat and hairnet. 'The papers say you are one to watch rising star!'

'Did you see the show?'

He scrunched up his face. 'I can appreciate culture, but Maria!' He jerked his head back as he tutted. 'She like nothing but the Coronation Street and the EastEnders. What can I do?'

'I'll try to get Avi to get me on those shows and then she can see me,' Sean said.

The big man laughed heartily and clapped his hands. 'Now, why you haven't been in for so long?'

'Strict diet. You wouldn't believe the crap I've been eating for the last four months.'

'Oh, that's no good. What can I get you today?'

Sean patted the scripts under his arms. 'Well, it looks like I'm employed for a little longer, so I think I should splash out and treat Emily to a nice leg of lamb.'

'I have just the thing.' He walked off into the back room.

Sean paced around while he waited, and that was when he saw the cash register was open. He looked to the back room and saw no sign of the friendly butcher. He quickly reached around and helped himself to a selection of notes from the till. He left enough so it wouldn't look obvious when the Italian looked in his drawer. Sean stuffed the wad of notes into his pocket just as the smiling man came back in carrying the leg of lamb with all the care of a new-born. He showed it to Sean like a proud parent. Sean nodded and he wrapped it up. When he rang it up, the butcher rounded the cut of lamb down to the nearest even number. Sean thanked him and reached the smiling Italian his own money back.

They said their goodbyes. Tony shouted, 'You give my best to Emily,' as Sean left the shop, and walked straight into Robin.

'You were very careful never to tell me your address, but I knew you'd show up here at Avi's eventually.' Robin folded his arms and gave him an accusing stare.

'Thank god you tracked me down. You'll never believe what's happened,' Sean said, taking him by the arm and leading him to the nearest alleyway. Robin looked at him and a spark of hope flared in his eyes. Maybe one of the many improbable explanations for Sean's behaviour he'd imagined was true. Maybe he really did love him and it was all a misunderstanding. When they got far enough down the alley and Sean checked that no one was watching, he jabbed the protruding bone from the leg of lamb into Robin's stomach.

The skinny man folded in half and dropped to his knees. Sean hit him on the back of the head with the lamb's leg and sent him face-first into the tarmac. He set the dismembered appendage aside and knelt down next to his former lover. He grabbed Robin by the hair and slammed his face into the ground repeatedly. When he finished, Robin's face was a bloodied mess.

'Are you still conscious?' Sean slapped him around the face until he got a reaction. 'Do you hear me? Can you understand me?'

Robin tried to answer but his jaw was broken. He managed a partial nod.

Sean moved closer and whispered in his ear, 'You come near me again, or mention to anyone else what happened between us, and I'll find you, and next time I'll really hurt you. Do you understand me?'

Robin made some incoherent noises.

'Do you believe me?'

Robin forced one of his swollen eyes open and tried to blink away the blood. He looked up at the insane eyes staring back at him. He nodded. Sean let go of him and stood up. Robin hoped that meant it was over, but Sean leaned down again and patted him over until he found his wallet. He took the notes from it and dropped the wallet beside the bleeding man. Sean picked up his leg of lamb and kicked Robin twice in the stomach.

Robin curled further into the foetal position and watched through blurred vision as Sean stood over him, wiping the blood from his hands onto his trousers. When he was finished, he looked down and threw a final kick at Robin's head, relieving him of consciousness.

04.

Avi paced around the small office. Occasionally he tried to perch on Aileen's desk, but couldn't settle. They'd heard the sirens and then looked out the window and seen the ambulance. They had both feared the worst about their friend Tony and his dodgy heart. He'd had a stint put in two years ago, but he kept on eating red meat and smoking like it was going out of fashion.

Avi heard the slow but steady plod of Aileen's heels coming up the stairs. He lit a fresh cigar, preparing himself for the worst. He and Tony had dinner together at least once a month. Apart from clients (and his lover), Tony was probably the closest thing Avi had to a friend in this country.

The door opened and Aileen stepped inside and took her coat off her shoulders and hung it up. She shook her head.

'Well, how is he? Did they get to him in time?'

'It wasn't Tony.'

'It wasn't?'

'No, Tony found him when he stepped outside for a smoke. It was a young lad. Looks like a mugging. A pretty bad one too.' Aileen shivered. 'I never thought this area was that bad for that sort of thing. I suppose you never know. You should've seen his face, Avi.'

Avi opened his arms and Aileen walked into them for a comforting hug.

'You know what was weird.'

'What's that?' the old man asked. He was still calming down from knowing it wasn't Tony being carried away by the ambulance.

'I overheard them calling him Robin. I couldn't tell for sure because of all the blood, but I'm pretty sure it was that young lad that starred opposite Sean in the gay soldier play.' She looked up at Avi. 'The police are down there now. Do you think I should mention it to them?'

Avi let those facts sink in and then considered the timing of Sean leaving. 'No, don't do anything yet. We'll see if it is him for sure when it's in the paper. And if it is, then I'll call the police and tell them. Half of this game is publicity. You say the wrong thing in the wrong place and it all falls apart.'

'OK. If you think it's best.'

Avi slapped her bum. 'OK, back to work.' She smiled and went back to her desk.

Avi went into his office and closed the door. He lifted a script he had been sent for Sean. He read the first page at least half a dozen times but it just wasn't going in. He threw the script back into his inbox and leaned back in his chair. He smoked his stogie slowly, and in silence.

Just thinking.

'OK, that's it for today, everyone. Good work. I'll see you all tomorrow,' the first A.D. called to the set. Within seconds lights were going out and people were wandering off the sound stage.

'Sean Black, as I live and breathe.' He grabbed his hand and started shaking. 'How are you doing, babe? I heard you were on this picture too.'

Sean winced at him. 'Do I know you?'

He laughed. 'Of course you know me! Paddy Hancock! We met on the set of *Saint Jude's*.'

Sean nodded slowly. 'Right, the agent who tried to poach me.'

'And I don't apologize for that, Sean. I knew talent when I saw it and here you are, proving my instincts were right.' He stopped shaking his hand and patted his shoulder like they were old friends. 'I bet you thought I'd never get anywhere, but here I am, on the same set as you.'

'One of your clients is working on this movie? Who?'

'Norm. Norm Speckles. You know Norm, right?'

Sean shook his head. 'Maybe I don't have any scenes with him. Who does he play?'

'He plays Corpse#3. No lines, but that's kind of a blessing with Norm.' He leaned in close and said, 'He's got a bit of a stutter.' He leaned out again. 'But listen, babe, since we're both here, we should have dinner and I can try to talk you into my stable. We're heading for big things, Sean. You'd be a fool not to at least hear me out.'

'I think I'll be that fool, Paddy. I'm still happy where I am.' He started to walk away.

'Well, if you change your mind, just look me up,' he shouted across the stage. 'We have a website now. If it doesn't work first time, just click refresh a few times and it'll come good. OK, babe? Yeah, email me,' he shouted for the benefit of anyone listening.

Sean had just got out of earshot when one of Jenna's personal assistants (she had four) stopped him by the props table.

'Hi, Sean,' she said in her irrepressibly perky Californian accent. 'Jenna asked if you could meet her in her trailer quickly to go over tomorrow's scene.'

Sean saw the prop master smile and shake his head while collecting his bits and pieces from the table. 'Sure. Now?'

'That would be ideal.' Perfect white teeth framed in designer lipstick.

The prop master gave Sean a quick wink and nod as he walked away.

'OK, lead the way,' Sean said.

Sean followed the bouncing ponytail out to the trailers closest to the set.

Her name was Jenna Michaels. She had been the star of one of those US teen drama shows about kids with too much money who have complicated love lives. This was to be her breakout movie, and if the current sexiest women on the planet lists were anything to go by, she was going to be a star whether she could act or not. Fortunately, she was a competent actor, though Sean did find her constant consultations with her on-set acting coach quite annoying. But if she was giving teenage boys boners in the numbers those magazines suggested, then this movie might just hit it big.

The ponytail stopped bouncing outside the biggest trailer in the grounds. She knocked and said loudly, 'Jenna, I have Sean Black here to see you.'

'Send him in,' came the muffled reply.

She opened the door and held it like a limo driver, only with a better smile. Sean climbed in and the door closed behind him.

Her hair was damp and she was wearing a short, red silk kimono. Her legs had won some magazine leg award or other and Sean could see why. 'Hi, Sean. You're a hard man to get hold of. I've knocked your door in the hotel a few times and you're never in. Living it up in London?'

'Something like that.'

'Do you fancy a drink?'

'Sure. Whatever you're having.'

'I'm on vodka after a day like that. I mean, am I right? What a fucking slave driver!' She poured them both a generous vodka and gave it a dash of coke. She reached it to him with her perfect smile turned up to ten. Her kimono came open slightly as she leaned forward and he caught a brief glimpse of her breast. She saw him looking and didn't seem to mind. She sat down and crossed her legs on the small sofa. She patted the space next to her. 'Come sit next to me.'

Sean did as she asked.

She winced. 'Wow, I guess you didn't have time to shower yet.'

'No.'

'You can use mine if you like.' She reached over and felt his bicep. 'I can even help you wash hard to reach places, if you like.' She smiled.

'No thanks.' Sean downed his drink and stood up. 'Was that all?'

Jenna Michaels looked like someone had thrown a bucket of ice water over her. Her mouth fell open, but no words were coming out. She finally managed: 'Are you blowing me off?'

'Looks that way. It's nothing personal, but my character wants to fuck you the whole way through this movie. If I fuck you now I'll be in totally the wrong…'

'Are you a fag?'

'No, I'm not. I just can't, at this particular…'

'So *you're* blowing *me* off?' She smiled, shaking her head slightly.

'I'm sorry, but…'

'Don't you fuckin' say that! Don't you feel sorry for me,' she screamed. She was breathing hard when she stepped close to him and said, 'You're nobody. Understand? Do you know how many A-list actors want to fuck me?'

'You should call one of them.'

Sean didn't see the slap coming, but he felt it, and it stung.

'You'll never know what you missed out on,' she whispered. 'Now get out!'

Sean grabbed her around the throat and threw her back against the wall of the trailer. She couldn't speak. He edged closer, his lips almost brushing hers. She let out small gasps as he loosened his grip. With his free hand he ripped her kimono off and let it fall to the ground. Her eyes were dancing with excitement and fear. Their lips were still close. She opened her mouth to him. He stepped back, keeping his hand around her throat, but now backing up to arm's length. He held her stare for a long time, and then looked down at her naked body. It was as good as she'd bragged; as smooth and perfectly curved as any Greek goddess carved in marble. Sean looked her up and down, remembering every curve. He released his fingers slowly. She still gasped in short, sharp breaths.

Sean stepped towards her and whispered, 'Now I know what I'm missing.' She looked at him, not sure if he wanted to fuck her or kill her. He backed away towards the door, smiling. She suddenly became very aware of her nakedness. She knelt down and lifted the ripped kimono from the floor. She stood up, holding it in front of her, covering herself as best as she could. 'Get out,' she whispered. Oddly, there was no anger in her voice now. She turned away from him, looking for something better to hide her nakedness. Sean lifted a gold watch from her dresser and slid it into his pocket. She felt the night breeze on her bare back and when she heard the door slam, she turned to confirm he was gone before sitting down on her sofa and pulling her legs up to her chin.

She bit her nails. For the first time since she was a teenager, she chewed on her $600 nails as she replayed what had just happened and tried to figure out how she felt about it.

She really didn't know.

The old bastard in the pawn shop only gave Sean £200 for the gold watch. The guy knew it was worth at least £3500, but he also knew it was stolen, so Sean took the ten twenty-pound notes and showed the old git his middle finger as he was leaving.

He didn't feel like breaking any of the twenties, so he nipped into a little corner shop and stuffed some chocolate bars into his pockets. The old man behind the counter saw him making for the door and yelled for him to stop. Sean broke into a run and was soon well out of the overweight shop-keeper's range. When he was in a safe spot, he knelt down and put five twenty-pound notes into each shoe. Where he was going, no one had that much money, and people were killed for far less.

He passed through an area he had nicknamed Queer Street. It was populated exclusively by men, some in drag, some not. Every time he had walked past this area he was propositioned and heckled. Fucking fags made him want to throw up, but as long as all they did was shout, he'd ignore them. But if any one of them dared to lay an AIDS–infected hand on him, he'd beat the living shit out of him without thinking twice about it.

He continued on his way, eating the chocolate. Eventually the high-priced shops and homes in central London gave way to more modestly-priced suburban homes, and further still led him to the slums. There was a bridge he'd found a couple of nights ago where all manner of refugees, immigrants and runaways congregated. He wasn't sure of its name, but it wasn't a famous one. Not the sort of one you'd get on postcards. It was a good place to hear stories of how these people survive, and they usually had a couple of fires going in metal barrels to keep warm.

Sean was just polishing off the last of his liberated Mars bars when a girl approached him. She was painfully thin with dark rings under her eyes and straggly, greasy hair. It was hard to guess her age.

Somewhere between eighteen and thirty, Sean thought, though he might be wrong.

'You got any more of that chocolate?' she asked with a Manchester accent.

'That was my last one.'

She hung her head.

'Sorry, I would've nicked more if I'd known you'd want some. What's your name?'

'Chrissie. Have you got any money? I haven't eaten for three days now.'

Sean shrugged and shook his head.

'Are you sure?' She opened her denim jacket and showed him a tight T-shirt covering her small breasts – there was no bra underneath, she didn't need one – and Sean was pretty sure he could make out her ribs through the thin material too. Usually he wouldn't look twice at this girl, but his encounter with Jenna in the trailer had given him an itch he was dying to scratch. She looked up at him with eyes that had seen too much. 'Please, I'm so fucking hungry. I have to eat. I'll do anything you want.'

Sean smiled at her. 'OK. My name's Connor, by the way. Do you have somewhere we can go?'

The somewhere they went was a disabled toilet. Chrissie had swiped a handbag a few days ago and had found a key that opened all disabled toilets in London. She had been sleeping in a different one each night since she discovered what a lucky find this had been. She kept the key on a string around her neck. It was the most valuable thing she owned. If anyone found out about it, they would take it from her in a heartbeat.

Unlike most public toilets, the disabled toilets were usually pretty well kept. There wasn't two inches of piss on the floor and they were rarely out of toilet paper. But they were still cold, so Chrissie took off only what she needed to. The hollow sound of her stomach growling echoed in the small space as she slid off her jeans. Neither of them commented on it. She kept the top half of her clothes on. If Sean wanted to feel her up he would have to go under the tight I-shirt, but he had no plans to do so. Not only because it might trigger another mood-breaking belly roar, but also because even if he did climb the rungs of her ribs with his fingers, there was little to be found up there. Sean sat down on the toilet and she straddled him. The burger and chips Sean promised her gave Chrissie a fresh boost of energy, and she did her best to give him value for money. He even caught her smiling and wondered if she was enjoying it. More likely she was just picturing that burger and chips sitting before her. Either way she got him there in record time.

Sean had barely got himself zipped up when he noticed Chrissie had put her pants, jeans and boots back on, and was eagerly waiting on him with her hand on the door handle.

They hurried down the street towards the nearest McDonalds. Chrissie was pulling him along like an enthusiastic child. When they got inside there was a long queue and most of the tables were taken. Sean looked up to the mezzanine level and saw it was quite busy too.

'MacDonald's was always my favourite. I love a Big Mac. Can I have a Big Mac?'

Sean nodded. 'Sure you can.'

'Can I get it super-sized with the large fries and large coke?'

'Of course. What about dessert? Apple pie or McFlurry?'

'Oh, apple pie. I couldn't stand to get any colder.' She smiled widely and he saw a hint of how pretty she might be under different circumstances. She closed her eyes and inhaled the stink of the lukewarm food and sweaty bodies like it was a field of wildflowers on a summer day.

As they got closer to the counter, she looked concerned. 'Do you think we can stay inside to eat? It's nice and warm in here.'

Sean looked around and saw no free tables. 'Why don't you go and check upstairs and see if there's a table. Or if you see someone who's nearly finished, hover.'

She nodded and turned to go, and then turned back. 'You know what I want?'

'A Big Mac meal with coke, super-sized, and an apple pie.'

She smiled and nodded. He watched her run up the stairs.

When she was out of sight, he left the queue, walked out of McDonald's, and never looked back.

05.

Avi stood by the edge of the set smoking a stogie. He checked his watch. 9.20am. The cameras were supposed to start rolling at 9am. He was hoping he'd get to see Sean in action before he caught his flight home. He looked around the set and saw a lot of people checking their phones and watches. They sipped from coffee cups and talked amongst themselves. Avi closed his eyes and listened to the multitude of voices all speaking in his native accent. These were Hollywood people, not New Yorkers, but still, being in the midst of this many other Americans was comforting. It was the closest thing to being home he'd felt in a long time

'Hi, excuse me.'

Avi opened his eyes and looked at the young man standing before him. His dark hair was held in place by a generous amount of gel. He was clean shaven and well-tanned. His suit fit him like a store mannequin. He looked like a life-size Ken doll in search of Barbie.

Avi took the cigar from his mouth and gave him a brief upward nod.

He extended his hand and said, 'You're Avi Goldman, right? Sean's agent?'

'That's right.'

'I'm Dan Braddock, Jenna's agent.'

Avi smiled, took the proffered hand and shook it. 'Good to know you.'

'You too, Avi. Listen, Jenna's flipping out about your boy.' He looked at the ground and shook his head. He glanced up occasionally while continuing, 'I don't know what's gone on between them, but it doesn't take a genius to guess, right?'

Avi put the cigar back in his mouth and nodded. Same old Sean.

'Anyway, she's creating this whole big stink and wants him fired and replaced. She even says she'll reimburse the production out of her own pocket to reshoot his scenes, but she doesn't realise it's not just about the money, it's about time. Half this crew are booked on another job as soon as this one finishes, and this film already has a set-in-stone release date that can't be changed.'

'What do you want me to do?'

'Can you talk to him? Maybe get him to talk to her and apologise for whatever the fuck she thinks he's done.' The young guy shrugged, his shoulders falling back into his perfect posture almost immediately. 'The producers aren't going to recast him at this stage, but if I tell her that she's just going to flip out even more and probably stay in her trailer for the next week.' For the first time he looked Avi in the eyes and held his stare. He gave the old man a tight-lipped smile. 'We're both on the same team here, Avi. If this film falls apart it doesn't do either of us, or our clients, any good. So, what do you think? Will you try to talk to him?'

Avi gathered from the chatter on the set that the producers and director were in Jenna's trailer trying to talk some sense into her. Sean wasn't in his trailer. The production manager said he was probably in make-up. Avi wandered around backstage looking for the make-up room for nearly twenty minutes. He was just about to grab someone to ask when two words stopped him in his tracks.

'Murray Weiss?'

Avi looked ahead, wondering if he should run but seeing no exit sign. His heart rate increased quickly. Within seconds he was already having trouble breathing. He needed to piss, badly. He feared his bladder was going to release any second. Feeling eyes burning holes in his back, he slowly turned and faced the thing he had feared for all these years.

The man standing before him, half in and half out of a doorway, must've been in his early fifties. His hair was almost totally grey, as was his goatee beard, but despite the greying and the wrinkles, Avi knew who he was looking at. 'Frankie?'

Frankie 'Lightfoot' Carino was the half-brother of Tony Carino, a very well-connected and feared wise guy in Albany. Tony had wanted Frankie to join the family business when he was old enough, but by his mid-teens it was clear Frankie was not cut out for that life. When the cops busted him and another guy in a parked car with their pants down, he was involuntarily outed for all of Albany to see. He went to college to study dance after high school. That's when Tony's rivals nicknamed him Frankie Lightfoot. It was a sign of disrespect to begin with, but over the years everyone came to call him Lightfoot and he didn't seem to mind.

Avi used to do business with the Carino family, so he saw Frankie a lot over the years. He'd even gone to see him in an off-Broadway show. Tony had made it clear that he wanted his brother's creative endeavours supported, and he wouldn't look favourably on anyone who didn't see his kid brother's stage debut at least once.

And now here he was. Standing before Avi in a black leotard and tights. Of all the people Avi thought might come looking for him one day, he never thought he'd run into Frankie Lightfoot.

Avi rushed forward and pushed him back into the room. He slammed the door closed behind them and looked around. They were alone.

Frankie edged backwards towards the far wall as the older man rested his head against the door. Avi took a pill from his box and put it under his tongue. He took some long deep breaths before turning to face his past.

'You're looking good, Murr.' He was trying to sound casual but Avi could see the fear in his eyes and hear the catch in his voice.

'Frankie, what the fuck are you doing here?' he wheezed, still trying to regulate his breathing.

'There's a little dance scene in the movie. I'm the choreographer.'

'Is that what you do now?'

The goateed man nodded. His mouth had gone too dry to answer.

Avi lowered his head and said, 'Fuck,' under his breath.

Frankie lifted a bottle of water from his dressing table and took a long drink. It fortified him as if it had been vodka. 'No one needs to know, Murr. I won't tell anyone I saw you. I swear on my fucking mother. You know I never wanted any part of that life and I still don't.'

Avi shook his head lightly.

'You don't need to do nothin', Murr. We can just go our separate ways and pretend like this never happened.'

'Shit.'

'Please, Murray. I'm seeing someone now. Three years. We're talking about adopting.' He sniffed back hard and tears ran down his cheeks. 'I swear on my life, Murr. I'll never tell Tony. I'll never tell no-one. Please, I'm begging you.'

Avi stood up straight and took a step away from the door. He lifted a large pair of scissors from the nearest table and looked at the choreographer. 'I'm sorry, Frankie. I wish it didn't have to be this way.'

Frankie sized up the approaching man for a few seconds and then charged at him. He grabbed Avi's wrist and pushed the scissors into the air. The force of the impact drove both men back across the room and against the door. Frankie was holding the scissors up with one hand and had his forearm pressed into Avi's throat with the other. Avi brought his knee up hard into Frankie's balls, taking full advantage of the minimal protection the tights provided. Frankie buckled and dropped to his knees. The downward jerk pulled the scissors from Avi's hand and sent them skidding across the floor.

145

With his right hand free, Frankie threw a punch into Avi's stomach with all the strength he could muster. Avi gasped, trying to inhale. He flattened his hand and thrust his fingers forward into Frankie's eye. He felt his forefinger penetrate the eyeball and withdrew it quickly. Frankie screamed in hitherto unknown pain. Avi caught a breath, but didn't have time to wait to see if another would follow. He fell on Frankie and tried to cover his mouth. Frankie bit at the bony fingers and continued screaming, but this time for help. Avi put both hands around his throat and tightened his grip. He leaned the full weight of his one-hundred-and-twelve-pound frame down on his hands. Frankie wasn't able to speak now. He tried his hardest to whack Avi's hands away, but the old man held firm. Outside in the corridor, Avi heard voices approaching. He looked at the door and realised he hadn't locked it. Frankie's hand reached out towards the voices, trying desperately to attract attention. The voices stopped outside the door. He could see the shadows of their feet through the crack. They talked in hushed tones. One male, one female. If either one of them was on their way to this room, Avi had a much bigger problem. Frankie squirmed under him. Jerking his body upwards like a rodeo horse. Avi's mildly arthritic hands held on even though it hurt. He looked at the shadows under the door again. The whispers stopped. The two sets of feet remained. Then the pair on the left walked away. The other pair remained. Avi pushed down harder on Frankie's throat. He wouldn't be able to keep this up for much longer. He looked back at the door. The remaining foot shadows turned. Stopped. And then walked away. Avi listened to the footsteps disappear back the way they had come.

When he looked back, Frankie, the boy who had wanted no part of his family's business, had stopped fighting. Avi readjusted his right hand and checked for a pulse under his jawbone. There was none.

Only then did Avi go to the door and lock it. He slid down to the ground and rested his back against the door. He looked at the body lying before him.

What the fuck had he done?

06.

When Avi finally tracked down his client, he was at the craft services table filling his pockets with food. Avi took his arm firmly and whispered, 'I need to talk to you, alone.'

'OK. We can go to my trailer.'

'No, come with me. I need your help.' As Avi led him towards the deceased dancer's dressing room he couldn't help but notice the stink. He guessed Sean had been wearing the same clothes since he started filming. He was about to ask why when he realised he already knew.

When they got to the corridor Avi slowed their pace, allowing two other crew members to clear the space before he pulled out the key and unlocked the door. He pushed Sean inside and then followed. Once inside, Avi locked the door and left the key in the lock.

He stayed by the door. Sean walked over to the body and knelt down. He leaned in close and examined the face of the dead man. He must've stared at it for a solid two minutes before getting up and facing Avi.

'Did you kill him?'

Avi nodded.

'Self-defence?'

'In a way.'

Sean turned around and looked at the body again. 'OK. We can sort this out. This is what I do. Three hundred.'

The old man's brow furrowed. 'What?'

'Three hundred and I'll make it all go away.' He turned to Avi. 'This is why you called me, right? I know how to make these things go away.'

Avi gave him the subtlest of nods, not knowing if he was being serious or not.

Sean started to look around the room. He ran over to the window and found it was sealed. 'Getting rid of him isn't the problem. Getting him out of here is.'

'I had an idea about that.' Sean turned to him. 'Jenna Michaels wants you off the movie. Her agent says if you apologise and kiss her ass a little, she might back down.'

Sean closed his eyes tightly and rubbed his forehead with his hands.

'I suggest you do it... just maybe not today.'

His interest now piqued, Sean opened his eyes and looked at his agent.

Two hours later the last member of the *Shard* crew turned out the lights and left the set. Two of the stars of the film had had a blazing row and stormed out. After it became clear neither of them was coming back, the production was shut down for the rest of the day. The crew were told to come tomorrow morning as usual, when hopefully everything would be back to normal.

While Sean and Avi waited in the choreographer's dressing room for everyone to leave, Avi had wiped his prints from the door handle and the scissors. Holding the blades with his handkerchief, he then got Frankie's prints all over them. Sean helped him drag the dead man to the door and put his prints all over the door handle as well. A wiped-clean handle was glaring evidence of someone covering their tracks and this had to look natural.

Sean's prints would be easily explained if they were found, but he took no chances and got a pair of rubber gloves from the craft services area. Sean hadn't been involved in the dancing scene they had shot and had no personal contact with this man. He was sure he could make up some bullshit if he was questioned, but it would be much better to leave no trace at all.

The two men sat there for hours together. They both knew from reading the script of *Savage M.D.* that rigour mortis sets in four to six hours after death. They also knew that keeping the body as cold as possible would slow this down, so they had turned off the heating in the room. They had put Frankie's coat, shoes and street clothes onto the body and put him in a chair. He sat there like he was waiting for a bus, with his mouth hanging open in a silent scream.

They said little once they had removed all traces of Avi from the scene and dressed the body. Avi didn't even dare have a cigar for fear the aroma would linger, but his breath misted in the cold air before him as if he were smoking. When they saw the main lights turned off under the door crack, they waited ten minutes and then Sean left. He returned twenty minutes later and they both hooked a lifeless arm around their necks and carried Frankie out to the stolen car like a drunk.

They sat him up in the backseat and put a seatbelt on him to stop him falling over. When Avi slammed the door he caught sight of the security camera looking down on them. 'Shit, the cameras!'

'It's OK, I threw the trip on the fuse box inside. They're down.'

'Won't that look suspicious?'

'Only if the cops come looking. I'm hoping they won't have to go as far as getting security footage if we do this right.'

Avi shivered. Maybe it was the night air, or maybe it was the cold detachment Sean was showing towards a murdered man. He got in the front while Sean ran inside and turned the heating back on in the room.

Sean glanced around the room checking if anything jumped out at him as odd or out of place. It didn't. He locked the door and ran back outside. After putting the keys in the dead man's pocket, he pulled the outer door to the studio closed and it locked automatically. Then he got in and started the car. He turned the heater to cold and drove off.

The alleyway was close enough to Queer Street to be used on a regular basis. By the stains on the walls and condoms on the ground, it had already been used several times that night. Fucking disgusting faggots. But no one was here now, so Sean quickly grabbed the body from the back of the car and carried it to the darkest corner of the alley. He propped the body against the wall and undid the dead man's belt and trousers before pulling them and his jockey shorts down to his ankles. He let the body fall to the ground. He checked his pockets and found Frankie's wallet. There was eighty pounds in notes which he helped himself to and then dropped the wallet next to the body.

Sean looked around the ground and saw a used condom. He lifted it and put the open end into the dead man's mouth. He squeezed the contents of the condom into the mouth, leaving a dribble on the lips for the cops to see, and then dropped it next to the body.

He gave his work one last look before turning and walking away.

Sean drove Avi to the nearest taxi rank, stopping at an ATM along the way so he could give him his three-hundred-pound fee. Avi never questioned the payment, but as he sat in the back of a taxi heading for Heathrow he again began to wonder about his client. Sean hadn't even asked him why he'd killed Frankie. It was like he didn't care about the murder or the possible consequences of helping to cover it up. Like his character in the movie, all he cared about was getting paid.

Avi looked at his watch. He had missed his return flight hours ago. He would just have to show up and hope there was something available on stand-by. He wanted to get home. It was a pity that

Aileen's husband wasn't travelling this week. Tonight, he really needed to hold her. He doubted he'd sleep even when he did get home. In the old days he never slept after a hit, and that's what this was. He could dress it up any way he liked, but he'd just committed his first hit in over twenty-five years.

The taxi driver said he didn't mind if Avi smoked. He lit up a stogie and was thankful for small mercies.

Sean drove the stolen car to a patch of wasteland where he set fire to it. When he was at least a couple of miles from the fire, and many more miles from where they had left poor Frankie, he took off the rubber gloves and threw them into a bin on a residential street.

It was still only half past seven when he got back to the hotel. He showered and changed into clean clothes. He was just pulling on his shoes when the phone in the room rang. He lifted it. 'Hello?'

'My god, where have you *been*? I've been going crazy, here.'

'Sorry, Em. I haven't been using this room much.' He lay down on the bed. 'At nights I went out walking to get a feel for how this guy lives. I got some really great stories hanging around the homeless.'

'That's no reason not to answer your mobile.'

'This guy wouldn't own a mobile. I *had* to go without it. Besides, the places I've been hanging out they'd kill you for a phone if they got the chance.'

'Oh, well *that* puts my mind at ease!'

Sean laughed. 'Don't worry. I'm almost done. I might even be home tomorrow night.'

'Really?'

'Yeah, all I have left to do is a few pick-ups, reverses and inserts – nothing I even have to act for really; a shot of the back of my head, my hand picking up a gun, that sort of stuff. If it all goes smoothly I should be done by lunchtime.'

'Good. I sort of missed you a little, you know.'

'Well of course you did. Who could blame you.'

She laughed. 'You really think you'll be home tomorrow?'

'I'll try my best.'

'OK. I love you.'

'I love you too. Bye.' Sean hung up the phone and went to the minibar. He grabbed a bottle of Champagne and headed for Jenna Michaels's room.

The following morning everyone was back on set and back to work.

Everyone except the dance choreographer.

07.

Phone calls in the middle of the night are never good news, so when Emily's mobile rang at just after four a.m., in the seconds between waking and picking up the phone she had already assumed the worst; Sean had been out researching the London street people and had been stabbed by some psychotic for the phone that she had guilted him into carrying.

UNKNOWN NUMBER

That was even more damning. It had to be the police. Or a hospital nurse. She reluctantly pressed the green Accept button. 'Hello?'

'Is this Emily Black?'

'Yes.' Gooseflesh on her arms. Hairs standing up.

'Are you Sean Black's wife?'

Mouth dry. 'Yes.' Barely audible.

'Could I speak to your husband, please?'

Relief. 'He's not here. He's on location in London.'

'Has he changed his mobile number? There's no answer when we call.'

We? When *we* call? Who the hell is we? 'No, it's the same number but he doesn't... sorry, who is this?'

'This is the staff nurse at Sycamore Acres. His uncle is here with us.'

'Oh, right. Ronnie. Yes. Is he OK?'

'I'm afraid not. He's had a bad infection in his lungs for several weeks. We've tried our best but he isn't responding to treatment. Over the last few days he's gone downhill fast. The doctor suggested... since Sean's his only family...

'He has a brother too, Sean's dad.'

'Oh right. Do you have a number for him?'

'No. Sorry. Sean hasn't spoken to him in years.'

'And you say Sean is in London?'

'That's right.'

'Well, you're under no obligation. We'd all certainly understand if you decided not to, but if you want to be with him, at the end, I suggest you come right away.'

The line was silent for almost twenty seconds. Then Emily said, 'OK, I'm on my way.'

As soon as the hospital hung up, she tried Sean's mobile and his hotel room and got no answer in either. He was probably out walking the streets again. Emily pulled on some clothes and left the house.

The guard had been told she was coming and hurried her through the security gate. As soon as the nurse saw her come through the doors, she came out from behind the desk and led her quickly to Ronnie's room. It wasn't the same nurse as before. This one looked sympathetic, or was at least was faking it well.

Ronnie hadn't been in great shape the last time she saw him, but the old man was little more than a skeleton now. His skin was wrinkled and yellow. His eyes were sunk into his skull. He had an oxygen mask on but still seemed to be struggling for breath.

The young Asian doctor at his bedside walked over and squeezed Emily's arm gently. 'It won't be long now,' he said.

Emily didn't know how to react. She had only met this guy once before and he had tried to pull his penis out when he saw her. But, technically speaking, they were family. She sat down in a chair next to his bed and took his cold and liver-spotted hand in her own.

'Hello, Ronnie. Do you remember me? I'm Emily. Sean's wife.'

In barely more than a hoarse whisper he repeated, 'Sean.'

Emily nodded and smiled. 'That's right. Your nephew Sean.'

The decrepit man tried to lean forward and only made it about two inches off his pillow. Emily stood up and leaned over him. He opened his mouth and she turned her ear towards him and leaned closer.

The words were barely louder than breaths, but she could make out: 'Tell him. Tell him. Under the blue elephant. Sean. Tell him I'm sorry.' He lay back on his pillow and closed his eyes.

Those were the last words he said. He didn't die for almost another hour, but he wasn't conscious. Emily made small talk with the nurse and doctor. She asked them about him saying 'blue elephant' but neither of them knew what it meant. Probably just incoherent ravings.

When he finally passed, they were very business-like. Ronnie had made arrangements for his own funeral many years earlier and had given the hospital the relevant details. Emily felt bad for being relieved that she and Sean weren't going to have to foot the bill for his burial, but money was tight enough at the moment and dying wasn't cheap. The hospital said they would forward Emily and Sean's contact details to the funeral home, so they could be notified when the burial was to take place.

She had some forms to sign and then she was given a shoebox of Ronnie's personal belongings. She told the staff to do what they thought best with his clothes. If they would be of use to any of the other patients, they could have them, but if they weren't, they could just bin them.

The hazy winter sun was just rising on another cold day as she left the hospital carrying a shoebox of belongings. She got into her car and started the engine. The windscreen was frozen, so she turned the heater to full blast and waited for the engine to heat enough to melt it. She opened the shoebox and had a look inside. There was an old fob watch and some old coins that might be worth something.

What a horrible way to think when he wasn't even cold yet.

There was also a bundle of letters and some photographs, held together by a rubber band that had long-since lost its elasticity. She searched through the photos. Some black and white, some colour. People posing holding babies. Standing in front of houses and cars. A child running out of the sea apparently screaming. Faces from the past frozen in time.

But the last photo was different. It was different because it had been taken with a Polaroid camera. It was different because the man in the picture had taken it himself with an outstretched arm. It was also different because Emily knew the people in this photo. Despite being much younger, the man in the photo was undoubtedly the man she had just watched die. The woman in the photo she also recognised, because Sean had shown her photos of his mother.

In the photo they were in bed together. Sean's mother was holding a sheet up to cover herself but it was clear that they were both naked. And laughing.

Sean's mother and Uncle Ronnie.

Emily lifted the bundle of letters and started reading.

08.

Sean arrived home two days later just in time for the funeral. He had stayed an extra day to do the audition Avi had set up at the BBC. Emily thought he was quiet and distant during the service and wake, and put it down to shock, though she didn't know why. They

153

definitely weren't close. A couple of the staff from Sycamore Acres attended and one other patient in a wheelchair. Emily tried to strike up a conversation with him at the wake, but the old guy kept dozing off and didn't seem to know who Ronnie was when he was awake. She came to the conclusion that the home had just brought along a docile patient to make it look like Ronnie had at least one friend in the world.

Emily also thought Sean's mood might be because he expected his dad to show up. Ronnie's obituary had been listed in several newspapers, so there was always the outside chance that Dessie Black had seen one of them. But despite the lure of free tea and sandwiches in the hall next to the church, he didn't show. Sean asked Emily to fill him a plate at the wake as he stared blankly ahead. He really did look like he was in shock. Emily wondered if he needed to cry. Maybe that would help him accept Ronnie's passing. Maybe he was wondering if his own dad had passed. It had been so long since he had seen him, and they had parted on such bad terms the night he had come backstage to Sean's play.

You're a fuckin' disgrace!

It was hard to know what was going on in Sean's head. He ate what she handed him on the plate and drank the tea, even though she later remembered she had forgot to put sugar in it.

That night he was much the same. He sat in the armchair staring ahead. The TV was on, but he seemed to be looking through it. He was normally very selective about what he wanted to watch. Usually anything with actors in it that he admired and could study, but tonight he handed the remote to Emily and he never objected to even the worst reality show drivel she put on.

She initiated sex that night. He lay on his back as she writhed on top of him; his body participating, but his mind elsewhere. She tried her best to engage him but she felt like she was fucking a coma patient. She climbed off him, determined to get to the root of what was wrong. Thinking she was finished, he leaned over and kissed her cheek. He smiled and turned on his side.

She lay back and stared at the ceiling. She was too frustrated to sleep. There was too much going on in her head. She always wondered if he would find someone else when he went off on these location shoots. She didn't want to ask him about it, because she didn't want to become one of those untrusting wives that can't let her husband out of her sight for five minutes without worrying if he's cheating. But what was she supposed to think when he came home like this? Jenna Michaels had been on that film. She was beautiful. But surely she was out of Sean's league. He only had a small part in the movie. Jenna Michaels only dates B-list or higher, and as much as she loved Sean, she knew he wasn't in that class. Yet.

Maybe it *was* just Ronnie dying. Not his passing specifically, but death in general. Funerals are definitely a time to look at your own mortality. Maybe that was it. Maybe Sean had looked at his life and decided he wasn't where he expected to be at this age. If that was it, she wished he'd talk to her. Even if that wasn't it, she still wished he'd talk to her.

Maybe if she told him what she knew about his mother and his Uncle Ronnie it would snap him out of this fugue. She had toyed with telling him as soon as he came home, but it would only hurt him, and she couldn't see any upside in him knowing. She let him see the contents of the box minus the letters and the Polaroid. He hadn't shown much interest and just told her to do whatever she thought best with the stuff. She'd hid the letters and photo in a box among many other boxes in their unused second bedroom. Sean had joked that the bedroom was like the warehouse at the end of *Raiders of the Lost Ark.* That was back when Sean had made jokes.

She knew what she wanted to do with that second bedroom, but she daren't broach a subject like that until she understood what Sean's malady was about. Her fingers drummed on her stomach, like she was knocking on the door of an empty house. She needed to wait until he snapped out of this. Until she knew if they had a future together.

It might not have been Jenna Michaels he had met on set. It could've been anyone. There were plenty of stories of famous actors hooking up with some lowly crew person and falling in love. Emily turned her back to Sean and closed her eyes. Despite her best efforts to stop thinking about it, all the worst possibilities bounced around her head for hours before sleep finally found her.

For the next two days Sean was like the patients at Sycamore Acres. He slept, he ate when Emily gave him food, but he rarely spoke, and when Emily tried to start conversations he just smiled at her. The only time she saw any sign of the old Sean was when the phone rang, but when it wasn't Avi calling, he quickly went back to his semi-comatose state.

Then, late one afternoon there was knock on the door. Emily was up to her elbows in washing in the kitchen and shouted for Sean to answer it. Sean walked to the door and found a very nervous young man on the other side of it.

'Hello, Mr Black, sir,' he babbled out. He was short and quite pudgy. His cheeks were red and he was sweating profusely. He swallowed hard a couple of times before continuing, 'My name is Lenny... er, Leonard! Leonard McCain. McCain, like the chips. Not that I'm... I live... Well, my aunt, she lives. Just down the street from you, there.' He pointed. Sean looked out and saw a head duck inside about fifty yards down the street.

'OK.'

The boy nodded and smiled. He seemed pleased that this part of his story had checked out and Sean believed him. He kept smiling, but said nothing.

Sean eventually said, 'Was there something your aunt needs help with?'

'No, no. Not her. Me. I... well, I'm sure you get this all the time and please feel free to say no if you want to. I won't be offended. I'm sure you're busy. I only came here on the off-chance. My aunt told my mum you lived on her street, so I thought why not? Nothing ventured, nothing gained, right? I'm sure you remember being in this position. It's not that long ago that you were at uni. I'm sure you chanced your arm a few times too. So that's why I'm here.' He exhaled, thinking his pitch was complete.

Sean's brow furrowed. 'Sorry, you still haven't told me what you're doing here.'

'Oh, fuck. Right. It's this!' He pulled a wad of A4 pages folded in half from his back pocket. 'I'm at Queen's studying directing. This is the script for my end of year short film and I was...'

'You want me to be in a film?' Sean grabbed the script and opened it. 'What's the story? What's the part?'

'Er, it's about this young girl who tries to seduce her English Literature teacher.' Sean looked over the top of the pages at him and raised an eyebrow. 'Seen it before, right? But here's the twist, Mr Black. He doesn't succumb to her advances. He's married and loves his wife. He's basically a good guy, but the shunned girl spreads the word on social media that he's touched her up, you know, out of spite, and the guy suffers the same consequences as if he had done it. It's... kind of a social comment on the dangers of social media and mob mentality, and how people are always wanting to believe the worst of...'

Sean stepped back, still looking at the script pages, and pushed the boy's shoulder inside as he kept talking. 'We call it *The Teacher's Pet*, but it's got a double meaning, you see, we mean pet like petting, you know, like heavy petting, that kind of pet. So it's kind of a play on...' The door closed.

After a couple of read-throughs, it became clear that the script needed some work, and soon after the writer arrived and joined Sean and Lenny in the living room. The writer's name was Leroy Lewis. He was a good-looking young black man with his long hair in cornrows. He had been born and bred here and his thick North Belfast accent seemed at odds with his appearance when he first started talking. His mother had been a dancer and he had inherited her slim physique. He was very serious about his writing, but was open to Sean's ideas, and soon had his laptop out working on a new draft.

Sean came into the kitchen to get some soft drinks for everyone. Emily saw him genuinely smiling for the first time since he had come back from London. He closed the fridge door with three cans of Coke in his hands.

'How's it going?'

'Great. They're good kids with good ideas.'

She gave him a wry smile. 'I thought you vowed never to do another student film as long as you lived.'

He shrugged and smiled back at her. 'It's actually a really good story, and they've got access to great equipment at the university. And the young black fella's not a half bad writer. After we clean up the dialogue a bit, I think it could be really good.'

She reached forward and touched his smiling lips. 'I've missed this.'

'Listen, we're on a bit of a roll. Do you have enough food if the lads stay for dinner? I think we can get this knocked into shape tonight if we push on.'

'Of course.'

He was about to turn and leave when he stopped himself. He stepped forward and kissed her. Properly kissed her. He reached around her and she jumped and pushed him back with a laugh.

'What?' he asked, smiling.

'Cold cans on my back,' she said pointing at his hands.

He leaned in and kissed her quickly with his hands behind his back. 'I love you, Em.'

She was shocked, but managed to repeat the sentiment back to him. As she watched him dance back to the living room with the soft drinks, she knew he really meant it.

09.

Emily was seriously wondering if she should look up the Guinness Book of Records to see what the record was for most orgasms in a twenty-four-hour period, because she was pretty sure she was close to beating it.

Since Sean had got involved with this student film he had been a lot more active in bed, and now that they'd started shooting he seemed insatiable. The previous night had been the sort of night erotic novels spend whole chapters on. She'd never thought Sean capable of it. From the Champagne and strawberries that had met her when she came out of the bathroom, to undressing her slowly, to touching her gently and thoroughly in all the right places while reciting Yeats. They had made love three times last night, and as if that wasn't enough, they'd had another quickie (but goodie) before he left that morning.

Emily lay on the bed smiling. She replayed the events of the previous night over in her head, not wanting to forget a thing. She even toyed with the idea of writing it all down so she wouldn't forget a single kiss or touch, but her cheeks flushed red at the thought of anyone accidentally finding it and reading it.

She giggled again. She needed to get up soon, but she'd just replay the night a few more times first. Just to be sure she didn't forget anything.

Sean knocked the door and entered. She looked round, saw him, smiled, and then returned to doing her lip-gloss. 'This is the big day, then,' she said through stretched lips.

'Yeah, I thought we should discuss how we're going to do this. The blocking.'

She turned to him and raised her eyebrows. 'Don't you think we've rehearsed this moment enough over the last week?' She smiled her shiny lips.

He walked over behind her chair and combed his fingers through her strawberry blonde hair and down to her shoulders. 'Yeah, but we can't do that in front of the students.' His right hand slid under the strap of her nightdress towards her breast. 'We'd scare them to death.'

She spun quickly towards him in her chair just before his hand reached its destination. 'Don't you go getting ideas, mister, or you'll be popping out of your...' She smiled. 'What *are* you wearing?'

Sean opened his robe to show the skimpy pair of red Speedos he had on.

She almost laughed. 'Very nice. Very Baywatch.' She rubbed her fingers down the front of the swimming trunks and felt him stiffen inside. She took her hand away and whispered in his ear, 'That's a down payment on later.'

There were two quick knocks on the door. Sean retied his robe and she spun round towards the mirror again.

The door opened and Lenny stuck his head inside. 'Oh, great, you two have met.'

'Well, we've talked on the phone before, but this is the first time... in the flesh.' Sean extended his hand towards her. 'Hi, I'm Sean. I'm your husband.'

She shook his hand, smiling. 'Nice to meet you, Sean. I'm Rhonda. I'm your wife.' Lenny laughed and they chuckled with him.

'So,' Lenny said, sucking air through his teeth, 'these sorts of scenes are always a bit embarrassing. Do you guys...?'

'That's why I asked for her number, Lenny. We've been talking about how to do this so it looks realistic but doesn't make anyone uncomfortable. So we came up with this.' Sean opened his robe and showed Lenny the Speedos. Rhonda stood up. Her sexy nightie came down to her knees. She lifted it up by the hem and showed Lenny she was wearing a pair of cycling shorts underneath. The young lad looked like he was filing the image in his wank-bank for later, and at the same time seemed more embarrassed than either of his actors.

He regained the power of speech soon afterwards. 'Yes, that all looks fine.'

Sean and Rhonda covered up again. 'We figure you strategically place a duvet over my arse to hide the Speedos, and we just bump and grind as if we're going at it. That way it won't look like one of those movies where the guy seems to be having sex with the woman's thigh.'

Rhonda laughed at that. Lenny still looked a little nervous but eventually forced a smile and nodded. 'OK. That sounds good. Well, whenever you're ready.'

'I'm good to go,' Sean said.

'I'll just be a minute,' Rhonda said.

Lenny opened the door and Sean followed him out with a coy backwards glance at his screen-wife just before the door closed.

Lenny addressed the assembled crew in the bedroom of his mum's house. 'OK, everyone. I need you to be professional now. For those of you who haven't seen the latest draft of the script, this scene was added to show that the teacher actually is tempted and attracted to his student. It's only his sense of right and wrong that's stopping him from going through with it, so we thought if we showed him having really passionate sex with his wife...'

Leroy stepped forward, 'Like she's a surrogate. He's taking his desires out on his wife because he can't take them out on his student.'

'Right,' Lenny agreed. 'So this scene will show that instead of the priest confessional scene where it was all dialogue. That's cut now. OK, everyone clear?'

The collection of spotty faces and greasy heads nodded. Rhonda walked in wearing only her nightie. Lenny moistened his lips and said, 'OK, first positions everyone.' The crew obeyed and got into place. 'Let's try to get this in one.'

Sean dropped his robe and got into the bed under the duvet. Rhonda walked over to the ensuite and got out of sight. Lenny looked around.

'OK, sound?'

'Rolling.'

'Camera?'

'Rolling.'

'OK, action.'

Rhonda stepped into the doorway of the ensuite, framed like an erotic work of art. 'Well, how do I look?'

'Beautiful.'

She started to walk slowly towards him. 'I can't remember the last time you bought me clothes, and you've never bought me anything like this. What's the occasion?' She stopped at the edge of the bed, looking down at him.

'Just horny.' He grinned.

She slipped under the covers with him. 'Well, I can help with that.'

He brushed the hair from her face and looked her in the eyes. 'I love you so much. I don't tell you that enough.'

'I love you too.' They kissed passionately and his hands explored her body.

She wasn't here today.

The girl playing the student.

Sean had been shooting scenes with her for the last couple of days. Lenny had cast perfectly, whether by design or accident. The girl had big, brown, butter-wouldn't-melt eyes, long blonde hair, small firm breasts, and inviting legs that disappeared into a short school skirt. She had adopted the trait of always sucking a lollipop when she was trying to tempt him. Again, Sean didn't know if this was a stroke of genius on Lenny's part, or if the actress had come up with it, but it worked. It was as suggestive and seductive as Lolita sucking her Coke through a straw in Kubrick's movie.

Sean kissed Rhonda more passionately. He squeezed her left breast and pinched her nipple. He could hear her breathing quicken in short gasps. He climbed on top of her and she opened her legs. Even with his Speedos on he quickly realised she wasn't wearing her cycling shorts. He saw a mischievous look in her eyes, quickly followed by a subtle nod. Under the duvet, her hand reached down and pulled his Speedos to one side. Without missing a beat, he thrust forward and she moaned with pleasure. Slowly at first, and then with increasing vigour they performed the scene as if the cameras weren't there.

Lenny looked over at Leroy and gave him the thumbs up. Leroy smiled back at him. Lenny turned and whispered to the producer, 'This looks so real!'

10.

Sean stayed in touch for the next few weeks because Lenny said they would need him for some ADR.

It was a Thursday morning. Sean was sitting in the living room after breakfast reading a library copy of *Great Expectations* when the post arrived. There was nothing with the BBC logo on the envelopes, but there was a brown envelope addressed to him. He opened it and saw a solicitor's letterhead. That made him pause briefly, but then he unfolded the letter and read.

Emily was on her way to the door with her coat and bag. She had to do breakfast club at the school this morning so was going in early. Sean was frozen to the spot where he had picked up the letter, blocking her way. She sidled up next to him.

'What's that?'

'It's from Uncle Ronnie's solicitor. Apparently, he left me everything in his will.'

'Wow. Really? Not your dad?'

Sean shook his head. 'I'm supposed to go in and see him at my earliest convenience.'

'You could do that today.' Emily didn't want to seem like a vulture, but she was anxious to know. 'Did he *have* much to leave you?'

'It says here I get the contents of his bank account – after death duties – and his house.'

'A house? We own another house, outright?'

Sean turned to her and winced. 'Don't get too excited. It's a right shithole from what I remember.' Sean wandered over to his chair and sat down.

'Still, it's a house,' Emily said. 'What's it like? Where is it? Is it fixable?'

'I was only there a couple of times when I was young. It's a little farmhouse out in the country. Somewhere near Bangor, I think. I remember how much it stank. Lord knows what he did in there. And it didn't even have indoor plumbing. The toilet was across the yard. There were some old outbuildings full of junk that I used to like to explore. I remember finding a stack of old Page 3 calendars he had saved. And there was a big garage with an old car and motorbike in it.'

'Well, it sounds like it's a fair size plot. Even if it isn't worth fixing up the house, the land might be worth something. Can we go and have a look after school today?'

'I don't know the address.'

'The solicitor will tell you that when you go to see him about the money.'

'I suppose. Yeah, OK. Let's go have a look, but seriously, don't get your hopes up. If it was a shithole when he was living there, god knows what it's like after sitting empty all these years.'

'I won't. I'll be totally objective,' she said, even though she was smiling widely. Emily kissed him on the forehead. 'I have to run. I'll see you after school.' She hurried to the door.

'Why would he leave it to me and not my dad?'

Emily stopped and looked over her shoulder at him. She thought of the Polaroid. She shrugged with a smile. 'I don't know. See you later.' She closed the door as she left.

Sean phoned the solicitor and got an appointment for noon. Emily had taken the car to work so he would have to get the bus into town. He was consulting the timetable when the phone rang. He fully expected it to be the solicitor apologizing that it had all been a mistake and he wasn't entitled to anything. But it wasn't. It was Avi.

'Are you sitting down, kid?'

'No. Why?'

'Because I just had the BBC on the phone and you've got the fucking lead in *Savage*,' Avi said with enormous restraint in his voice.

Sean screamed with joy. 'That's amazing, Avi. Thank you so much for all you've done to make this happen. Shit, this must be my lucky day.'

'Why, what else happened?'

Sean told him about the inheritance and then got the details of when he was due to start shooting. 'Now, I know you said if you got this you only wanted to see one episode at a time, but I've read all six, and I strongly recommend you do the same before you step in front of the camera.'

'But that would be like the character knowing his future, Avi. No. That doesn't work.'

Sean could hear a few awkward breaths on the other end of the line. 'I'm trying not to give you spoilers, kid, but let's just say, what happens in the last episode directly relates to what happens throughout the series. So, you kind of need to know where it's going. I know how you work, and I know you'll think you played it wrong if you don't have the full picture before you start.'

This time there was a long pause on Sean's end of the phone. 'OK, Avi, I'll trust your judgement on this. Email me all six episodes and I'll read them.'

'It's the right thing to do, believe me. OK, I'll let you go pick up your windfall.'

'It's probably just a few quid of interest on his last dole cheque.'

'Well, even if it is, Emily's right about the house. The land at least has to be worth something. Good luck with it, and keep an eye out 'cause good things always come in threes.'

'OK, I will.' He hung up and immediately lifted the receiver again. He dialled Emily's mobile. It went to voicemail. Of course, she'd be in class by now. He called the school and asked if someone could go get her.

He heard the receptionist clicking her keyboard. 'I don't think she's due back until after lunch.' She stopped typing. 'Yes, that's right. After lunch.'

'Due back? She's not there? Where is she?'

'I don't have that information,' the nervous girl answered.

Sean hung up. He lifted the receiver and dialled again. 'Lenny, how's the short coming along? OK, listen I need to wrap today. Something else has come up that'll need my attention. Can we do this ADR today? Well, I'm sorry about that, but I'm going to be busy for the next few months at least and probably not in the country, so we either do it today or it doesn't get done. Great. OK, I'll see you then.'

Sean put on his coat and shoes and headed towards the door. He tried Emily again on her mobile. Voicemail again. He ran out the door to catch the bus.

He was in the solicitor's office for half an hour, listening to the official reading of the will and then signing various documents. When he left, he had the address and keys to Uncle Ronnie's house, and was carrying a cheque for £33,641.39p.

Where the hell had Ronnie got that kind of money? Sean assumed he was getting some sort of state benefits while he was in Sycamore Acres, but he also assumed most of that went to the facility for his care.

His dad had sometimes told stories which suggested Uncle Ronnie was sort of a minor criminal. Someone who had profited off The Troubles with various protection rackets and scams, and had even committed some low-profile robberies all in the name of The Cause. The truth was, his only loyalty was to himself and the only cause he ever fought for was his own. He bandied around the name of whatever paramilitary organisation he needed to, but none of his actions were sanctioned by any of them. Was this money the remains of his ill-gotten gains? Something he'd stashed away before the demons in his head had taken over?

Sean went to the bank and deposited the cheque in his account. He tried calling Emily a few more times and got her voicemail. He had lunch in a sandwich bar and then went to the nearest library, found a copy of *Great Expectations* and picked up where he'd left off at home. He sat in the quiet space and continued reading until it was time for his bus to take him home.

Blue skies had fought and won their battle with the grey clouds by the time he got off the bus. There was still a chill in the air, but the sun was trying its best to heat up the world. Sean took the long way home through the park.

Why wasn't Emily answering her phone? Why wasn't she at work? He had been so excited to tell her about getting the part of Savage, but now the news seemed tarnished. She was excited about the inheritance this morning too, so why wouldn't she keep her phone on? She must've known he'd call when he found out how much they were getting. None of it made any sense. Maybe she was seeing someone else.

That would explain a lot.

He just didn't think she was capable of it. He laughed out loud. Famous last words. How many people who are cheated on think their partner would never do that? It's the oldest cliché in the book. Of course you never suspect them. He wondered if depositing the cheque into their joint account had been a dumb move. What was the difference? If she was seeing someone else and they were heading for divorce, she'd take half his money anyway.

Sean wandered home, the double dose of good news now being eclipsed by his own doubts and fears. When he got to the end of the street, he saw her car sitting outside the house. He checked his watch. She shouldn't be home from school yet. So she'd seen all his missed calls on her phone and had decided whatever she had to say needed to be said face to face. Reluctantly he walked down the street and opened his front door.

She was sitting on the sofa. She turned when he came in the door. Her eyes were red. Sean took off his coat and hung it on the hooks by the door. He leaned against the door and gave her a thin smile. 'I tried to call you.'

'Yeah, I saw. Sorry, I had my phone off.'

'You're home early.'

She sniffed back hard. 'I took a personal day. I was feeling… Sean, come and sit down next to me.'

Sean walked over and sat next to her. She took his hand in both of hers. 'The reason I wasn't at school when you rang… is because I was at the doctor.'

'Are you sick?'

She shook her head and smiled. She took his hand and placed it on her stomach. He looked at her again and saw her eyes were full of tears. She smiled at him and nodded.

'A baby?' Tears were blurring his vision now too. He wiped his eyes. 'Really?'

'I know we said we wouldn't start trying again for a while, but… how do you feel about it?'

He touched her face and smiled. 'I think it's the third piece of good luck I've had today.'

'Oh god, yes, Uncle Ronnie's will. It totally slipped my mind with all this. What happened?'

'Thirty-three grand.'

She laughed. 'Well, that's better than nothing! Where did he get that sort of money?'

'I have no idea.' Sean still had one hand on her stomach and was gently rubbing it like he was Aladdin.

'Wait a minute, what's the third thing?'

'That's what I called you about the first time. Avi called. I got the part of Savage.'

Emily's mouth dropped open and her eyes went wide. 'Oh my god! You're going to be famous.' She hugged him and they kissed. Emily laid her head down on his chest. 'Everything's falling into place.' She popped her head up and looked at him again. 'What about Ronnie's house?'

'I've got the keys and the address.'

'Shall we go and have a look? The sun's come out. It'll be a nice day to drive out to the coast.'

Sean wiped his cheeks. 'Let's have a cup of tea and stop crying first.'

Emily laughed and hugged him tightly.

11.

They used the sat-nav on Emily's phone to guide them to the road, but they weren't surprised that the sat-nav had no record of the house. The closest house was three miles away and the road barely classified as such. Though it had been almost twenty years since he had been here, Sean recognised the place as they got close. It was a small two-storey surrounded by out-buildings. It had probably been a family-run farm many years ago before the profession required large numbers of livestock and machinery in order to stay profitable.

'I suppose it's picturesque in its own way,' Emily said as they got closer. 'There's a little copse of trees over there and you can just about see the sea over those fields. It's an ideal country retreat.'

'There's a river behind the house too. We used to fish there.'

'Well, there you go. We fix it up and hire it out to stressed, city-types who want to get away from it all and go fishing for the weekend.'

Sean said nothing. He was getting a queasy feeling in his stomach the closer they got to the place. He'd had the feeling ever since they set out on this journey, and had just put it down to nerves about becoming a father, but now he wasn't sure. It was definitely getting stronger the closer they came to the abandoned property. Something inside him was yelling for him to turn around and never come back here. He looked at the ever-optimistic Emily and wondered how he could explain this feeling to her without seeming mad. He kept his mouth closed and pulled up to the gate.

The keys he had been given included one for this padlock, but it was rusted so badly the key wouldn't even go inside. Sean was prepared for this and got the bolt-cutters from the boot of the car. He snapped the lock and the little voice inside him seemed to be screaming now. *Don't go in there!*

He looked back at Emily, smiling in the passenger seat. He threw the padlock aside and opened the heavy gate. There was a badly pot-holed lane which led to the house about a quarter of a mile away. He got back in the car and threw the bolt-cutters on the back seat. He started the car.

The car sat idling. Sean was looking at the house in the distance.

'What's wrong?' Emily asked.

Ghosts.

That's what he wanted to say.

167

Ghosts of the past. They're here. Everywhere.

He turned to her and forced a smile. 'Nothing.' He put the car into gear and they slowly trundled down the lane towards the house.

Everything looked smaller than he remembered, but still familiar. Despite the car's heater being on full-blast and the sun chipping in as much as it could, Sean was shivering when he turned the ignition off. He wiped the sweat off his brow and looked at the house.

'Well, with a little TLC and a little TNT, I think it could be... Sean? Sean! What's wrong? Sean!'

He was visibly shaking now. 'I can't... I can't breathe,' he gasped. He opened the door and fell out of the car. By the time Emily ran round to him his body was jerking violently on the ground.

She knelt next to him. 'Sean! What is it? What's happening?' Tears were running down her cheeks. 'Help,' she screamed.

Sean looked at the panicked face looking down at him. Her mouth was moving but he couldn't hear what she was saying. There were spots of light piercing through reality all around him. And then inky blackness closed in from all sides.

The crash wakes the boy.

He gets out of bed and immediately feels the cold. He is only wearing his pants. There's another crash from downstairs. It sounds like glass breaking. He walks over to the chair with his school clothes sitting on it and pulls on his jumper. He opens his bedroom door and creeps over to the top of the stairs.

The sounds are louder. So are the shouts. They're saying the bad words that the older boys at school say in the playground. He knows the voices. Not strangers. He creeps down the stairs to the halfway point and can see into the living room.

His dad throws his uncle across the room. His uncle's face is already bleeding and bruised. His dad lifts the poker from the fireplace and hits the bleeding man repeatedly with it. His uncle isn't fighting back. He's crying. The boy has never seen a grown-up cry like that before. His dad drops the poker, breathing hard, and slouches down the nearest wall to the ground. He puts his head in his hands and whispers more bad words. His uncle keeps crying.

Intrigued, the boy readjusts his position for a better view and the stair creaks. Both men look over at him. Neither of them says a word.

168

The boy is in the back of the car. It is night and raining. His dad is driving. His uncle whimpers in the passenger seat. It is a long drive and the boy falls asleep. When he awakes the car is in the yard of his uncle's house.

The two men are standing outside in the rain shouting at each other. They see him watching. His dad opens the back door of the car and shouts at him to stay in the car until he gets back. He says this with much more force and anger than is needed for such a simple command. The rain is running down his face making him look like he's melting, and the lightning crashing behind him just makes the whole scene more intense.

The boy stays in the car. He gets cold again and wraps the back seat blanket around him. It's very dark out here in the country. There are no street lights. But there is lightning and he sees brief flashes of what is going on.

He sees enough to make him close his eyes and lie down on the back seat. He wraps the blanket around his head.

'Sean? Sean?' Emily was lightly slapping his face when he woke. He quickly raised a hand and stopped her. 'Oh, thank god. I didn't know what to do. We're so far away from anywhere, and I couldn't lift you into the car, and I didn't want to leave you while I went for help, and I couldn't get a signal on my phone. Sean, what the fuck just happened? You scared the shit out of me!'

He sat up. 'How long was I out?'

'Just a couple of minutes, but they were the longest of my life. What happened to you, Sean?'

Sean looked to the bottom of the yard and saw what had once been flowerbeds, but were now overgrown with weeds. He got to his feet.

Emily had to grab him to stop him falling over. 'Whoa, wait! Slow down.'

Sean took a few deep breaths and his balance seemed to return. He broke free of Emily's arm and hurried to the bottom of the yard. Emily ran after him.

Sean tore through the high grass, ripping handfuls of it from the ground. Near the back of the flowerbeds he found a concrete elephant with some blue paint still left on it. He dropped to his knees and pushed it to the side. He started digging with his hands. As he ripped at the hard ground, Emily could see some of his fingernails had bent backwards and were bleeding.

'Stop, Sean, stop! You're hurting yourself. What are you…?'

Sean stopped digging and sat back on his feet. Emily looked down and stared at the skull staring back at her out of the dirt. She turned to Sean. Her mouth hung open but the words wouldn't come. Sean walked backwards on his knees and started digging three feet lower and to his right. Emily could do nothing but watch in horrified awe. Pretty soon Sean uncovered the skeletal left hand of the body. It had two rings on its third finger. Sean brushed the dirt off them to get a better look, and then sat back.

Emily didn't know what to say. She looked at her husband for a long time. He was staring at those rings. She eventually managed to get up the courage to ask, 'Sean, who is this?'

He answered in a very matter-of-fact way, 'It's my mum.'

They sat in silence for about ten minutes before he spoke. 'Ronnie used to come round to our house all the time. He stopped when mum left. He always said he was coming to see me, but it was her he was coming to see.' He looked over at Emily. 'I was here the night they buried her. That's how I knew where she was. I don't know how I blocked it out until now, but I was here. He came to our house in the middle of the night and told my dad. They'd been rowing and he'd hit her and… he said it was an accident. But with Ronnie's record he knew the cops would never believe that. My dad beat the shit out of him… but he still helped him in the end.'

Emily edged closer and put her hand on Sean's arm. 'We have to call the police. It doesn't matter now. Ronnie's dead, and now we know what he was saying sorry for on his death bed. Sean?'

'What?'

'We need to drive until we get a signal and then call the police.'

Sean nodded vaguely. She helped him to his feet and led him to the passenger's side of the car. 'I'll drive. You're in no state.'

Emily drove to the end of the lane. 'Take out your phone and check.'

Robotically, Sean did as he was told. He looked at the screen and shook his head.

'OK, keep an eye on it. I'll just head for Bangor. It's not that far away. It shouldn't be long before you get a signal.'

They drove for a couple of miles in silence. Sean had the phone in front of him, but she didn't know if he was looking at it until he raised it and dialled. She heard it ringing and looked for a place to pull over.

'Hi, it's me. Something's happened. I don't know what to do.'

Emily pulled the car into a lay-by and stopped. She looked at Sean with knitted brows. He ignored her stare.

'No, this is bad. Really bad, Avi.'

Avi? What the hell had he called Avi for? Emily sat in silence as Sean recounted the whole story to his agent. When he was done, she heard frenzied talking from the old American that she couldn't quite make out. Sean was nodding and saying OK every once in a while. Eventually he hung up.

'Why did you call Avi?'

'We need to go back to Ronnie's place and cover her back up.'

'What? Sean, we've just discovered a murder scene. Your *mother's* murder scene! We need to call the police.'

'I'll explain it to you later, but for now we just have to...'

'No, you explain it to me now, Sean,' she shouted.

Sean took a deep breath. He looked straight ahead, through the dusty windscreen. 'Do you think the BBC are still going to hire me if this comes out?'

'Why not? You didn't do anything.'

'Oh, come on, Em. It's guilt by association. Mud sticks. All that shit.'

'So we just leave her out there?'

'No. Not forever. Avi has a plan and I trust him.' Sean turned to her and took her hands tightly in his own. 'You just have to trust me. Can you? Em? Please?'

12.

They were back home by early evening. In addition to covering up the remains again, they'd also put back the blue elephant and tried to rearrange the grass and weeds as best they could. Then they'd driven to the nearest petrol station and bought a new padlock for the gate.

When they got back to the house Sean hurried upstairs. Emily followed him up and watched from the door of the bathroom as he quickly washed himself and scrubbed the dirt and blood from under his nails. Sean had done the majority of the work, but she felt much dirtier.

'What's your rush?'

'I have to meet Lenny to do the voiceover, remember?'

'You're still going to do that after everything?'

'I have to.' He rubbed himself over quickly with a towel. 'Avi said don't do anything out of routine or character. I made this appointment so I have to keep it.' He edged out past her and into the bedroom. He pulled on some clean clothes. Emily sat on the bed. She didn't know what to say. She thought of that skeleton lying out there in an unmarked grave, miles from anywhere. She looked at Sean and was troubled by how normal he looked. Now the initial shock had passed, discovering his mother's body didn't seem to be bothering him at all.

Sean pulled on a jacket and kissed her cheek. 'I'll take the car, OK? Shouldn't be more than a couple of hours. Don't wait for me to eat. I'll grab a sandwich or something on the way.' He smiled, briefly touched her stomach and then ran out of the bedroom and down the stairs. Emily heard the front door slam and the car start seconds later.

She didn't feel like eating. She needed a long soak in the bath. And then she needed to call her mother.

But first, she needed to cry.

Sean ran into the university sound room. 'Hey, guys. Sorry I'm late.'

Lenny stood up and shook his hand. 'That's no problem. We were just finishing up with Rhonda.'

Sean gave a nod and smile at his co-star. She glared back at him before grabbing her bag and coat and rushing out. 'What's with her?'

Lenny looked embarrassed, which was getting to be his default setting. 'She was asking a lot of stuff about you. I think she might have a bit of a crush. Sorry.'

'Hey, it's not your fault, Lenny. You told her I was married, right?'

'Yeah, I told her but...'

'You don't think it sunk in?'

Lenny shrugged.

'Well, shit like this happens on set, Lenny. Get used to it.' Sean took off his jacket. 'Now, what are we doing here?' He sat down next to the sound editor and Lenny pulled in a chair next to him.

An hour later the dubbing was complete and Sean was walking back across the university car-park when the door of a small Renault opened and Rhonda asked him to get in. Sean considered it for a few seconds and then decided it was best to deal with this now rather than let it drag on. He got into the passenger's seat and closed the door. 'What can I do for you?'

'I've been trying to call you.'

'I blocked your number.' He turned towards her. 'Look, I thought you knew what this was. I told you the first time we…'

'I'm pregnant, Sean.'

Sean slowly sat back in his seat and stared straight ahead.

'And before you ask, yes, I'm sure, and yes, I'm sure it's yours.'

The seconds passed by slowly, like onlookers at an accident site.

'Well?'

'Well what, Rhonda?'

'What do you think?'

He turned to her quickly. 'What do I think? What do I *think*? I don't know what the fuck to think. You drop this shit on me and you expect me to…' Sean punched the dashboard of her car repeatedly, screaming Fuck! with each punch. When he was finished he lowered his head and covered it with his hands. After a few seconds he raised his head up, leaving his hands folded as if in prayer before his face. 'You think you want to keep it?'

'I do,' she answered. She let that hang for a while before adding, 'And I want us to be together, as a family to raise it.'

She reached over to touch his face but he raised his hand and stopped her. 'I need to think about this.'

'Sean, I moved to Belfast to be an actress. I have no one else here and I can't go back to my family like this. They'd… Well, let's just say it would just prove them right about a lot of shit we argued about.' She took his hand. 'Those times we were together, it was more than just… You felt it too, didn't you?'

Sean gently released her hand from his. He shook his head. 'I don't know, Rhonda. I don't know anything right now. I have a wife; you *know* I have a wife. I have to think about this.' He opened the car door and put one leg outside. He turned back to her. 'Are you at home tomorrow?'

She nodded, spilling tears from her eyes.

'I'll come by your place tomorrow afternoon and we'll talk properly. OK?'

She nodded and more tears escaped. He leaned over and kissed the trails of saltwater on her left cheek. He saw the hope blossom in her eyes. Sean leaned back before she could initiate further physical contact. He got out and said, 'Tomorrow then,' before closing the door and walking back to his wife's car and driving home.

Sean got in and picked up the laptop from the sofa on his way to the kitchen. He left the computer to boot-up as he filled a glass of water under the tap.

'Did you get something to eat?'

Sean turned and saw Emily standing in the kitchen doorway in her pyjamas. 'No. I didn't really feel like it. I'll grab some biscuits with this.'

'Aren't you coming to bed?'

'No, I don't think I'll sleep.' He looked her in the eyes. 'It was a big day. Lots to digest. Lots to think about.'

'Lots to talk about at some point too,' Emily said.

Sean nodded.

'What are you going to do? It's still early if you want to watch a movie or something.'

Sean nodded towards the laptop. 'Avi emailed me the *Savage* scripts. I was going to take a look at one or two of them.'

Emily smiled. 'My husband the star of *Savage M.D.* I always knew you'd get your shot.'

He walked over to her and put his arms around her waist. 'I couldn't have got here without you.' He kissed her lightly. 'Oh, and I think they're just calling it *Savage* now. They've dropped the M.D. from the title.'

'*Savage*.' She tried the new title out loud. 'Isn't that a misleading title for a crime-fighting doctor show?'

Sean shrugged. 'I'll tell you after I read the episodes.'

She kissed him again. 'OK, don't stay up too late.' He watched her leave. He got his glass of water and sat down in front of the laptop. He found Avi's email, opened the attachment, and began to read.

Emily woke the next morning to the sound of the smoke alarm going off. She jumped out of bed and ran downstairs to find Sean flapping a tea towel under the living room detector with a cigarette hanging from his mouth.

'What the hell's going on, Sean?' she shouted over the incessant beeping.

'This fucking thing's gone mad.' His accent was different. He was talking like Richard E. Grant in *Withnail & I*. He flapped harder with the tea towel. The beeping stopped. He shook his head and threw the tea towel onto the nearest chair. He sucked hard on his cigarette and exhaled with some minor coughing.

'Why are you smoking?'

'It's just for a few weeks. In episode one Savage has just quit smoking. It's why he's so irritable and can't sleep, and works on the case to kill the dark hours.' The alarm started beeping again. Emily was getting a headache. She took Sean by the shoulders and directed him towards the door, then pushing him out onto the street. She went to the kitchen and opened the window, creating a thru-draft with the front door to clear the smoke from the house. The beeping stopped. She went out the front door and joined Sean. Neighbours were poking their heads out of their doors up and down the street.

Emily waved to them and smiled. 'It's nothing. False alarm. Thank you all.' When the last one had gone back inside, she gave Sean a bewildered look. 'What the hell are you playing at?'

'All part of getting into character, my dear. You know this.' He smiled and moved to go back inside.

She put her hand on his chest and shook her head. 'No more smoking in the house. Apart from the alarms, did you forget about this little one?' She pointed to her stomach.

He raised a finger in exclamation. 'Ah, excellent suggestion. Stupid of me not to have spotted that.' He flicked the cigarette into the street. 'These really taste disgusting. I'll be glad when I have to quit. Now, what about breakfast, my dear?'

She couldn't help but smile. She hadn't seen him this excited in a long time. 'I take it the scripts were good?'

'Better than good. Incredible.' He kissed her.

'OK, let's get you a bacon butty. You can't fight crime on an empty stomach.'

'Oh, sorry, stupid of me not to have mentioned it. I'll be a vegan now, for the duration of the shoot.' Inside, the alarm started beeping again.

'A vegan?' Emily exhaled. She should've known this was coming. Couldn't someone just write a part where the character ate normally for once? 'OK, you're going to have to give me a list of what to buy to suit a vegan. Can you have some tea and toast?'

'Savage only drinks camomile tea. I'm not sure about toast. We may have to Google that. I've got a big day planned so I hope you didn't need the car.'

'No, it's fine. As long as you drop me at school and pick me up afterwards. What do you have to do?' The beeping stopped.

'New haircut, some new suits – Savage always wears suits, even at home – I also need to get some old Motown music to listen to, and as many books on forensic science as the library will give me.'

'You haven't finished *Great Expectations*.'

'I don't have to now.' Sean smiled and went inside. The alarm started beeping again. 'What, I'm not smoking! I put it out! What more do you want from me?'

Emily heard him shouting at the sensitive device. She shook her head, took a deep breath and went inside.

'You don't mind if I smoke, do you, my dear?'

Rhonda shook her head against his bare chest. Their naked bodies were nestled together on the bed in her small flat.

'Of course, I probably shouldn't, what with the bun in the oven.'

'My mum told me my dad smoked around her the whole time she was pregnant. It never done me any harm.' She combed her fingers across his chest. 'I can't believe you're here, like this. That we're together.'

'Get used to it, my dear. You're going to be seeing a lot more of me over the next few decades.'

She smiled. 'When will you tell Emily?'

'After we've finished filming the series, but before it airs.'

'That seems like a long way away.'

'But you understand why it has to be this way? If a divorce scandal gets out now, it'll be all the BBC will need to go with their second choice. Whoever that is. And then we'll just be two out of work actors raising a baby on benefits while trying to squeeze in auditions when we're not exhausted.' He changed position so he could look her in the eyes. 'The money from this series is going to set us up with a good life in a new place, so we can't blow it. Just don't say anything to anyone until the money's in the bank.'

'I don't know anyone in the city except you.' She broke contact with his eyes and looked down at his chest again. 'Sean, can I tell you something?'

'Of course, my love. You can tell me anything.'

Despite his reassurance, she was hesitant. 'When I found out I was pregnant... I didn't think you'd want to know. I was in a pretty dark place for a while. I had no one to talk to and... a couple of weeks ago... I took some pills. A lot of pills.'

Sean squashed out his cigarette on the ashtray next to the bed, and then pulled her closer. 'What?'

'I regretted doing it as soon as I... and I called an ambulance and they pumped my stomach. I'm fine now.'

'And the baby?'

'Yeah, it's fine. No harm done.' She looked him deep in the eyes. 'I didn't know what else to do. I couldn't see any happy ending at that point. I knew what my family would say if I...'

Sean hugged her tightly. 'Don't worry about that now. In a few months we're going to show up at your parents' house in the biggest fucking limo they've ever seen and show them just how well their little girl's done.'

Rhonda laughed and they kissed.

13.

Dinner was on Avi to celebrate the signing of the contracts for *Savage*. Shooting would begin in three weeks' time and Sean would be living in Manchester for the next two months. Avi had brought Aileen with him tonight. Her husband was in Barnsley on business. That still wouldn't make it safe under normal circumstances, but Aileen had told her husband about it and sold it as sort of a work-outing to celebrate Sean's success. So the couple were safe if any of her husband's friends spotted her out with her employer. She'd told her husband it was basically a little bonus, in addition to the raise she was getting, so he told her to milk Avi for everything she could. He even told her to order a starter and a dessert in case the old Jew tried to skinflint her.

Sean was looking every bit the doctor in his new suit and sporting his new haircut. He even seemed to have got the hang of smoking. He wasn't coughing as much as he enjoyed a post-dinner cigarette at the table. He held it away from Emily, who made a big deal about flapping away his unwanted cancerous fumes, but indulged his eccentric approach to his upcoming job.

'He thinks he's going to be able to stop just like that,' Emily said, smiling across the table.

'That's what I thought fifty-odd years ago too,' Avi said.

'It could be worse,' Aileen added. 'He could smoke those horrible cigars like this one.'

'I've cut back a lot,' Avi said.

'Didn't I quit after the play? The soldier I played smoked. But when the play was done I quit, no problem.'

'You were irritable for days afterwards, and then you were only smoking a couple of those little skinny rollies each day,' Emily said, and added to Aileen: 'Wartime rationing, you know.' Aileen laughed.

'Look, I'm not even a smoker. I'm just suffering for my art,' Sean said. He still had the accent, but they were all getting used to it now. 'I'll quit on day one of shooting and never look back. You'll see. All a question of willpower.'

'Famous last words,' Emily said, sipping her orange juice.

The waiter arrived at the table to clear the plates. 'Did you enjoy the Masala Dosa, sir?'

'Very tasty,' Sean said. 'This vegan thing's still a bit new to me, so thanks for the suggestion.' The waiter nodded and continued clearing.

Emily lifted the dessert menu. 'OK, now we get to the main event. What are you having, Aileen?'

'Oh, I really shouldn't.'

Emily put on her best sad-face. 'Come on. Don't make me look like I'm the only one pigging out. We're celebrating. Besides, I'm going to look like a whale in a few months no matter what I eat, so fuck the calorie counting.'

'You're right. The Milan catwalks will just have to get by without me this season,' Aileen said.

The ladies laughed and the men smiled, admiring their reasoning. Emily settled on the Strawberry Cheesecake, Aileen on the Chocolate Fudge Cake, Avi went for the butterscotch ice-cream and Sean went for his usual Pecan Pie.

The women dug in as soon as the desserts were delivered and immediately made orgasmic sounds the men could only dream of eliciting. Avi and Sean took a more detached approach to eating the food and talked over the details of the upcoming shoot.

'They've got you a little flat to yourself. It's not much, but I assumed you didn't want to blow all your wages on five-star accommodation.'

Sean cleared his throat. 'You were right. All I'll need it for is sleeping anyway.'

'You're probably right. These are going to be long days. I suggest you stay off the drink and clubbing.'

'Savage doesn't drink.'

Avi had to think about that for a second, then realised what he meant. 'OK. Just don't get tempted. The cast and crews on TV shows drink like fish, every night. Don't get sucked into that scene. Save it for the wrap party.'

Sean coughed and then smiled. 'No worries there.' He coughed into his hand again. 'I'm looking forward to...' He stopped and took a deep breath. Emily paused her love-affair with her cheesecake to pat his back. 'Are you OK, mister non-smoker?'

Sean nodded. 'Yeah, I just must've...' He coughed hard and she patted his back harder.

'Is something stuck in your throat?' Emily stood up. The other diners were looking concerned now. The waiter was back at the table looking very worried.

Sean shook his head. He grabbed his throat and rubbed. He jerked to his feet, causing the cutlery and glassware on the table to clink in alarm. 'My throat's closing in,' he said in a raspy voice. By now they could all see the swelling on his face too. One of his eyes was almost closed.

'He's having an allergic reaction,' a female diner cried. 'Call an ambulance!'

The waiter ran to the girl in charge of the takeaway counter and grabbed the phone from her. He had just dialled nine-nine-nine when there was a crash behind him and Sean collapsed on the table. He clutched at the tablecloth and pulled everything on top of him as he fell to the floor amid screams and yelling.

Aileen was the only one who kept her head in the crisis. As soon as she realised what was happening, her years of watching medical soap operas sprang into action. She asked the restaurant diners if anyone had an EpiPen on them. No one did, so she ran out of the restaurant and across the street to their competitor, almost getting hit by a car along the way. They had one in their First Aid box. The heavy-set

179

woman ran back across the road with it and jabbed it into Sean's thigh without stopping to explain to anyone.

The paramedics said she likely saved his life.

As they sat in the corridor of the hospital, Avi had never been prouder of her. She was resting her head on his shoulder and he had his arm around her. Emily had finally stopped crying after the nurse telling her Sean was out of danger, but Avi thought she looked like she might start again soon.

The doctor came towards them reading his clipboard. He was middle-aged, skinny and wore round glasses. Emily got to her feet and faced him. 'Your husband's out of danger now. We're going to keep him overnight just for observation, but you can come and get him in the morning.' All the tension rushed from Emily and she hugged the doctor. 'You can thank your friend here. She did all the work.' He turned to Aileen. 'That was quick thinking with the adrenaline. If you hadn't done that, I don't think he would've made it to the hospital.'

A chill ran up Emily's spine and she exchanged solemn looks with Avi and Aileen. Emily took a few deep breaths. Now they had cheated death, she wanted to make sure it didn't happen again. 'What caused it?' she asked the doctor.

'We're running some tests now, but I'll put money on the pecans.'

Emily shook her head. 'But he was never allergic before. He's had Pecan Pie before. Loads of times. It's his favourite.'

The doctor shrugged. 'Allergies can spring up at any time in life. A lot of the time they just come out of the blue.'

'They're a tree nut, aren't they?' Avi asked.

The doctor turned to him. 'I'm sorry?'

'Pecans, they're a tree nut, right?'

'Yes. Pecans, almonds, walnuts, pine nuts, Brazil nuts – they all grow on trees I believe.' He turned back to Emily. 'Now, we've sedated Sean so he'll be out all night. I suggest you all go home and try to get some sleep. Come back in the morning and get him.'

'OK. Thank you, doctor,' Emily said as he walked away. She sat down on the opposite side of the corridor from Avi. The old man had a concentrated scowl on his face. 'What's wrong, Avi? What was all that tree nut stuff about?'

180

Aileen raised her head too. Now both women were looking to him for an answer. 'In episode four,' Avi said. 'Savage says he's severely allergic to tree nuts.'

14.

'You can't prove a thing!'

'I'm afraid I can, Mrs Whelan. I not only know it was you who killed your husband, I know you did it at your own personal shooting range at your country estate.'

'You're fishing, Savage.'

'Am I? You were quite clever buying an unregistered weapon to commit the murder. No way for the ballistics to trace it back to you, but those six shots you fired into your husband's chest and abdomen didn't kill him immediately. And he used the last few seconds of his life to identify his killer.'

'This is pure fiction, doctor. You have no evidence.'

'Evidence is what I do have. Or maybe you'd like to explain why a man shot six times has seven bullets inside him?'

'What?'

'At first I just thought two bullets had gone in almost the exact same place. You did use quite a large calibre weapon and the resulting holes were exceptionally large. But one was flattened more than the rest, and one had very different rifling marks from the others. There's only one way that seventh bullet got inside him. As your husband lay dying on the ground, he picked it up and swallowed it.'

'No!'

'The six bullets you shot him with are untraceable, but the seventh leads right back to you. Your favourite weapon; the one you told us you never let anyone else fire. Your husband swallowed one of the many flattened bullets lying under your metal targets for one reason and one reason only, to identify his killer.'

'Fuck you, Savage!'

'Put the gun down, Mrs Whelan. There's no way you can... do you smell something?'

Rhonda sniffed the air. 'Shit, the veggie bake!' She threw the script down and jumped out of bed. Sean watched her bare ass as she ran for the kitchen. He reached over to the bedside table and grabbed another cigarette. He had just lit it and filled his lungs with noxious fumes when she came back.

'Charred remains?' Sean asked. 'Another case for Savage?'

She smiled. 'No, it was on the critical list but I think it'll pull through. Do you want it now or do you want to finish reading through the episode?'

'Let's eat, my dear. I only have two more lines and I know them.'

'OK, but I need a little cuddle first.' Rhonda lay down next to him and hugged his chest.

'It's good having a proper actress to run lines with.'

'Wasn't Emily an actress back in the day?'

'She wanted to be, but it never happened. She never really had the chops or the stamina to stick at it. Now she's spent so long teaching kids, I think she's just happy if they know their lines and hit their mark. She doesn't care about the nuance of performance anymore.'

'The nuance of performance. I like that.' She psyched herself up for a few seconds before continuing, 'Maybe there's a part for me on the show. If you think I'm good enough.' Her head was resting on his chest so she couldn't see his face when he answered.

'Yes, I'm sure of it, my dear.' He patted her stomach. 'Maybe not this year, though. You'll be starting to show by the time we start shooting.' He sat up and turned her so they were facing each other. 'But if we get a second series, I'll insist on it!' He smiled and kissed her.

Sean walked up behind her as she was washing the dishes and put his hands around her waist. 'Hey, I'm all soapy.'

Sean reached forward and put his hands into the dishwater. 'I'm all soapy too. Don't worry about it.' His hands moved through the warm water and found hers. She dropped the bundle of cutlery she was holding and stroked his hands under the bubbles. He nestled into her neck and kissed her.

'I thought you had to go. Don't start something you can't finish.'

'I don't know what you're talking about. I'm just helping out with the dishes like any well-trained twenty-first century male.'

'Really? I think you know exactly what you're doing.'

'You must be mistaken, my dear. I keep passing you stuff to wash but you aren't taking it. Instead you're giving me... what the fuck!'

The mood was broken instantly when Rhonda looked into the sink and saw the water was red. Sean pulled his hands from the water and wiped the bubbles on his jeans. He checked his hands, back and front. 'It's not me.'

Rhonda lifted her hands from the water and they both saw the blood running down her arm from the cut on her left wrist. She looked at Sean, the fear evident in her eyes.

'Shit! What the fuck happened? What did you do?' Sean grabbed a tea towel and wrapped it around the wound. 'Keep it upright and keep pressure on it.' He was already ushering her towards the door.

Within minutes they were racing down the dual carriageway towards the hospital in Emily's car. The tea towel was now soaked through with blood. Blood was dripping off Rhonda's elbow into her lap. 'Are you OK? Rhonda!'

She nodded, still too shocked to speak.

'Jesus Christ, Rhonda, what the fuck did you do?'

She was shaking her head. 'I didn't do anything. I swear. Why would I? It just must've been an accident... one of the knives in the sink must've... The water was so hot I didn't even feel it. Sean, I feel really tired.'

'Don't you fucking fall asleep! We're almost there. You have to stay with me, Rhonda, because you're going to have to go in by yourself.'

She was fighting to keep her eyes open. 'What? Why?'

'If I come in with you the police are going to ask questions and it's all going to come out about us.'

'But, Sean...'

'No, listen, Rhonda, this is important. This BBC job is the only way we're going to be able to build a life together. If that gets fucked up...'

'What?'

'Never mind. Look, we're here. I'm going to drop you off as close as I can, but I can't be seen. You have to go the last little bit yourself. When you get in there you just tell them exactly what happened only don't mention I was there, OK? Rhonda? Do you understand me?'

She nodded. Sean pulled the car in around the corner from the Accident & Emergency drop-off point. She was really pale and her eyes were flickering. Sean leaned over and kissed her cheek. 'Go. Now. Every second counts. I love you.' He opened her door and she almost fell out. She climbed her hands up the wall to get herself upright and then staggered round the corner.

Sean drove the car into the car park where he could see the doors to A&E. He watched her claw her way around the corner, leaning against the wall. Then, like a novice ice-skater letting go of the side for the first time, she started towards the double doors. There was no one around. She was staggering badly, all the time trying to keep her arm elevated. She was only a few feet from the door when she stopped and swayed back and forth. Sean leaned forwards. He was gripping the steering wheel so tightly his fingers were tingling.

Rhonda dropped to the ground. Sean's hand shot out and grabbed the door handle, but he didn't pull it. Not yet. Someone would come out. Someone would find her in time. He was sure of it. He was sweating so much the car windows were steaming up. He wiped the windscreen with his hand. She was still lying there, not moving.

Sean looked towards the entrance for incoming cars. He looked around the car park for anyone who might be waiting for a loved one. Surely there had to be someone. His hand tightened on the door handle. He couldn't judge how long she'd been lying there. It seemed like a long time. She hadn't moved since she dropped.

He pulled the handle and opened the car door a couple of inches. He looked around the entrances, the car park, the doors. Still no one. He pulled the keys out of the ignition and stepped out of the car.

The A&E doors opened and he ducked down behind the car. He could see inside. There was an old woman in a wheelchair with an unlit cigarette in her mouth. A porter was holding the handles of the wheelchair while talking to a nurse inside. They were laughing. Rhonda lay only a few feet away, but they wouldn't be able to see her until they came outside. Sean watched the porter flirt with the nurse. Her body-language indicating she welcomed his advances. The old lady in the wheelchair would be able to see her if she just turned her head. The nurse changed her posture, like she was preparing to stand there for a long time. The porter let go of the handles and turned to face her.

The old lady saw her! She waved to the porter. He held a hand up to her. *Yeah, I'll be there in a minute.* The old lady turned to him and grabbed for his sleeve. She pointed at Rhonda with the other hand. Sean watched the old lady over the roof of the car. The porter shook off the withered hand without breaking eye-contact with the nurse. The old lady grabbed him again, her frail gestures trying desperately to convey urgency. The porter shook his head and pulled the wheelchair back a few inches. The automatic doors closed.

Sean looked at Rhonda lying on the cold cement.

He came out from behind the car and hurried towards the A&E entrance. The automatic doors opened and the old lady came wheeling forward on her own. The porter rushed after her. Sean ducked behind the nearest car. The porter stopped the forward momentum of the wheelchair and then began reprimanding the old lady. She pointed behind him and he finally looked.

The porter rushed over to Rhonda and quickly checked her before running back inside. Seconds later the flirty nurse and another nurse came running out. Seconds after that the porter pushed an emergency gurney out the double doors. The three of them got Rhonda onto it and rushed inside with her.

Sean breathed a sigh of relief.

He stood up and saw the old lady in the wheelchair having a smoke. He walked back to Emily's car and decided to do the same.

When he'd crushed his second cigarette out in the ashtray, he got the bag from the glove-box. He pulled the blood-stained cover off the passenger's seat and stuffed it into the yellow hospital bag with BIOHAZARD printed on it in large black letters. He did the same with the plastic sheet that was under the cover and had caught the blood that seeped through. He tied the bag and then walked around to the back of the hospital where he found a stack of similar yellow bags in a cart next to the incinerator. He added his bag to the pile and left.

He would go back to Rhonda's place and clean it from top to bottom. It would be a nice surprise for her when she got out.

The nurse turned out the lights. Emily took hold of Sean's hand and squeezed it tightly.

'OK, this might feel a little cold.' The nurse squirted the gel onto Emily's lower abdomen and then smoothed it around with the transducer probe. They all looked expectantly at the monitor. Emily's hand tightened around Sean's. There was complete silence for a few seconds. 'OK, there's the heartbeat. Seems strong.'

Emily gasped. Sean looked down at her and saw her cheeks were wet with tears. She was smiling like he'd rarely seen her smile before. He looked back up at the blurry images on the monitor and failed to see what the nurse was pointing out. He obviously wasn't feeling what Emily was feeling either, but that he could fake. He smiled.

'I'd say you're about eleven weeks.'

Emily sniffed back hard. 'Yes, that's what we thought.'

'What about the nuchal translucency?'

'I was just about to... do you have some specific reason to worry your baby might have Down's Syndrome?'

'No.' Emily turned to her husband. 'Sean, what are you doing?'

'Can you just check?'

There were more tense seconds as the nurse studied the screen and took some measurements. 'No, it looks fine. No reason to... Hang on.' She smiled. 'Are you a doctor?'

Emily laughed, more with relief than anything. 'He soon will be. Sort of.'

'That explains it,' the nurse said. 'Doctors know too much for their own good. They always find something to worry about.' She shook her head in mock exasperation. 'I'll print you out a copy of your first baby photo.'

Emily wiped her cheeks again and turned to Sean. 'She thought you were a real doctor. All that research must be paying off.'

Sean didn't look amused.

15.

'When will you be back?'

'I don't know. Two or three months maybe.'

Rhonda lay across his chest looking up at him smoking. 'Don't you even get home for weekends or holidays?'

'I don't know. It's my first time on something like this. I think a lot of it depends on the weather. There's quite a lot of exterior stuff to do, so my guess is if it gets postponed because the weather's dire, we'll have to reschedule. That makes it hard to give you a set-in-stone timetable, my dear.' He kissed the scar on her wrist.

The hospital had let her out after three days. Most of that time was spent convincing them that it really was an accident and not a cry for help. She hadn't said a word about Sean, and for that he was grateful. A couple of weeks later she had got her stitches out and now the wound had almost disappeared to a thin white line. Sean kissed it again, and then turned to her. 'Are you going to be OK while I'm away?'

She took a deep breath. 'I've been thinking about getting in touch with my family again. After the scan next week. When I know everything's OK. You're right, I'm not going to get any acting work in this condition, and the big city isn't all I thought it would be if I'm honest.' She smiled and kissed his chest. 'Except for meeting you.'

'How do you think your parents will take it?'

'A strict catholic family having an unmarried daughter up the spout? They'll be over the moon.'

'It's 2004, Rhonda.'

'Not in their world. I'll be lucky if they don't make me wear a scarlet letter around town. It's not going to be fun.'

'Maybe you should wait for me to come back and we'll tell them together.'

'Sit in this little flat alone for the next three months waiting for you to call? No offence, darling, but that doesn't sound like a lot of fun either. No, I've thought about it. I'll reach out to my sister first. She's the most open-minded of them.'

'Are you close?'

'Not especially. She hasn't called or visited once since I've been here. But I think she's my best shot to act as peacekeeper between us while the news sinks in that their little girl isn't a virgin anymore.'

Sean chuckled. 'Jesus, how old's *that* news?'

Rhonda slapped his chest and laughed. 'None of your business!' His phone rang. He lifted it and looked. He turned the screen towards her and she saw it was Emily calling. He declined the call. Seconds later it rang again. He declined again, and then made a point of showing her he turned the phone off. They lay there for a few minutes in silence, and then she watched him squash out his cigarette. She put her head down on his chest again. 'How much longer can you stay?'

'Not long. What are you going to do with the rest of the evening?'

'I think I'll take along soak in the bath and listen to The Corrs' new CD.'

He pushed his fingers through her hair. 'Sounds nice. I wish I could stay.' He gently lifted her head and slid out from below her. She watched him walk towards the bathroom.

He came back a couple of minutes later and started dressing. 'I've started your bath. I can at least get you settled before I go.'

Rhonda dropped her robe and looked at herself in the bathroom mirror. She turned sideways and sucked in her stomach. She released her breath and ran her hand over the barely perceptible bump. She smiled as she turned and eased herself into the hot bath. Track one from *Borrowed Heaven* started playing in the living room.

'Is that loud enough?' Sean shouted.

'That's fine.'

Halfway through the first track Sean came into the bathroom with a glass of milk. 'Here you go. This is probably the last thing I'll be able to do for you until I get back. Drink it all down. The calcium's good for the baby.'

Rhonda drank it down in one. She smacked her lips. 'Tastes chalky.' She handed the glass back to Sean and he left the room with it. The steam was causing her to flush. She heard him turning the kitchen taps on and tried to shout for him not to bother with the dishes, she'd do them later, but she didn't have the strength. She saw him walk past the door a few times carrying a black bin bag.

The bathroom was spinning now. She felt sick. The bathwater must be too hot. The steam was making her feel like she couldn't breathe. 'Sean,' she managed to say.

He walked in and looked down at her. With his thumb and forefinger he opened one of her eyes and looked closely at it.

'Sean, I don't feel well. I think something's wrong. Maybe something's wrong with...' She noticed his blue hands. 'What have you... why are you wearing gloves?'

Sean knelt down next to the bath. Her head lolled over to the side as she tried to see what he was doing. He was leaving an empty pill bottle on the floor next to the bath. Why would he do that? It didn't make sense. Nothing was making sense.

'Sean, I feel really sick and I don't understand anything. Why aren't you talking to me?' Her words were slurring and barely audible. She looked down at the floor and saw something else scattered next to the pill bottle. Little black rectangles. All spilled out like a fan. She looked up again and saw Sean looking down at her. Was that Sean? Didn't Sean leave? He had one of those little black rectangles in his hand. He lifted her limp arm out of the bath and hung it over the side. Then he lifted the other hand out of the bath and patted the towel with it. He squeezed her fingertips against the smooth surface of the thin black rectangle, making her grip it. The other arm had gone cold, leaning over the edge of the bath, but now she felt warmth flow down it. He helped both arms back into the warm water. She saw the rectangle she had touched lying on the floor next to a red stain. What was the red?

She felt so tired. Sean was blurry above her. She couldn't focus her eyes. It felt like she was falling asleep. She probably shouldn't fall asleep in the bath. It's dangerous. But she'd be OK.

Sean was here.

They were digging up the road on his way home. Belfast City Council had decided it was less disruptive to do this sort of work at night, but there was a long tailback of angry motorists waiting for temporary traffic lights to change who would disagree. Sean looked at his phone and saw it was still turned off. He turned it back on and waited for it to boot up and find his network.

When it had, he saw twelve missed calls from Emily and eight missed calls from Avi. Something was very wrong. Had the BBC pulled the plug on the whole project? He called Emily and got her voicemail. He called Avi.

'Jesus, kid, where've you been? We've been trying to get hold of you for the last hour.'

'I was at the... it doesn't matter. What's wrong?'

'Kid, I'm sorry.'

'What, Avi, what?'

'Emily had some pain earlier and... She tried to call you, but... She's at the hospital now. I'm sorry, Sean, she's lost the baby.'

Sean had seen this scene many times in TV shows and films. He knew how he was supposed to react. 'I'll be there as soon as I can.' He hung up.

He didn't mind the traffic lights now. He needed the time to think. He was supposed to be leaving for Manchester tomorrow to start rehearsals. Emily would expect him to stick around now after this. He had to play it just right.

She looked pale and weak when he stepped into the hospital room. Her eyes were red and puffed up. Avi was sitting in a chair in the corner. When Sean came in he got up and gave his client's arm a squeeze as he left.

189

Tag, you're it.

Sean walked over and climbed on the bed next to her and hugged her. She started crying again. 'I'm sorry, Sean,' she said through her tears.

'Hey, you did nothing wrong. I spoke to the doctor. He says this happens a lot with first pregnancies, and he also said there's no permanent damage so we can try again whenever you feel ready.' He kissed her forehead.

'Where were you?' she asked. 'I called you when I first thought something was wrong, and I kept trying.'

'I know. I'm sorry. I was in the library with my phone on silent.' He pushed the hair back from her forehead. 'I was reading baby books if you can believe it. I wanted to look like I knew what I was doing when...' He gave her a flat smile. 'Let's not think about that now.'

She wiped her tears on the back of her hand and looked into his eyes. 'We'll try again, Sean.' And then added. 'Some day.' This came as a relief to him because it sounded like she was thinking long term. In the immediate future he had other things to concentrate on.

He turned quickly to the door. 'Shit, I should catch Avi before he leaves.'

She sniffed back hard. 'Why?'

'So he can tell the BBC I won't be there tomorrow. I can't go now. Not after this.'

'But they could fire you.'

Sean shrugged. 'Fuck 'em if they do.'

'But this is your big break. This is what you've been working towards for all these years. You can't blow it now.'

'I'm not leaving you in this state.'

She smiled at him and touched his cheek. 'They said I could get out in the morning. How about I come with you to Manchester? Just for a few days. It would do me good to be away from the house for a while.'

'What about work?'

'I can take some personal days.'

'And you're sure you're OK to fly?'

She actually managed a giggle. 'You're the doctor, you tell me.'

He hugged her tighter. 'OK, if you're sure.'

'I am, and there's no point in you hanging around here all night watching me sleep. Go home. Try to get some rest and come back for me first thing in the morning. Your flight isn't until the evening so we'll have all tomorrow to get packed and get me on the flight too.' She kissed his lips.

The hospital administrator hurried down the corridor. It was cold at this end of the hospital. He never came down here if he could avoid it. He hadn't even had his first cup of coffee yet. He didn't know what was so important it couldn't wait. His portly frame was waddling towards the mortuary with a full head of steam, intent on giving the attendant a lesson in not using the word 'emergency' lightly. His demeanour changed when he saw a police officer standing outside the entrance. After explaining who he was and showing his swipe card ID, the officer let him inside.

There was a middle-aged female detective and a younger male taking notes. The mortuary attendant nodded towards him when he entered and the detectives turned. The female walked towards him with her hand out. She wore no jewellery and no rings burdened her fingers. She had blonde hair tied back in a ponytail. An inch of dark roots showed she wasn't a natural blonde and also how busy she had been recently. The athletic figure she had held onto during her twenties was getting insulated a little more every year. Her tightly-fitting trousers and blouse betrayed the fact that she didn't eat regularly or healthily and grabbed whatever was handy whenever possible, but it also showed a woman who thought she could lose the excess weight and wouldn't admit defeat by buying new clothes.

'D.S. Agnes Finn,' she said, shaking his hand.

The administrator looked over at his subordinate. 'You called the police?'

'I'm afraid he would've been breaking the law if he didn't, sir. I'm sure you wouldn't want that.'

The bewildered man looked around for signs of vandalism. 'But what's happened?'

Finn nodded for him to follow her over to a gurney containing a body with a sheet over it. She gave the man a sombre look before lifting the sheet. It was the body of a man in his fifties. There was a large Y incision in his chest where he had been autopsied and then sewn back up.

'This man died in the early hours of this morning on your coronary ward. Heart disease. No suspicious circumstances. No reason for an autopsy.' She lowered the sheet.

The administrator looked around those present. 'Then who did...?' His sentence froze as he realised what the police were doing here. 'Are you saying someone did an unauthorized autopsy on this man?' He shook his head vehemently. 'That's impossible. The family must've arranged for an independent examination. We get it sometimes.'

'The family don't know anything about it.'

'But we have security measures.'

'One of the cleaners had his swipe card stolen. We've already talked to him. He doesn't know when he lost it, and doesn't remember anyone bumping into him.'

'But the cameras!'

'Shaving cream. Stolen from the hospital shop.' Finn pointed upwards and the administrator saw the camera covered with foam. Finn nodded towards the door. 'Same as those in the corridor leading here.'

'But why? Why would someone do such a thing?' He swallowed hard. 'The body hasn't been... interfered with... sexually, has it?'

'No, as far as we can tell, someone just came in, did an autopsy; took everything out, put everything back in, sewed him up and left.'

'It must be one of our people,' the administrator said, finding the nearest chair and sitting down. 'Someone trying to get ahead on their workload. Doing it during the night so they can take the morning off, maybe, and they just autopsied the wrong body?'

Finn nodded to the attendant who stepped forward and lifted the sheet again. 'It's not professional. Whoever did this knows the procedures and the theory, but look at these cuts. That's not an experienced hand making those incisions.'

The administrator shook his head and then covered his face with his hands. He could only imagine the scandal and the paperwork this incident was going to create, not to mention the legal liability of the hospital. He looked up from his hands to the detective. 'Do you have any idea who might've done this?'

'We'll look through your CCTV to see if we can spot anyone scoping out where the cameras are or stealing the shaving cream, but hundreds of people come through this hospital every day, maybe thousands, and this one's careful.' She looked up at the shaving foam covered cameras. 'We'll give you some tips on how to improve your security. Whatever thrill this individual is getting from doing this means they're very likely to do it again. We'll alert the other hospitals to tighten security too. We'll get them. Don't you worry. Someone who does something like this doesn't just do it once.'

16.

Sean and Emily were already in Manchester when Avi got the email inviting them all to the premiere of *The Teacher's Pet* at Queen's Film Theatre. Avi thought it was his duty to go and represent Sean. He was also on the lookout for new talent. For the last couple of years, the other half-dozen clients he had on his books had taken such a back seat to Sean's career, that they had either chucked in the business altogether or found a different agent. If everything went as planned, Sean's career would no longer be about chasing parts, but deciding which roles to do from the offers that came in. It was time for Avi to take on another client and see if he could piggy-back on Sean's success, and freshly graduating students were ideal.

There were six short films playing that night. Avi didn't know until he got there that *The Teacher's Pet* was scheduled last, but he happily sat through the other films and made some notes of names when the cast list rolled.

The final film was undoubtedly the best of the bunch. Even if Sean hadn't been in it, Avi would still have thought so. As the credits rolled, he made a note of the name Rhonda Boyle. She had held her own against Sean on-screen. That's something the old man had rarely seen. *The Teacher's Pet* got the longest and loudest applause too. Avi smiled. The cheers were just dying down when Lenny walked out onstage with a microphone and then a fresh volley of praise erupted.

Lenny nodded and held up a hand to stop them. 'Thank you. And thank you all for coming.' He took a deep breath. 'This screening is bittersweet, as you all know. Since this was filmed, we've lost the wonderful young actress you saw up there playing the teacher's wife. So I've had a word with the other directors and the manager of the QFT and they've all agreed that all proceeds from tonight should go to PIPS, the charity that provides suicide prevention and bereavement support services, counselling and therapies across Belfast and throughout Northern Ireland.' He wiped his eyes with the back of his hand before concluding, 'Let's stop this happening.' He lowered the mic and walked off the stage to another round of applause.

Avi didn't stay for the drinks, nibbles, and backslapping afterwards. He had planned to meet some of the names on his list, but since the most promising young actress he had seen tonight wasn't going to be there, he walked out into the rain and found the nearest bar.

'Jim Beam. Double. Straight.'

The barman obliged.

'Leave the bottle.' The young barman looked unsure until Avi produced a roll of notes and peeled some off for him. The cash caught the attention of a middle-aged woman at the other end of the bar. She sidled over to the old man.

'Hey, there. Buy a girl a drink?'

'Not tonight, honey.'

'Oh my god, you're American. That's so cool. I've always wanted to go to America. Can't you buy me just one teensy drink and tell me about it?'

'I said not tonight, so why don't you fuck off.'

Her soft face turned to granite in seconds. 'Ignorant bastard!' She stomped off towards the poker machine.

Avi poured himself another and smiled.

Ignorant bastard.

When he moved here it was one of the first things he didn't understand about the Northern Irish. When they say ignorant they don't mean ignorant, they mean rude. Somehow those two words had become synonyms in this country but nowhere else. Avi had definitely been rude to the woman, but he wasn't ignorant.

Sometimes he wished he was, but he knew far more than he cared to.

He downed the drink and poured himself another.

LOCAL ACTRESS FOUND DEAD

The police have now confirmed the name of the woman found dead in her flat by her landlord last Friday morning as Rhonda Boyle, 22, from Newtownabbey.

Rhonda had come to Belfast in hopes of pursuing an acting career and had landed roles in a few short films, including one with Sean Black, star of *Wee Barry*.

The coroner's report revealed that Ms. Boyle had died from a combination of sleeping pills and massive blood loss from a self-inflicted wound on her wrist.

The deceased's sister, Caitriona, said the family were unaware of Rhonda's state of mind, and are angry that social services didn't do more to help. Her hospital records show the troubled actress had made two previous attempts to take her own life.

The coroner's report also discovered Rhonda was almost three months pregnant, but her family were unaware of a boyfriend and the landlord reported never seeing anyone visit her. The police believe the most likely narrative, based on the facts they have, is that Rhonda got pregnant on a one-night stand and was too ashamed or scared to tell her family, and this situation led her to a state of depression and despair.

Sean Black is currently filming a BBC series in Manchester, but a statement released through his management said: 'Sean is deeply upset and shocked by the loss of his colleague, Rhonda. She was a very talented actress who he remembers fondly. On-set she was a delight to work with; always prepared and professional, but also funny and friendly when the cameras stopped. He was sure she would've had a long and distinguished career and is saddened that he didn't see the signs of her depression in time to help. His condolences go out to her family and friends.'

Rhonda left no suicide note, but when the police broke in they found the song *Long Night* by The Corrs on constant repeat on her stereo. The song was written by Sharon Corr about the loneliness felt after a break-up.

Belfast Echo, 22 May, 2004

Whatever Happened To...?

Q: I was totally enamoured of Shelly Marcus, the Northern Irish actress who played Sandra McGuigan in boxing biopic *Wee Barry*. I've been patiently waiting for her next film. Please tell me we're going to be seeing more from this talented lady soon.

Gerard Wiley, Portsmouth.

A: I'm afraid the majority of critics didn't see what you saw in Marcus's performance, Gerard. Her role in *Wee Barry* was almost universally panned, and this is probably the reason she found it hard to get further work on the big screen. In a rare interview with an Irish newspaper in January 2002 she blamed her poor performance on not getting along with co-star Sean Black, who she described as 'extremely arrogant' during the shoot. She couldn't give any more details because of a non-disclosure agreement she had signed.

Marcus played Sandy in a revival of *Grease* in her native Belfast the year after *Wee Barry*'s release, but reviews and audiences were apathetic, forcing her to eventually find work with Bank of Ireland as a loan manager. She married her long-time boyfriend Brendan McComb, *Fair City*'s bad-boy Lothario, in August 2002 and has since had a child, Declan, with him. Her agent's website no longer lists her as a client, so it looks like she's thrown in the towel on acting for the moment at least. Sorry, Gerard.

Imperial Magazine, September, 2004

Arrogance is thinking you're better than everyone else. Confidence is knowing you are.

Sean Black (actor), Quotables Vol. 7

THE TEN BEST TV SHOWS NO ONE IS WATCHING
#2. Savage.

We're only two episodes in, but this is shaping up to be the best British show of the year, so why aren't more of you watching it! The writing is clever and the performances are amazing. Sean Black and Sarah Alexander play a forensic pathologist and detective respectively, and the chemistry between the pair is undeniable as they bicker their way through the episodes like jealous siblings fighting for attention. This banter gives the show just the right balance of humour to even out the dark subject matter of the episodes. Everyone I've recommended this show to can't thank me enough, so trust me when I say, this is something special! We can only hope the ratings pick up over the next few weeks or this show may end up as another corpse in the BBC's single-series graveyard.

Tellyaddictz.com, 23 September, 2004

I'm here supporting my wife tonight. Her wonderful sitcom *Plus One* is nominated for Best New Comedy, but I'm also going to shamelessly promote my own show, *Savage*, starring the incredible Sean Black, because the BBC have been doing such a poor job of it. People keep saying to me, when's it on? I tell them it started two weeks ago, and they say they haven't seen any ads for it. What can I do but try to spread word of mouth when I can.

Barry Needham, creator & writer of Savage, Comedy Awards,
25 September, 2004

SHALLOW GRAVE FOUND IN ACTOR'S YARD

Police were called to rural premises outside Bangor on Saturday when *Wee Barry* actor Sean Black discovered human remains on a property recently bequeathed to him by his uncle.

Ronald 'Mad Ronnie' Black was a known underworld figure during The Troubles, and spent the last years of his life in Sycamore Acres mental health facility after a severe breakdown. Ronald died in March of this year, leaving the property to his nephew, but because of work commitments, Black only got a chance to visit the property this weekend.

Black and his wife Emily arrived at the property and saw a stray dog digging in the flowerbeds. When Black chased the dog away he saw the human remains and called the police.

Though no formal identification has been made, there are rumours that the remains may belong to Sean Black's mother, Madeline, who Black believed abandoned him when he was seven.

A spokesman for the police said they didn't want to comment on the circumstances of the victim's death at this point, but also added that it is very unlikely that a body would be buried in this manner if foul play wasn't involved.

Sean Black, who is currently playing a forensic pathologist in BBC1's *Savage*, is said to be very distressed by the findings and eager to find out if the remains are indeed his mother's, and if so, how she died.

Belfast Echo, 27 September, 2004

TV'S SAVAGE IN REAL-LIFE MURDER INVESTIGATION!

Actor's mother believed murdered by his uncle. See page 4 for full story.

Daily National News, 1 October, 2004

LIFE IMITATES ART FOR STAR OF BBC AMERICA'S 'SAVAGE'.

Sean Black, the Irish star of hit TV show Savage, is at the centre of his own forensic mystery after the remains of his murdered mother were discovered on a property on the outskirts of Bangor in Ireland. (Turn to centre pages for full story.)

Hollywood Plus, 1 October, 2004

DNA CONFIRMS BLACK'S UNCLE WAS ACTUALLY HIS FATHER!
After a judge agreed to exhume the remains of Ronald 'Mad Ronnie' Black, a DNA test was rushed through and has now confirmed that Sean Black is the biological child of Ronald Black and Madeline Black née Mullan.

Sean always believed Desmond Black was his father and Ronald was his uncle, but this macabre discovery suggests that Ronald and his mother carried on a long-term affair until her disappearance in 1981.

Sean Black nor his management were willing to comment on this revelation at the time of going to press.

Weekend Gossip, 3 October, 2004

I TOLD YOU SO!

Well it seems, thanks in no small part to my blog, the ratings for *Savage* have sky-rocketed. The show that I championed from the beginning is now catching on at a national and even international level, becoming the most talked about programme on TV.

The ratings for episode three: *The 7ᵗʰ Bullet*, were ten times what the first two episodes combined had, and episode four: *Allergen Zero* (the best episode yet, IMHO), received a staggering 8 million viewers. The BBC have a definite hit on their hands, and unless this series goes badly off the rails in the next two episodes, I think we can safely say a second series is guaranteed. You're welcome, Barry Needham.

Tellyaddictz.com, 7 October, 2004

@2scared: sean black is a violent self-hating gay. i used to be his lover but he ended things with me by almost killing me and telling me never to reveal his secret. none of the papers will believe me but this story is true!!!

LetsOutCelebs.com, 8 October, 2004

SAVAGE: SERIES FINALE REVIEW

The credits are still rolling as I start to type this, because I can't believe what I've just seen, and I can't wait to share it with you! I'll try to keep this review spoiler free for those of you who haven't seen it yet, but I'm still in a state of shock, so forgive me if I slip.

This has been one of the most unforgettable series in recent memory. Not only were the weekly episodes exceptionally well written, but there's a twist in the last episode that none of us saw coming.

Oh, fuck it! I can't go on without **SPOILERS** so if you don't want to know, don't read on.

The twist goes right back to episode one where the bad guy, the extremely menacing Maximilian Randall (Jay Walker), literally got away with murder and there was nothing Savage (Sean Black) could do about it... or was there? Throughout the series there have been strange little diversions where we saw Savage do something completely bizarre that seemed to have nothing to do with that episode. I put this down to whimsy on the writer's part, but something much cooler was going on. Savage wasn't going to let Randall get away with killing those girls, and has been plotting his revenge since episode two.

In tonight's finale, aptly titled *The Long Game* we found out that all those strange little asides for the last four weeks were part of Savage's plan to kill Randall and make it look like suicide. No doubt the cerebral forensic scientist could've killed him any number of ways with his vast knowledge of poisons, but he chose to play the long game and created the groundwork for a suicide scenario that no one could argue with. It was sheer genius, and he would've got away with it too, if Gina (Sarah Alexander) hadn't followed him and walked in just as Randall took his final breath. The look on Gina's face sent chills up my spine... and then it ended!!!

I am dying to see where this goes in series two. I don't believe we have ever had a character like this on TV before. He's a pacifist vegan who never carries a gun and only ever defends himself when it comes to fisticuffs, but he's also a brutal killer when his logic dictates that it's the only way justice will be served.

Come back soon Savage and Gina. Tuesday nights just won't be the same without you. I'll be counting the hours until you return.

Tellyaddictz.com, 19 October, 2004

Sean doesn't like doing interviews. He does the absolute minimum that the publicity department will let him get away with. I think he likes being a bit of an enigma. But when we're filming he's totally there, twenty-four/ seven, he *is* Savage. Savage's problems are his problems. Savage's goals are his goals, and he attacks them with incredible tenacity. I just hope they never cast him as a Bond villain!

Sarah Alexander, Friday Night with Jonathan Ross,
12 November, 2004

The less people know about the real me, the more likely they are to believe what I show them.

Sean Black, Parkinson, 4 December, 2004

BBC Drama Dept. confirms *Savage* will return. Series two to air in September 2005.

Radio Times, 12 December, 2004

Sean Black has signed up to play a scheming London banker along with Ewan McGregor and Emily Blunt in *The Crash*. Black will shoot his scenes after filming is complete on the much-anticipated second series of *Savage*.

Imperial Magazine, May, 2005

DESMOND BLACK ARRESTED

The estranged father of Sean Black, who the *Savage* star recently found out *isn't* actually his father, was arrested late last night after showing up at the gates of the exclusive apartment block where Sean Black and his wife Emily live.

There had been an altercation between the pair when Desmond showed up begging for money earlier that day. Black Sr. returned later that night in an intoxicated state and started breaking windows by throwing rocks.

Manchester police arrived promptly and Desmond Black assaulted them both physically and verbally. He was arrested for public intoxication, drunk & disorderly behaviour, damage to private property, and assaulting a police officer.

Sean Black's management issued a statement saying: Sean and his wife have been made to feel very welcome in Manchester, and they hope to live in this great city for as long as Savage continues. He deeply regrets what happened and trusts the police and the legal system to deal with it as they see fit.

Manchester Bugle, 14 June, 2005

I have got some other interesting pet-projects on the back-burner, but it's hard to get experimental stuff like *Manhattan Wasted* financed. I know a drama about heroin addiction isn't going to pull in the audiences that *Star Wars* or *Harry Potter* do, but these little movies only cost a fraction of what those blockbusters do, so they don't have to earn hundreds of millions of dollars to make a profit. These issues are important, and I think those holding the purse-strings have a social responsibility to help get films like this made. But as far as I can see, every producer in the world wants to be second in line to back an original idea.

Sean Black, Up Close, 22 November, 2005

STORK VISITS SAVAGE

Savage star Sean Black's wife Emily has given birth to their first child; a girl they're naming Madeline. She was born in St. Mary's Hospital in Manchester late on Saturday night (26th) weighing in at 7lbs 2oz. Both mother and baby are doing fine. Sean is said to be over the moon at the birth of his daughter.

Manchester Bugle, 28 November, 2005

SAVAGE S3 ANNOUNCED, BUT CAN IT POSSIBLY TOP SERIES TWO?
(click here for full article)

Tellyaddictz.com, 2 December, 2005

SAVAGE SWEEPS THE BOARD AT NATIONAL TELEVISION AWARDS

Hit TV show takes home 9 statues, including Best Actor, Best Actress and Best Writer.

Wotz on the Box? Magazine, 25 January, 2006

Sean Black is currently in LA filming *The Forgotten Place* with *Buffy* star Sarah Michelle Gellar. Black plays a psychologist specialising in dream therapy who is trying to cure his patient (Gellar) of her night terrors, but all his PhDs can't prepare him for the disturbing truth that lurks in *The Forgotten Place*.

Bump in the Night Magazine, 20 February, 2006

NO SERIES 4 OF SAVAGE!

The BBC website today announced that their hit show *Savage* will NOT return for a fourth series, instead moving to a feature-length format and giving us a single Christmas special every year.

The producers say the writer and stars agreed it was time to slow down and explore other projects, but they still want to keep the characters and the show alive, and assure us the Christmas specials will be worth waiting for.

Personally, I doubt the BBC wanted to put this cash-cow out to pasture. *Savage* has proved a massive hit both here and in the US, where an American remake is already in the works. I suspect this downshift has more to do with the lucrative movie offers Sean Black is being bombarded with. You can hardly blame the guy for wanting some ridiculous American paycheques in his account.

I wish him all the best... as long as he promises to keep doing *Savage*.

Tellytaddictz.com, 9 December, 2006

Rumour has it that Sean Black has been cast in Martin Scorsese's upcoming crime thriller *New York Minute*. The project is scheduled to shoot in the city that never sleeps this autumn. It's thought the Northern Irish actor will play a NYPD beat cop who discovers an assassination plot when he pulls over a car, and has only hours to prevent it. Scorsese is said to be still working on the script with screenwriter William Goldman so any or all of that may change, but the release date is set in stone for July 2008, so mark your calendars now.

Scorsese and Black working together sounds like a dream pairing to us. Just take our money now.

Imperial Magazine, 3 March, 2008

2008

01.

The faces change but the streets remain the same.

Avi walked the pavements of New York without ever having to consult a street sign. It had been a long time since he had been home, but New York is somewhere you don't forget. The clothing stores were selling hoodies instead of Members Only jackets now, and over-sized sunglasses instead of Ray-Bans. The music stores had actually gone backwards; CDs had just come out when he left New York in 1983 and the music stores were phasing out their vinyl, now CDs were gone and vinyl stores were back.

Something else was different as well. When he'd walked these streets as a young man he was full of swagger and bravado, but now he was nervous and looking over his shoulder. Even back in Belfast he couldn't relax. Ever since that thing with Frankie Lightfoot, he'd been waiting for the day when someone else from his past would cross his path. And next time it might be someone he couldn't silence so easily.

It was time for that fear to end.

He walked into a Dollar Store and bought an ice-pick, and then found the nearest Internet Café. He gave a kid twenty bucks and a name. Less than a minute later, the kid gave him an address. Avi took a cab.

It was a quiet, residential street. Not what he expected. He got the cab to drop him off a block away so he could scope the place out from a distance. Trees lined the street. Kids rode bikes and screamed in delight as they chased each other. The house looked like every other one on the block; well kept, big garden. Just another anonymous house. Tony was laying low in his old age, but Avi knew he was probably still pulling the strings for the organisation. Some jobs you never retire from.

He watched the house for a long time and saw no activity. He took the ice-pick out of its plastic wrapping and kept hold of its handle as he stuffed it in his pocket. If Tony could get to his gun before Avi could get close enough, he didn't stand a chance. But guns were loud and messy. This had to be quiet and discreet if he was to get away. He couldn't sprint like he used to.

He popped a pill in his mouth to slow his heart down and then crossed the street. There was a very good chance this was a terrible idea. He'd spent the last twenty-four years avoiding these lions and now he was voluntarily walking into their den.

He opened the gate and walked up the path to the front door. He was about to knock when he heard music. He followed it around the side of the house to the back yard.

There he was. He was sitting on a lawn chair next to a little table with a radio on top. An oldies station was playing. Sinatra was telling us if he could make it there, he could make it anywhere. Tony looked much older than his years, but Avi would know that face no matter how much time tried to disguise it.

His hand was sweaty on the handle of the ice-pick. He pulled it out and wiped it on his coat. When he stuck it back into his pocket, the force poked the ice-pick through the bottom of his pocket. He gripped the plastic handle again, tightly. He swallowed hard and started towards the old man.

There was no one else in the garden. Avi manoeuvred himself behind the man in the chair. He looked back at the house and saw no other signs of life. He moved towards him. He focussed on the centre of the wrinkled neck ahead. Just a quick thrust upwards into the skull cavity and it would all be over in a matter of seconds. As Frank reached his climactic note and the song reached its crescendo, Avi lined up the ice-pick. He was right behind him now.

And then he saw something that stopped him.

The old man had a wet patch on the crotch of his pants. Avi lowered the ice-pick and walked round to face him. He knelt down. Tony saw him and blinked a few times as his eyes adjusted. He opened his mouth and smiled. He didn't have any teeth left and wasn't wearing dentures. He reached forward to hug Avi. Avi obliged and hugged him back.

'You remember me, Tony? You know who I am?'

The old man just kept the same open-mouthed smile on his face. Occasionally he smacked his mouth closed to moisten his lips, but he didn't speak, and his eyes showed no sign of recognition.

'Dad, are you ready to come...?' The woman in the summer dress saw Avi and looked suspicious. 'Can I help you?'

Avi stood up, smiled and extended his hand to her. 'Jerry Greene. I knew Tony a long time ago, back in the old neighbourhood. I heard he was living out here and since I was passing... I'm sorry. I hope you don't mind. I was going to ring the doorbell and then I heard Sinatra and I figured that's where Tony would be.'

Still a little suspicious, but trying her best to be friendly, she shook his hand. 'Well, I'm sure dad appreciates it. Don't you, dad? Wasn't that nice of Mister Greene to visit you. Oh, dad, look at you! We're going to have to change those pants again before dinner.'

'Is he...?' Avi left it hanging, not knowing how to phrase it so as not to offend.

'Always like this? Yes, I'm afraid so. He had a stroke a couple of years back and hasn't said much since.' She turned and looked at Avi closer. 'I don't remember you from the old days, Mister Greene.'

'Sure you do. My dad ran the deli where your dad used to get a bear claw every morning.'

Her eyes widened and she smiled. 'Oh my god, yes! Jeremiah!' She hugged him and then looked at his face closer. 'Of course it's you. I see it now. My god, how long has it been?'

'Longer than I care to count. And you're little Marie, I bet.'

'Yes, sorry. I didn't even... Yes, I'm Marie.'

'Last time I saw you, you were terrorising the kids on the street with that little purple bike of yours.' She laughed. 'You were dangerous on that thing.'

'Well, you'll stay for supper, right. My husband will be home soon.'

'No, I got a plane to catch. I live in Canada now.'

'Aw, that's a shame. Gregg would've loved to meet you.' She lowered her voice. 'Between you and me, he's a little bit *too* interested in the things dad used to get up to in the old days for my liking. I think he wants to write a book... or a screenplay, one day.'

'What does your husband do?'

Odds on she says 'construction.' If she ain't carrying on the family business, you can bet her old man is.

'He's the manager of the biggest branch of Staples in the area.'

'That's great. Listen, I better get going. I only stopped in for a quick hello. Next time I'm back in town I'll take you up on that meal. If you can cook meatballs half as well as your mom used to, it'll be worth it.' She smiled, proudly. Avi knelt down to the old man again. 'I'll see you, Tony.' He was answered with the same open-mouthed, toothless smile. Avi hugged the old man, and while he was close to his ear, he whispered, 'I'm sorry for everything.' He kissed the old man's cheek and got up. He gave Marie another hug and walked away.

As he walked down the suburban street towards town he felt lighter and freer than he had in years. He could finally close the book on that part of his life. The old man was knocking on heaven's door, his daughter was taking care of him, and his son-in-law was selling paper clips for a living. There was probably still a few of the old gang kicking around who might hold a grudge, but old was the key word. They'd all be drawing social security by now and probably more concerned with living out their remaining days quietly. He doubted they had the time, money or inclination to chase an old rat who disappeared almost thirty years ago. Avi figured if he didn't look for them, they wouldn't find him.

Jerry Greene actually did live in the old neighbourhood and did move to Canada many years ago when he fell in love with a girl from Ontario. Back in their reckless teenage days Avi (or Murray as he was then) and Jerry looked so similar that Avi had sometimes used him as his alibi. He would loan him some of his clothes and his car and get him to drive around somewhere lots of people could ID him, far from the crime he was actually committing, and the cops couldn't touch him. The NYPD had to let him go at least half a dozen times when Jerry alibied him. They knew he was guilty, but they could never figure out how he could be in two places at once. Now Jerry's identity had saved him again. Even though Tony's family were out of the old business, he suspected the name Murray Weiss was known by all members, young and old, by blood and marriage. You don't forget the name of the guy who sent your dad to prison for twenty years. They probably had a bonfire every year and burned his effigy.

Avi looked in the vague direction of Canada and sent a prayer of thanks to Jerry Greene, wherever he was.

He dropped the ice-pick in the next trash can he passed.

02.

When Avi picked up his room key-card from reception he was handed a message with it. Sean wants to see you as soon as you get back. Avi walked to the elevator and was ushered inside by the man in uniform who also relieved him of the inconvenience of pressing his floor button. This was five-star living. Avi was glad the studio was footing the bill.

The elevator operator delivered Avi to the fourteenth floor with no diversions or complications. Job well done. The old man wanted to get inside and have a stiff drink, but he knocked on the room adjacent to his instead. The door wasn't answered and he re-knocked. Still nothing. He was about to leave when Sean answered the door wearing a towel.

'Oh, it's you, Avi. Come on in.'

Avi walked in and Sean closed the door behind him. 'You've got that accent down. You sound like you were raised in The Bronx.'

Sean was heading back to the bathroom. 'Help yourself to a drink while I get dressed.' He disappeared inside and closed the door.

Avi walked past the room-service trolley and saw the remains of a steak and enough crumbs to identify Pecan Pie on the plate next to it. He opened the minibar and helped himself to a large scotch. He wandered around the suite. It was at least three times the size of his apartment back in Belfast. He found a set of four hand-carved chairs sitting around an equally impressive table and sat down in one, letting him look out over the city. He never tired of that skyline and those millions of lights.

Sean came out wearing jeans and a Knicks shirt. 'You enjoying being home?'

'More than I thought I would. In fact, I was just thinking I wouldn't go back with you in the morning. I thought I'd hang around for a few days and get the new draft of the script. Maybe take in a ball game or something while I'm here.'

'Sure, whatever works for you.'

'So, why'd you want to see me, kid?'

Sean sat down opposite Avi and leaned forward, resting his damp arms on the table. The old man turned his attention from the New York lights to his client. 'The last time we were here you were able to get me some heroin.'

'Yeah. I was against it, but I did.'

'You were scared I wouldn't be able to kick it if I tried it, but I did. I only needed to do it once to know what it felt like.'

'But now you want more, right?'

'No, not at all. This cop I'm playing doesn't use drugs. Why would I need them? No, I...' Sean turned away from the old man's eyes. 'I need you to get me a gun.' He flicked his eyes up for Avi's reaction.

He considered his response and then said, 'What for?'

'This guy's a cop. I need to know how to use a gun.'

'I can take you to the range downtown. They'll give you a gun and you can shoot 'til your heart's content.'

'No, that's not going to work. I need to know what it feels like to carry it. I want to go out walking with it, tonight, before I leave. I need to feel that power, that anticipation. How it feels to know that if someone tried to hurt me or rob me, I have a gun and I'd have the option to defend myself.'

'Kid, guns aren't that hard to come by in this country. You don't need me for this.' Avi started to get up.

Sean jumped up and stopped him. 'I do. I'm not a US citizen, so I can't buy one legally, and I can't afford the waiting time even if I could. So I need one by other means. If you could get me H, I'm sure you can get me a gun.'

Avi stared into the eyes of his client, looking for ulterior motives. 'Yeah, I can. But I don't suggest you go out walking in this city at night. At least let me tell you the areas to steer clear of.'

'Fine. Fine. Whatever. Look, I'm not looking to get into anything, Avi.' He gave a little laugh. 'I just want to know what it feels like to walk around carrying a gun.'

'OK. Two conditions.'

'Name them.'

'You stay away from the areas I tell you, and you throw the gun in the Hudson when you're done. And you let me know when you get back, so I know you're safe.'

'That's three conditions.'

'I should be giving you three hundred conditions for this sort of stupid fuckin' idea. Do we have a deal?'

'We do.' Sean extended his hand and Avi shook it.

'OK, I won't be long. Wait here.' Avi walked out of the room.

Half an hour later, the very talented elevator man was ferrying him to the fourteenth floor again. This time Avi had a snub nose .38 in his pocket.

The gun had been a lot easier to procure than the heroin three years ago. He'd had to go down some shady alleys and meet some even more shady people just to get one hit of heroin, but the gun just required a visit to the nearest pawn shop. Avi got out of the elevator and paused. The doors closed and the elevator man went off to lend his expertise elsewhere.

Avi reached into his pocket and was about to pull out the gun when he looked around the ceiling and saw cameras watching his every move. He hurried to his own room and went inside. He didn't even turn the lights on. He just released the barrel on the .38 and emptied the bullets into his hand. He dropped the bullets into his pants pocket with his loose change, and then closed the barrel and left to go next door.

Avi wrote a list of places to avoid on hotel paper while Sean examined the gun gleefully. It only took him seconds to work out how to open the barrel. 'Where's the bullets?'

Avi didn't look up from his list. 'You don't need bullets. It's just to carry around, right?'

'Well, yeah, but I have to know it's there if I need it. That's how cops feel. Without bullets I might as well be carrying around a fuckin' squirt gun. Why the fuck didn't you get bullets for it, Avi?' Sean's voice had got steadily louder. He exhaled now as Avi set down the pen and stood up straight. 'Where can I buy bullets? I don't need to be a US citizen to buy bullets. They sell them in every fuckin' Walmart, don't they?'

Avi studied the agitated young man before him. Sean stared back at him, as solemn and serious as he'd ever looked. Avi reached into his pocket and dropped the bullets on the fancy table. 'The conditions still apply.'

Sean's eyes danced at the sight of the bullets.

'Hey!' Avi snapped his fingers and Sean looked away from the six little life-takers on the table. 'The conditions still apply.' Avi poked his finger down hard on the hotel paper. 'You stay away from these places. You throw the gun in the river when you're done, and you tell me when you get back, capiche?'

Sean nodded.

'I'll talk to you later, then.' Avi left and went to his room. He poured himself a very large drink and put on some music. He didn't want to hear Sean leaving, but even Gershwin's melodies couldn't distract him tonight. He paced the suite with a bottomless drink in his hand.

He sent a text message containing a single **?** to Aileen. This was their signal. He was asking if it was safe to call her. That way, if it wasn't and her husband saw the message, they could put it down to a mistake or a butt-text. He was surprised when she called him back immediately.

'Hey, I didn't think you'd be up. What time is it there?'

'It's almost two a.m. The text beep woke me.'

'Sorry.'

'It's OK. I always sleep light when Harry's not here. Are you all right? How's New York?'

'Yeah, it's fine. Sean's just out doing something stupid and I can't settle.'

He explained what had happened and then told her how New York had changed in the quarter century-plus since he'd been here. When he'd visited a couple of years back for *Manhattan Wasted,* he'd stayed in the hotel when he wasn't in various offices taking meetings, but this time he felt safe visiting old haunts and even doing some of the cheesy touristy stuff. They were winding down the phone call when Avi asked: 'Anything happening at the office that can't wait a few more days?'

'No, I can handle it. Oh, the contracts came in today for *Diamond Geezer.'*

'*Diamond Geezer?* We turned that down,' Avi said.

'That's what I thought, so I called them up and they said Sean came back to them afterwards and said he'd do it.' Three thousand miles of silence connected them for a few seconds. 'Avi, are you still there?'

'Yeah, I'm here.'

'What do you want me to do about it?'

'I don't know. I'll call you tomorrow at the office after I've spoken to Sean. Love you.'

'Love you too.'

Avi hung up and refreshed his drink. *Diamond Geezer.* What the fuck was Sean thinking? They had laughed at this script when it had come in originally. It was one of those British movies that thought it was being really gritty and edgy by using F-words and C-words thirty times per page. The cockney rhyming-slang was probably there to make it seem authentic, but it was so badly over-used it was just laughable. Avi had watched a couple of the director's short films online and saw nothing redeeming about his style or approach. This feature script was the story of a low-level tea-leaf (thief) who uses the proceeds of a robbery to set himself up as a jeweller and go straight, but then his sister gets hooked on smack and O.D.'s, so the brother reverts to his old sadistic ways and goes all Charles Bronson on every drug dealer he can find. It was tacky, exploitative crap. Avi walked to the window and looked out over the city. There were a lot of drug dealers in New York.

03.

A couple of hours later Avi's door was knocked and he hurried to answer it.

Sean stood there, looking at his feet. 'I'm back. The gun's in the river. I'll see you at breakfast.'

'Wait a second!' Avi grabbed him by the arm and pulled. 'Get in here.' He closed the door. 'Where've you been? What've you done?'

Still looking at the ground, Sean answered, 'Nothing.'

Avi grabbed him by the shirt and pulled him close. 'Don't give me that shit. I want to know!'

Sean looked up and Avi saw the coldness in his eyes. 'Do you?' Sean slapped the old man's hands off his shirt. 'You *don't* want to know, Avi. You've *never* wanted to know, so don't pretend you care now.'

Avi walked away and looked out the window over the city.

Sean looked at the little man, dwarfed by the city outside. 'I can tell you've had a skin-full, so why don't we just forget this happened, OK?'

When Avi spoke now his voice was low and controlled. 'You agreed to do *Diamond Geezer*?'

Sean exhaled. 'Yeah, I did. So what?'

Avi turned to him with a furrowed brow. 'Why? It's a piece of shit.'

Sean stepped forward, angry again. 'You left a six-week gap in my schedule. What was I supposed to do? I need to work. You're supposed to keep me working. That's your job.'

'I figured you'd want to spend some time with the baby. You've hardly had a minute since she was born. And I know Emily wants to move back to Northern Ireland and you need a break, so I just thought...'

'When I want a break, I'll tell you I want a fucking break, OK?' He stepped closer. 'You don't make those decisions, *I* make those decisions. Your job is to keep me working and you work for *me*, understand?'

Avi nodded gently. 'Yeah, I understand.'

Sean turned and marched toward the door. He opened it and then stopped. He took a deep breath and didn't turn around when he said, 'What we've been doing is working, Avi. Let's not fuck that up.

Let's just keep going the same way we have been. You do your thing, I'll do mine, and we both get rich. OK?'

'Sure, kid.'

Sean walked out and closed the door after him. Avi sat down in a soft chair and took out his pills. He slipped one under his tongue and sat in silence for over an hour.

They missed each other at breakfast. Avi had troubled sleep when he finally did go to bed, and slept late the next day. He ordered breakfast in his room (got to love that studio tab), so by the time he was polishing off his Eggs Benedict, Sean was already on his way across the Atlantic.

He called Aileen later that day and told her to go ahead with the paperwork for *Diamond Geezer* and that was the last time he thought about business for the next three days.

He went to Yankee Stadium and watched them trounce Cleveland 10-3. He saw *Wicked* on Broadway. He visited museums, comedy clubs and even went to hear Woody Allen playing clarinet with the Eddy Davis New Orleans Jazz Band at the Café Carlyle. He ate in a different restaurant for every meal, and savoured every second of The Big Apple.

The day before he was due to leave, he went back to the hotel to change before heading out to see *The Producers*. Another perk of being here on the studio's dime was they wanted to impress you, so they could get tickets to shows that had been sold out for years with only a few hours' notice, and Avi was taking full advantage of their generosity. He got his key-card from reception and they reached him a fat A4 envelope with it.

Avi weighed it up in his hands. It could wait. It would give him something to read on the plane home tomorrow. There was a time when a huge project like this would take all his attention and everything else would be secondary, but after his little spat with Sean, he no longer felt like sacrificing his personal time for his client's career. He was going to see Mel Brooks's stage show, and nothing was taking precedence over that.

Avi Goldman was the only person on the plane that afternoon who was smiling.

They had been sitting on the runway for forty-five minutes waiting for the torrential rain and gale force winds to stop shaking the plane. The captain had just come over the intercom and told the passengers he thought they'd have a window in twenty minutes' time and they'd try to take off then. Avi heard a collective groan from behind him. Back in coach. Here in First-Class there was nothing to make you groan except the exquisite pastries and champagne. He was warm, had plenty of leg room, and all the food and drink he could ask for brought to him by beautiful women. The plane could sit here all day with the studio's meter running for all he cared.

He slid the fat A4 envelope out of his briefcase. He had planned on waiting until they were in the air to begin reading, but since they were going nowhere for at least twenty minutes, he decided to make a start. There was a note paper-clipped to the cover.

Latest draft. We've emailed a copy to Sean. Any suggestions, let us know. M.

Avi opened to the first page and began.

The blonde stewardess quickly hurried around making sure everyone had their seatbelts on. She saw Avi pull out his mobile phone. 'I'm sorry, sir. You can't use your phone.'

'I'll just be a minute. It's important.'

'I'm sorry, sir, but I can't let you make a call. It's dangerous. We're preparing for take-off.'

'Just fucking chill, honey. I'll be done before we start moving.'

The stewardess reached over and snatched the phone from his hand. 'I'm sorry, sir, but it's against our regulations *and* the law. I can't let you...'

Avi lurched for the phone and she stepped back. 'Give me that fucking phone. This is an emergency.'

'I'm sorry, sir, but...' Avi undid his safety belt and got up. She took a few steps back. 'Sir, I'm going to have to ask you to get back in your seat!' Avi grabbed the phone but the stewardess wouldn't let go. She started shouting, 'Sheila! Tim! I need some assistance.' Avi got a good hold on the phone and pushed her to the ground. He hurried to the First-Class toilet. The stewardess had put herself in a defensive posture on the floor, but now she realised she wasn't being attacked she started to get up. Avi pushed the folding door to one side and ducked inside. By the time the stewardess got back on her feet he had already closed and locked it behind him. She banged on the outside. 'Open this door now, sir, or you *will* be arrested.'

A clean-cut man in a steward's uniform arrived at the door next to her. She turned to him. 'He wouldn't turn off his phone. Now he's locked himself in the bathroom.' The brunette stewardess arrived. 'Sheila, go get the Air Marshal – quietly.' The brunette ran off. 'You watch the door and keep trying to get him out.' The young man nodded. 'I'll inform the captain.' The stewardess ran to the nearest internal phone.

Avi wiped the sweat off his brow with his sleeve. He was waving his phone around the corners of the bathroom trying to get a signal. He got one bar and dialled Sean's home. CALL FAILED. He held the phone high and low and it connected again. He redialled. This time it started to ring. And ring. And ring.

'Come on!'

The phone continued to ring.

The marshal arrived and used his master key to unlock the door. Avi sat down on the toilet, braced his back against the wall and put his feet against the door. They pushed, trying to unfold the concertina door, but it bounced back on them. The men charged at the door with their elbows. The old man's legs were taking the hits like rusty springs.

The phone kept ringing.

And then was picked up. 'Hello?'

'Hello? Hello! Sean, can you hear me?' Avi screamed. He couldn't hold the door much longer. 'Sean!'

04.

Sean was watching the movie *Fracture* on DVD. Anthony Hopkins and Ryan Gosling were both giving compelling performances, but he was pretty sure he'd figured out how it was done already, so he was watching the clock more than the movie. They had lived in this furnished apartment for three years now, but it still didn't feel like home. It was decorated to someone else's taste and they were surrounded by furnishings that weren't their own. Like that old-fashioned clock on the wall. Its pendulum swung back and forth, hypnotic in its rhythm. The minute-hand crept towards the twelve camouflaged by time and tension. He wiped his brow with the back of his hand. The label on the bottle said twenty to thirty minutes, so he would give it the full half hour to be safe.

The minute-hand finally made it to the top. He paused the film and got up. It was time. He walked to the master bedroom. Emily was lying on top of the covers with one boot pulled off and her jeans halfway down her legs. He removed the other boot and then pulled the jeans the rest of the way off. She groaned a few times but didn't wake. She wasn't going to wake.

He took off her sweater, T-shirt and bra, and then pulled on her nightshirt and got her under the covers. He lifted the glass from the bedside table and ran a finger around the inner rim. The powdery residue was a dead giveaway. He took it to the en suite bathroom and rinsed it out thoroughly. He dried the glass and refilled a small amount of water. He brought it back out and left it next to her on the bedside cabinet.

He lifted her clothes and put them in the en suite hamper, just like *she* did every night. He walked to the bedroom door and looked back at the room. Nothing was out of place. Everything was just as it always was. Just another Friday night. He turned out the light and left the door half-open. Just like always.

He walked to the hall cupboard and opened the door. He reached up and around to the ledge above the door lintel. He felt the cold steel with his fingertips and gently lifted the weapon down.

The weight of it surprised him. He hadn't felt it since he put it up there. This wasn't a prop gun full of blanks or a rubber gun used in wide shots, this was the real thing. A Smith & Wesson .38 Special. He held it up and looked at it. The nickel finish reflected his face around the gun's curves like a fun-house mirror. He released the cylinder and checked all six bullets were still there, and then closed it again.

It had been a lot easier to get a gun in New York. He could probably even have got one back in Belfast without much trouble, but in Manchester he'd had to visit all the worst areas of the town and drink with all the nastiest people (wearing a wig, coloured contacts and a false nose so his fame wouldn't betray him). Eventually he bought enough drinks to the right guy to get directions to another guy who would be able to sell him what he needed.

And now he held it in his hands.

He pulled back the hammer. This was much easier to do on prop guns. Instead of cocking it with one thumb like he had seen so many of his heroes do, he had to pull it back with his thumb and forefinger until it clicked. He cautiously removed his finger from the hammer,

217

and once he was sure it had locked in place, he lowered the gun to his side and walked down the hall.

He entered the nursery and saw the baby was awake and sitting up in its cot. It looked up at him and smiled. He smiled back at it, and then stepped forward and lowered the gun into the cot and set it down between the baby's legs. He stood up and the baby's gaze followed him. They just stared at each other for a few seconds, and then the baby glanced down. It tentatively put its hand forward, and then looked up again, wondering if it was going to be reprimanded. When it wasn't, it took hold of the cold steel with both hands and tried to lift it.

His heart rate started to race. It was so heavy the toddler could barely move it. It fumbled with it and got the barrel pointing upwards under its chin. It leaned down and bit the end of the barrel and his heart jumped, expecting the inevitable. The baby continued to bite the end of the barrel. Drool ran down the frame, eventually causing the gun to slip from the child's grasp and fall. Again, his heart jolted. The baby looked up at him. It had the same look on its face as it did when it crawled towards the living room wall with a crayon in its hand. The baby flopped forwards and grabbed at the gun. Its small fingers touched the trigger and he jerked backwards anticipating the blast. He put his back against the wall. Sweat was rolling from his forehead into his eyes. His breaths were fast and shallow. He tried to take deeper breaths to calm his pounding heart.

The baby pulled the gun towards itself by the trigger guard and his heart jumped again. Its slippery hands slid over the gun's surface trying to get purchase. Three fingers curled inside the trigger guard and the baby tightened its grip.

The phone in the other room started ringing.

The baby froze and looked up at the noise.

He ran to the door and looked down the hall. Through the partially open door he could see her stir slightly in the bed. The phone was screaming for attention next to her.

Even with what he'd given her, the irritation might be sufficient to wake her, at least temporarily. He looked down at the baby again. It looked back at him as if wondering why he wasn't doing something about the ringing phone. Its hands were still on the gun but not moving. Could he risk ducking out and grabbing the phone? He didn't want to miss it when it happened.

The phone kept ringing.

He looked back at the master bedroom again. Emily seemed to be turning in her sleep more now. She was going to wake.

He bolted down the hall and into the guest bedroom. He snapped the cordless phone from its cradle. It continued to ring as he ran back to the nursery. He looked over his shoulder into the master bedroom and saw her rubbing her eyes, but still lying down.

He ran back into the nursery and pressed the answer button. He raised the phone to his ear and said, 'Hello,' just as the baby's fist tightened on the trigger.

'Hello? Hello! Sean, can you hear me?' Avi screamed. 'Sean! They changed the script. Do you hear me? They changed it! The cop doesn't have a kid who died in a gun accident anymore. It… it… it's been done too many times before. It's a cliché. They've changed it, Sean. Do you hear me? They've changed it. The cop doesn't have a dead kid anymore, Sean. Do you hear me? Sean!'

'Yes, I understand. Thank you, Avi.' He hung up. The baby had frozen, seemingly fascinated by seeing her father talk on the phone. Sean leaned down and took the gun from her reluctant grip. She looked confused, but didn't cry. He put the gun back in its hiding place, and then went back to watching the movie.

'OK! OK! Stop!' Avi shouted through the aeroplane bathroom door. His heart was racing. 'I'm coming out. Just give me a second.' Avi quickly texted Scorsese's people: *Sean loves the script. So do I. Maybe cop with dead kid is a cliché, though? Up to you.*

He sent the text and it actually went first time. Cliché. That one word was enough to send most writers into a tailspin, so he hoped it worked. He also hoped he'd got through to Sean in time. He'd call Emily from one of the air-phones when they took off to make sure. His heart was still pumping like a Gatling gun. He reached for his pillbox and found his left arm was tingling. 'Oh no,' he said quietly. He started to rub the arm with his right hand. Panicking now. The pins and needles persisted. Got stronger. He couldn't restore feeling to it. He reached for his pills and flipped the lid open. Pain hit his chest like he'd stood in front of a speeding truck with his arms open. His whole body jerked in pain. The pills spilled over the floor. The sweat was running down his forehead, stinging his eyes. He could hear his heart pounding inside his chest.

'Help me,' he whispered at the gap in the door.

'I'm sorry? Sir, did you say you need help?'

The pain kicked him in the chest again. Avi fell forward against the door and slid to the ground.

'He's down. We need this door open now!'

'Call an ambulance.'

'Tell the captain to abort take-off.'

'He's blocking the door. I can't get it open.... Get help.... Jesus, we're losing him... What do we do? Get help for Christ sakes! What's he saying? Who's Aileen? Check the passenger manifest for anyone called Aileen. Help's coming... You hang on, OK? Do you hear me? Hang on. There's no Aileen on the flight. Is he still alive? I don't think he's breathing... Can you feel a pulse? *Attention all passengers. If there is a doctor on the flight could they please make themselves known to.........*

'DIAMOND GEEZER' – SHOOTING SCRIPT (FINAL#3). APR07

02. INT. DOG FIGHTING PIT. NIGHT .02

There's forty or fifty punters inside a big shed making bets on the two dogs in the pit that are ripping the shit out of each other.

Enter Danny 'SPOCK' Manson. He got his nickname at school because of his big fucking ears and it stuck. He walks around like he owns the fucking place. He's a lairy little cunt in his mid-twenties who would sell his own grandmother's arse if he thought there was a profit to be had.

He approaches TEL, a 40ish fat fucker with thick glasses, who's running the fight.

> SPOCK
> Wotcha, Tel, you speccy cunt.

> TEL
> Spock, you toe-rag shit-stain.
> What the fuck you doing
> 'round this manor?

> SPOCK
> I'm planning a little job.
> Could be very tasty. I need the
> right crew. No fuckin' muppets.

> TEL
> You cleared it with Big Mike?

220

                    SPOCK
Fuck Big Mike. He's past it.
Time for a new guv'nor on this
patch.

                    TEL
And that's you, is it? Listen,
Big Mike might be getting on,
but he's still connected, and he
eats little cunts like you for
breakfast. So if you take my
advice you'll go see the man,
kiss his fuckin' arsehole, lick
it clean if you have to, and
offer him a piece of the action
before you do anything.

                    SPOCK
When did you become such a scared
cunt, Tel, you fuckin' numpty?

                    TEL
Listen to me, fuckstick, we all
heard about your little score. The
snatch and grab at Hatton Garden.
You're doing all right, making a
name for yourself around the manor,
but there's no way Big Mike's going
to let a little upstart cunt like you
operate without oversight. Bigger
cunts than you have tried and failed.
So fuckin' forget it, you cunt.

05.

The door of the trailer was knocked and Sean threw his script aside.

'What the fuck you want?' he shouted at the door.

Timidly, the door opened and the First A.D. poked her head inside. She smiled and clutched her clipboard to her chest like a shield. Her name was Tasha. She had dark skin and big brown eyes that would make your average man melt. Sean thought she was a fucking stunner. He wondered what the fuck she was doing on the wrong side of the camera and very much hoped to get nuts-deep in her Jack n' Danny before the shoot was over.

'Hi, Sean. Sorry. I know this is a horrible thing to ask, but would you mind changing trailer?' She smiled crookedly.

'Do fuckin' what?'

'I know it's a crap thing to ask when you're already settled, but...' Her eyes twinkled and her smile widened. '...*he's* here.'

'Who's fuckin' here?'

'Vinnie. Vinnie Jones. He's here. He's actually on the set right now.' She looked over her shoulder. 'We offered him the most expensive trailer, but it turns out he actually prefers this kind, so...' She smiled and raised her shoulders.

'You're having a fuckin' laugh, intcha?'

Her smile dropped. 'No.' She pulled the door closed behind her so the star couldn't hear. 'I think the producers and director, they all just want to keep him happy because... it's Vinnie Jones!' she finished through gritted teeth.

Sean got up and walked towards her. 'You tell the producers, and the director, *and* Vinnie fuckin' Jones, if they want me out of this trailer, they can come in here and try to fuckin' drag me out! You tell them *that*, you fuckin' slag! Now fuck off!'

The smile wilted, and those beautiful brown eyes filled with tears. She hurried out.

The door was still flapping against the trailer when he grabbed it and put his head inside. 'Sean, babe, hi! I don't know if you remember me, it's Paddy Hancock.'

'Oh, for fuck's sake!'

He held up his hands. 'First can I just say: congratulations on *Savage*. Big fan.'

Sean rubbed his face with his palms. 'Paddy, now is *not* a good time.'

'Listen, I know you've turned me down in the past, but my profile's really risen since last we spoke. I've got three, count them, *three*, of my actors working on this film and one of them has lines as well, so just hear me out.' He started to climb inside.

Sean held up a hand to him. 'No. I'm sorry, Paddy, but the answer's still no.'

'Are you sure, babe? I heard things weren't great between you and Avi, and you were looking...'

'Who the fuck told you that?'

Paddy shrugged. 'I don't remember exactly. Word gets around.' He reached into his pocket. 'Listen, babe, why don't I leave you my card and...'

Sean got into his face. 'Because I don't fuckin' want it. Awright? Do I need to spell it out for you any fuckin' clearer, Paddy?'

He swallowed and shook his head. 'No. OK. I'll catch you around, Sean.' He stopped at the door and looked back. 'You don't know who's representing Vinnie Jones at the minute?'

'No, I fuckin' don't. Now fuck off!'

Paddy left and closed the door after him.

Sean picked up his script and tried to find his place. He flipped through a few pages and then threw it against the nearest wall with all his rage and screamed, 'Fuck!'

He sat down, took out his phone and looked at it.

06.

The doctor examined the stitches down the centre of Avi's chest. 'That seems to be healing nicely, Mr Goldman. How are you feeling?'

'Like thirty miles of bad road.'

The young surgeon smiled. 'Well, that'll pass. We've fixed you up almost as good as new, but you have to lay off the booze and cigars, or cut down at least, or this is just going to happen again.' Avi nodded. 'You have a stressful job too. Have you thought about retiring, or at least cutting back your hours?' Avi shook his head. 'Consider it. I'm going to give you a heart-smart eating plan to follow for the first couple of months and I want you to stick to it.'

Avi nodded and smiled. 'Well, that's drinking, smoking, working and eating ruined. What the hell's left? What about women, are they off the menu too?'

'We recommend six to eight weeks after surgery before you resume a normal sex life.' He scribbled on his chart. 'But that's just a guideline. You'll know yourself if you feel up to it.' He hung the chart on the end of the bed and looked at the old man solemnly. 'This was close, Avi. I don't know if anyone's told you just how close you came to getting your wings. You were hanging by a thread in surgery. Don't forget that.' The doctor nodded and walked towards the door.

'Hey, doc.' The doctor stopped and turned to him. 'Thanks. Thanks for not letting go of that thread.' The doctor nodded and left.

Avi took a deep breath. He looked around his private room and felt the silence. In a city of eight million people, he'd never felt so alone. Sean was doing his shitty movie, Emily couldn't fly because of the baby, and Aileen couldn't leave the office unattended or fly to America to visit her boss in hospital. How would that look to her husband?

223

At least the airline had dropped all charges against him. He had bluffed his way out of being arrested or sued by saying it was a medical emergency; he had chest pains and was trying to call his doctor for advice. Ironically, the airline was now scared he was going to sue them for almost causing his death by denying him medical advice, so they were picking up his hospital tab. It made him smile. He'd forgotten how crazy this country was; everyone was either suing, being sued, or lived in fear of getting sued.

The bedside phone rang and he turned as slowly as he could to get it. 'Hello?'

'Mr Goldman, I have Sean Black on the line for you. Would you like to take the call?'

'Yeah, I'll take it.' There was a brief click. 'Sean?'

'Awright, Avi, how are you?'

Despite his cockney accent, he sounded subdued. 'I'm OK, kid. The docs think everything's looking good and healing how it should, but they say I can't fly for at least four to six weeks, so it looks like I'm stuck here until then.' He thought he heard a sigh but it was barely audible. 'How's the shoot?'

He took a deep breath. 'It's fuckin' horrible, Avi. You were right; this is a fuckin' shitty movie.'

'How long do you have left on it?'

'Nine more humiliating days.'

'Ah, well, we live and learn, eh? Sean...'

'Yeah?'

'Shit, kid, there's no easy way to say this so I'm just going to say it, the Scorsese picture fell through.'

'What? How?'

'There was a shake-up at the studio. A lot of suits got fired and replaced by a lot of different suits. When that happens, they usually try to kill any projects their predecessor had going so that their tenure only gets judged on projects they green-lit. It's something that happens more often than people know.'

'But how the fuck can anyone tank a Scorsese picture? Are they fuckin' mad?'

'You got to wonder. Marty still thinks it'll get made at some point. He says it's on "indefinite hiatus" at the moment. He thinks he might have to make one for them before the studio let him do it, so we're probably talking about a couple of years at least.'

'By that time I'll be king of the straight-to-DVD movie.' Sean sighed loudly this time. 'I've fucked this all up.'

'No you haven't, kid. This shit happens. We'll find you something else.' The silence burned in Avi's ear. 'Sean? Are you still there?'

'We had five months set aside for the Scorsese project. That means I have nothing now when this shit wraps. I've got six months before we start shooting the next *Savage* special. Fuck, Avi, I've got nothing to do for most of the year.'

'Now just calm down, kid. I'll speak to Aileen at the office and we'll see what we can come up with. Sean? Are you still there?'

'They're calling me to the set, Avi. I have to go. Bye.' The line went dead.

Avi checked the time. Aileen should still be in the office. He asked the switchboard to make a long distance call for him.

So much for cutting back on the work. He had nine days to find Sean something to keep him occupied.

Being in hospital was a lot like being in jail for Avi. He watched the clock a lot. He counted the roof tiles in his room. He looked forward to mealtimes to break the monotony. He even looked forward to the nurse changing his catheter bag, just so he would have someone to talk to for a few minutes.

What he did mostly was read, and when it was too dark to read – again like prison, the nurses were strict about lights-out time – he'd think. He had begun to formulate a plan regarding Sean. He knew he would never accept the fact that he needed help if confronted, but he trusted Avi's judgement on scripts. Probably more than ever if *Diamond Geezer* was still going as badly as it had been when they'd spoken last. That was Avi's ace card. That was his way in.

Avi couldn't do a lot while he was on a different continent, so he needed to find his client something to keep him busy until he got back. A little rom-com or heart-warming family drama would keep Emily and the baby safe in the meantime, and then he needed something very specific. He needed a script about a guy who talks to a therapist about his previous misdeeds. True to form, Sean would want to research the part by living it, and would ask for some therapy sessions to be scheduled to find out how it feels to confess all the things he'd been holding inside.

Then they would find out if Avi's fears were justified. He'd suspected Sean for a while, but he didn't know how far back it went, or how far he'd gone on how many occasions. When Avi couldn't sleep at night, he replayed every part he'd got for Sean and tried to think of anything suspicious or out of the ordinary that had happened around those times. He was fairly certain about a couple of things, but there were others he could only speculate on. His imagination took him to some dark places and no amount of hospital blankets could chase away the chills he got thinking about what Sean might've done.

The rom-com part would be easy enough to find. Since *Savage* had hit big, Sean had become something of a sex-symbol. He was offered those sorts of parts all the time, but Avi had always turned them down because they were simplistic and predictable. Still, he was pretty sure he could convince Sean to do one now. He could tell him it was the price they had to pay to get Sean considered for romantic leading man parts in better films.

The other script would be harder to find. It had been three days since he'd had a very long phone call with Aileen, at the airline's expense, and taken notes on all the scripts currently waiting for a yay or nay from Sean. Avi had read most of them, so just needed a title for him to remember the gist of it. He wrote the names of all seventy-seven scripts down on a page as Aileen went through them in the Belfast office. The few he hadn't read, he asked Aileen to read and he'd call her in a few days so she could give him an idea of the storyline. The standard of writing didn't matter to him as much as finding the right story.

For the last three days he'd pored over the names of those scripts and whittled them down to nine. He made phone calls and asked who else was attached before narrowing it down to two; the lead in a romantic drama with Kate Winslet, or a smaller part in a Woody Allen ensemble comedy. They were both wholesome characters. He'd tell Aileen to present them both to Sean and let him decide.

The other scripts weren't completely disregarded. He remembered some of them for their writing more than the story or the part offered to Sean. If he couldn't find a script to suit his needs, he'd commission one. He'd pitch it as a Northern Irish version of *The Sopranos* where an ex-paramilitary would unburden his soul about crimes he'd committed to some sexy psychologist. There were plenty of starving writers out there who would jump at the chance of paid work, and Avi figured if he kept the budget low enough, he would be able to find the financing to get it made too.

'You know, you supposed to be resting, Mr Goldman.' The nurse wandered in, barely clearing the sides of the door as she passed through. 'This look more like an office than a hospital room.'

'Working is relaxing to me. It's staring at these walls, doing nothing, that stresses me out.'

She brought him a fresh jug of ice-water and set it on his locker. 'Doctor going to be upset if he sees you with all this paperwork.'

'I won't tell if you don't.'

She changed his catheter bag, re-tucked his bedclothes and adjusted his pillows. 'OK, I ain't your mama.' She finished her chores and headed for the door. 'Anything else you need?'

'A pack of cigars and a bottle of bourbon.'

She gave him a flat smile. 'Yeah, I never heard that one before. Take it easy, Mr Goldman,' she said as she edged out the doorway.

A half-hour later the nurse came back looking concerned. 'You OK, Avi? We got an alarm on your heart rate monitor at the nurses... Avi?' She ran to the bed as fast as she could. The old man was pale and sweat had drenched his pyjamas and the bed sheets. She glanced at the heart monitor and her concern deepened. 'Can I get a doctor in here, now!' she cried at the door. 'Avi? Avi, look at me. I need you to take some deep breaths for me, OK?' The look of fear was undeniable in the old man's eyes.

Avi grabbed his chest and looked into the eyes of the kindly face looking down at him. He tried to speak, but couldn't get his breath.

She put her hand on top of his. 'No, Avi, it's not your heart. It's a panic attack. You have to take some deep breaths and calm down. Your heart is fine.'

The doctor rushed into the room and grabbed the print-out from the heart monitor. He scanned it quickly and apparently came to the same conclusion. 'Let's get some O2 on him.'

The nurse put the mask over his mouth and nose, and Avi felt the cold air filling his lungs and his heart rate started to calm. He saw the doctor pointing at the stacks of papers on and around the bed, and bawling the nurse out. They must've slipped him a sedative as well, because before he had time to apologize for getting her in trouble, sleep had taken him.

227

Having missed his evening meal the night before, Avi woke the next morning with a hunger that a hospital breakfast was never going to sate. He ate the bland food and drank the OJ. He begged for coffee and was refused. He couldn't wait to get his autonomy back.

When the nurse came in to take his breakfast tray away, he asked, 'Hey, where's all my notes?'

'Confiscated. Doctor's orders. You can have them back when you leave.' She put one hand on her hip. 'You know how much trouble you got me into?'

'Sorry. I'll make it up to you. What kind of car do you prefer; Porsche or Ferrari?' Avi smiled at her.

She immediately took on a look of faux-anger. 'You crazy? You can't go parking no Porsche or Ferrari in my neighbourhood.'

Avi laughed and put a hand gently on his stitches.

'OK, now you going to relax this time. You going to read some books and watch some TV, and that's all. No more panic attacks, understand?'

'Yes, ma'am.'

'I check in on you in a little while.' She waved a hand over her shoulder as she left.

Avi picked up the phone and called the office in Belfast. 'Aileen, OK, here's the two scripts I want you to show to Sean. They're called...'

'Hello, Avi. Yes, I'm fine, thank you. How are you?'

'What? Oh. Yeah, sorry, thanks, all that stuff, whatever. Listen, the two scripts are called...'

'No, Avi,' she said firmly.

'No what?'

She took a deep breath. 'I called to see how you were last night and they said you'd had a panic attack because you were working too hard when you should've been resting.'

He sighed quickly. 'That was nothing. Don't worry about that. I just need you to...'

'No, Avi. The office can function perfectly well until you get back. There's nothing that can't wait.'

'But you don't understand. Sean...'

'Sean is fine. I've spoken to him and we both agreed, so don't try ringing him either because I told him not to answer. Everything will be fine as long as you're fine.' She sniffed back hard. 'I don't want to lose you, you silly old fool.' She cleared her throat. 'So no more shop talk. You may still call to talk about non-work-related matters, or flirt within certain limits, but work is going to wait until you get back. Sean and I have things covered. That's the last word I'm going to say on the matter. Now, is there anything else?'

Avi considered this for a few moments and then said, 'Yeah. I love you.'

'I love you too.'

'I'll call you tomorrow and see how much dirty talk I can get away with on an international line.'

'You do that.'

Avi hung up with a smile on his face, but it soon fell. *Sean and I have things covered.* What did that mean? There was no way to find out either, except to get better. He lifted the remote and switched on daytime TV. The banality of the programmes distracted him almost to the point of sedation, but in the back of his mind he still worried about what Sean might do.

07.

A couple of weeks later, Avi was walking unassisted and able to piss without a tube. They had moved him into the recovery ward after his stitches had come out. His tests had all come back as well as could be expected for a man his age. He was even allowed out of the ward on his own to walk in the hospital gardens.

He'd been lying in that bed for weeks dreaming about having a smoke, but now he had the opportunity, he didn't buy a pack. The way he looked at it, he was through the withdrawal phase; where his body no longer craved the poison it had become accustomed to, so now all that was left was the psychological phase. His body didn't need them anymore, but his mind still wanted them. The heart-attack had scared him. He never wanted to go through that again. And Aileen always hated him smoking. Every logical reason told him not to smoke, but a voice in his mind still screamed for him to buy a pack. The fight raged on. He hoped the longer he denied it, the quieter that voice would become.

He was sitting on a bench in the hospital gardens. It was a clear, New York day. The flowers filled his nostrils with some of the sweet smells smoking had masked for decades. He breathed it in.

Two candy-stripers came out and sat on the bench opposite him to eat their salad lunches. There was a brunette and a redhead, both with their hair tied back. Avi couldn't help but notice their shapely, tanned legs. God, it was good to be alive.

'No, he wasn't Irish in the film, he had a different accent. I think he was like, from New York in the film,' the brunette said. 'He was in a TV show too.'

'Colin Farrell?' The redhead asked.

'No, not Colin Farrell. He's from the south of Ireland, this guy's from the north of Ireland.'

'What's the difference? Isn't it all Ireland?'

'No. Yes. I don't know. It's just different, trust me. This guy, if I could only think of his fucking name, is from the north of Ireland. They have a *way* different accent.'

'Like what?'

'I can't do accents.'

'OK, what did he do in the TV show he was in?' the redhead asked.

'I don't know. I didn't see it. It's on BBC America or something.'

'You're not talking about Liam Neeson, are you?'

'No, a younger guy. Hot. Nice ass. Dark hair.'

Avi had been watching this whole exchange with a smile on his face. He now decided he was going to go over and put these girls out of their misery, and maybe even score an extra dessert if he told them he was this actor's agent and knew him personally. He got up slowly from his bench and started towards them.

'Ooh, the Batman guy with the eyes. Gillian something!'

'No, not him,' the brunette said. She shook her head. 'It'll come to me later. Anyway, he's dead now. That's what I was trying to tell you. He committed suicide a few days ago.'

Avi froze on his way towards the girls. All heat disappeared from the bright spring day and he shivered.

'Oh my god. How'd he do it?'

'It said on the Internet that he drove to a forest and hooked a hose-pipe up to the exhaust of his car and then fed it through the window.'

'Oh my god. That's horrible. You think these actor types have money and fame... I guess you just never know what's going on in someone's head.'

The brunette nodded. 'I think he had a wife and kid too.'

Avi ran across the garden and back into the hospital. He hurried up the stairs as fast as he could and made his way towards the patients' common room. By the time he sat down at a computer the sweat was running down his cheeks. He typed the keywords "Irish, actor, dead" into a search engine and found an article published only hours earlier.

LOCAL ACTOR FOUND DEAD

The body discovered by a couple walking their dogs early Tuesday morning in Belvoir Park Forest has now been identified as the actor Ciaran Feagan, 25, originally from East Belfast.

Feagan is best known for his role in the Irish TV series *It's Your Round,* where for three series he played Gerry McCann, the lovable bartender striving to become a professional boxer. After a few low-budget British and Irish films, Hollywood came calling and he beat fierce competition to land the starring role in the film adaptation of Christy-Marie Schultz's best-selling novel *The Crying Garden*, for which he won a BAFTA and was nominated for an Oscar. He had returned to Belfast just ten days ago to prepare for a local film, due to start shooting around the North Coast in a few weeks' time.

Feagan divorced eighteen months ago but remained close with his ex-wife Leona, with whom he has a two-year-old son, Carter. No official statement has been made by the family or Feagan's management as to what could've prompted the young actor at the beginning of such a promising career to take his life.

Northern Ireland, and the world, has lost one of its brightest and most promising stars of the silver screen. Online tributes have been pouring in from fellow actors and fans alike. His peers describe him as a delight to work with, while fans are telling stories of how he never refused a photo or autograph no matter how busy or tired he seemed.

Belfast Echo Online, 22 June, 2008

Avi sat back in the chair. He was relieved to some extent, but also anxious. Feagan had been Sean's biggest… competition, for want of a better word. Could it be possible that…? No, Sean would be back in Manchester when they finished shooting in London, wouldn't he?

Avi marched back to his room and started getting dressed.

The nurse came in and was startled. 'What you doing, Mr Goldman?'

'I'm leaving. I'm sorry. I can't stay here any longer. Give me whatever A.M.A. forms you need me to sign and I'll sign them, but I'm going. I need to get home right away.'

The nurse shrugged. She shuffled off to get the doctor and the forms to say he was leaving the hospital Against Medical Advice. Avi slowly ran his finger down the rough stitch marks on his chest and then he pulled his shirt on and started buttoning it up.

He called Aileen from the taxi and asked if Sean was still in Manchester. Once she learned he was on his way home, she saw no reason to protect him from work stresses any more.

'No, he's back in Belfast. The whole family came back about a week ago.'

'OK, I'm heading for the airport now. I'm going to get on the first flight I can. Can you pick me up in Belfast when I land?

'Sure.'

'OK, I'll call you when I know what flight I'm on and when I'll be landing. I'll see you soon, honey.'

08.

D.S. Agnes Finn was breathing heavily by the time she had climbed to the top floor of the abandoned mill. She thought of the StairMaster she had bought from a late-night infomercial to combat this very problem. Buying the thing was the crucial first step to getting her figure back. Unboxing it and using it would've been the logical second step, but she hadn't reached that stage yet. It sat in the hall cupboard gathering dust until she had the time to get into a proper routine.

She leaned over and put her hands on her knees as she got her breath back. She noticed a button had popped off her blouse at some point and wondered how long she had been walking around with part of her bra on display. She also saw a stain she hadn't noticed before. It looked like burger relish. She stood up straight and tried to pull her jacket closed far enough to cover the gap and the stain.

'You OK, ma'am?' Millar, her latest DC, asked. He was twenty-five and almost robotic in following the letter of the law. He took notes of everything. Finn suspected he would be promoted before long. He was just the sort of model detective the PSNI liked to fast-track. And after all those stairs, he wasn't even a little out of breath. Maybe he was a robot.

She nodded and pointed towards the door ahead. Millar went through first and Finn forced her aching legs to follow him.

The roof of the old mill had several large holes in it which had allowed many pigeons to enter and use the place as a toilet. Finn looked at her shoes – less than a month old – and shook her head before wading into the carpet of pigeon crap. It was a huge empty space apart from what the pigeons had left; easily half the size of a football pitch. About three quarters of the way down, two uniformed officers stood over a familiar shape covered with a sheet as the SOCO packed up his bag.

Finn addressed the officers, both of whom looked experienced. 'Who found the body?'

'A couple of teenagers, ma'am,' the one with the grey moustache answered.

'You get their details?'

'Yes, ma'am,' the other replied and showed his notepad to Millar. Millar copied down everything on the page quickly.

'What were they doing up here?'

The officer with the grey moustache cleared his throat and nodded towards the corner. The little nook they had created was far enough away from any of the roof holes to stay dry, even in bad weather. They had also cleaned the crap from the floor in a vague circle and thrown down some blankets and cushions.

'Drugs?' Finn asked.

'Not that I can see,' the SOCO answered. 'Just getting jiggy.'

Finn turned to her DC. 'Millar, when we get back, I want you to check the archives and find out the last time someone used the term jiggy.'

The SOCO gave her a sarcastic grin.

The DC was already scribbling when he realised what she had said and slowly stopped. He gave her a flat smile, flipped the page, and poised his pen for the next relevant piece of information.

Finn and the SOCO exchanged a look and smile. She nodded at the sheet. 'OK, let's hear it.'

'No ID on the victim. I guess she's early twenties. No signs of drug abuse or rape. Clothing is good quality and she's clean, so she's not homeless. She's also wearing a gold ring and a pretty expensive watch which weren't taken. Her phone is lying over there.' He pointed to the evidence marker ten feet away. 'You should be able to get her ID from that once you crack the PIN code.'

'Not robbery, not rape, not drug-related? That's weird.'

'It gets weirder.' The SOCO exchanged solemn looks between the two uniformed police officers.

The look on their faces was already making her skin crawl. 'What?' Finn asked. 'What aren't you telling me?'

The SOCO took a deep breath. 'Cause of death.' He knelt down and lifted the corner of the sheet.

Finn took a few steps closer and knelt down opposite him. She saw what the SOCO had refused to say out loud. 'Jesus Christ,' she whispered. 'Is that...?'

The SOCO nodded.

Millar came and looked over her shoulder as Finn tried to get a handle on what she was seeing. Millar saw what had left her speechless. His pen touched the paper but he didn't know what to write.

Finn stood up and turned to the uniformed officers. 'Did the kids see that?'

The moustached man shook his head. 'She was lying face down when we arrived and her hair was covering it. We only saw it when we turned her over. The kids were gone by then.'

'OK, no one mentions this, understand? No one! I don't want the media getting hold of this until we know what the hell we're dealing with and we've had time to talk to her parents.'

Everyone present nodded their agreement.

'Has the area been photographed?' The officers nodded again. Finn turned to the SOCO. 'OK, get her back to your lab as soon as you can and tell me... tell me what you can.' The SOCO took out his phone and started to walk away. 'And tell your people the same,' she shouted after him. 'No one leaks this or I'll throw the fucking book at them.' The SOCO nodded and walked on.

Finn walked to the side of the huge space and looked out through one of the holes in the roof. The overcast sky made it feel much later than afternoon. A grey mist hung over the city, giving Belfast the look of Dickensian London from some old movie. She took a deep breath, but it didn't chase away the feeling of unease in her stomach.

It's an honour to be asked to play Ciaran's part in this film. The media liked to say we were rivals, but the truth is, we'd always meet up and have a drink and a laugh together if we were in the same city. I am extremely saddened by his loss, but I also know how much he loved acting, so I know he would be the first to agree that the show must go on. It is for this reason that I've stepped into this role; so a project I know he was passionate about will now get completed.

Sean Black, 23 June, 2008

09.

The first face Avi saw when he walked out of baggage claim was Aileen. There were dozens of expectant faces popping their heads up like Meerkats, looking for their loved one, but as far as Avi was concerned there was only one person at the gate. They kissed and walked towards short-term parking. When they got there Avi saw her small car was full of luggage.

'Going somewhere?'

She looked over the roof of the car at him, summoned her courage and said, 'I'm moving in with my boyfriend... if he'll have me.' She looked so vulnerable in that moment.

Avi hurried round the car and took her by the arms. 'You sure? What about Harry?'

'I left him a note.' She laughed, more from relief than humour. She stepped close to Avi. 'You really scared me. When I thought I was going to lose you... it just put things in perspective.' She still looked unsure. 'So, what do you think?'

'I think I love you, and I always have.' He kissed her. 'Let's go home.'

Aileen wiped the tears from her face and nodded. She got in the driver's seat and Avi went back round to the passenger side.

Avi closed the door and looked over his shoulders. 'I'm going to need a bigger place.' Aileen laughed and started the car. Avi put his hand on hers and turned the car off again. 'Wait, first tell me what's going on with Sean. What script did he pick?'

'Oh, he didn't pick any of the scripts in the office. He said they were all in pre-production. He needed something now. It was lucky... well, not lucky, but you know what I mean, that young fella died. Sean sent an email of condolence to the production company and they jumped on him right away.'

Avi sat back in the chair and looked at the roof. God, he really wanted a smoke.

'What's the matter, Avi?'

'What's the picture?'

'It suited everyone. Emily and little Maddie got to come home, and Sean got something to fill…'

'What's the picture?' he said, slightly firmer.

'It's called *Vampire Dawn*. Sean plays this vampire called Kaaliz. It won't interfere with *Savage*, I checked.'

The old man put his head in his hands. 'Oh, Christ,' he said quietly.

'Avi, I don't understand. Have I done something wrong?'

'No. Just give me a minute.' Avi got out of the car.

Aileen watched as he paced around the car park for fifteen minutes. Then he strode back quickly towards the car and opened her door. 'Avi, what is going on?'

The old man nodded towards her stack of luggage. 'Go through that lot and get yourself enough stuff to do you for a few days. One bag, OK? Then come inside and find me.'

'But I don't understand. Where are we going? I don't have a passport.'

'You won't need one. Just pack a bag and get inside.' Avi looked at her bewildered face. He knelt down beside her and took her hand. 'I haven't got time to explain this to you now, but I need to get you out of the country for a little while. Just to be safe.'

'To be safe? From what? Where are we going?'

'I don't know yet. And it's not us, it's just you. I have something important to do, and then I'll come get you in a few days.'

'Avi, I don't understand any of this.'

He kissed her hand. 'I know you don't. Just know I love you, and I'm doing this *because* I love you. Please, trust me.'

She shook her head and shrugged. 'OK.'

He kissed her lips as he stood. 'OK, pack quickly and lightly. Come inside as soon as you're done.'

'What about the car? Should I move it to long-term?'

'No, I'm taking the car,' he said, running towards the terminal. 'You just hurry!'

She watched him running back inside the airport and wondered what could've got him so worried.

10.

Agnes picked through her salad, looking under every lettuce leaf hoping there might be some fried chicken beneath it. She wondered how the hell vegetarians were able to muster up the strength to answer the door, let alone anything else. She continued to poke at the rabbit-food while she perused the case file sitting next to her.

A tray piled high with chips, beans and sausages plopped down opposite her. 'Hey, Agnes, how goes the diet?'

'It's a laugh a minute, Sam.' The scruffy detective was probably twice her weight, but he also had a wedding ring wedged on one chubby digit, so he no longer seemed to care. Finn closed the file and rubbed the bridge of her nose.

'What you working on?' he asked just before the first forkful of delicious, unhealthy food was crammed into his mouth.

'That dead girl we found.'

'The one with…?' He poked two fingers into his neck.

'Yeah. It doesn't make any sense. No signs of drugs in her system. No signs of struggle. Her college tutors all say she was very clever. Why would she go willingly with someone to a place like that?'

'She knew them,' he said through a mouthful of half-masticated food.

'That was my first thought too, but she's from across the water, so she doesn't know many people and didn't seem to have many friends. Her acting teacher said she was fine on-stage, but off-stage she was quiet and shy. She just doesn't fit the profile for someone easily coerced; we found a rape alarm and pepper spray in her bag. She was cautious, so why… who, would she lower her guard for?' Finn abandoned her plastic fork into her salad and rubbed her tired eyes. 'What are you working on?'

'That actor who killed himself,' he said, biting a sausage in half.

'Another actor?' Finn furrowed brows that were in dire need of plucking. 'Anything weird about it?'

Sam opened his can of Coke and took a long swig to clear his mouth. 'No note. No apparent motive that we can find. And the day he died he agreed to give a talk to the drama students at his old high school, *and* he'd booked himself a holiday in Mauritius for after this shoot completed.'

'You think the suicide was staged and he was murdered?'

'Feels like it, but we can't find anyone with a motive.'

'Who got his part in the film after he died?'

Sam shook his head, smiling. 'Maybe if it was a *Star Wars* movie or something – I might even kill to be in that, but this is a little local

237

movie. He wasn't getting paid very much and it's not the sort of film you kill over. It's a little horror movie.'

'So who got the part?'

'Sean Black. Don't you read the papers?'

'Does he have an alibi?'

'Couldn't get hold of him, but I spoke to his lovely wife Emily, and she said they were both in bed sleeping.'

Finn lifted her fork again and started pushing a cherry tomato around the plate. 'Emily Black. Why do I know that name? Is she an actress too?'

Sam shook his head with his cheeks restocked.

'Then where do I know that name from?'

Sam shrugged. Finn got up, grabbed her file and left.

11.

'Hello? Emily?'

'Avi! How are you? You feeling better?'

'I'm fine. Factory reconditioned.'

'We were so worried about you. Did you get the flowers I sent?'

'I did. Thank you.'

'It was the first time I'd done it online. I thought I might've screwed it up.'

'They were great. How's the little one?'

'She's great. She's actually letting me sleep a few hours every night now.'

'That's good. Listen, I've just landed and I thought I might call round on my way home. Is Sean there? I need to talk to him about a few things and he's not picking up.'

'Oh, sorry, Avi, we're not at home. I'm in Antrim staying with my mum and dad. They haven't seen Maddie since she was born and Sean said he wanted some time alone. I think Ciaran's death's hit him hard. To be honest, I didn't even know they knew each other. I don't think he ever mentioned him. But he says they were pretty close. I think he needs to take some time with that and to prepare for this film.'

'Is he at the Belfast house?'

'No. We were there for a few days, but we weren't counting on how famous *Savage* had made him. There were people knocking on our door twenty-four/ seven. Struggling actors looking for an in, struggling writers wanting to give him scripts, reporters, TV people, autograph hunters... it was just never-ending. So we thought it was a good time for me to visit my folks and for him to get out of town for a while.'

'Do you know where he is?'

'He said not to tell anyone, but I'm sure that doesn't mean you. He's at his Uncle Ronnie's old place.'

'The place where they found his mum's remains?'

'Yeah. Creepy, right? I guess he's taking this horror movie seriously. He said he was going out there so he could get used to being nocturnal, since the shoot was going to be mostly nights and he didn't want to seem tired. Oh, god! Do you know he got a dentist to make him a custom set of teeth?'

'You're kidding.'

'No. He said if you look at all those old Hammer movies, the vampires always have to walk around like they're catching flies, because the actors couldn't close their mouths with the prosthetic teeth in. So he wanted a set that fit perfectly over his own so he could talk and eat and everything without them falling out or affecting his speech.'

'That sounds... Listen, do you know why he's not answering his phone?'

'I'm not even sure there's electric out there, so he's maybe just out of charge. Let me get you the address. Hang on, it's on here somewhere.'

'Take your time.'

'Of course he might just think a vampire wouldn't carry a phone. You know what he's like.'

'Yeah. I do.'

TEN QUESTIONS

Seven years ago we asked Sean Black our famous Ten Questions, so we thought it was time to catch up with him and ask them again. As he prepares to take over the late Ciaran Feagan's role as a psychotic vampire in the upcoming *Vampire Dawn*, we find out if huge success in TV drama *Savage,* as well as multiple movies roles and more awards than you can shake a stake at, has changed the Northern Irish actor's tastes.

01. Favourite Film: The first VHS I owned was *The Lost Boys*. I love it. I could recite it. I also love Neil Jordan's film of Anne Rice's *Interview With The Vampire.*

02. Favourite Band/ Musician: I find it hard to get into new music, so I tend to just like stuff I got into when I was younger. Def Leppard, Guns n' Roses and Bon Jovi are the most played on my iPod. I saw Pearl Jam live this year and they were awesome.

03. Favourite Food: Steak, very rare.

04. Favourite TV Show: I can't really say *Savage*, can I? [laughs] I'm really enjoying *Lost*, though I can't see how they're ever going to satisfactorily resolve everything. I've also been watching the DVD boxsets of *Buffy* and *Angel*. They're both great shows. I'll always watch *The X-Files* if a repeat is on TV.

05. Favourite Drink: Blood! [laughs] No, it sounds boring but I drink more tea now than anything. It comes from being on movie and TV sets so much. Someone's always pushing a cup into my hand.

06. First Celebrity Crush: I remember being very much in love with Diana, the leader of the aliens who invade Earth and try to steal all our water in the classic TV mini-series *V*. She was played by an actress called Jane Badler. I don't know if it was the bad girl thing, or the big 80s hair, or the uniform, but I thought she was hot. Even if she did eat rabbits alive.

07. Person You'd Most Like To Meet: Christopher Lee. I've seen him interviewed and he seems like a very intelligent man and a true gent. I'd love to pick his brain about *The Wicker Man* and all those Hammer *Dracula* movies.

08. Last Time You Laughed: I've been watching the news series of *Saxondale*. I love that show. It's great if you're a fan of classic rock.

I'm a big fan of [Steve] Coogan. I think Alan Partridge is genius. Also loving *The IT Crowd*.

09. Last Time You Cried: When I heard Ciaran [Feagan] had died. It was such a shock. He was so young and talented. Everyone who knew him can't believe he did what he did. We all thought he seemed so happy. I wish we were all more educated about looking for danger signs of depression.

10. Favourite Quote: I'll choose one of mine. 'The movie business is dog eat dog. The key to success is knowing when to bark and when to bite.'

Wotz on the Box? Online, 23 June, 2008

Avi hadn't driven for over ten years, and the cramped confines of Aileen's little car weren't making things any easier. He wondered how a woman of her proportions managed to operate this little lunchbox on wheels. Darkness had now fallen and his eyes weren't good either. He needed his other glasses and he hadn't packed them. After much honking from aggravated motorists, he was now out of the city and less likely to get pulled over by the cops.

Aileen had tried to explain the sat-nav to him before he put her on the plane, but it hadn't sunk in and he was just stopping and asking people whenever he had the chance. He was getting close now. He was sure of it.

The next plane leaving had been bound for the Isle of Man and he hoped that was far enough away for her to be safe. Neither of them had any connections over there, so Sean couldn't possibly second-guess that's where she had gone. Aileen was his only way of getting to Avi indirectly. Now he had removed that possibility.

On the drive Avi had tried to convince himself that this whole idea was nuts. Maybe Sean wasn't doing what he thought he was. Maybe he would reach this old house and find Sean sitting with his feet up watching old Hammer movies.

The old man squinted and saw the gate Emily had described. It was open. He slowed down and pulled in. As the little car bumped and rattled down the lane, Avi saw no lights on in the house and no car parked outside. Maybe he'd lied to Emily about staying out here. Maybe he was just shacked up in a luxury hotel in Belfast, screwing some goth chick with vampire fantasies. For once, he really hoped Sean was just being unfaithful.

Avi stopped the car and got out. It was eerily quiet. There was the distant sound of traffic, but apart from that, it was as still as a graveyard. He looked towards the end of the yard, to where the cops had dug up the flowerbed. There was a crater at least twenty feet across and ten feet deep. It seems when they had dug up Sean's mum, they had checked to see if any of Uncle Ronnie's other acquaintances had ended up in the same resting place. There were still some fragments of police cordon tape clinging to branches and caught in hedges around the hole. Avi pulled his coat tighter to chase away the chill.

He walked up to the front door of the house and gave it a gentle push. It swung open. He stepped inside and felt the cold air, and smelled decades of damp. It was dark. He flipped the switch by the door and the darkness remained. He saw his breath mist before him. He walked inside. His eyes adjusted to the darkness and he was able to make out the 1970s décor and the religious pictures and ornaments dotted around the cramped living area. The sofa was covered in mould. Avi took another step and a mouse scurried across his foot and ran for cover. His heart was beating hard. He took some deep breaths and tried to slow it.

'Sean? Are you here?' His voice cracked when he said it, and for the first time he considered the fact that maybe Sean wasn't here, but some murderous hobo might be. He looked around for a weapon and could see nothing. He continued forward and proceeded up the steep, narrow stairs. The upstairs floorboards were spongy and creaked, even under his modest weight. He slowly walked along the landing, checking rooms as he went. All the doors were open except the one at the end of the landing. He reached that door and took a deep breath before knocking.

'Sean? Are you in there? It's Avi.' When there was no answer he added, 'I'm coming in, OK?' He twisted the brass doorknob and pushed the door open. The first thing he saw was the bed and mattress turned on their end and pushed against the window. That made this room even darker than the rest of the house. Avi reached into his pocket and produced his lighter, which he still carried in case he needed an emergency smoke. He flicked the wheel of the Zippo several times before it produced a flame and illuminated the space.

The room was empty... apart from the coffin at the far end.

The flame of the lighter flickered as if fighting an unnatural cold. Avi hadn't seen his breath mist for a long time. His heart was banging in his chest. He started towards the coffin. He cupped a hand around the flickering flame as he moved deeper into the room.

He stood over the coffin and swallowed hard. He knelt down with his aged knees and sense of self-preservation protesting every inch of the way. He ran his fingers over the top of the polished wood and found several finger-sized holes drilled into the lid where the head would rest. Avi held the lighter as steadily as he could with one hand and slid the fingers of his other hand under the lid. Something behind him caught his eye and he turned quickly. He saw only the imposing shadow the lighter and his silhouette were creating. It trembled against the wall and ceiling. He turned back to the coffin and started to raise the lid. He only lifted a few inches when it slipped out of his grasp and slid into the gap between the coffin and the wall. It made a loud noise for such a quiet room. Avi looked behind himself again. The coffin was empty. But unlike the rest of the fabrics in this house, the lining was clean and smelled new.

Avi stood up. His worst fears seemed to be confirmed. But what was even more worrying was Sean's absence. If he wasn't here, then where was he, and what was he doing?

12.

Finn screamed into her pillow.

She turned over and stared at that same semi-circular crack in her ceiling that had been smirking at her since she lay down. The novel she had been enjoying for the last few nights was lying on the other side of the room. She had thrown it there after reading the same page a dozen times and still not knowing what was happening. Then she had put three discs into her CD changer; T'Pau's *Bridge of Spies*, Transvision Vamp's *Pop Art* and Fleetwood Mac's *Rumours*. She had hoped these familiar albums would sing her to sleep, but as the final moments of *Gold Dust Woman* faded and the CD player rested, she was still wide awake.

She flicked on the TV and tried to get interested in some old movie, but she couldn't concentrate long enough to follow it. For the umpteenth time that night, she got out of bed, fluffed her pillows and straightened her bed clothes. She got back in and smoothed the duvet down by her sides. She took a deep breath and closed her eyes.

She jumped into a sitting position and shouted, 'Emily Black! That's where I know that name from. Fuck!' Finn jumped out of bed and ran downstairs.

13.

Sean pulled into the yard and saw the little yellow car.

It was Aileen's car, but he doubted Aileen was inside. He turned off the lights and engine of the rented 4x4. He sat there for a few seconds, and then turned the rearview mirror towards him and checked his face and teeth were clean. He got out and walked towards the front door.

There was a faint glow of light coming from inside. He opened the door and saw Avi sitting in a wooden chair facing the door. He had his hands folded in his lap and his legs crossed. 'How are you, kid? I hope you don't mind me dropping in like this.'

Sean stepped inside and looked around.

'Found some candles,' Avi said. 'Hope you don't mind. I think it suits this whole... vibe you're going for.' He looked at Sean's all black attire and long black overcoat.

Sean stepped over and leaned against the wall. 'What are you doing here, Avi?'

'Just checking in on my client. That so odd?' They studied each other. 'Come closer, kid. Let me see you.' Sean exhaled and then took a couple of steps towards the old man. Avi squinted through the candlelight. 'Red irises, huh? Contacts? Let me see those teeth Emily told me about.' Sean opened his mouth like a petulant teenager at the dentist and showed him the pointed incisors.

'Is that it? Inspection complete?'

Avi shook his head. 'What are you doing out here, living like this?'

'I'm sure Emily told you, I'm just getting into character like I always do. I can't do that in the city, surrounded by humans always bothering me.'

'Humans?'

Sean winced. 'You know what I mean. Assholes, always knocking on my door.'

'I'm sure no one knocks on your lid out here.'

Sean swallowed and looked upwards briefly. 'Don't look at me like that.'

'Like what?'

'Like I'm fucking crazy,' he shouted. 'I'm just living how my character would live.'

'Blocking the windows?'

'I can't rightly be a vampire with a fucking tan, can I?'

'They can make you pale with make up,' Avi said.

'Look, I'm staying inside for a few weeks, out of the sun, so I get pale before the shoot. It'll give me an authentic look that make up can't replicate. Wolfgang Peterson did the same thing with his actors when he was making *Das Boot* and I'll bet no one gave him shit about it!'

'I'm not giving you shit, kid. I'm just looking out for you.'

'Well, I'm fine, thank you. Now fuck off.'

Avi didn't move except for a slight nod towards the kitchen. 'No food in the cupboards. What've you been eating?'

Sean stared at him. 'I drive to get something. Domino's don't deliver this far out. You believe that shit?'

'It's hard to believe.' Avi looked him up and down. 'I heard on the radio on the way over here some girl was killed in Belfast. In an old mill. Police are clamming up about the particulars for some reason. Almost like there's something weird about it. You know anything about that?'

'Why would I?' Sean looked at him with a cold intensity.

'I can't let you keep doing this, kid.'

'I haven't done anything, Avi.'

'Really? So you don't mind if I bring the cops out to talk to you? Maybe take a mould of your teeth with that prosthetic in and see if it matches any of their active cases?'

Sean glared at him silently. Avi was close enough to see the candlelight reflecting off his red contact lenses. 'You do whatever you have to do, Avi, and I'll do what I have to.' Sean held his stare for a few more seconds and then took a step back and gestured towards the door. 'If that's all, I'm tired and...'

'Yes, it's getting near dawn. Your bedtime, right?'

'For the next few weeks, yes,' Sean answered through gritted teeth.

'Right, well, I'll leave you to it.' Avi got up and Sean saw a wooden crucifix in his hands. 'Oh, right. I knocked this off the wall while I was stumbling around in the dark. Here, you can put it back where it belongs.' Avi held out the cross. He thought he saw him flinch slightly in the flickering light.

Sean looked from the proffered wall ornament to the old man's eyes, and then back at the cross. 'Keep it. It's a gift.' He raised his gaze and stared at Avi.

'Jewish, remember?' He was still holding the cross out to Sean.

'Then burn it. Bin it. Shove it up your arse for all I care.' He walked past the old man, keeping his distance from the cross. Avi heard him run up the stairs. He lowered the cross and walked outside.

Avi got into the car and looked at the cross in his hands. He dropped it onto the passenger's seat and started the car. He took a deep breath and once again asked himself if quitting smoking was really a wise decision. He wondered where the nearest garage was that sold...

Sean came running out of the house and slammed into the side of the car with his shoulder. The door panel dented inwards. The car rocked, throwing Avi one way and then the other. The old man instinctively slammed his palm down on the lock. Sean pulled at the door handle until it ripped off in his hand and he staggered backwards. He ran to the car again and looked inside at the terrified old man. His breath was misting the window. Avi saw those red eyes, filled with hate and evil. Only a couple of millimetres of glass separated them.

Sean reached down and grabbed the car under the door sill and began to lift. Avi's heart was pounding. He grabbed his chest and felt it thumping under his hand. He was struggling to breathe. The car started to tip. Avi scrambled over to the passenger's seat and fumbled around the floor for the cross. He almost had it in his grasp when the car flipped over onto its roof and Avi's world turned upside down. His head smacked against the roof and he couldn't focus his eyes. He saw a blurry figure walk around to the back of the car. Avi felt around the dark interior for the cross.

Sean started pushing the car along the yard on its roof. The mud was slick and the yard was on a slight angle, so it gathered speed until he pushed it into the hole left by the police excavation. The little car crashed down into the pit with a cacophony of twisting metal and breaking glass.

And then silence returned to the night.

Sean knelt down and looked inside the car. He saw his ex-agent lying there, clutching his heart. He wasn't moving. There was a large cut on his head which had masked half his face in blood. Sean licked his lips. On another night he might've indulged, but tonight he'd already had his fill.

He looked across the fields at the slowly brightening sky and walked back to the house, closing the door tightly behind him.

14.

The DCI had only just hung up his coat and turned his coffee percolator on when Finn bustled into his office with a stack of pages. 'We need to bring in Sean Black.'

'Good morning to you too, Finn. Are you wearing slippers?'

Finn looked down at her feet. 'Yes, I am, sir. I couldn't sleep last night so I came in and chased something down.' She sat down opposite her superior. 'Yesterday Sam told me he had spoken to Sean Black's wife Emily in regards to the Ciaran Feagan suicide, and that name bugged me. I couldn't figure out where I knew it from, but last night in bed it hit me.' She got up and started to pace the office.

'And that's why you came to work in your slippers?'

'Exactly. Now, remember a few years ago we had the incident at Altnagelvin Hospital with the body being autopsied by persons unknown?' She sat down and pulled her chair close.

The DCI switched on his computer and waited for it to boot up. 'Yes, I remember. We never got anyone for that, did we?'

'No. I was sure they'd do it again, but they didn't. Totally against all the profiles we have for this sort of thing. We looked at everything back then, including a list of patients admitted at the time and we interviewed almost all of them. A few we didn't get to for various reasons and Emily Black was one of those names. We couldn't interview her because she moved to Manchester and none of her neighbours had a forwarding address at that time.' The light went out on the coffee machine and Finn got up and went to it while still talking. 'Do you know why she moved to Manchester? Because her husband, Sean Black, had just landed the role of Savage and he went over there to film it.' Finn brought them both over a cup of coffee.

The DCI took his and nodded at her cup. 'How much of that have you had?'

'Don't you see, sir? His wife was in hospital, so that meant he was very likely in the hospital on the date the body was fucked with, and then he went over to Manchester to play...' She got up and pointed to the DCI.

'Savage?'

'Right. A pathologist.' She raised her eyebrows.

'Is that your only grounds for wanting to bring him in?'

'No.' Finn sat down and drained her coffee cup before continuing, 'He got the job on this new movie because Ciaran Feagan died, but Sam says the suicide doesn't add up. Black claims he knew Feagan, so he could've easily lured him out to that forest and staged the suicide.'

'For a part in a movie? Is it a well-paid part?'

Finn got up and went to the coffee machine for a refill. 'No, it isn't and that's the only thing I can't figure.' Finn poured herself more coffee, spilling some over her wrist and ignoring the burn. She turned back to the DCI and hurried back into her seat. 'But also consider this, Sean Black gets cast as a vampire and then we find that girl with the bite marks in her neck.' The DCI sat back in his chair, looking more concerned. 'We were trying to figure out why a smart girl like that would go off with a stranger. She was training to be an actress. If a famous actor asked her to go for a walk with him, she would've jumped at the chance. It all fits.' She slammed her cup down on his desk, spilling some coffee.

The DCI sat back, scratching his freshly shaved chin. 'OK, look into him, but *quietly*. If we're going to pull someone like Sean Black in, we better have more than you have right now.'

Finn jumped to her feet. 'Yes! Thank you, sir.'

The door was knocked and they both looked round as Millar popped his head inside. 'Sir, ma'am, there's been another one.' He tapped two fingers against his neck.

Finn turned to the DCI. 'If I'm right about this, sir, we have to grab him fast or this is going to keep happening.'

'Then bring me enough evidence to satisfy the CPS.'

Finn nodded and exited quickly, taking Millar with her. They strode across the station to Finn's office. Once inside she closed the door.

'Are you wearing slippers, ma'am?'

'Yes, I am. OK, here's what I need you to do.' Millar pulled out his notepad and pen as Finn interlaced her fingers and tapped her hands against her chin. 'Find out everything you can about Sean Black.'

Millar scribbled it down. 'The actor?'

'Yes. As far back as you can find anything. See if his name appears in any police reports first. Then I want to know where he worked and where he lived. As much information as possible. I want to try to create a timeline if we can. Then I want you to go through police and newspaper reports and see if anything happened when he was in the different areas. Anything that never got solved or anything connected to him even in the vaguest way. He won't be responsible for all of it, but I'm betting he did some of it.'

Millar nodded and turned to the door.

'And then…'

Millar turned back and lifted his pen and notepad again.

'…I want you to bring up anything you can find on him online. Interviews, articles, anything that'll help tell us who he really is. Maybe he let something slip or hinted at something he was proud of.'

'He famously doesn't do many interviews,' Millar said.

'I'll bet he doesn't.' She bit her lower lip and nodded at him. 'Just get whatever you can. Any mention of him. I hope you had a big breakfast, Millar. This is going to be a long day.'

Millar nodded and hurried out of the office. Finn was going to visit the latest murder scene. After she called home and put on some shoes.

15.

Sean awoke that night with a hunger gnawing at his insides. His body had now adapted to the nocturnal cycle. He no longer needed an alarm clock to tell him when the sun went down. His body knew instinctively. He sensed the change in temperature, even from within his coffin. He pushed the lid aside and rose. He had slept well, but now he needed to feed.

He went downstairs and outside. The cool night air filled his lungs. His heightened senses appreciating all that mortals ignored. He saw the wheels of the little yellow car sticking out of the hole, like a turtle on its back. He smiled as he walked towards it.

He knelt down and looked inside.

Avi wasn't there.

Sean stood up and looked around three hundred and sixty degrees. Even with his exceptional sight, he couldn't see the old man anywhere. He could've crawled out of there hours ago. Sean ground his teeth together as he ran to the 4x4. It was lucky he had kept the keys in his pocket or Avi could've taken his transport. They were still a long way from civilisation. There was still a chance Sean might be able to catch him before he flagged down a car for help. Avi couldn't move fast at the best of times, and now he was injured, he would be even slower.

Sean got into the 4x4 and brought it to life as he slammed the door. He took off up the uneven lane in search of his prey.

Avi watched him go. The old man crawled out from behind the outhouse when he saw the 4x4's headlights disappear out of sight. In reality, he had woken half an hour before dark, and it had taken him that long to climb out of Aileen's upturned car. He had only just got to cover when Sean stepped out the door.

At first, Avi found it hard to believe he had slept the whole day away, but he supposed the concussion and his panic attack were enough to keep him unconscious all that time. He touched his head. The cut had stopped bleeding long ago. He opened and closed his jaw to make sure it wasn't broken. The dried blood cracked and peeled off his face when he stretched his wrinkled skin.

He reached into his pocket and removed the cross. He had found it before leaving the car and decided to take it with him, but that wasn't what he needed right now. He took out his phone and looked at the screen. NO SERVICE.

There were miles of darkness all around, but at least he could hear traffic and see headlights in the distance. His aching body made its way slowly up the yard. Then he hobbled up the lane. Once he hit road he felt like he was on the home straight, but there was still NO SERVICE, and that traffic still sounded very far away.

Sean kicked in the door of the small house. He knew entering without an invitation might make him sick or weak, but he didn't care. All he was interested in was revenge. The house was dark. He walked through the rooms without turning any lights on. The thirst inside him was incredible. Humans only thought they knew what hunger was. He reached the kitchen and saw a note propped up on the table addressed to Harry.

Sean snatched it up and scanned it quickly. He ripped it in half and dropped the pieces. His teeth were gritted tightly. He looked around for something to vent his anger on. A family pet would be ideal, but there didn't appear to be one. He grabbed the table and threw it against the wall, smashing it to kindling.

They weren't at Avi's place and they weren't here. They wouldn't go to the office either; too obvious. Fuck it. They could wait until another night. He couldn't go on for much longer without quenching the thirst inside him.

As he walked towards the door, he punched a hole in the plasterboard wall.

The old lady who picked up Avi was very concerned about the amount of blood on his face and shirt. Not concerned enough to go more than forty miles per hour, but she did fuss and panic a lot for the entire journey to the police station. She tried to talk him into going to the hospital first, but the old man was adamant. He gave her a story about being run off the road by drunken teenagers in a car with a loud exhaust. She tutted, knowing exactly the sort of boys he meant, and for a few minutes forgot her mothering instinct to constantly ask him if he was OK. Avi appreciated the attention, but he was more focused on finding Sean and stopping him before he hurt anyone else.

For the hundredth time since he'd set off from Sean's lair, he grabbed his jacket and was reassured to feel the shape of the crucifix in his pocket.

The desk sergeant was shocked to see the elderly man in a suit come in with blood over his face and clothes. He offered to get a police car to run Avi to the nearest A&E but the old man waved away his concerns. 'Never mind about that. I'm fine. The girl. The body. The one you found in an old mill. I need to talk to whoever's looking into that.'

Finn had fallen asleep at her desk wading through the folder of clippings and print-outs Millar had brought her. The desk sergeant woke her with a shake of her shoulder.

Finn's head popped up quickly and she rubbed the sleep from her eyes. 'Yes. I'm awake. What's happened?'

'I've got someone at the front desk who wants to talk to you about the girl with...' The desk sergeant tapped her neck with two fingers.

Finn took a deep breath as the last remnants of sleep were chased away by reality. 'Credible or nut job?'

The desk sergeant swallowed hard. 'He says he's Sean Black's agent.'

Now the desk sergeant had Finn's full attention. 'Show him in.' As the desk sergeant turned to leave, Finn added, 'And issue a BOLO on Sean Black.' The desk sergeant nodded and hurried away. Finn started to straighten her crumpled clothes and hair. She saw the little man being led across the floor by the desk sergeant. It wasn't the amount of blood on him as much as the look they exchanged that convinced her she was right about Sean Black.

16.

She folded her arms and gave him *the look*. They had only been dating a few weeks, but he already knew that look meant it was her way or the high way. He was weighing up whether her drop dead gorgeous face, insanely hot body and expert technique she had shown while eating an ice-lolly were enough to counter-balance this annoying stubborn streak.

They couldn't sit in the car much longer. He'd have to make a decision. He looked across the road at the smattering of students going into the Queens Film Theatre. 'Doesn't look like we'll have any trouble finding a seat. You know, there's a reason they put this on at midnight.'

Her tight-lipped smile tightened, as did her folded arms.

'All I'm saying is, it's not very romantic, is it? It's not really a date movie.'

'It's an important film that I need to see.'

'I get that.' She worked in a drop-in centre for drug users. He knew it was a worthy vocation and he admired her for it, but seeing Sean Black wandering around New York doing depraved shit for his next hit of smack, wasn't going to get her in the mood to come back to his place afterwards. 'But you could argue the same thing about me seeing *The Bourne Ultimatum*.'

She turned and raised her eyebrows at him. 'You're a PSNI constable, not a genetically enhanced super spy.'

He shrugged. 'Close enough,' he mumbled. She had no respect for what he did, and he was about to tell her to get out, but then he remembered her skill with that lolly. 'Well, what about *Hot Fuzz*? It's still playing at the Movie House. Compromise?'

'How is another cop movie with guns and blowing stuff up a compromise?' She looked over at the doors and then checked her watch. 'Look, I'm going to see *Manhattan Wasted*. Are you coming or not?'

One hundred and seventy-nine minutes later, and he'd counted every single one of them, they stepped out of the QFT with around two dozen film and acting students. They were nodding at each other and discussing the possible symbolism of the albino man called H.

As they walked back to the car she looked smug. She hooked her arm around his. 'Well, didn't I tell you it would be good?'

'Good? You thought that was good?'

'You didn't?' She unhooked her arm from his. 'You didn't see the symbolism?'

'Oh no, it was brilliant. I think my favourite bit was when Sean Black shit himself and then smeared it all over his face. That was symbolic of him being shit-faced was it?'

'You don't like anything unless it has car chases and guns.'

'Well, there was that bit where he stuck a gun up his arse.'

She was giving him *the look* times a thousand now. 'I think I'm going to walk home.'

'And I don't think I'm going to try to stop you. Good night. Thanks for such a fun film.'

As she turned and stomped away, she shouted over her shoulder, 'It wasn't supposed to be fun, you fuckin' idiot!'

He turned from her and someone walked into him, banging his shoulder. 'Hey!' he shouted after him, but the figure kept on walking. When he passed beneath a streetlight, he thought it almost looked like Sean Black. Maybe he just had Sean Black on the brain after sitting through three hours of him, but the guy really did look like him. He walked back to the car.

Sean Black was from Belfast and he'd read in the papers he was back in town. It would be just like the egomaniac to attend a screening of his own film to get his ass kissed afterwards. Maybe that's why he'd gone off in the same direction as her. Well, he could have her.

He got into the car and slammed the door. He turned his phone back on. Just in case she wanted to call and apologize. He wasn't going to be an asshole about it. He'd let her apologize, and he was confident if they put their heads together, they'd find a way to make up.

When his phone connected to his network he found he had two messages waiting. One was from his friend, telling him what an awesome movie *The Bourne Ultimatum* was, having just seen it. The other was a BOLO from the station.

BeOnLookOut for the actor, Sean Black. Wanted in connection with at least two murders. Do not approach. Considered extremely dangerous.

He threw the car door open and raced down the street shouting her name. He rounded the corner and kept running, knowing the most probable route she'd take home. He almost missed the couple in the alley as he ran past, but he went back for a better look and saw they weren't kissing.

'Hey!' he screamed and started towards them. The figure turned around and his pale face was caught in the light. Sean Black. Red eyes. Sharp teeth. His mouth dripping blood. He dropped her and ran. The young constable ran to his date and knelt down by her side.

She looked up at him with panicked, unbelieving eyes. The blood was pumping from her neck. He put his hand over it and stifled the flow as best he could. 'Just hold on, OK? You're going to be fine.' With his free hand he pulled his phone from his pocket and dialled 999. As he waited for it to be answered he saw tears run down her face. Her eyes were so scared, pleading with him. He leaned closer to her. 'Just hold on,' he whispered. 'Help's coming.'

17.

The response to the BOLO sent all cars in the area rushing towards the suspect's last known location.

It was almost three-thirty a.m. when Finn and Millar got the call. As soon as it came through, they were on their feet. Finn got on the phone and requested the Armed Response Unit to the area.

Having told his story and compared notes with Finn, Avi had insisted on sticking around until he was found. He had got his face cleaned up, but his clothes were still partially stained with blood. The officers had got him some food and as much tea as he could drink. Now the old man was feeling rested and strong. 'I'm coming with you.'

'I think that's a bad idea, Mr Goldman,' Millar said.

'Look, I don't know if he'll listen to me, but I think there's a better chance of me talking him down than you. I want to bring him in alive if possible.' Avi looked to the ranking officer.

After a little consideration, Finn nodded. 'OK, but you stay in the car unless I tell you it's safe.' Avi nodded and followed them out.

The whole street had been bought by developers. It was due to be demolished and luxury apartments built there some time next year. The presence of half a dozen screaming cop cars with flashing blue lights had sent the usual collection of drug dealers and low lifes scattering like cockroaches.

The police had both ends of the street blocked and men watching the backs of all the buildings by the time Finn and Millar arrived. She hung her lanyard around her neck and walked towards the nearest car. 'DS Finn. Report.'

The officer glanced at the lanyard and then answered, 'We responded to the BOLO sighting and saw him on our approach, ma'am. We positively ID'd Sean Black. He ran down here. We pursued him in the car. Our colleagues cut off the other end of the street before he had a chance to escape. He must've gone into one of the buildings. We've got the place surrounded and air support on its way. ARU has been alerted, but they're on another call.'

'Good. Thanks.' Finn took a few steps forward and looked at the row of buildings on her left and right. It was a mixture of business premises and some residential. At least a dozen on either side. It would take time to check them all.'

Avi and Millar appeared behind her. They looked at the dark windows and partially bricked up doorways. That would at least rule some of them out. The best thing to do was to go through them all methodically from top to bottom. Finn took out her gun and checked it. Millar did the same.

'The movie theatre.' Avi nodded at the building three-quarters of the way down the street.

Finn turned to him. 'The old Palladium? Why?'

'No windows,' he said solemnly.

Finn considered this and then nodded. Avi saw her glance over at the uniforms and knew she was uneasy sharing with the troops how they'd come to this conclusion. They were all holding guns and twitching with nervous energy. 'OK, but we wait for ARU. I'm not going in there in the dark.'

Avi grasped the familiar shape in his pocket and took comfort that it was still there.

The Armed Response Unit took over two hours to get there. There had been a siege with a gang of armed drug dealers. They had taken hostages when the Drugs Squad had attempted a raid on their squat. The stand-off had ended without any shots being fired, and the ARU had come straight from that job to this one.

The leader of the ARU was sent to talk to Finn upon his arrival. 'DS Finn.' He shook her hand. 'Sorry it took us so long. We sit around for weeks on end with nothing to do and then there's two situations in one night. We were briefed partially on the way over, but... this guy's not armed?'

'Not in any conventional way,' she said, 'but he is suspected of killing at least two people and attempting to murder a third.'

'I heard about that. He really bit her?' He whispered the second part.

Finn nodded. 'We've been talking to the hospital. They think she'll pull through, but it was touch and go for a while there. Lucky she was a common blood group.' She pointed him towards the street. 'Let me show you what we're dealing with.' He followed her to the front of the lead car. 'He could be hiding in any one of these buildings, but our best guess is the old cinema.'

'Why do you think that?'

'Well, because of what he thinks he is... no windows in a cinema.' She looked at him, expecting the officer to scoff, but he remained stone-faced and sizing up the situation before him. 'That's why we didn't want to go in. You guys have night vision goggles, right?' He nodded, still keeping his eye on the building. She continued, 'We've been keeping an eye out for signs of movement but nothing so far. If he's in there, he's laying low.'

'If? How certain are you he's in one of these buildings at all?'

'Probably eighty to ninety percent sure. He was chased down here and they secured the area pretty quickly.'

The ARU leader surveyed the street silently for a few more seconds before turning to Finn and saying, 'OK. We'll sweep the cinema first. Tell your people to cover the exterior.'

As he turned to leave, Finn took his arm. 'Look, I don't want your men to be flippant about this. If I were you, I wouldn't even mention the... *stranger* aspects of this case. Just tell them you have an extremely dangerous individual in there with psychotic tendencies who *will* kill if he gets the chance. Ideally, we want him alive, but if he leaves you no choice...'

The ARU leader nodded his agreement. He hurried towards his men and briefed them. Finn looked back at the worried old man sitting in her car. She gave him a flat smile.

Finn, Millar and Avi watched with all the assembled uniformed officers as the six-man Armed Response Unit crossed under the cordon tape and made their way down the street in formation. They were dressed in full battle gear with their automatic rifles pointed in front of them. In preparation of the demolition, the street lights had been disconnected too, so the only light was coming from the car lights at either end of the street pointing at each other, and the small torches attached to the rifle barrels, which swung in front of each of the officers like a blind man's cane.

They reached the front of the old cinema and paused.

Finn spoke into her radio. 'ARU, what do you see?'

'The door's been forced. Recently. Wood is freshly broken. Proceeding inside.'

'Be careful.'

The officers watched as the old building swallowed the six men.

'We're in the lobby now. Two men stay here. Two up to the mezzanine. You come with me into the main theatre. Check your targets everyone. There could be homeless squatting in here.'

The air was thick outside. Finn could only bear to wait several seconds between updates. 'What are you seeing ARU?'

'It's a big space. Most of the seats are still here. We're checking them row by row. Mezzanine?'

'We're almost... Shit!!'

Everyone's grip tightened on their guns outside. They focussed their aim on the doors. 'Report, mezzanine, report,' Finn yelled.

257

'Sorry, it's nothing. My foot went through the stair. Continuing up.'

'OK, everyone watch where you put your feet. Building is not structurally secure.'

'Lobby, report.'

'Lobby clear.'

'Main theatre, anything?'

'We're about halfway down the rows of seats. Still checking. Plenty of rats, but nothing else so far.'

'Mezzanine, are you up there yet?'

'We're up here. The projection room is clear. Moving on to the seating area.'

'Lobby, report?'

'Nothing to...'

'Jesus Christ! He's on the wall, he's on the fucking wall!'

'Who's that? Mezzanine?' Everyone jumped as they heard the sound of muffled gunfire. 'All teams report!' Finn yelled.

'Man down! I repeat... fuck!' More gunfire. The uniformed officers looked at each other. The tension evident on their faces.

Finn looked at the nearest officer and shouted, 'Get an ambulance here, now!' The officer turned and started speaking into her radio immediately. Finn looked back at the doors of the cinema. 'Who was that? Mezzanine? ARU, report. Do you need backup?' Finn put her free hand on her gun. 'What's going on in there?'

'We think we tagged him. Hold your fire out there; one of ours coming out the front. Tell your officers we have an injured officer coming out.'

They were all patched into the same radio frequency, but Finn shouted to the officers to make doubly sure. 'One of ours coming out, hold your fire. Repeat, hold your fire.'

Seconds later two men came out carrying a third between them. Finn turned to the officer. 'Where's that ambulance?'

'Two minutes out, ma'am.'

'OK, go with these guys and make sure...'

'This is lobby. He's here! He's came out of the fucking ceiling!' Automatic gunfire echoed up the street. The two ARU officers carrying their wounded colleague broke into a run. They ran past her, breaking the cordon tape. Finn saw the officer's helmet had been pulled off and his throat torn open. 'Apply pressure to that until the ambulance arrives.' She pointed to the female officer. 'Tell the ambulance what's happened so they're prepared when they get here.' The WPC was fixated at the wound and amount of blood. 'Hey,' Finn shouted at her. The WPC looked up, her face pale and scared. 'Tell the ambulance what's happened,' Finn repeated. The WPC nodded and spoke into her radio. Finn could hear the ambulance was close.

'We have another man down.'

Finn turned back to the street.

'I think he's dead.'

'Get out of there,' Finn shouted. 'Do you hear me? ARU withdraw now!'

'Negative. We know where he went. We have him cornered.'

Finn held her breath. She glanced over her shoulder and saw the paramedics getting to work on the wounded ARU officer. More gunshots from inside the cinema made everyone tense on their weapons.

Finn let the echoes die before trying her radio again. 'ARU, do you have him?' The night remained still and quiet. 'Any ARU officer, please respond.' The airwaves remained silent. As the seconds crept slowly by, the inevitability of what had happened sunk in among everyone. Shocked faces looked to Finn for what to do next. She was so preoccupied trying to think of an answer, she didn't see the little Jewish man duck behind her and run slowly down the street.

'Mr Goldman, get back here!' Millar shouted. Finn turned and saw him.

The old man stopped and made eye contact with her. 'We tried it your way, now let's try mine.' Finn gave him the subtlest of nods. He continued down the street to the doors of the old cinema.

18.

It was pitch black inside. Avi's eyes had become accustomed to the darkness outside, because it never got truly dark in any city, but the blackness in front of him was total. He crossed the threshold and took a couple of timid steps inside before his foot hit something. He looked down and saw the gloved hand of one of ARU officers. It wasn't moving.

'Sean?' His tone wasn't as strong as he hoped it would be. 'It's Avi, Sean. Come on out and talk to me. Don't be scared.'

'You think I'm scared?'

Even though the voice was perfectly calm, it was so close it made the old man jump. Avi looked in the direction it had come from and thought he saw some movement. 'You need to come out now. Give yourself up. This has gone too far.'

'Still telling me what to do, Avi?'

'Still looking out for you, kid. You're not walking away from this one. Best thing you can do is go out there with your hands in the air and get a good lawyer.' He heard footsteps and jerked his head around but he couldn't see anything.

'Did you bring them, Avi? Did you tell them some tall tales?'

'I filled in some blanks, but they were already onto you, kid. You fucked up and they were closing in. It was just a matter of time.'

'I never fucked up!' The voice was closer now, and angry.

'It was the hospital. The autopsy you did before *Savage*. That's what tipped them off. I didn't even know you'd done that. Come on, kid. This doesn't have to end like *Butch and Sundance*. Give yourself up.'

'And what?' The voice had moved again. 'We get this misunderstanding cleared up and go back to work?' Avi tried to moisten his mouth, but he had no answer. 'Yeah, that's what I thought.' The voice had moved again. 'That's why I figure if my fame is gone, maybe infamy will have to do.'

'You going to kill me, kid?' The old man took the cross from his pocket and held it out in front of him.

Laughter echoed around the art-deco lobby, scaring the mice back into their holes. 'Are you serious, Avi? You think that's going to stop me?'

'Take it from me, then.' Silence. 'Come on, Sean. You've got the upper hand. The fact that you can even see what I'm holding, and all this moving around you're doing without stumbling once, makes me think you can see in the dark. Now whether that's because you've taken the night vision goggles off one of these guys, or... some other reason, the fact is you *can* see the cross. Surely you can pull it from the hand of a broken-down old man like me.'

'You're starting to annoy me, Avi.' Further away now.

The old man kept the cross held up. 'Think about Emily, Sean. Think about the baby.'

'Appeals to my humanity now? Really pulling out all the stops, aren't you? You should know by now that I...'

'Don't give a fuck about them?' Avi said. 'Yeah, I know. I know there's only one person you really care about. So let me make it real simple. Step out that door now and give yourself up, or I'll tell them to come back in here. With forty or fifty armed officers this time. After what you've done to their friends... they're not going to hold back.' Avi lowered the cross, turned his back and walked to the door.

He stopped just outside the threshold and stood to one side like a doorman. A few seconds later a figure came out of the dark. Avi barely recognised his client. His pale skin and red eyes he had seen before, but now the lower half of his face was covered in fresh blood too. He stopped next to Avi and gave him a small grin. The old man held a look that was more courageous than he felt. Sean turned and walked out into the street with his hands up.

Dozens of different officers started shouting commands at him. Too many to hear any of them clearly. Sean walked to the middle of the street with his hands behind his head, then turned to them and knelt down. He looked back over at Avi smiling as the officers came towards him with trigger-fingers poised for the slightest move that seemed suspicious.

The first officer to reach him pushed him forward to the ground and started cuffing him. Sean was still trying to keep eye contact with Avi, and he was still smiling. And then the old man saw his smile disappear and turn to fear.

'Get me out of here,' Sean screamed. 'Get me out of here, now!'

Avi looked around wondering what had caused this change in demeanour, and then he saw the first rays of the morning sun crowning over the city. Sean started to jerk and thrash his body, trying to get to his feet. The cuffs were in place but several other officers now came closer to subdue him.

'Get me inside! Get me inside!' he screamed.

'Hold him down, he's trying to run,' the first officer shouted. Through the circle of assembled police, most still with their firearms trained on him, a few rays of sunlight found their way through and hit his face. His pale skin started to redden rapidly. He screamed in pain.

Avi ran towards him, pulling his jacket off. He fought his way through the confused cops and threw his jacket over Sean's head. His client fell limply to the ground and started crying with relief. He stopped struggling.

Avi looked at the puzzled faces staring at him. 'Keep that over him until you get him inside and he won't fight you.' He gave them a nod which said 'just indulge him'.

The police got him to his feet and led him to a waiting prisoner transport van with the jacket still over his head. At least the windows were tinted on those transports, he thought. Avi knelt down and picked up the cross he had dropped when he pulled off his jacket. He was still Jewish through and through, but he was going to hold on to this all the same.

Finn and Millar approached him. Finn nodded to her car. The old man followed her back up the street where the sun was now well on its way to ushering in a new day.

ROYAL VICTORIA HOSPITAL A&E REPORT [POLICE COPY]

Two bullets removed from patient during surgery; one from upper right quadrant of back, one from lower left shoulder. Minimal damage caused and NO blood loss. To clarify: neither wound was bleeding from the trauma caused by the bullet. I am at a loss to explain this reaction without further case study.

Jonathan Carmichael FRCS 29/06/08

SEAN BLACK IN JAIL!

Local actor being held for questioning by Belfast detectives in murder investigation.

Belfast Echo, 30 June, 2008

SAVAGE STAR PRIME SUSPECT IN BIZARRE KILLING SPREE

Evidence is mounting as more witnesses come forward against the accused actor.

Daily News, 5 July, 2008

THE NIGHT SEAN BLACK ALMOST KILLED ME

Exclusive first-hand account of vampire killer's victim, attacked after she watched one of his films. (Turn to middle pages)

Sunday News, 8 July, 2008

SEAN BLACK CHARGED WITH MULTIPLE COUNTS OF MURDER
Actor's legal representation claims Black's unwillingness to speak is evidence of mental breakdown and asks judge for psychiatric evaluation.

Belfast Echo, 19 July, 2008

BLACK DECLARED: 'NOT FIT TO STAND TRIAL'
Psychiatric consultants for both prosecution and defence have agreed that accused star Sean Black is 'not in a fit mental state to stand trial.' The Portstewart born actor appears to have suffered a complete mental breakdown following his arrest and so, according to the law, cannot be tried without being aware of what he is being tried for. The court-appointed psychiatrist says he is not confident Mr Black is cognisant of what he is being accused of and has recommended the trial be postponed until such a time when he can answer his accusers.

Belfast Echo, 26 July, 2008

SEAN BLACK ADMITTED TO SYCAMORE ACRES
Sean Black is today being transferred to the same institute where his estranged father Ronald 'Mad Ronnie' Black spent a good portion of his life. Evidence continues to grow against the accused star, but he is said to be in an almost catatonic state and has not spoken since his arrest. One expert we talked to informed us these conditions can last days, years or even a lifetime, prompting the question: will Sean Black ever stand trial for his crimes?

Belfast Echo, 30 July, 2008

SYCAMORE ACRES [Patient: 29845 Update – Police Copy]
Patient has an extreme psycho-somatic reaction to sunlight. He cowered under his bed today during daylight hours, even when the curtains and blinds were closed. Patient has not spoken since his arrival and refuses to eat.

S. Coles (MRCPsych) 30/07/08

SYCAMORE ACRES [Patient: 29845 Update – Police Copy]
Repeated attempts to bite hospital staff have resulted in him being restrained until further notice. Still refuses to speak or eat. Glucose drip being given intravenously.

S. Coles (MRCPsych) 03/08/08

SYCAMORE ACRES [Patient: 29845 Update – Police Copy]
Fresh burns on his face today, likely caused by sunlight exposure. This was undoubtedly done by hospital staff, but whether it was out of error, curiosity, or some kind of retribution is unclear, as no one will admit to it. Sean Black has now been moved to a room with twenty-four-hour camera surveillance. Tests for erythropoietic protoporphyria (EPP) have come back showing his protoporphyrin levels are normal, supporting my original claim that this condition is psycho-somatic; the result of the patient's own belief that sunlight will harm him and nothing else.

S. Coles (MRCPsych) 09/08/08

SYCAMORE ACRES [Patient: 29845 Update – Police Copy]
Patient's former manager visited today. Mr Goldman allowed me to sit in on the visit. Black refused to converse with him, but Mr Goldman showed him a magazine which reported the role of the vampire he was due to play has been recast.

After Mr Goldman left I asked the patient if he minded if I opened the blinds and curtains. He showed no signs of the hysteria or panic this question usually evokes. I opened the curtains and blinds until sunlight was hitting his bare arm. There was no reaction, so I opened them fully. He winced a little, probably just because he has been avoiding sunlight for so long, but showed no other adverse effects and his eyes soon acclimated.

S. Coles (MRCPsych) 11/08/08

SYCAMORE ACRES [Patient: 29845 Update – Police Copy]

With his aversion to sunlight apparently gone, we removed the restraints today, but still warned all hospital staff to be careful around him. He shows no signs of violence and when his food tray was brought he ate and drank normally. Glucose drip discontinued.

S. Coles (MRCPsych) 14/08/08

SYCAMORE ACRES [Patient: 29845 Update – Police Copy]

Several weeks have now passed since he has had any negative reaction to sunlight; physical or otherwise. The burns on his face have healed. Patient now eats and drinks when meals are brought to him, but the rest of the time he spends huddled in the foetal position on his bed.

He still has not spoken to anyone, despite many doctors and solicitors visiting him. One of my colleagues suggested: 'He's like a puppet whose strings have been cut,' but I think a more apt analogy is: *He's like a robot without software.*

S. Coles (MRCPsych) 12/10/08

SYCAMORE ACRES [Patient: 29845 Update – Police Copy]

Today Emily Black visited. His wife allowed me to sit in. Patient refused to talk to her despite her emotional pleas. She asked if he wanted to know about Maddie (patient's daughter). She told him she was moving to another country where she wouldn't be hounded constantly by the press and where he wouldn't be able to find Maddie if he ever got out of here. She asked him if all the stories in the press were true and why he did it. He ignored all of this. Even when she physically attacked him, crying, and had to be escorted from the room, he continued to ignore her.

S. Coles (MRCPsych) 23/10/08

SYCAMORE ACRES [Patient: 29845 Update – Police Copy]

This note was found by a nurse today while changing the patient's sheets.

01. INT. PSYCHIATRIC HOSPITAL - DAY

Sean Black lies curled up in bed, motionless. To the rest of the world he is an empty shell of a man, but little do they know he is making a plan to free himself of this place.

The missive was written on a tissue in crude handwriting that is not Sean Black's usual hand, but given his condition, we cannot rule out that this was written by him. Review of the security tapes shows no unauthorized visitors giving him anything. This may be the only way the patient knows how to communicate. I am going to make further writing materials available to him to see if I can stimulate this avenue of communication.

S. Coles (MRCPsych) 06/11/08

SYCAMORE ACRES　　　　　**[Patient: 29845 Update – Police Copy]**
It has now been three months since the patient has had any violent outbursts. I have decided to try to introduce him to the common areas of the facility and let him come and go from his room as he pleases within designated times. For the first three hours he did not want to leave his room, but after that he went up to the common room and sat in a chair by the window. I had two members of our support staff monitor him at all times. When it was time to go back to his room he did so without protest. The paper and pen I left in his room are still unused. Maybe social interaction will help him to communicate again. I have recommended to the court that he stays here for the time being and I will review his case again in six months.

S. Coles (MRCPsych) 11/11/08

19.

Sean heard the heavy footsteps and jangling keys coming down the corridor and swallowed the piece of tissue containing the instructions. It didn't matter. Since he'd found the note last night, he'd read it so many times it was memorized. His door unlocked and the fat guard stepped inside.

'Come on, Sean. Time for you cuckoos to go free-range for a few hours.'

Sean got up from his bed and gave the fat guard a thin smile as he passed him. He did just as the note instructed him and went to the games room. For an hour he interacted with the crazies in there; playing draughts and Connect4 like children, but he was always keeping a discreet eye on the clock. When the time came, he was able to slip out without anyone noticing.

As he made his way down the corridor, he looked up at the glass eyes watching him. The note said they would be down for maintenance, but they still scared him. He reached the door the note had indicated. There was a sign on it saying: NO PATIENTS BEYOND THIS POINT. KEEP DOOR LOCKED AT ALL TIMES. Sean tried the door and found it unlocked. He slipped through and closed it after him.

He found himself at the top of a spiral staircase. He followed the metal stairs downwards, round and round, to the basement. He felt the warmth of the boiler and walked towards it. This was as much as his instructions had told him to do. He looked around the large room and saw no one.

'You're a hard man to get a meeting with these days, Sean.' The voice echoed around the pipes and concrete. Sean looked for its source and saw a man emerging from the shadows.

'Paddy Hancock?' His voice sounded weak and alien even to himself. He cleared his throat and made his next statement louder and more confident. 'What the hell are you doing here?'

'So you *can* talk. I thought as much.' As he came into the light Sean recognised the agent. He was a little heavier, wearing a newer cheap suit and had more product in his hair, but there was no mistaking him or his stainless-steel briefcase.

'You're the one who's been sending me the notes? How? And how'd you get in here?'

'Come on, Sean. How much do you think the guys who work here make? A few quid in the right palm goes a long way. I just hope my investment was worth it.'

'Well, here I am. What do you want?'

'It looks like Avi's given up on you. I'd never do that. I'm here to make you an offer, babe. I'm here to get you back to work.'

Sean laughed. He actually laughed. After lying on that same bed for months staring at the same walls, it was something he never thought he'd do again. 'That's great, Paddy. What's the part? Where do I sign?' He laughed again.

'You think your career's over, don't you?'

Sean nodded. 'I think that's a pretty safe bet. My final role – as a dribbling mute simpleton – is the role of a lifetime, and it's the only thing stopping me from getting shivved, or fucked in the ass, or both, in prison, so I think I'll stick with it.'

'You see, that's all those years of Avi's influence. Making you think small. I can get you out of here, Sean.' He smiled his inordinately white teeth. 'Just say the word.'

Sean walked up close to him and looked for fear in his eyes. He saw none. 'Do you read the papers, Paddy? Do you know what I'm accused of?'

'I know, and I couldn't care less whether you did it or not. That's where Avi and I differ. Whatever you need, I'm here for you, and whatever you need to do to get into character is no concern of mine.'

'Avi was right about you. You're a real piece of shit, Paddy.'

He laughed. 'Well, thank you. So, are we in business?'

Sean looked him up and down. 'You get me out of here with no charges pressed and I'm your client.' Sean sat down on a crate and folded his hands. 'Let's hear it.'

Paddy pulled up another crate opposite him and opened his briefcase on his knees. 'You have no idea how much shit I had to read to find this.' He took a script from his briefcase and passed it over to Sean with all the ceremony and care of a priceless museum artefact.

Sean looked at it and read the title. 'The Whole Truth.' He looked up at Paddy.

'It's a legal thriller. About this guy who gets sent down for these crimes, and while he's locked up he uses the library and Internet to read up on the law, especially the difference between real, tangible proof and circumstantial evidence.'

'I suppose in the end you actually find out he did it,' Sean said.

Paddy smiled. 'Of course he did, but who cares. He still gets off.' He pulled his crate closer. 'You see, I *have* been reading the papers, Sean, and it seems to me, ninety-five percent of the stuff they've got against you is circumstantial. You were in the same city when something happened. You have some vague connection to this person. The truth is, Seany, babe, for all the big stuff, they don't have shit but hearsay. They're hoping you crack and confess to it. And the other stuff... well, it can be dealt with, one way or another.'

'Even if you could get me out, and that's a hell of a big if, what makes you think you could get me work?'

'Because I've been putting out some feelers.' Sean looked alarmed. Paddy put his palms up. 'Very discreetly! But if I can get you out, and get you off, which I think I can, it's all on a plate waiting for you. Publishers want you to write a book telling your side, studios want the movie rights to that book before it's even written. Studios want you for any movie you'll do, acting-wise. They know the free publicity is going to be incalculable. Think of the papers, the protests, all free publicity. This thing could be fuckin' huge. All you have to do is say yes.' He raised his eyebrows, waiting for a response.

Sean looked at the script in his hands. 'I'll never be able to get this back to my room.'

Paddy stood up. 'Read it here, now. We've got time.' Sean smiled at him. Paddy winked at him. 'I wouldn't ask you to commit to any project you weren't a hundred percent invested in, babe. I know how much you like to prepare for a role, and I'd expect no less on this.'

Paddy stepped away and lit a cigarette as Sean turned to page one and started reading.

Paddy couldn't help but smile as page after page, minute after minute, he watched Sean Black slowly disappear.

[CURTAIN]

The next book in The North Coast Bloodlines series is…

*** Coming 2022 ***

Printed in Great Britain
by Amazon

78873989R00159